Spire Publishing

www.spirepublishing.com

Causeway

Shadow Lands: Book Two

by
Simon Lister

Spire Publishing
www.spirepublishing.com

Spire Publishing, January 2008

Second edition. This edition first published in Canada 2008 by Spire Publishing.

Spire Publishing is a trademark of Adlibbed Ltd.

Note to Librarians: A cataloguing record for this book is available from the Library and Archives Canada. Visit www.collectionscanada.ca/amicus/index-e.html

Printed and bound in the US or the UK by Lightningsource Ltd.
Cover photo/design © S Lister

ISBN: 1-897312-63-6

Simon Lister was born in Twyford and raised in Berkshire. He studied and lived in London for several years before travelling and working around the world. He now lives and writes on the North shore of Loch Tay. His Arthurian saga comprises of *Shadow Lands*, *Causeway* and *Haven*.

**For information on ordering the books in this series please visit:
www.simonlister.co.uk**

Causeway

is for

Anna, Tish, Bren & Mark

- for all the support and encouragement

Acknowledgements

Thanks to Rick who co-wrote the earlier Shadow Land stories when we were kids and who helped editorially in these later versions. Thanks also to: Anna and Stan for Loch Tay. Tish and Bren for all the support and encouragement, and Mark too, who was there with the original inspiration back when I was doing a primary school essay. Paul Biggs and Jenny Grewal for the valuable feedback, and Steve Forrow for the re-reading, critical assessments and editorial input. And a final thanks to the folks at PABD for all the effort and patience in getting these books to print. Any errors that remain are, of course, solely of my own doing.

Characters

The Wessex

Arthur – Warlord of Wessex
Merdynn – Counsellor to King Maldred
Ruadan – Arthur's second-in-command and brother to Ceinwen
Trevenna (f) – Arthur's sister, married to Cei and a warrior in the Anglian war band
Ceinwen (f) – healer and ex-tracker for the Wessex war band, sister to Ruadan
Morgund – Captain in the Wessex war band
Mar'h - Captain in the Wessex war band
Balor – Wessex warrior
Morveren (f) – Wessex warrior
Ethain – Wessex warrior
Cael – Wessex warrior
Tomas – Wessex warrior, married to Elowen
Elowen (f) – Wessex warrior, married to Tomas
Tamsyn (f) – Wessex warrior, sister to Talan
Talan – Wessex warrior, brother to Tamsyn
Llud – Wessex warrior
Laethrig – the Wessex Blacksmith
Kenwyn – Wessex Chieftain

The Anglians

Cei – Anglian Warlord, childhood friend to Arthur and married to Arthur's sister, Trevenna
Hengest – Cei's second-in-command, son to Aelfhelm
Cerdic – Anglian warrior
Aelfhelm – Anglian warrior, father to Hengest
Elwyn – Anglian warrior and boat captain
Aylydd (f) – Anglian warrior and boat captain
Lissa – Anglian warrior and boat captain
Leah (f) – Anglian warrior

Saewulf Anglian warrior
Cuthwin – Anglian warrior
Berwyn – Anglian warrior
Roswitha (f) – Anglian warrior
Herewulf – Anglian warrior
Osla – Anglian warrior
Wolfestan – Anglian warrior, brother to Elfida
Elfida (f) – Anglian warrior, sister to Wolfestan
Godhelm – Anglian warrior
Thruidred – Anglian warrior
Wayland – Anglian warrior
Ranulf – Anglian warrior
Leofrun (f) – Anglian warrior
Aelfric – Anglian youth
Henna (f) – Anglian healer
Aelle – Anglian Chieftain

The Mercians

Maldred – King of the southern tribes
Gereint – Mercian Warlord, brother to Glore
Glore – Mercian warrior, brother to Gereint
Dystran – Mercian warrior
Unna (f) – Harbour master of the Haven

The Uathach

Ablach – Uathach Chieftain of the lands to the North of Anglia, father to Gwyna
Gwyna (f) – Uathach warrior, daughter to Ablach
Ruraidh – Uathach Captain
Hund – Uathach Chieftain of the lands to the North of Mercia
Benoc – Uathach Chieftain of the lands to the far north

The Cithol

Venning – Cithol Lord and ruler of the Veiled City, father to Fin Seren
Kane – Commander of the Veiled City
Fin Seren (f) – daughter and heir to Lord Venning
Terrill – Captain of the Cithol

The Bretons

Bran – Chieftain of the Bretons
Cardell (f) – Advisor to Bran
Charljenka (f) - Breton child
Nialgrada – Breton child

Chapter One

Winter held the dark forests in frozen silence. The only thing moving in the stilled landscape was Cei's band of warriors as Merdynn led them ever eastward. They had left Arthur's camp in the Shadow Lands some five weeks ago and in that time they had seen no other living thing; the forests had been abandoned to the long months of winter darkness.

They had been travelling for several days before Cei had told them the true nature of their undertaking, that they were journeying far into the Shadow Lands to the City that supplied the massed Adren army that was poised to invade Britain. Somewhere in that city there was a power source, a legacy from the last Age that was similar to whatever powered the Veiled City in the Winter Wood. It was their task to wreck that ancient relic and deny the Adren the ability to support their army.

He explained it had been necessary to keep the objective from them until after they had left Arthur's camp as the less who knew their real purpose the more unlikely it was that the enemy would learn of their plan. He offered that anyone who no longer wanted to go on could return if they so chose. No one said they wanted to return.

Cei was not surprised that they all chose to go on but he was relieved that they all seemed to relish the task ahead. Despite the apparently casual way he had selected them during the clamour back at the camp they had, in fact, been carefully picked for the journey ahead. Merdynn would obviously be their guide, Trevenna would not have suffered to be left behind and Ethain had volunteered and been accepted as a representative of the Wessex and his exceptionally good eyesight would doubtlessly prove to be an asset for them as they travelled deeper into the Shadow Lands. On their first day's travelling Cei had introduced Ethain to the others who all came from the Anglian war band and whom were mostly unknown to him. Ethain had feigned an interest but he let the names go by him in a blur and by the time Cei had finished he realised he could only put one or two names to the new warriors he was committed to travelling with, but it was clear that the Anglians fell into three distinct groups.

Herewulf led the first of these groups. He was in his mid-fifties and the oldest amongst them, a few years older than Aelfhelm who was Cei's second-in-command. Herewulf was an experienced, tough warrior who had often travelled in the Shadow Lands in winter. His small band included four others among them Cerdic and Osla, and Cei hoped Herewulf's experience would curb the younger men's invaluable but impetuous bravery. The other two, Roswitha and Leah, were both older than the young warriors and the two women had fought alongside Herewulf in many raids against the Uathach. Cei had wanted to make sure Roswitha was with them because of her skilled use of healing plants and powders. Before leaving the camp she had talked to Ceinwen and they had divided out their supply of curative medicines to make sure they both had what they might need. Leah had always fought alongside Herewulf so taking one meant taking the other but she would have been chosen for her ability to fight in any case.

The two remaining groups were sharply divided by age. Wolfestan led the youngest group and he was only twenty-three. His sister Elfilda and their two friends Leofrun and Cuthwin were all younger. Cei felt that their youth and strength would more than counter their inexperience although he had concerns about Leofrun. Her strength was one of character and resolve rather than body and limb but her speed with the sword allayed any fears he had for her in battle. In training duels she would defeat the much bigger and stronger Cuthwin nine times out of ten but Cuthwin had a calmness of temper that the older warriors approved of, knowing he would be a good man to have alongside them in the fierce confusion of battle.

The last band of friends was just such a group of experienced warriors. Between them, Wayland, Thruidred, Godhelm and Ranulf had fought in countless skirmishes and repelled dozens of Uathach raids. Each had travelled in Britain during the winter darkness before and it held few fears for them. Indeed they feared nothing and years of fighting, patrolling, drinking and womanising together had bound them into a tight-knit group that neither Cei nor Aelfhelm would have wanted to journey without.

Most of them had no real concept of either where they were going or how far they had to go. They understood that they were to travel the Shadow Lands in the darkness of winter. They understood that the journey would take them to the Adren City and that they had to destroy whatever magic it was that was used to feed their seemingly endless armies. They did not understand how they could do this but they trusted in Cei and they trusted his faith in Merdynn.

Ethain held no trust in either and was horrified by the revelation of their undertaking. He thought he had volunteered for the same kind of ambush warfare of the last month. The reason he hadn't paid much attention when Cei had introduced him to the others, and why he purposefully kept himself to himself, was that he didn't plan to be with them for too long. He had thought that he would be able to slip away from the group unnoticed during one of the raids and make his way back across the Causeway. Once he reached the Gates he planned to contrive to be carrying some message from Arthur for those at Whitehorse Hill. His plan became more vague afterwards but that did not bother him. If he got that far he could bury himself deep in Wessex somewhere. He just knew he could not face up to any more of this constant fear.

He had to stop himself from being physically sick when Cei had told them where they were truly going. With his stomach churning he prayed to the gods that someone would take up Cei's offer of the option for anyone to return and inwardly cursed the same gods when no one spoke up, damning the folly of those around him and damning his appallingly bad fortune. Instead of the opportunity to slip away from these relative strangers during an ambush, where they would assume he had been killed, he had volunteered to go ever further away from the Causeway on some ill-starred journey to the ends of the Earth.

To make matters worse Cerdic admired Ethain's bravery in volunteering to join Cei's band, suspecting that he had some pre-knowledge of their destination, and was forever by his side affording him no opportunity to double back. Now it was too late. He could not find his way back even if a chance presented itself for him to slip away. He realised with a now familiarly sickening feeling that he was in a worse position than before, stuck with a band of warriors whom he didn't know and who were mad enough to volunteer for this kind of folly; and he knew his chances of survival now depended entirely upon these strangers around him. He forced himself to make the effort to at least get to know their names and went out of his way to assist whomever he could in an attempt to make himself indispensable, or at least not expendable when they finally found themselves in trouble. Ethain had long since run out of curses to scream in his mind at these turn of events but he was not averse to repeating his curses and, as they trudged mile by mile through the dark forest, repeat himself he did.

Merdynn confidently led them eastward and as the days and miles slipped behind them the forest gradually began to thin allowing the moon to light more and more of the ground before them and they started to come across the first signs of wildlife in the frozen forests. Once they startled a small herd of deer but after a moment of mutually transfixed surprise the deer had reacted the quicker and hastily bounded off into the deep forest. The eerie cries of a wolf pack began to follow them but never seemed to get any closer. When they stopped for meals they could hear the wolves baying in the depths of the forest, their baleful howling echoing through the trees and muffled by the snow, making it difficult to discern exactly which direction it was coming from. Merdynn seemed unconcerned by it but Cei's warriors frequently made the sign to ward off evil remembering the tales they had heard of souls damned to wander the Shadow Lands, lost to this world and denied the next.

As the trees became fewer and further apart Merdynn called another stop. As the others set up a camp and began preparing a meal, Merdynn led Cei and Aelfhelm onwards across the iron-hard ground that rose before them and which lay exposed to the stripping wind.

He stopped at the crest of a ridge and the other two looked at the landscape before them. The land gently fell away before them for several miles and beyond that lay a scene unlike any they had seen before. It appeared to them to stretch from horizon to horizon, a desolate broken uneven land. In the bright winter moonlight they studied the snow-covered terrain. Even where the ground lay under a deep blanket of snow they could tell the landscape was no product of nature. The ruins of an ancient city lay before them for as far as their eyes could see. The sparse stunted trees and straggled undergrowth could not hide the collapsed stonework or mask the linear edges that were set in relief by the winter snow. Among the rubble-strewn remains shattered towers stood out like the fingers on an upturned hand of a corpse, no longer pointing with any purpose towards the hard stars above.

'What is this place?' Aelfhelm asked, looking at Merdynn with wonder and fear.

'A city from another age. There were wondrous things in the world once, Aelfhelm, beyond wonder even. I never saw these things; never saw the glory of the world in that time. I travelled once more in Middangeard only after their downfall and as high as these people of old had risen, so did they fall. Only ruins are left of what they accomplished, desolate reminders of a time we cannot comprehend.'

'Perhaps they got too close to the gods and were cast down,' Cei said, still trying to take in the scope of what stretched before them.

'Perhaps. Perhaps they were gods, of a kind,' Merdynn replied softly.

'What could cause the downfall of gods?'

'Only themselves,' Aelfhelm said staring at the ruins.

'Or perhaps fate. Not even the gods can stop fate,' Merdynn added quietly.

'What happened to the people of this city? There must have been a countless number of them,' Cei asked.

'Dead. Dead a long, long time ago. Only a fraction survived that downfall. Some of their descendants still inhabit the ruins, a desperate shadow of those gone before, poisoned and deformed many thousands of years ago. Now they scrape what living they can from the country around here in the summer and retreat back to their stone tombs when the winter snows come.'

'Ruins, graves and ghosts,' Aelfhelm suppressed a shudder.

'Our road lies through these ruins,' Merdynn said, pointing with his staff to the distance beyond the ancient city.

'Is there no other way? Can't we take the East Road?' Aelfhelm said, his brow deeply creased with anxiety as he surveyed the immense graveyard stretching out before them.

'The great Aelfhelm scared? Three decades riding with the Anglians and a son who stands second-in-command of the spear riders and you baulk at ruins?' Cei was smiling at him as he spoke.

'It's not right. Not right to ride with ghosts through their graves.' Aelfhelm spat on the ground then kicked snow over his spittle to stop the evil spirits stealing it.

'Quite right. But it's not the ghosts that worry me,' Merdynn said.

'No?' Asked Aelfhelm, still kicking snow over his spittle and now wishing he had not spat at all. Merdynn remained silent as he stared down into the ancient city.

'Well? What does then?' Cei asked no longer smiling.

'It's the shadows of those who still live,' Merdynn finally replied and then turned to make his way back to the camp leaving Cei and Aelfhelm looking at each other.

'Come on, don't look so worried. I've seen you stand before Uathach raiders and grin, what are shadows to us?' Cei said and clapped a hand on Aelfhelm's shoulder before following after Merdynn.

Aelfhelm started after Cei then turned back and swept some more snow over where he had spat before trudging back to the camp muttering to himself.

Merdynn told them to collect some firewood while they could, as there wouldn't be any to be found in the city, so Cei handed his large war axe to the diminutive Leofrun. She scowled at Cei then slung it over her shoulder and strolled off with Roswitha and Herewulf chuckling behind her.

They ate quickly then crossed the bare ridge before starting down the long gentle slope towards the ruins of the city that spread for miles before them. Merdynn led the way with Cei and Trevenna. Cerdic brought up the rear with Ethain and Leah.

As they passed the first of the levelled stone buildings, Leah loosened her spear and touched the wooden shaft for good fortune. Cerdic noticed the unconscious act.

'There's nothing to fear from ghosts,' he said.

'If old Aelfhelm's concerned then so am I,' she answered.

'Aelfhelm's not afraid of the dead,' Cerdic stated flatly, 'nor is our Wessex warrior,' he added, mistaking Ethain's silence and steady gaze for resolve and determination.

'Perhaps Aelfhelm isn't but I've never seen him look nervous before and perhaps those in Wessex are accustomed to walking among ghosts,' she replied, glancing at Ethain for a moment.

Ethain came out of his trance and turned his tired, reddened eyes to Leah. She did indeed look nervous as her blue eyes darted from side to side of the broad path they followed, searching the shadows for movement. He took heart from someone else showing fear and began to fight the fatal resignation he had felt approaching the city.

'People lose their courage as they get older, particularly the women,' Cerdic said to Ethain.

Leah scoffed in derision, 'You'll lose more than your courage if you say that again, boy.'

Ethain looked at them both finding it hard to imagine that Cerdic was ten years younger than Leah was. He acted with so much confidence and seemed so self-assured that he had forgotten they were about the same age. He felt himself to be no more than a frightened boy in comparison. His nervousness and uncertainty transmitted itself to his horse, which skittered sideways, bumping into Leah's horse before he could bring it under control. Leah scowled at him and he held up a hand to apologise, feeling foolish and out of place.

They began to pass by more and more of the collapsed buildings until ruined stonework continually lined their path and rose high to either side of them. The column paced on through the snow-covered avenue, veering to one side or the other to go around the frequent large mounds of collapsed stonework. The debris sprouted wiry shrubs and shallow-rooted trees, winter-bare except for the precarious lines of snow balancing on the emaciated branches that reached towards the black sky. Ethain looked on their twisted trunks and saw the spirits of tormented souls and their thin branches seemed to him like the begging arms of starved children. He shuddered nervously and tried to mask it by scratching at the beginnings of the sparse beard on his chin.

The moon still shone brightly casting irregular shadows across the track they were following and causing the snow and ice to glisten and shimmer like the stars in the skies above them. Ethain was subsiding back into his lonely trance when Cerdic swung his horse around quickly and drew his sword. Leah reacted to his sudden movement and did likewise. Ethain watched them almost disinterestedly, barely feeling as if he were involved in any way with anything that might happen here. They stared back down the track they had come along then searched the broken land to either side before Cerdic shook his head and sheathed his sword.

'There's something evil about this land,' he said quietly as if in explanation for his actions.

Leah looked at him but did not chide him for his nervousness. She felt it too. Ethain watched her as she chewed her lower lip. He studied her face briefly, the pale blue eyes set wide of her long straight nose, the paleness of her full lips and the leather collar that encircled her throat with the glinting silverwork embedded in it. He had found her attractive the first time he had seen her, sitting on the ground with her long legs stretched out before her and laughing with her head thrown back. Unfortunately for him Morgund had felt the same way.

He quickly turned away and set his horse plodding after the others. He felt a stab of bitterness at his idle attraction to her. She was older than him, more confident, braver, taller and probably stronger, indeed, altogether more of a warrior than he would ever be. He felt attracted to the qualities and strengths he saw in her and which he knew to be absent within himself. He felt there was less chance of her liking him than there was that he would make it back to Wessex alive, and he put those chances at nothing. In a strange way it was only the resignation that kept him going. He had already accepted his certain death. It was only a question of when and where. The sooner it happened, the sooner he could stop fearing it.

Despite Cerdic's newfound kinship with Ethain, based largely on the mistaken assumption that he shared his own bravery, they only truly had one thing in common and that was their feelings towards Leah. Cerdic was not fearless, he had felt fear standing before Arthur when he had questioned the staking of the Adren heads and he certainly did not feel comfortable now, but he had courage. He had been with the Anglian Spear Riders for three years now and his dreams of heroic deeds had not diminished. In fact they had redoubled and he looked upon this venture to the East as an excellent opportunity to reinforce his growing stature within the Anglian war band. He felt that if he could perform some great unspecified deed on this quest then he would be nearer to realising his ambition of becoming the warlord before he was thirty. Perhaps even the foremost Warlord of Britain, Arthur would be fifty by then and he could not live forever. He respected Cei as his leader and looked upon him almost as a father but like many sons he felt the time was coming when he should take over his father's position as head of the family. Cerdic had plans for the future.

The head of the column entered an open space surrounded on all sides by the piles of ruinous dwellings that had risen in height the further they had travelled into the city. Merdynn called a halt by raising his staff in one hand.

'Is there something wrong?' Trevenna asked.

Merdynn, standing up in the stirrups of his pony, faced each side of the square in turn.

'We aren't alone here,' he finally answered.

'Danger?' Cei asked quickly, signalling his riders to draw together.

'There! In the tower!' Herewulf said pointing to the crumbled remains of a building that stood taller than its surroundings.

They followed his gaze and saw movement in an opening near the top of the tall and dangerously leaning tower. A solitary and slowly rhythmic clanging began on the opposite side of the square. The warriors turned their horses toward the source of the sound and someone in the tower took up the dull beating of iron on iron. They looked back to the tower and gradually, one by one, the clashing tattoo was taken up by others on all sides of the square until the dull clanging filled the air around them like a malevolent heart beat.

The Anglians had drawn together in the centre of the open space and were fighting to control their horses in the din being created around them.

'There must be a hundred or more of them!' Cei shouted above the noise to Merdynn as he turned his horse first one way then another to watch the shadows emerging from the ruins.

'I don't understand! The creatures who inhabit this tomb never join together in numbers!' Merdynn shouted back.

'What do they want?' Trevenna cried as her horse reared up under her.

'Horsemeat! They must want our horses!'

The Anglians drew their weapons as the hunched and raggedly clothed figures leapt from the ruins and began encircling them. Still beating their crude iron bars together they began to close in round Cei's riders.

'Get us out of here, Cei, it's not just the horses they want!' Herewulf shouted above the deafening clash of noise.

Cei looked around urgently. He saw what might be the beginnings of an avenue between the heaped stones in one corner of the square.

'Follow me!' he cried and spurred his horse towards the shambling figures that blocked their way.

The others pulled their horses around and in a cloud of trammelled, powdery snow they sped after him. A desperate wail went up from the square as Cei rode through the advancing throng with the others close behind him. They raced blindly along the linear depressions between the mounds, unconcerned with where they were heading only intent on leaving behind them the nightmarish scene of the misshapen shadows that the ruins of the city had birthed.

Eventually Cei pulled his horse up and the riders came to a halt around him. He passed back among them, checking through the clouds of steam and pluming breaths of the horses to make sure everyone had gotten away. He realised Merdynn was missing and cursed himself for not remembering that he rode only a pony.

'Did you see Merdynn?' he asked Leah.

She shook her head, out of breath. Cei cursed.

'Wait here,' he said and then, lashing his already lathered horse, sped back the way they had come. Cerdic turned to Ethain,

'Come on!' he cried and dug his heels into his horse's flanks.

'But Cei said to...' Cerdic was already out of earshot and Ethain turned helplessly to Leah.

'We'll wait here for you,' she said, indicating it was all right for Ethain to go on after Cerdic.

Ethain swore and seeing no other alternative, followed Cerdic. Cei was already some way ahead of them and he was still cursing himself for leaving Merdynn behind when he heard a crashing cascade of rock ahead and saw one of the precarious towers collapse in a billowing cloud of snow. He reined his horse in and leapt to the ground then scrambled up the broken masonry in front of him. He peered over the edge at the scene below.

Merdynn was standing in the pathway with his staff raised. The tower had toppled onto the rear of the assailants who had pursued him. In the clouds of settling dust and snow he faced the crouching figures that had survived the carnage of the tower. They were slowly advancing upon him. Cei was about to race down to his side when Merdynn drew himself up to his full height and the countless years that had weighed him down seemed to slip away. His voice rang out clear and strong and a deep rumbling echoed from the heaped mounds of rubble to either side of the avenue. Stones and blocks of masonry slid and tumbled down the steep slopes. The advancing figures wavered as they warily watched the unsettled slopes to their right and left. Merdynn took a step forwards and raised his staff once again. They fled before him.

Cei ran back down to his horse as Cerdic and Ethain arrived.

'Is he safe?' Cerdic asked.

Cei nodded to a bend in the pathway as Merdynn came into sight on his pony, sedately plodding towards them.

'Weren't you just a touch too hasty in getting away, perhaps?' he asked when he arrived.

'Are they following?' Ethain asked.

'I shouldn't think so.'

'What was that? The tower? How did...' Cei gestured to Merdynn's staff as he spoke.

'Oh, saw that did you? Well, just lucky I suppose. The tower could have fallen at anytime – must have been all the commotion caused by your speedy retreat.'

'You can do that?' Cerdic asked.

'Do what?' Merdynn asked and stared at him for a second then nudged his pony onward. When they met up with the others Cei turned to Merdynn for directions.

'Don't look at me like that. I've no idea where your headlong flight has taken us.'

'You have no idea at all?' Cei asked.

'Well, we're deeper into the city and we need to be heading south but I don't know the paths from here.'

Cei looked up at the winter stars in the moonlit sky. He picked a broad way that headed south between the tall broken buildings. They resumed their journey with more urgency, wanting to distance themselves from the starved inhabitants of the ancient city.

Despite their sense of urgency, their progress was slowed by the snow that had drifted deeply between the endless lines of ruins in this part of the city. At times they had to resort to digging through the snow, using their shields as shovels. It was tiring work and when they came to a ravino that ran straight across their path they stopped, leaning heavily on their shields and trying to take only shallow breaths in the frozen air.

'It looks like it might be deep,' Cuthwin said as he tried to brush off the snow that stuck to his winter cloak.

'Probably a collapsed tunnel. There are many that run under the ruins,' Merdynn replied.

Cei looked about them for a place to rest for a few hours.

'Do you think they will be following us?' he asked Merdynn.

'I'd be surprised, but then I was surprised by them banding together like that. As far I know they've always avoided intruders, hiding in their underground lairs until the city is theirs once more.'

'Well, we'll need somewhere to eat and rest. Elfilda, Wolfestan! Scout the area for a place to camp for a few hours,' Cei said and Elfilda and her brother climbed sprightly up and into the ruins.

'That's youth for you,' Aelfhelm said watching them disappear quickly as he bent his tall, lean frame from side to side to ease the aches the digging had brought on.

'Trevenna, take Cerdic and scout back down the path, see if there's any sign of pursuit,' Cei said.

'Whatever my Lord commands,' Trevenna replied and gave him a mock bow.

'Told you not to marry within the war band,' Aelfhelm said once Trevenna had ridden off with Cerdic.

'No point telling Cei that, he had no choice in the matter, you should have told Trevenna,' Merdynn pointed out.

Elfilda and Wolfestan came back quickly and reported that there was shelter in a building next to a frozen river not far from where they were. It took them longer to reach it as they had to find a route their horses could take but when they did they stood silently in front of the ruin, staring at it.

Most of it had collapsed to lie in haphazard mounds of broken stone with snow-covered coarse grass prying its way between cracks and fissures. One corner of the building still rose fifty-feet into the air and sloped buttresses spread from both walls. The roof had given way a long time ago and no evidence of it remained but the structure had collapsed in such a way as to afford them a space inside like an unnatural cavern.

'Gods, it's a tomb. It has to be cursed,' Aelfhelm muttered.

'Are there ghosts in there, Merdynn?' Leah said, crossing her hands to ward off the wandering souls of the dead.

'If there are ghosts then they'll have our company for a few hours because that's where we're eating and resting,' Cei replied not waiting for Merdynn's answer as he made his way across the rubble to the entrance. Trevenna went with him and one by one the others stoked their courage and followed. Two of the group remained where they were, staring at the shelter. Osla shifted uneasily and the proud Leofrun had drawn her sword as if it would give her extra courage but they were unable to overcome their fear of the spirits that might haunt the building. They both would have been happier if Cei had ordered them to turn back and face the shambling creatures from the square, at least they could fight them. It was not until Trevenna walked back out to reassure them that it was not beset with the spirits of the dead that they allowed themselves to be led inside. There was enough room inside for both the warriors and their horses and Cei quickly set guards as others started a fire deep inside the cavern with the wood they had carried from the forests. They drew lots for who would take the wider patrol around their shelter and Cuthwin trudged back out wrapping his cloak around himself once more.

Soon they were eating a frugal but hot meal with a hot drink to wash it down and as they warmed up, their spirits rose and they began speculating upon the ruined city around them, thoughts of ghosts and tombs temporarily abandoned.

Cei watched Trevenna as she joked with Leofrun and Osla, her smiling face lit by the firelight and he felt a warm surge of love for her. He had known her for almost as long as he could remember. He had been born into the Anglian war band where both his father and mother had been spear riders. His early years, like those of the orphaned Arthur and Trevenna, had been free from the chores that bound the children of the villages. Weapons training could always be postponed for a lone visit to the Wessex camps to meet up with Arthur and Trevenna. In later years Ceinwen and Ruadan would join their group and the four friends from Wessex would travel frequently to the Anglian lands to meet Cei.

Merdynn had originally brought the three of them together and as children they had ridden their ponies far and wide across the southern lands of Britain and they were known in most of the villages before they even left childhood. They were welcomed too because children of a war band invariably became warriors themselves and most villagers reasoned it never hurt for a warrior to have good memories of you and your village.

It was not until his mid-teens that Cei realised two things about his constant companions. He hopelessly loved Trevenna and while everyone treated Arthur with respect, no one and no village had ever seemed genuinely pleased to see him or welcome him to their homes. Cei did not understand why that was but once he had noticed the difference in the way they looked upon Trevenna and the way they acted towards Arthur he saw it everywhere and every time. Either Arthur didn't notice or didn't care because Cei never saw him react to it and he never seemed to resent or hold it against his sister or his friends.

By the time Cei was seventeen, and after a year of debating the matter with Ceinwen and Ruadan, he had declared his love to Trevenna and sought Arthur's approval. Arthur had been happy enough for them and Cei had thought that golden summer the best of his life. In his memory it seemed to stretch on for years. Cei had been too involved with Trevenna to see that it was around that time when people began to fear Arthur, seeing in the adult what they had suspected in the child. People talked among themselves when he was far away from them, trying to voice what it was they felt. Most could not define it but others agreed quietly that it was in his lifeless, gray eyes, something different from themselves, something alien to their nature, something they could not reach. These fears and nameless suspicions were only strengthened by the amount of times he was seen travelling with and talking to Merdynn. Cei never really understood why others feared Arthur so much and their friendship had lasted and grown over the years. His love for Trevenna had never waned. As Merdynn crossed towards him with a plate of food he wondered if he or Trevenna would ever see Arthur again.

'Lost in bad thoughts?' Merdynn asked folding the robes of his cloak as he sat down.

'No, not at all, they were good thoughts, happy ones. At least I think they were,' Cei replied and pinched his nose, frowning.

Merdynn laughed, 'Gods, you don't even know your own thoughts!'

Cei joined him, 'It's a complicated business this thinking. Not really a warrior's best quality.'

Merdynn chuckled and offered Cei some food from his plate. Cei helped himself to a piece of dried meat and started to chew it laboriously.

'Let me guess where you were,' Merdynn said.

'Go on then,' Cei replied smiling. It was a game Merdynn used to play with them when they were children. Merdynn rubbed his old hands together, his eyes twinkling.

'It was summer?' he asked, Cei nodded cautiously and Merdynn continued, 'Hmmm, you, Trevenna and Arthur. Maybe with Ceinwen and Ruadan? No? Just the three of you then, when you were children?' Cei narrowed his eyes and nodded again. 'Right, it was the time when the three of you stole that cow from a village then lost it and yourselves on the moors!'

Cei laughed, 'Yes, you can still do it.'

Merdynn looked at him and offered his food once more. 'I'm not so old that you have to humour me you know. And you used to be either a touch more honest, or a touch more subtle.'

Cei shrugged in reply. Merdynn sighed and looked up at the winter sky through an arched opening halfway up the high wall.

'You were thinking about your love for Trevenna and why people acted the way they did around Arthur.'

'Gods! You can still do it,' Cei said staring at him.

'Did you reach any conclusions?'

'Only that I still love her and that I can't remember anyone ever loving Arthur.'

'I think Ceinwen might have, once. But people can't love what they fear. They can fear what they love but not vice versa.'

Trevenna came and sat cross-legged in front of them, 'Dispensing eternal truths and worldly wisdom?' she asked Merdynn.

'Pearls before swine, I'm afraid young lady. Pearls before swine.'

'Young?' Cei asked.

'But you got the swine bit right,' Trevenna added sharply.

'Oh, you're not going to argue are you? Or worse, make up?' Merdynn asked, equally appalled by both prospects.

'No, don't worry,' Trevenna said smiling brilliantly at him.

Confronted with that smile and her laughing, turquoise blue eyes, Merdynn could not stop a slow smile forming on his own lips.

'You have an extraordinary power you know,' Merdynn said to her. She winked at him in acknowledgement.

'So do you it seems,' Cei said, 'What was it that you did back there?'

'Something simple Nature did to stop those Irrades getting themselves into trouble.'

'Who?' Trevenna asked, puzzled at the exchange.

'Irrades – it's what the poisoned descendents of this city call themselves.'

Trevenna still looked bewildered.

'Beautiful but not, perhaps, the brightest star in the sky,' Merdynn muttered.

She looked daggers at him.

'Those shambling iron-beating creatures we came across! Good heavens woman! The Irrades!' Merdynn cried, disturbing those around him who were attempting to sleep. He continued in a quieter voice, 'Though in truth I think I'm the dullard. No idea what possessed me to start fooling around this far from our own land. I'll kick myself if it leads to ill.'

'Well, if you need help just give me a nod,' Trevenna said and got up to find a place to rest for a while.

'She's got the right idea,' Cei said standing up too, 'About resting that is – not kicking you.' He picked his way over the sleeping figures, following Trevenna and leaving Merdynn to absently chew over his food and his own misgivings.

Cei woke suddenly as Herewulf's strong hand shook him by the shoulder. Still half-asleep he stared up into the grey bearded face.

'What is it?' Cei asked, working his eyes to focus on his surroundings.

'Come,' Herewulf said simply and led the still groggy Cei to the lip of the entrance to their cavern.

The sky was still cloudless and strewn with the brilliant hard winter stars but the wind had picked up and it was beginning to trail snow from the broken ruins. It looked as if fires burned deep under the whole of the city and the wind was whipping the smoke from the remnants of the surface. The icing wind brought tears to Cei's eyes and he quickly wiped them away to stop them from freezing on his face. He was completely awake now and scanned the alien landscape for signs of danger. Then he heard it, faintly at first then more clearly as the wind subsided then strengthened. The distant tolling of a bell. He lowered and cocked his head to one side, frowning at the stonework before his face as he listened intently.

It did not have the clear tones of the great bell at Caer Sulis but it was unmistakably the tolling of a bell. Herewulf pointed in the direction he thought it came from then pointed off to the right. Cei nodded, there were two bells tolling with a haunting rhythm that denied the possibility that it was the work of the wind. He swore.

'Wake the others, we need to leave here. Quick.'

Herewulf left to rouse the others so that they could get the horses saddled and ready to leave. Merdynn appeared at Cei's side and crouched down with surprising ease.

'Bless me, that wind's cold. What is it?' he asked, wrapping his cloak tightly around himself.

'There are bells tolling out there. From at least two different directions. Your Irrades appear a lot more organised than the last time you were here.'

Merdynn's levity vanished instantly. 'We must leave here now.'

'That's what I thought,' Cei answered and signalled the lookouts to return. As they passed into the cavern Cei asked if they had seen any sign of the Irrades from their vantage point. Ranulf and Roswitha had thought they had spotted distant figures on the higher piles of rubble but the wind-blown snow made it difficult to be sure. Cuthwin had not seen any sign of them at all.

Within minutes Cei was leading his band across the frozen river, which embraced their temporary shelter. There was a deep layer of soft snow covering the ice and they laboured across in single file with the lead horses frequently sinking up to their flanks before they could thrash a way forward again.

Cei urged them on desperately. To be caught here would be fatal and they all realised the danger. The wind was gusting over the flat reach of the river and scything off the top layer of snow, reducing visibility to only a few yards. They pushed onwards and were relieved to reach the far bank safely.

Cei was the first to reach the far side and his horse laboured up through the deep snow covering the sloping bank of the frozen river. He pulled the reins around and watched as his riders emerged from the blasting snow that was being picked up and driven relentlessly across the flat surface of the frozen river.

The riders milled about on the bank as their horses snorted great plumes of hot breath that were immediately snatched away by the rapacious wind. Cei signalled Merdynn and Aelfhelm to take the lead and then searched the opposite bank for any signs of movement. He shuddered and pulled his sheepskin cap down over his raw, stinging ears but it was not just the cutting wind that made him shiver. The broken carcass of the ancient city that was laid out before him was both eerie and unreal. The winter stars shone down on the endless lines of heaped rubble and the half-collapsed towers stood out from the littered bones of the dead city like the ribcage of some enormous beast. The air close to the ground was thick with wind-hurled snow, which made the higher mounds and towers appear to be drifting across the landscape.

Cei could still catch the tolling of the cracked bells, their sullen message borne over the dead city by the storm. Then he saw the figures crawling over the buttressed ruins of the shelter they had just left. He cursed and turned his horse to hurry after the others who were already disappearing into the flying snow.

'Close up and keep moving! They aren't far behind us!' he yelled to the riders as he passed by them. As he overtook Trevenna he stabbed a thumb over his shoulder and she understood. Leaving Leah and Ethain she moved to the back of the small band and joined Cerdic. Together they kept a watchful eye behind them while urging those in front to increase their pace.

'Are we heading in the right direction?' Cei shouted to Merdynn when he was alongside him.

Merdynn looked up through the swirling snow at the constellations ahead of them then back towards the way they had come.

'Ish.'

'What?' Cei shouted above the wind.

Merdynn shrugged and nodded which Cei took to mean he did not really know, but this way was as good as any other. It didn't comfort him. It was no good escaping from those behind if they had no idea what was ahead. He left Aelfhelm and Cuthwin to forge the path onwards and passed back down the file of horsemen, telling them to keep close together and ride two abreast so that they could keep a watch on either flank.

They travelled that way for an hour, covering no more than two or three miles through the labyrinth of snowed gulleys before the wind carried to them once again the clanging of the iron bells. Minutes later Ethain gave a muffled shout, pointing to the high ruins on their left flank. His softly spoken voice did not carry to the others and Leah bellowed out the warning. Misshapen figures were shambling across the hills of rubble, tracking parallel to them and matching their pace.

They pulled their horses up and Leah swung her bow off her shoulder but Cei stopped her from shooting. Their trackers were over a hundred yards away, the wind was strong and their supply of arrows was limited. Cei was unsure what to do. He could not attack the pursuers without clambering up into the ruins and leaving their horses behind, and clearly they were not able to outpace the Irrades in this terrain.

'Why are we waiting? We should attack them!' Cerdic yelled out hefting his sword. Ethain gave him a surreptitious look of heart-felt hatred.

'Daft bugger, they'd have our horses away and scoffed before we got anywhere near them,' Leah remarked leaning in close to Ethain who regarded her with renewed fondness.

'They can watch from that distance all they like!' Herewulf shouted over to Cei who nodded and ordered them to continue onwards. They had not gone more than two hundred yards when a yelp from Ethain told them that the Irrades were now shadowing them on both sides. Cei urged them onwards but the deep snow made it impossible for them to put any distance between themselves and their shadowers.

Herewulf spurred his horse to the front and Roswitha joined him. Together they took the lead from Cuthwin and Aelfhelm's tiring mounts. Herewulf turned to Cei and voiced his concern that if the path they were following narrowed it would provide their pursuers with an excellent ambush point. Cei agreed and prayed silently to his gods that the route would not close in on them. Perhaps his gods listened to him because the path became steadily wider until it was almost two hundred yards between the lines of chaotically stacked debris that edged their improvised route, but his prayer of thanks died on his lips.

Stretching across the roadway ahead of them waited a line of black armoured Adren. They stood shoulder to shoulder, motionless in the wind-driven snow with their shields interlocked and curved swords raised. Behind the shield wall were three mounted Adren Captains, their silver helmets glinting in the starlight.

Cei and Herewulf pulled on their reins and stopped in their tracks. At the rear a cry went up from Trevenna and Cerdic, who had not yet seen what was waiting ahead of them. Behind Cei's band the Irrades were swarming down from the high ground of the city's ruins and cutting off their retreat. Cei's riders bunched together turning back and forth assessing the threat that bracketed them.

The path behind them was now thick with the hunched and shambling figures of the Irrades and still more were spilling down from the hills of rubble to either side.

Herewulf turned his horse from the gathering Irrades and pushed his way to Cei, 'There's hundreds of those bastards!' he yelled above the constant wind.

Cei looked from the waiting Adren and back to Herewulf whose greying beard was now white from the flying snow. They both realised the only way out was through the Adren line. Cei was about to give the order when Aelfhelm shouted and pointed towards the Adren.

A lone Adren Captain was pushing his way through the Adren ranks and slowly making his way towards the Anglian riders. The snow swept across the open space between them in thin veils giving the impression that the earth beneath was steaming.

Cei looked at Merdynn who shrugged and they both nudged their mounts forward to meet the approaching captain. They met halfway between the two groups and stood regarding each other. The Adren Captain was well equipped for the dark winter and both his clothing and weapons appeared to be new. His silver helmet slanted down on either side of his head, covering his face and had narrow slits for his eyes. The high helmet was squared at the forehead and overlarge to allow for the thick fur padding on the inside. A design had been worked into the front. He wore a thick, black fur cloak and Cei wondered what type of animal it had come from.

'What is it that you want?' Cei asked as his horse bucked its head and stamped at the snow.

The silver helmet turned directly to Merdynn and the captain spoke in a language Cei had never heard before. Merdynn turned to Cei, 'He's actually speaking your tongue – though you'd never know it for the accent.'

Cei waited for Merdynn to continue.

'Yes, well, he says that you are all free to return to your land if I surrender to them.'

'I didn't think the Adren made any deals.'

'Whether they would let you go or not is another matter but I doubt it and even if they did, I doubt the Irrades would be so keen to see their four-legged feast walking away. Or the two-legged one either come to that.'

The Adren Captain repeated his offer again but his voice was angry and his hand was on his sword hilt.

'They must be keen to get their hands on you and keep you alive,' Cei said levelly.

'Fairly keen to stay alive myself as it happens.'

'That could prove difficult,' Cei said gesturing to the Adren line behind the captain.

'Tempted then?'

'No, not in the least. Tell him.'

Merdynn faced the captain and began speaking in the singsong, staccato variety of the language that the Adren used. Before he could finish the Adren Captain snarled and in one movement spurred his horse to Merdynn and drew his sword, sweeping it towards Merdynn's head. With a speed that belied his age, Merdynn brought his staff up to meet the Adren's broad, curved blade.

Cei watched on in horror expecting the sharp blade to slice through the staff and kill Merdynn but there was a flash of light and the sword was flung backwards without leaving so much as a notch in the oak. A split second later Cei felt and heard an arrow speed past his shoulder and

31

the Adren Captain was jerked from his saddle as if he had been plucked backwards by an invisible force.

Ethain's horse skittered sideways then finally lost control under the fear of its rider and bolted. Ethain, already panicked, let out a thin scream and tried desperately to haul on the reins to bring the beast under control. In seconds he was flashing past the still twitching Adren Captain and heading straight for the Adren shield wall. Behind him Cerdic let loose a battle cry and sped after his companion whom he thought was incensed into leading a lone charge against the enemy. Others followed the pair in two's and three's and Cei cursed as the ragged charge swept by him. He and Merdynn had no choice but to follow the others with Herewulf and Wolfestan bringing up the rear on their slower mounts.

Ethain had only just realised where his blindly racing horse was heading and he screamed curses as he fought to stay on the beast and haul back on the reins at the same time. Ahead of him the Adren line tensed, shields raised before them as they waited steadily.

Ethain was only yards away when his horse finally realised what was ahead of it, obeyed his commands and tried to stop. It slid onwards through the snow then reared up in panic as it reached the Adren wall, its hooves flailing desperately as it crashed into the shields. The madly sliding horse smashed through the line sending several Adren sprawling in a tangled, thrashing mess of hooves, swords and shields. Ethain was sent sprawling in the cloud of snow and he lashed out blindly as the nearest Adren slaughtered his horse and cut at him.

Cerdic roared as he saw Ethain break the line and he raced into the chaotic breach with the others thundering in a broken line behind him. He laid about him with his sword in a mad battle rage, searching for his fallen friend. Around him other horsemen were joining him and the shield wall was collapsing. Those Adren at either end of the line raced in to surround the riders. The Irrades had started their chase as soon as the charge had begun and were closing in on the melee.

Cerdic saw Ethain duck under an Adren blade then stumble backwards over his dying horse. Cerdic spurred his horse forward and his sword swung down onto the Adren's helmet and glanced off. The Adren reeled away dazed and Cerdic yelled to Ethain with his hand outstretched. Ethain grasped it and Cerdic hauled him up into the saddle.

Cei was roaring above the noise of the frantic battle for them to ride onwards. One by one they fought their way free of the breach, using their horses to bludgeon a way through. As Cei swung his axe repeatedly down on the Adren surrounding him, he tried to see who was free of the mess and who was not. He saw Trevenna battling one of the Adren Captains, their swords flashing at each other as they fought to control their horses. Leah swept past them and her spear tore the captain from his horse and was wrenched from her grasp as she and Trevenna kicked their horses free of the confusion. Cei buried his axe deep into the shoulder of an enemy below him then, having to use both hands, tugged the heavy weapon free and spurred his horse after the others.

Once clear, he glanced back over his shoulder. The Adren and Irrades were all racing to the point where the riders had broken through the line and where the fighting still continued. He could see at least two of his riders unhorsed and still enmeshed in the battle. He recognised Herewulf by his long grey ponytail, which swung back and forth as he hacked about him with his long sword. Cei turned his horse to go back when he saw Herewulf's sword cut deeply into one of his attackers and momentarily bury itself in the Adren's guts. As he jerked it free others leapt at him and he fell under a rain of curved swords.

Cei checked his horse. Whoever else had been left behind must also have been killed as the Adren were leaving the churned mess of snow, blood and bodies and were now being marshalled by the remaining Adren Captain to give chase to the fleeing riders. Cei turned and sped after the others, yelling for them to regroup and ride together.

Aelfhelm had halted his horse's break-neck dash about a mile from the ambush and was collecting the straggled group when Cei arrived with Cerdic who bore Ethain behind him. Cei cast his eyes over the group, frantically looking for Trevenna. He saw her with Leah and let out a long breath of relief. Merdynn was with Roswitha, helping to bandage Elfilda's badly gashed thigh. She would not remain still and kept calling out for her brother, Wolfestan, who was not among the group.

'Anyone see Herewulf?' Cerdic asked loudly.

'He's dead. They cut his horse from under him,' someone answered.

'He died bravely, laying about him and taking some of the bastards with him,' Cei added as he searched the faces to see who else had not survived.

'Wolfestan?' he asked.

'He went back to try and help Herewulf and Ranulf but one of their captains rode him down.'

'Ranulf too?' Cei asked.

Both Thruidred and Wayland nodded. Cei cursed then went to see the injured Elfilda. Three dead and they were not out of the city yet. As he knelt by the squirming Elfilda they heard a horse galloping towards them. The mounted riders readied themselves but it was one of the dead men's horses. Trevenna went to retrieve it and Cei turned his attention back to Elfilda. Roswitha was shaking her head behind her.

'I've lost too much blood,' she said and cursed, voicing what Roswitha was implying. The snow around her was soaked dark red. Cei looked at Merdynn who just pressed his lips together and shrugged miserably.

'You'll recover Elfilda, we'll rest here a bit. Cerdic, take Wayland and go back down the roadway, join Wolfestan and make sure there's no pursuit.'

The others all looked at Cei for a second then looked away. Elfilda grabbed Cei's arm fiercely.

'My brother's alive? He's safe?' she said through gritted teeth.

'He's fine. Hacked down three of the bastards. Now, rest easy, we need to stop this bleeding.'

Cei examined the sopping bandage that was wound tightly around her thigh. Blood was seeping out in great pulses as each heartbeat pushed the life from her. She was weakening quickly and lay back in Cei's arms.

'Tell him he's a great useless bastard but that I love him,' she said softly and smiled as the pain ebbed and the last of the life drained from her.

'You can tell him yourself now, Elfilda,' Cei said, gently closing her eyes. He looked up at the sound of drumming hooves. Cerdic and Wayland raced up through the still swirling snow.

'They're coming!' Cerdic yelled.

The warriors mounted and Ethain took the spare horse. As they were preparing to leave Ethain cried out to them, 'We can't leave her here, not for them!'

Cei looked down at the dead girl and realised what Ethain was implying. They could not afford to carry her, it would slow them down but after what they had seen at Branque they could not leave her here for the Adren either.

'Get moving, Cei,' Merdynn said, taking the responsibility from him.

As the riders cantered away Leah stole a glance backwards and saw Merdynn standing over the body of her friend. As she watched flames began to flick around the lifeless body. She shuddered and prayed to the gods that they would not hold it against Elfilda when she arrived at their gates.

She turned away from Merdynn and stared in disbelief as Wayland slowly toppled from his saddle in front of her, a crude arrow sticking incongruously from the side of his face. Suddenly there were rocks, stones and iron bars raining down around her. An iron bar caught her across the shoulder and head and the world darkened as she slumped in her saddle. She felt hands holding her against her horse and a distant voice screaming at her from what seemed a different world. Gradually the voice became nearer and clearer and her horse's ice-rimed mane came into focus before her eyes.

Ethain was trying to shield them both from the missiles that were hurling down upon them from the high ruins on either side of the roadway. She could not make out what he was saying and put it down to her confusion when in fact he was just incoherently cursing. Above the noise around her she heard Cei roaring for them to ride on. The Irrades had put little faith in the Adren trap and had set their own ambush further along the road. Winter food was rare and never walked willingly into their city and they were not prepared to lose the opportunity of adding to their winter store.

No sooner had Leah sat up straight than she was thrown forward onto her horse's neck again as a large rock cracked into her back. She grunted at the force of the blow but the shield she had slung across her shoulders took most of the impact and it served to jolt her back into awareness. Ethain was trying to lead her horse out of the narrows and after the others who were already racing ahead and away from the trap but the Irrades had abandoned their missile assault and were now leaping down onto the roadway.

Leah yelled a warning to Ethain as the figures closed on him in a shambling rush. Ethain did not seem to hear, his head was down and he was furiously kicking his heels into his horse's flanks in an effort to get clear. Leah drew her sword just as she was tumbled from her saddle by an Irrades who had taken a mighty leap from the ruins.

Together they sprawled in the snow, grappling to get on top of one another. Leah could feel its foul breath on her face and she twisted violently, driving the attacker off her. She scrambled on top of him and bringing her sword's edge to his throat, pressed down with all her weight. Through the shower of blood she saw his face clearly for the first time and she recoiled in horror.

She stumbled to her feet and doubled over as an iron bar thumped into her stomach. She lurched sideways to avoid the following down swing and the heavy bar crashed into the snow beside her. She stood bent over fighting for breath, momentarily winded and unable to move and she looked up to face her death just as her assailant's head flew from its shoulders. As the creature fell she saw Ethain standing behind it, his sword dripping blood into the snow and a wild look in his eyes.

The Irrades were rushing into the narrows all around them and she looked on, still gasping for air as Ethain charged headlong into them swinging and hacking with the madness of desperation. Three of the Irrades fell in mutilated heaps of severed limbs and pooling blood before Ethain's legs were hooked from under him.

Leah covered the short distance screaming a war cry with her sword held high. They backed away long enough for Ethain to regain his feet and they stood back to back as the Irrades circled them beyond sword's length. Leah could hear Ethain muttering to the gods in a trembling voice. Thirty or forty of the Irrades surrounded them and there could only be one outcome. She reached behind her and took Ethain's hand.

'Thanks for trying to save me. We'll take some of these hideous creatures with us, eh?'

If she was looking for encouragement and bravery in the face of death then she would have been disappointed by the mewing whimper which was all Ethain could manage. She did not appear to hear though and freed her hand from Ethain's tight grasp so that she could unsling her shield.

Some of the Irrades had already slaughtered their horses and were dragging them away leaving long trails of blood in the furrowed snow. The others were intent on taking the two warriors as well. Two dashed at Leah who took one blow on her shield and cut at the other with her sword. They took turns to sporadically lunge at her as they mustered themselves for closing the circle.

Two more lunged at Ethain. He met one of the clubs with his sword but was unable to stop the other attacker jabbing a bar into his groin. He collapsed to one knee and the Irrades cried out. Leah felt Ethain go down beside her and thought the cry that went up signalled their end but suddenly there was the thunder of horses all around them and the Irrades were being trampled and hacked in a furious charge as Cei and the others smashed into and through their crowded ranks. Leah was knocked aside as one of the horses cannoned into her and she scrabbled on all fours to throw herself over the prostrate Ethain and protect him from the carnage.

Seconds later and the charge had taken Cei's horses through the narrowed roadway and the surviving Irrades were scrambling back up and into the ruins. Leah lifted herself off Ethain and gently turned him over.

'Ethain? Are you wounded?' she said scanning his bloody body then seeing where he clutched himself added, 'Is any of this blood yours?' She carefully took his hand away as he shook his head. 'You'll live,' she said with a smile and helped him to his feet.

She too was covered in blood and gore and absently brushed at the mess as she looked around the killing ground. The horses were thundering back towards them.

'Quick! The Adren aren't far behind!' Cei shouted to them both.

Roswitha offered her hand to Leah and she leapt up into the saddle behind her. Trevenna offered Ethain a place and he mounted gingerly, grimacing as he sat in the saddle. As they rode off, Cerdic came alongside Trevenna and thumped Ethain on the shoulder.

'Didn't think we'd leave behind the hero who broke the Adren ranks did you?' he cried grinning at him. Ethain just closed his eyes, held Trevenna tightly round the waist and rested his head against her back as they rode through the ruined city under a waning moon.

As the moon sank behind a growing bank of clouds they finally left behind the last outlying ruins of the city. They left behind the Irrades who ravenously feasted upon horseflesh, their own dead and Cei's fallen warriors. They left behind the ominous remains of once great dwellings and the sullen tolling of the iron bells. They also left behind six of their own number as Osla too had fallen, unseen by Ethain and Leah, in the ambush on the narrow roadway. But they did not leave behind the Adren or their remaining Captain, who had orders to take Merdynn no matter what the cost, for the Adren followed Cei's tracks through the city and out onto the white plains beyond.

Cei's riders travelled on for several hours after leaving the city, across a gently rolling country of low hills, frozen river valleys and clusters of small woodlands. Eventually Cei called a halt and they hastily set up a camp on the edges of a small wood that provided them with some protection from the wind, which still scoured across the white winter-locked land.

They spread what canvas they had to shield the fire from the wind and to hide their presence in the lifeless land. The warriors huddled around the fire trying to warm their tired bodies and dry their sweat-soaked winter clothing. Their mood was a strange mixture of joy at surviving and having killed some of the enemy, and grief for the loss of their companions. Only twelve of them remained and they only had ten horses. Both Merdynn and Cei were acutely aware that their journey had only just begun and countless leagues stood before them and the Adren City.

They ate frugally and made a weak but hot gruel. Some were talking excitedly, their bodies still coursing with adrenaline as they relived the skirmishes. Others sat silently watching the fire, dwelling on the fates that took in battle a warrior like Herewulf and yet let them live. Leah and Cerdic were among those who talked and laughed about the events back in the city.

Cerdic raised his broth in toast to Ethain, 'To the hero who wouldn't wait for the order and who charged the Adren wall alone - and broke it alone!'

Others raised their drinks in salute to Ethain's bravery.

'How on Earth did you manage to get your horse to charge into the Adren swords?' Trevenna asked.

'And to his horse that was just as brave as him,' Merdynn added.

Ethain could not meet their eyes and his gaze shifted about on the ground before him. He darted a look at Merdynn just to confirm that he was smiling exactly as he thought he was. He was.

'And for standing by me when these bastards were running away!' Leah added to quiet laughter and put a hand on Ethain's shoulder, 'Thank you, Ethain.'

Ethain could not stand it any longer and shrugged off Leah's hand and jumped to his feet staring at the faces around the fire.

'We're all going to bloody die out here! You treat it like a child's game!' He was going to add more but stopped in exasperation and stormed off into the darkness between the trees.

The others were silent, astonished by Ethain's words.

'He's a serious warrior. Brave to madness yet he feels the loss of his friends as if it were his fault,' Cerdic said and shook his head in quiet admiration. Others grunted their agreement and raised their steaming drinks once more. Leah stood up and pulling her thick cloak around her, walked off after Ethain.

'Give a dog a good name...' Merdynn muttered into his soup. Only Cuthwin heard him and he frowned at his words.

Conversations started again around the fire and Cei drew Merdynn and Aelfhelm to one side to discuss their situation. They quickly agreed it was not good.

'And there's only twelve of us now,' Aelfhelm added unhelpfully, his brow furrowing even more deeply than was usual.

'And only ten horses. The lighter ones can share - Roswitha, Leofrun, Trevenna and Ethain - but still, it'll slow us down,' Cei said.

'I don't believe the Adren or, more accurately, their Adren Captain will give up the chase,' Merdynn added.

'They want you, don't they?' Cei asked.

'Yes. Unfortunate that.'

'How's our food lasting?' Cei asked Aelfhelm who just grunted.

'And the horse feed?'

'Almost as bad but we'll be eating them before we run out of food for them,' he said, his close-set eyes looking levelly at Cei.

Cei sighed heavily.

'How much further do we have to go?' Aelfhelm asked.

Merdynn shifted uneasily, unwilling to let him know the bad news.

'That bad, eh? Well, what choice do we have?' Aelfhelm shrugged, resigned to their situation and still shocked by the death of Herewulf.

'What choices do we have, Merdynn?' Cei asked. He was torn between the reality of their situation and the faith Arthur had put in him.

'Well, we can't go back to the Causeway. Too many Adren there. No longboats on the Belgae coast. Arthur would have taken them by the time we can get there – if the Adren haven't already destroyed them.'

'Perhaps not all of them?' Aelfhelm asked with hope.

'He'd burn those he didn't take,' Merdynn continued, 'So. We can carry on, though admittedly the going will become harder the further we travel into the Shadow Lands,' Merdynn paused and then voiced what he had been thinking since their encounter with the Adren Captain, 'or we can abandon our quest and make for the Breton lands.'

'And where are they?' Cei asked.

'They're across the sea from Wessex. Good people.'

'Would they have boats to take us to Wessex?' Aelfhelm asked, his hope flitting from one option to another.

'The main village is on the coast, and yes, they fish the seas so they'll have boats,' Merdynn answered.

Aelfhelm studied Cei who still wrestled with the opposing responsibilities of keeping his warriors alive and trying to carry out Arthur's plan.

'Let me think about it,' he finally said.

'We can't stay here long. I fear the Adren will be nose-down to our tracks,' Merdynn said standing.

Aelfhelm wanted to stay to help Cei decide but Merdynn gently led him back to the fire. In truth, Cei knew the quest east was all but finished, especially now that the Adren knew Merdynn was with them. Merdynn had come to the same bitter conclusion. Cei did not see how they could continue in worsening conditions with the provisions they had while being hunted down. Still he remained undecided. He knew how much depended on Arthur's plan. Everything did.

Leah found Ethain leaning with his back against a cold tree trunk and his head hung down resting on his chest. She was not quiet approaching him but he jumped nonetheless when she rested a hand on his shoulder, which still felt thin even under the thick layers of winter cloaks.

'Are you angry?'

He turned slowly to face her, his eyes red and watery. Her hand was still on his shoulder and she felt him shaking. He realised that she had noticed and looked away wretchedly.

'You're cold, shivering. It's always the same after the heat of battle,' she said, lying to comfort him a little. She led him to a clump of fallen trees where the upturned broad tangle of roots offered more protection from the searching wind. They sat down side by side.

'It's not the cold. I'm scared. And I'm scared of showing that I'm scared,' he said with his chin once again resting on his chest.

Leah looked sideways at him, surprised by his honesty and surprised by the warmth she felt for him. She saw a tear form on his long eyelashes and track down his nose where it hung for a moment before a second swelled it and began a steady drip onto his cloak. He made no attempt to hide his silent crying and she admired him for it. She put an arm around him and drew him closer to her.

'At your age I was scared too. Still am. We all are. We've just learnt to hide it,' Leah said, wondering briefly why she was lying to this boy.

She loved battle and like most of the warriors she lived for fighting and the sheer joy it brought. But something about this young man's honesty and vulnerability made her feel suddenly very attracted to him. Unlike most of the men she knew there was no sense of having to compete with him and no need to prove anything to him either.

He certainly was not trying to prove anything to her or impress her yet she felt impressed by his self-abasing truthfulness and he had already proved himself when he stood by her in the city. She realised it must have taken an awful effort for him to have tried to help her when he could have just bolted without anyone judging him the worse for it.

He took his sheepskin cap off and wiped it across his nose and scruffy, sparse beard. He glanced at Leah, 'I only wish I had your courage. And strength,' he muttered in his soft voice.

'Perhaps you can have both,' Leah said and leant across and kissed his lips. She could taste the salt of his tears. She changed her position so that she was facing him.

'Are you recovered now?' she said smiling.

He nodded uncertainly and wiped his finger back and forth under his nose, sniffing back his tears.

Leah stroked the side of his face and laughed softly, 'I see you have recovered.' She kissed him again, brushing her tongue across his lips.

He shook his head.

'Why not? We could be dead by the time the moon next wanes! And there's nothing better after cheating death – trust me!' she said grinning at him.

Ethain could not speak but his eyes were wide and he shook his head slightly again.

'Have you not done this before?' Leah asked quietly and judged she was right by his embarrassed look.

'Don't worry. I have,' she smiled again, her pale blue eyes keen with anticipation.

Chapter Two

The wind was from the southwest and it brought rain. It was the first heavy rain in Britain since the sun had set in autumn. Arthur sat on the steps of the Great Hall and watched as it swept through the darkness of Caer Sulis in dense, torrential curtains. It clattered on the roofs of the buildings and washed away the accumulated snow of winter. The roads and pathways about the town ran like streams as the water quickly pooled on the frozen ground.

Morgund stood leaning against a pillar behind Arthur and he too watched the deluge, mesmerised by the sight after months of snowfall. All around the town people leant out of windows or stood in doorways and watched the driving rain. They stared in silence as the white mask of winter was slowly stripped from the land.

Sunrise was still a month away and the rains were unusual for this time of year. Normally winter would die fiercely, hurling snowstorms and blizzards blown on gales from the East. Throughout the town those who wanted to read evil signs into the sudden rains did so and those who wanted to take encouragement from the early retreat of winter argued the point with them but they all shared the same sense of foreboding. No one felt the jubilation usually associated with the coming of spring, for with the spring would come the Adren.

Morgund shifted against the post, 'Never thought I'd be unhappy to see the end of winter.'

Arthur looked up at him and saw anxiety in the pale eyes that contrasted so starkly with his dark face. He grunted in reply and with his hands on his knees levered himself to his feet. His leg was still stiff from the arrow wound he had received at Branque and he wondered absently how long it would be before he was free from the nagging pain. He was about to go back into the hall when Morgund started to chuckle. He looked around to see what had made him laugh and smiled too.

Ceinwen was splashing her way across the courtyard in front of the hall. The water already stood two-feet deep in places and it swirled around her thighs as she waded towards them. With her wavy hair bedraggled and her sodden clothes hanging on her slight frame, she looked more like a lost child than a warrior. She was swearing with each laborious step and when she finally climbed the steps and saw Morgund grinning at her she slapped him wetly across the side of the face and stamped on into the hall leaving a trail of water behind her. Morgund just laughed and he and Arthur followed her in.

The hall had served as Arthur's main base during the last two months although he had made frequent trips to Caer Cadarn to coordinate all the necessary preparations for war being undertaken by Laethrig, the war band's blacksmith. At any one time there were usually fifty or so warriors in the hall, a mix of Gereint's Mercians and Arthur's company. The tension between the two groups had been high at first but over the weeks they had become more accustomed to each other and gradually mutual respect and friendships had developed.

The warriors spent most of their time preparing themselves for what lay ahead and despite their experience they nonetheless practised and trained incessantly, always eager to learn and perfect a new feint, ploy or tactic that they might use in the months ahead. The half-empty town was usually quiet during the long winter darkness but in recent weeks it had rung to the clash of steel and the endless hammering from the forges as new swords, spears and arrowheads were added to the growing stockpiles of war.

Yet despite the increased activity a subdued atmosphere had settled on Caer Sulis. It was as if the whole town passed the darkness under a veil of grief, as if everyone had lost someone close to them and in the middle of a conversation or a shared laugh they would suddenly remember their loss and a heavy quietness would fall upon them. Each day took them nearer to a future filled with uncertainty and fear. The warriors had become anxious to start the journey to the Causeway and to face the Adren that waited on the far shores. The townsfolk fretted and worried about their own safety. Both the warriors and the people of Caer Sulis watched the swaying curtains of rain knowing that the uncertain future would soon be upon them.

Arthur gazed around and saw Ceinwen standing by one of the fires furiously rubbing her hair dry. He strode towards her forcing his stiff leg to work.

'How are the preparations going at the camp?'

Ceinwen had just returned from their base at Whitehorse Hill where Laethrig had the families of the Wessex and Anglian warriors working on the provisions for war.

'Going well,' she answered as she first tipped her head one way then the other, twisting a finger in her ears to clear out the water.

'Arrows?'

'Thousands. Wrapped, dry and ready for transport. Unlike me.' She self-consciously peeled off her soaked trousers and jacket and draped them near the fire where they immediately began to steam. She hunted around for some dry clothes among her few possessions. Modesty and privacy were luxuries that all the warriors had learnt to live without but she was still unused to living so closely with relative strangers, and those nearby, appreciating how she felt, either ignored her nakedness or made a point of turning away. Arthur watched her impatiently.

'Supplies? Meat, corn?'

'Yes, all ready to be loaded onto the wains.' She finally found the long woollen shift she was searching for and quickly pulled it over her head, belting it at the waist.

'Everything's ready, Arthur. Everything. They're just waiting for your word to begin taking it to the Causeway.'

Morveren walked across to them, 'You look like a drowned dog,' she said, smiling as she handed Ceinwen a hot drink. Ceinwen shook her still wet hair in Morveren's face by way of a reply.

As Arthur turned to leave them he heard his name being called out from the front of the hall. Several warriors were gathered around a cloaked figure by the doorway and Morgund was waving him over. Arthur looked to see if anyone else had arrived with the newcomer for he knew who it was even before he threw back the hood of his cloak. Terrill, Captain of the Cithol, had come from the Veiled City to Caer Sulis but he had come alone.

Arthur sat with him at the top table and beckoned Gereint and Elwyn to join them. He introduced them to Terrill as representatives for the Mercians and Anglians. Gereint had seen Lord Venning at the King's Council but Elwyn had not seen a Cithol before and struggled to keep the amazement from his face as he stared at the black eyes and the strange washed-out pigment of his skin that looked that it should be as dark as

Morgund's but actually seemed more grey than black.

The Cithol Captain in turn looked at the thickset, pale-skinned Anglian with his short-cropped sandy hair that stood up in wet spikes. They each found the other strange and alien and when Terrill turned his black eyes to study Gereint it took all the Mercian's self-control to keep his expression neutral.

'Have you travelled alone?' Arthur asked and Terrill looked to him and nodded slowly as if answering the real question behind the enquiry; Fin Seren remained in the Veiled City.

Arthur breathed in deeply, unsure whether he was disappointed at not being able to see her yet or relieved that at least one complication was delayed until later. His formal marriage to Gwyna, the daughter of Ablach the Uathach chieftain, was only a matter of weeks away now. He would have to decide whether to send this news back to Seren via Terrill or wait until he had the chance to tell her himself. Both Elwyn and Gereint realised that more was being said in the silence than was actually being spoken.

'Has there been any news of Merdynn?' Terrill asked.

Arthur shook his head. Only a few knew of the real purpose behind Merdynn and Cei's quest in the Shadow Lands and the pivotal role it played in the defence of Britain. Those who were not aware of the true intent were becoming increasingly concerned over their continued absence.

Once again the other two were aware that the question asked more than was apparent to them and they were relieved when Ceinwen interrupted the uncomfortable silence by bringing a pitcher of hot drink and plates of food to the table. She had met Terrill previously at the Veiled City and he nodded to her in recognition. Arthur waved her to take a chair and she sat next to the Cithol Captain. Although she did not share the mix of amazement, fear and curiosity that the other warriors in the hall clearly felt, she still did not entirely trust the Cithol or their motives and she welcomed the chance to join in the meeting with Terrill.

Arthur was asking about Lord Venning's preparations for war and for the first time Terrill looked uncomfortable. His calm face became troubled and a brief frown creased his forehead as he looked away. Ceinwen watched with interest as he hesitated, clearly struggling to find the right words. She sensed that there was a serious disagreement among the Cithol regarding the part they had to play in the inevitable war and that the compromise they had settled for did not please Terrill. Finally he met Arthur's eyes and answered.

'Lord Venning does not yet feel the need to commit us to war.' He quickly raised a hand to stop Arthur's retort, 'It's not a view that I, or some others, share. Many of us feel that the numbers of the Adren host make it plain we must help you, and help you now before it is too late. But even among those who feel this, it is unclear how best we can aid you. We are not warriors. We have no experience of battle. Many are reluctant to even leave the Winter Wood and few are ready to stand by you in war. I am doing what can be done to convince the council and my people that it is not a matter of choice for war is coming and we either stand and fight for everything we have, or we flee and leave behind everything that is dear to us. We cannot do the latter and many won't accept the former; they hope that the Adren will not cross the Causeway or that you will hold them there for long enough.'

'We'd stand more chance of that if the Cithol stood with us at the Causeway Gates,' Ceinwen blurted out.

'I know this. It is hard to convince my people that they must stand by you for they've seen you and know you are warriors while they are not. It shames me that many think only to defend the Winter Wood, they cannot see that the Causeway is the gate to both your home and theirs. I have not given up the attempt to convince them otherwise and the matter is debated everywhere you turn in the Veiled City. There is still time, perhaps only a little, but some time nonetheless.

'The council has agreed on two things at least. We can provide your peoples with food from the crops grown in the caverns of the Veiled City. If you are to arm and train your people for war then at least in this way you will not have to concern yourselves with the summer harvest.' He sensed that Ceinwen was about to launch a protest at the suggestion and once again he held up his hand and hurriedly continued, 'I realise that this seems only to serve our ends, that we are willing for all your people to go to war while we merely send you food and stores but whether we stood by you in battle or not, you would need your farmers armed and trained and not tending fields.'

'How much can you provide?' Arthur asked.

'As much as you will need.'

'You can feed all the peoples of Britain?' Ceinwen had seen the caverns in the Veiled City where they produced the crops but she hadn't realised they were so extensive.

'Indeed.'

Gereint ventured a question, 'How long will this take?'

'We are already increasing our production. You will have the supplies as you need them.'

'It's how the Shadow Land City can provide for the Adren armies,' Arthur said to his nonplussed companions before continuing, 'You said there were two ways you could help us?'

'Yes, the second way is with weapons. Or one type of weapon to be precise. I have an example outside.' Terrill stood up and left to fetch the weapon.

'We need more than food from the Cithol!' Ceinwen said once he was out of earshot.

'At least we can put every able person to arms,' Gereint said reiterating the point that Terrill had made.

'That's if we can trust the Cithol to deliver the food,' Ceinwen muttered under her breath as Terrill returned.

He laid a crossbow on the table.

'We rarely hunt in the Winter Wood but when we do we use this. It takes years of training and great strength to wield your longbows but anyone can learn to use this in only a few days and a child's strength is all that is needed.'

Elwyn was inspecting the weapon and offered it back to Terrill, 'Show us how it works.'

Terrill took the crossbow and laid two ten inch, metal tipped darts on the table. He wound the twine back using a small handle underneath the bow and slotted a dart onto the centre groove then settling the stock into his shoulder he squeezed the trigger and the dart shot into the wall thirty-feet away. The other warriors in the hall had gathered around to watch and Terrill demonstrated once again how the handle pulled the twine back by a series of gears and how the trigger released it. The warriors passed the crossbow amongst themselves, inspecting it closely.

'It is not as accurate as your longbows, nor is it as powerful - so its range is obviously shorter. A bowman can fire arrows at a quicker rate too, but with this a child or old man, or in fact anyone who has never used a longbow before, could kill an Adren at twenty paces and continue doing so for as long as he had darts. We can give you hundreds of these and we are making more.'

The warriors who were now gathered around the table voiced their approval. Not a single one of them would ever contemplate exchanging their longbows for these new crossbows but they could see their value. They were light, it was easy to wind the twine back with the handle and the darts would be deadly at twenty paces. With this weapon then farmers, craftsmen, mothers, children, all could take their place in the battle against the Adren.

Arthur had taken Terrill to one side away from the crowding warriors and talked to him about where to send the food trains and the weapons. He offered him a place to rest before he returned to the Veiled City but with a quick look around the hall Terrill hastily declined. Arthur thanked him for his help and urged him to keep trying to persuade Lord Venning that the Cithol were needed at the Causeway. The Adren attack would begin before anyone had the chance to train on the new crossbows and any of the Cithol who were already familiar with the weapons could help in the defence of the Causeway.

Just as Terrill was about to depart, Arthur put a hand out to stop him. They stared at each other for a second, 'Tell Fin Seren that I do what I must and not what I would.'

Terrill looked at Arthur a moment longer then slipped out into the darkness where the cold rain still hammered down on Caer Sulis.

Arthur grew more impatient as spring edged closer. The peoples who had crossed the Western Seas were expected back soon but still no word of their arrival had come from the Haven. Mar'h and Lissa, whom he had sent across the seas to bring back the people earlier than was normal, would have told the King's Council of the news from Britain but Arthur was unsure how they would react. The counsellors and people had little choice but to accept him as the Warlord of Britain but the Mercian warriors who were with them might be harder to convince. He had sent Gereint and Elwyn on to the Haven to be there when the tall ships landed so that the returning Mercians and Anglians could hear what had unfolded from their own people.

When the rain finally eased he sent supplies of both arms and food to Ruadan and the warriors at the Causeway. He kept most of the new weapons at Caer Sulis for the training and arming of the people but the thousands of arrows that had been made at Whitehorse Hill and Caer Sulis were sent on to the Causeway.

A messenger from the Uathach arrived at the Great Hall declaring that Ablach would be there in ten days time with fifty of his warriors for the marriage of his daughter, Gwyna, to Arthur. Time was running out and Arthur sat brooding in the Great Hall, growing ever more impatient for word from the Haven. There had been no news from the Causeway either and Arthur despatched ten warriors to set up a relay across the country so that any word of the Adren moving across the Causeway would reach him as soon as possible.

Finally he could no longer sit idly by and he decided to ride to the Haven. He left Cael, who was making a determined effort to replace the bulk he had lost whilst travelling in the Shadow Lands, to see to the arrangements for the forthcoming wedding and he rode out of Caer Sulis with Morgund, Ceinwen and Morveren.

The unseasonable rain had passed by leaving the hillsides with only patchy remnants of the winter snow. The wind was still from the southwest and it pushed against them as they left behind the warmth and smoke-filled air of Caer Sulis. Long trails of thin dissipating clouds, still carrying the vestiges of the rain from the Western Seas, streaked the dark skies. Between the tattered clouds the last stars of winter stood in defiance of the coming dawn that was already evident on the western horizon.

All four of them were glad to be on the move again and Morveren was unable to resist the urge to spur her horse into a gallop as they travelled the still frozen Westway through the hills and valleys towards the Haven. Ceinwen's horse wanted to respond to the challenge but she checked it and the three of them rode abreast talking of the Shadow Lands, the Adren and the friends they had already lost in the fighting across the Causeway.

'Seems to me that Terrill and the Cithol are doing everything to allow our men, women and children to stand by us in battle against the Adren without risking any of their own people,' Morgund said during a lull in the conversation.

Ceinwen agreed wholeheartedly but kept her silence waiting for Arthur to respond. The silence extended and Morgund cast a glance at Arthur. Their horses walked on at an unhurried pace and the only noise on the Westway was the sound of their hooves on the hard ground and the gentle, rhythmic creaking of their saddles.

'The food and weapons will make a difference,' Arthur finally said.

'But enough of a difference?'

'It depends. It depends how long we can hold the Adren at the Causeway. It will take at least two months to turn farmers, fishers and craft workers into any kind of useful fighting force – even with the crossbows. If the Causeway falls before they can be brought to reinforce us then it will be too late.'

They both looked at Arthur.

'You think the Causeway will fall?' Ceinwen asked thinking of her brother, Ruadan, who was organising the defences there.

'We have to hold the Causeway,' Arthur replied flatly.

'Against the numbers we saw in the Shadow Lands I don't see how we can hold it forever,' Morgund said.

'We don't have to hold it forever. Just long enough,' Arthur replied and then told Morgund of the true nature of Merdynn and Cei's quest east, to destroy whatever relic of the past it was that allowed the Adren to produce the enormous amounts of food that were needed to keep their armies supplied.

Morgund nodded when Arthur finished, 'I thought there must have been a greater purpose than just ambushing the enemy food trains. Poor old Ethain. Bet that was more than he bargained for.'

'My village, my family, Tomas, Elowen, Talan – we've all got more than we bargained for,' Ceinwen pointed out.

'How good are their chances of success?' Morgund asked looking straight ahead.

Again long minutes passed before Arthur replied, 'It's our only chance of success.' He nudged his horse ahead of them both, wishing to be alone with his thoughts of Merdynn, Cei and his sister.

Morgund watched him ride ahead then guided his mount closer to Ceinwen, 'How will we know if they succeed or fail?'

'If we all die then they probably failed. If some of us live then they must have succeeded.' Ceinwen shrugged, the matter was out of their hands and they had their own course to follow.

'Right. Good. That's fairly clear then,' Morgund said.

'You sound like Merdynn,' Ceinwen answered, laughing softly at the memory of the old man.

'Someone has to carry his banner now he's gone.'

Clearly Morgund shared Ceinwen's private opinion that Cei and the others were more than likely already lying dead in the snow and ice somewhere deep in the Shadow Lands.

Arthur did not think that either Merdynn or his sister were dead. He would have been unable to explain why he thought that but he felt certain that if they had fallen then he would somehow know of it and that certainty gave him hope that they might yet succeed.

After several hours riding they caught up with Morveren who had stopped at a village that had been abandoned for the winter. She had started a fire in one of the roundhouses and they had seen the smoke rising into the night air from some miles away as it leant upwards and towards them, borne on the wind from the West that had softened to a breath. As they made their way down the main track through the village they could smell the food she had already begun to cook and they hurriedly saw to their horses' feed as the aroma from the roasting lamb tantalised their empty stomachs.

The rugs and pelts that hung in the roundhouse were still cold and dank despite the blazing fire that Morveren had lit some hours ago so they spread their thick winter cloaks on the floor around the fire and sat down. They settled contentedly around the warmth and started on the roast meat and thick vegetable broth that Morveren had prepared. The previous summer had provided a good harvest and there had been more than enough to send with those who crossed the Western Seas and still have ample left for those who wintered at Caer Sulis.

It was not always so. About ten years ago two ruinous summers in succession had stretched the food stocks extremely thinly and everyone, except the king's entourage, had gone hungry. The Uathach raids had been numerous and desperate; if the organised farmlands of the South were struggling then the ragged agriculture of the northern tribes would have been on the brink of collapse. If it had not been for the surplus harvests of the Western Lands that were brought back to Britain at the time of Imbolc, the festival to celebrate the return of the sun, then hunger would have slid to starvation, and if it had not been for the southern war bands then the Uathach would have plundered what little they had managed to store.

The meal was good and they paid Morveren the compliment of eating hungrily and in silence.

'So, where's the wine then?' Morgund said sitting back and wiping his greasy fingers on his trousers. Morveren told him just where he could look for the wine and he laughed.

'Did you manage to see any of your brothers before they left for the West?' he asked her.

'No, they'd already gone by the time we got to Caer Sulis.'

'Do you think they've forgiven you yet for not marrying that farmer?' Ceinwen asked, remembering a conversation a few weeks ago when Morveren had explained one of the reasons behind her joining the war band.

Morveren shrugged as she tied back her long black hair, 'Probably not. They think I ought to be married already, preferably with two or three children.'

'So why aren't you? That Anglian, Elwyn-something-or-other, he seems decent enough for a straw head and he's taken a liking to you, how about him?' Morgund asked, smiling at her as a blush crept into her thin, pale face.

'Leave the girl alone, Morgund,' Ceinwen said coming to her defence.

Morgund cast a quick glance at Arthur, who, as rumour suggested, might have been her true father but he was lying back lost in his own thoughts and ignoring the conversation by the fire.

'He's a fair bit older than you,' he pressed on enjoying himself. 'Not that there's anything thing wrong with having a few years behind you,' he said, smiling at Ceinwen.

'That's why he acts like an adult, unlike some,' Morveren replied then added, 'He's a good man.'

'He's a short man,' Morgund replied, leaning back with his hands behind his head.

'I don't think I'd be comfortable being with a man shorter than me,' Ceinwen said rejoining the attack.

'You couldn't find a man shorter than you,' Morveren pointed out and Morgund laughed.

'At least I don't lose track of who I'm supposed to be with,' Ceinwen said, turning on him much to Morveren's delight.

He just blew her a kiss.

Arthur stretched and stood up. On his way out of the hut he put a hand on Morveren's shoulder, 'Would that the Adren were so easy to divide and conquer.'

She lowered her head and flicked her eyes between the other two, smiling at them innocently. Morgund grunted and placed another log on the fire. Ceinwen checked over her shoulder to make sure Arthur had left the hut then turned to the other two, 'Why do you think the Uathach are only bringing fifty of their warriors to Caer Sulis for the wedding?'

'I thought they were going to turn up with all their warriors and then we'd all make for the Causeway,' Morveren added.

'Unless they don't plan to go to the Causeway. Maybe they're just going to sit up in the North and hope for the best,' Morgund said and resumed picking at his unusually white teeth with a splinter of wood.

'Gods, that's a sobering thought. No Cithol and no Uathach.'

'Just us and the Adren,' Morgund said it lightly enough but the thought settled in their minds and in the silence that followed he regretted saying it.

Morgund, like the other warriors, longed for battle, the madly unleashed joy and exhilaration simply couldn't be matched by anything else. All the warriors were experienced in battle and confident in their abilities, and every single one of them had at some time found themselves swaggering and strutting more than usual in front of the townsfolk of Caer Sulis over the last few months, taking pride in being all that stood between them and the Adren. None of those that had been in the Shadow Lands were naïve though and neither were they empty braggarts; they knew the time was coming when the swagger and posturing would have to be justified by standing firm against the enemy who would soon attack across the Causeway.

Even Ceinwen had found she had more in common with the warriors than with the townsfolk that she met in Caer Sulis. She didn't relish the prospect of fighting the Adren again but she knew that she couldn't just stay behind and await whatever outcome transpired.

Over the last few weeks she had noticed, and thought it strange, that the Mercians had shown more anxiety at the prospect of fighting the Adren than those who had already done so. When she mentioned it to Morgund he had put it down to the old adage that imagining something can often be worse than the reality. They had both quietly agreed that the old adage was rubbish. When Arthur returned they wrapped themselves in their warm cloaks and slept in front of the fire.

They set out as sporadic showers drifted in from the West adding to the collecting water that stood in the fields to either side of the Westway. The western horizon was clear of clouds and already the stars there were dimming as the first streaks of dawn touched the sky. They all noted it with the same mixed emotions and picked up their pace feeling a renewed urgency to reach the Haven. They alternatively set their horses to canter and walk and the miles slipped behind them.

For the most part Morveren kept her inclination to speed off in check and she rode with Arthur, talking and asking questions in an attempt to recapture the closeness she had felt when riding with him along the beach in Anglia but Arthur clearly had other matters on his mind and he answered her questions with an obvious patience.

At a casual pace it was another two days' journey to the Haven even if they cut across the estuary that divided Wessex from western Mercia. The whole of the estuary was subject to tidal flooding but the moon was waxing so the wide stretch of sand and mud could be crossed with care. Every month the high tide would build up against the silt deposits, laid down over the centuries by the river that meandered in sweeping curves across the breadth of the exposed estuary bed, until it finally breached the mud moraine that had been holding it back and then suddenly the tide would race over the thirty miles of the level expanse in little over an hour; within two hours the flats would be completely covered in over forty-feet of water as the Western Sea reclaimed the estuary.

They crossed the estuary on the second day of their journey and towards the end of the third day they at last approached the long stretch of grassland that swept down to the large bay of the Haven. It was half-encircled by a headland that reached out into the sea and then around the bay like a protecting arm, curling around the town that was spread all along the shore of the harbour. The glow of winter fires lit the warren of clustered huts, pens and roundhouses that were gathered tightly together on the grassland behind the dunes. The close-packed buildings edged the curved shoreline for over a mile. The grander and more official houses stood on the low headland and looked down on the maze of huddled dwellings from their perch above the deeper water where the wharves jutted out into the dark sea.

They brought their horses to a stop and looked down on the Haven, the bay from which the tall ships sailed for the Western Lands at the onset of each winter.

'Gods help us if we ever have to defend this place from the Adren,' Ceinwen said quietly, voicing the thoughts of the others; only Morveren had looked at the town without thinking how best to defend it from attack.

'If we ever have to defend this place from the Adren then the gods would have deserted us long ago,' Morgund replied and they made their way across the frozen but snow-free fields.

Like Caer Sulis, the Haven was half-empty during the winter months with most of the population farming the lands across the sea where the sun rose three months earlier than it did over Middangeard. It was a short growing season but a crucial one in the cycle for the southern tribes. When the tall ships returned from the West they did so with usually double the supplies of food that they had left with. It defined the difference between living on the margins of starvation, like the Uathach of the North, and living in relative comfort and security. Occasionally a ship would be lost on the crossing but it was rare and the last such loss was more than twenty years ago. Only once had none of the ships returned and every child had heard the legend of the Tribes of the Lost Crossing.

Arthur had sent Mar'h and Lissa to bring back the peoples earlier this year and he was angry that the beacon on the headland had not already been lit to guide the ships towards the Haven. They rode past the long, empty dwellings, which were used as brief accommodations for those preparing to embark, and onto the harbour master's house on the edge of the promontory. She had left in autumn with the ships but her second-in-command, a man called Juraman, had been left in charge.

As they approached the house Morveren peeled away on the pretext of finding Elwyn who was likely to be staying at one of the taverns on the beachfront. Both Morgund and Ceinwen wanted to join her but they felt obliged to stay close to Arthur in an effort to protect those who had forgotten to light the beacon from his worsening mood. A young boy in charge of the stables took their horses with a look of nervous fear. Everyone at the Haven had heard from King Maldred's messengers that Arthur had died in the Shadow Lands. Then the unbelievable news had followed that Arthur had returned from the dead, slain the king and fashioned a new treaty with the Uathach. Word had spread just as quickly that there was an Adren host waiting to invade Britain and that Arthur was to marry an Uathach princess to bind together the tribes of the South and North to stand against the Adren. The boy led the horses away quickly; he did not want to incur the wrath of the warlord ghost and certainly did not want to play any part in the great events that were to shape his own destiny.

Arthur called out angrily to the boy and he froze in his tracks. It was all he could do to turn around and face the three warriors. Arthur was asking him if Juraman was in. He nodded dumbly and then fled to the stables.

'Didn't you wash at Caer Sulis?' Morgund asked turning to Ceinwen.

'More likely to be your breath,' she replied.

Juraman had appeared at the doorway to the house and Arthur was demanding to know why the beacon was not already lit. The two warriors exchanged a quick look and leaving the hapless Juraman to answer to Arthur they headed off down the steep lanes to join Morveren in her search of the taverns. They had gone no more than ten yards when Ceinwen had the satisfaction of catching Morgund surreptitiously breathe into his cupped hand.

Within ten minutes the whole bay was flickering in the light of the blazing beacon that was set upon the edge of the headland. Arthur stood with his back to the towering fire, staring out across the dark ocean to the western horizon. The distant skies betrayed the first hints of the coming dawn but of the tall ships there was no still no sign.

Arthur spent several hours watching the dark, empty seas before seeking out the tavern where the others were staying and retiring to get some sleep. He repeated the pattern, taking his food to the headland and eating it there. The others joined him at different times and one of them kept the watch each time Arthur retired to sleep. None of them feared that the ships were lost but it was getting very close to the time when Arthur would have to return to Caer Sulis to welcome Gwyna and the Uathach and then march on to the Causeway. He needed to first answer to the council for the king's death and then set them to organising the people for war. He would depend heavily on Gereint being able to convince the returning Mercian warriors to accept him as Warlord of Britain and to follow him to the Causeway.

The wind still blew gently from the sea and Arthur could think of no reason why the ships should be so delayed. He grew more irritable as the time passed and for every four hours he slept he spent twenty more staring out to the West. Despite his vigil it was Ceinwen who saw the first ship. She sent word to the sleeping Arthur and within an hour he and the others arrived at the edge of the promontory. The waxing moon was bright and the skies were clear but it was another five hours of quiet frustration before Arthur too could make out the tiny speck on the distant surface of a sea rippling with the soft silver light cast by the crescent moon. The ship had long since seen the glow from the beacon and was making straight for the Haven. Arthur watched it for another two hours but it seemed stubbornly unwilling to get any closer and he returned to the tavern to sleep away the time before it arrived.

As he slept, the Haven became a scene of frenetic activity. The wharves were made ready for the ship to dock and wains were brought alongside the quay in preparation for unloading the stores from the ship's hold. The lines of low buildings were first aired then fires were lit to warm them and fresh bedding was laid out for the travellers, many of whom would be exhausted after the crossing. Juraman was working hard to make sure nothing was left undone and he even lit fires in the main room of his house and prepared food should Arthur wish to speak to the council there.

Ceinwen woke Arthur as the ship rounded the headland with several smaller craft guiding it to the first of the long wharves. Other ships had been spotted out to sea and over the next few days the Haven would become chaotically busy as the tall ships sailed in from the West one by one.

Arthur strode along the waterfront. Those that saw him coming hurriedly moved possessions, equipment and baggage aside. The entire wharf and surrounding area was well lit by dozens of burning brands, each one guarded by a youth. The tall ships were mostly oak and canvas and carelessness with fire could easily lead to disaster.

There was an order to the turmoil on the docks but to those unaccustomed to the unloading of the ships it seemed like madness had been loosed. Seagulls, having returned as winter moved away from the land, whirled and dived, competing noisily with the shouting of orders and the cries of welcome that rang along the quayside. The strong fresh smell of the salt air was expunged around the ship and supplanted by the stench of the animals that had been penned onboard for more than four weeks. There were hatches to the sides of the stalls that allowed the lower decks to be swilled clean but four weeks was more than long enough for the animals' reek to become all pervasive.

Arthur approached the group by the main gangplank where Juraman was reporting to Unna, the harbour master. She was a tall woman, young to be the master of the Haven but with a reputation for brooking no nonsense that she had inherited, along with the running of the harbour, from her father. She stood with her hands on her wide hips as Juraman told her what had been done and what still needed doing. Juraman was flicking nervous glances towards Arthur as he approached and Unna turned to see what distracted him. She tried to hide the sudden unease she felt at seeing Arthur. They had already heard from Mar'h and Lissa what had happened at Caer Sulis and what lay beyond the Causeway.

'Any problems on the crossing?'

'No, fair sailing once again,' she replied, wishing her voice sounded stronger in her dry mouth.

'I expected you here sooner.'

'We were surprised to be leaving earlier than normal, Lord,' she had not meant to add the title and her eyes broke away from Arthur's as she shifted nervously.

'Are the counsellors already inside?' Arthur gestured to her house above them.

She nodded and Arthur strode away and climbed the steps that led up towards the house on the promontory. Unna turned her attention back to

Juraman and spoke to him with a newfound sympathy.

Further along the wharf the others greeted Mar'h as he disembarked. Ceinwen glanced up and watched Arthur as he took the steps up to the house two at a time. Mar'h followed her gaze, 'He looks like he's in a hurry.'

'He's been in a hurry for the last two months but with nowhere to go,' Ceinwen replied.

'Come on, let's get to the tavern before it gets too full,' Morgund said and taking Morveren's arm led the way with the other two following.

The inn was already busy with people looking for beer or wine to help them rediscover their land-legs after the long voyage and Morveren made sure the landlord had kept their rooms set aside for them. As they settled around a sturdy table, one that had soaked up countless spills but not seen a clean cloth in months, Ceinwen asked Morveren where Elwyn was. Apparently he was with Gereint and the returning Mercian warriors explaining what had happened in their absence. There was much to explain and doubtless Arthur was doing likewise with the counsellors.

'You're looking better than when we last saw you,' Morgund said, clapping Mar'h on the shoulder.

'Still too thin though, you'll need to do some serious eating before you meet up with the Adren again,' Ceinwen added.

'Find Cael and follow his example,' Morveren suggested.

Mar'h did indeed look better. His skin had darkened further under the western sun and his broken, hooked nose seemed to have healed itself. He lifted his mug of beer and saluted his friends and Ceinwen noted he still could not use his left hand properly. The Uathach arrow that had smashed his forearm had left his hand with some movement in his thumb but little else. He smiled at them as they lifted their mugs in return and his recovery from the nightmare of his last weeks in Britain was clearly evident in his eyes. He had brought that nightmare upon himself with his own deeds but he appeared to have made a peace with his past.

He had spent long hours walking the coastline of the western shores debating all that had happened and his part in it. He had been consumed by guilt and more than once he had thought to end the slow torture by simply hurling himself off one of the cliffs but each time he found himself looking down into the churning waves, images of his wife and children came to his mind and each time he turned away from the precipice. He had told himself that he wanted to atone for the damage he had done. He wanted a chance to balance the harm with some good. As he dwelt on his actions and lingered over his guilt it seemed to him that perhaps fate had determined events.

If Breagan had not been on that raid so many years ago then he, Mar'h, would not have raped Esa. If he had not raped her then Gwyna would not have been born the person she was. She and the Uathach party may not have been in the Shadow Lands and Arthur would not have saved them. There would have been no one to confirm to Ablach, the Uathach chieftain, that the Adren were poised to invade all the lands of Middangeard. Ablach may not have had a daughter to use as a pawn in his ambitions and whom Arthur could marry in order to cement an alliance with the northern tribes to oppose the Adren host. In some strange twisted way, Mar'h felt that his rape of Esa had ultimately led to the unification of the tribes of Britain. If fate was to blame then perhaps he was not, but that did not lessen his desire to counterbalance the wrong he had done. He reasoned that he was merely playing a part on a greater stage, a stage he had little control over and that his part now was to try to achieve some measure of forgiveness, if not from Esa or the gods, then perhaps from himself. He could do no more than that and had accepted it but at the back of his mind lurked the nagging suspicion that his self-justification was no more than just that.

He realised he had drifted away from the conversation around him and tried to find its thread once more in the increasing noise of the tavern. Morgund was making his way back from the long tables that divided off one corner of the large room and which acted as a serving counter. Someone jostled him from behind and the beer slopped over the sides of the mugs as he placed them down on the table. He turned swiftly and caught the man by the shoulder. Seeing he had inadvertently bumped into one of the Wessex warriors the man hurriedly apologised and offered to fetch more beer.

Apparently mollified, Morgund sat down then winked to Mar'h who laughed, 'I see not much has changed. Morgund's still bullying anyone who can't defend themselves.'

'We'll see if he's as brave when it comes to the Adren,' Morveren said.

'Yes, well I'm sorry about that but I'm not going to the Causeway with you. Arthur's asked me to do an inspection of the wells in the far west of Wessex.' Morgund shrugged in apology as Morveren stared at him in disbelief.

'Wouldn't surprise me,' Ceinwen added.

Mar'h grinned at his friends and took a deep gulp of his beer, glad to be back with them. Elsewhere in the waterfront tavern the talk of the Adren was not so light and one rumour of impending disaster was quickly followed by another and more extravagant one. The luckless man who had bumped into Morgund returned with more beer and Morgund asked him his name, promising to defend the man's family personally if the Adren attacked his village. He had forgotten the man's name before he had even finished talking; his mind was on the snippet of conversation he had overheard at the bar.

'What's this I hear about coming across people in the Western Lands?' Morgund had to repeat the question before Mar'h could make it out in the surrounding din. Ceinwen and Morveren leant closer too, curious about the news or rumour that had swept through the Haven when the ship landed.

'Yes, that's right. A scouting party of about ten.' Mar'h was beginning to slur his words. 'Came across them a few days before we left, or rather they came across us. They were scouting new lands, said there was war in the West.'

'They weren't Adren then?' Ceinwen asked loudly.

'No, certainly not, just like us really, spoke the same language even.'

'Strange. Why haven't we seen them before now? We've been to the Western Lands every year for hundreds of years,' Morveren said, frowning into her drink.

'Don't know. Perhaps they were ghosts. Kenwyn and Aelle, the two chieftains, spoke to them before they left.'

'We know who Kenwyn and Aelle are you idiot. You're not with ignorant villagers now,' Morgund replied and they fell to insulting each other, dredging up past follies and humiliations. Ceinwen laughed at them and turned to Morveren to question her further about Elwyn.

As more beer arrived the conversation turned back to the dominant topic, 'when would the Adren cross the Causeway and could they stop them?' They discussed the matter in an increasingly fruitless way and eventually stumbled out of the tavern a few hours later roaring out a tuneless rendition of one of their many drinking songs. They were half-way to the jetties before Morveren remembered that they were actually staying in the tavern that they had just left. Undeterred and completely unashamed they simply turned around and reeled back the way they had come. As they turned, Ceinwen looked up to the harbour master's house where the lights were still burning inside; Arthur was still talking to the tribes' counsellors.

When they left with Arthur for Caer Sulis the next day the four drinking companions were very quiet. Mar'h had to get off his horse several times to be heroically sick but none of the other three taunted him as they were feeling a bit bilious themselves. Arthur was silent too but for entirely different reasons.

Chapter Three

Since leaving the camp in the woodlands Cei's band had toiled through the endless night of winter and left behind the gently undulating hills and valleys of the land beyond the ruined city.

At first they had made good progress despite having to share and change their mounts to spread the extra load the horses had to carry. They had even managed to cut through the ice on a large lake and catch some fish to supplement their dwindling supplies. It was during those days that hope rose once more in Cei that perhaps they could complete their journey deep into the Shadow Lands to the Adren City and at least attempt Arthur's plan. Trevenna's indefatigable hope was spreading once more through the company and although the miles passed by slowly the lingering sense of an impossible task gradually lifted from their hearts.

In the absence of any present danger, Ethain became more relaxed and chatted happily to the rest of the band and it was not long before they realised the reason why. Even travelling in a large company it was difficult to keep secret any coupling but it was a fruitless endeavour in such a small group. Not that Leah made any attempt to hide her affections, which did nothing to improve Cerdic's temper at first but he put aside his chagrin as he reasoned, in his own way, that Ethain's bravery in the city had merited such a reward.

The others looked on in amusement at the ill-matched couple. Leah was every bit the warrior, strong, proud and confident. Ethain did not seem to be any of these things but he had proved his shorter, wiry frame and nervous attitude were not any hindrance to his courage. Merdynn snorted in derision but otherwise kept his opinion to himself, wishing the boy well but thinking it would end badly for him. Leah was not known to be 'hearth-bound', as the Anglians said. Indeed, quite the opposite but they were practical and none held it against her that Herewulf, her previous lover, had been replaced so quickly. Each to their own they reasoned. None of them knew about Morgund, which was probably just as well. Ethain, naturally enough, was entirely blind to all of this.

When they were able to find enough shelter and stop long enough to light a fire, Merdynn would tell them tales from ages long past.

Everyone found them too fantastic to have any truth and Cerdic scoffed at the impossibly heroic deeds undertaken by such unlikely heroes but nonetheless they all sat enthralled as the tales unfolded. He spent one such stop teaching them a less ancient song and they soon altered parts of it to amuse themselves. Leah had been off with Ethain when she heard the singing and laughter and, unwilling to miss out and much to Ethain's annoyance, she had abandoned their tryst to return to the fire and see what the noise was all about.

She had sat among the laughing group just as the refrain started again. Cerdic started them off with a simple introductory beat on his shield then Cei began singing to Trevenna. The song revolved around the accusation that Arthur's sister was, without any doubt, the ugliest witch in the West Country and that no matter what she was prepared to offer prospective lovers in the way of riches none would succumb to her desires. Everyone joined in the chorus despite Trevenna liberally pelting everyone with handfuls of snow. The song ended with the witch casting vengeful spells against the young man who had callously refused and scorned her. The group around the fire laughed as Trevenna leapt on top of Cei and rubbed more snow in his face.

That had been the last day of their respite for even as Trevenna pummelled Cei, the abandoned Ethain had climbed one of the tall trees on the edge of the copse and was looking out onto the moonlit white plains that they had already traversed. He had just wanted to make sure they were not being pursued, but in the distance, perhaps ten miles away out on the plains, there they were. A slow moving group, little more than a black dot on the white landscape and they were heading straight for the trees.

He had rushed straight back to the camp and kicked snow over the fire as he stammered out the news that appalled him so much. The laughter had stopped suddenly and they were packed and on their way once more heading to the East.

The land they were now travelling through with such haste was flat and the masking snow rendered it almost featureless. Clumps of trees were rare and although they crossed streams and riverbeds they did not know it as the deep snow covered all.

Ethain rode ahead every time they approached one of the sporadic copses and climbed the highest tree to see if the Adren still pursued them across the plains. Every time the answer was the same and while the Adren drew no closer, neither did they fall any further behind. Under moon or stars their trail was easy to follow, there was no way they could disguise the passing of ten horses across the white plains.

Their previous attitude seemed almost carefree to them now and they withdrew into themselves, fighting their own personal battles with the cold and fatigue as they alternated between riding and leading their horses across the winter terrain. They kept their stops for rest as short as possible and as the days of pursuit lengthened desperation stole secretly back into their hearts and Ethain's world turned black once more.

Cei felt his hope beginning to drift away again. He could think of no way to shake off the distant but relentless pursuit. Ethain's best guess was that over two hundred Adren followed them. Cei was not to know that Ethain had doubled his true estimation, just to be on the safe side. They could not turn and face them, yet they did not seem to be able to out-distance them either. Their journey into the Shadow Lands of the enemy was hopeless indeed if they took with them a small Adren army hard on their tracks.

They had been watching the stars gradually disappear in the West for the last few hours as heavy cloudbanks rolled towards them. Finally the first flurry of fresh snow began to reach them, borne on the wind from the northwest.

Cei called a quick halt and as they sheltered behind their horses to take a fast meal of near frozen dried meat and fruit, he talked quietly to Merdynn.

'We can't do it can we?'

'It's looking less promising, and it wasn't very promising to start with,' Merdynn agreed, sucking on a strip of meat in an attempt to thaw it. He had already privately resigned himself to the impossibility of their task but felt that Cei had to make that decision for himself.

'It's just not possible to travel in this land in winter,' Cei said, looking for agreement from Merdynn, as he was still unwilling to forsake Arthur's plan.

'It couldn't get a great deal more difficult,' Merdynn agreed.

'And it looks like a snow storm is about to settle on us.'

'True, that'll make it a great deal more difficult. Being buried in snow and all.'

'At least it'll cover our tracks.'

'All trace of us more like.'

'So you agree then?' Cei finally asked.

'Absolutely,' Merdynn said, finally swallowing the meat, then added, 'What to?'

Cei stared at him, concerned for the old man's mind. 'To abandoning this venture and heading for those Breton villages you mentioned.'

'We can certainly try. I don't suppose it'll make much difference if we freeze to death heading east or if we freeze to death heading west. Matter of preference I suppose.'

Cei gave up on the conversation and told the others that they were going to head west. They had turned now and hopefully by the time the Adren arrived here, if they carried on in the growing storm, and no one doubted they would, their tracks would be obliterated and no sign would remain that they had turned from their course.

So where they had been travelling eastward they now turned their faces to the flying snow and with their horses strung together with rope, trudged through the storm heading southwest almost doubling back on themselves. Once they felt they were clear of the Adren they would veer to the northwest and make for the Breton land that only Merdynn among them had ever visited before.

Tiredness turned to exhaustion as they crawled across the landscape, the wind and snow constantly seeking to drive them backwards. Cei refused to call a halt despite two serious appeals for a rest, one from Aelfhelm and one from Trevenna. Now that his choice was made, he was determined to make it work and that meant putting as much distance between themselves and the Adren before they realised they had lost the trail. Cei hoped that when they made their inevitable discovery his riders would be far enough away to be free from further pursuit.

The hours passed in agonising exertion as they fought through the deep snow that was drifting across the plain. It hid gulleys and ditches and those in the lead, despite their broad snowshoes, would suddenly find themselves chest deep in a drift with their horses bucking and thrashing beside them. It became a stumbling, exhausting, frozen nightmare.

Without stars or moon they had no points of reference for navigation and Cei prayed that the wind from the West had not veered or changed direction. He kept them facing into it and blindly hoped they were making west.

Occasionally he would stop and wait as the line of bent, stumbling figures and struggling horses slowly passed him. The bundled figures, made bulky by the thick winter clothing, would appear out of the swirling storm with flecks of snow thick in the air around them and clinging to their backs and shoulders in a white outline. Cei would exchange a few words with each but the wind and exhaustion made talking nearly impossible so he tried to gauge their state by their frozen faces and their bearing.

Two of the group were struggling more than the others. They were all struggling but Ethain looked to be on the point of collapse and Leofrun had passed by Cei without seeming to realise he was there. He was more worried about Leofrun, a slight woman in her twenties who was lightning fast with her sword but who lacked the strength of her companions and it was beginning to show. Cei knew her well, as he did his whole war band, and knew she would not give up or ask for help. She had a stubborn and independent streak that was not uncommon among the warriors but it was leading her beyond exhaustion and Cei feared she would carry on staggering behind the others until she died, then and only then she might allow herself to fall behind.

Ethain had nothing like her resolution but he was stronger. He did not feel like it though and as the interminable hours passed and the storm raged around them he felt like curling up in the snow and drifting away. It became an increasingly attractive idea to him and the thought of a relatively painless and numb death began to compare favourably to the possibility of dying in agony with his guts spilled by a curved Adren sword. His feet were already numb to the cold but the aching in his thighs and calves sent white-hot jolts of pain up his body every time he lifted his feet from the deep snow to take another step. He clung to the stirrup of his horse as it too battled through the storm and forced himself to take one laborious step after another.

Two thoughts kept him going. They were heading away from danger and not into it, for the first time since leaving Caer Sulis. And the second was Leah. Someone had mentioned to him or he had overheard, he could not remember which, that she had been with Herewulf for the last couple of months. He had not realised that and had thought back to see if he could recall them being together in that way but he had been too preoccupied with his own safety to notice others' coming's and going's. He felt his ego being bolstered every time he thought about Leah choosing him after being with a man like Herewulf. He did not realise that he had appealed to her because he was the opposite of everything that Herewulf had been. It was a pity that Herewulf had died, he thought, but it was an ill wind that blew no good. Even this ill wind that drove into his face was at least masking their escape from the Adren pursuit.

He found a small reserve of renewed energy at the thought of meeting up with Elowen, Tomas and Morveren with the strapping Leah on his arm. He did not know that Elowen and Tomas were already dead and he had yet to learn that Leah's affections were quickly given and just as quickly taken away. Ethain was no doubt a fool but Leah was not playing him as such, everyone knew that was just how she viewed life. Everyone that is, except Ethain.

Leofrun finally collapsed. She simply could not make her legs do her bidding any longer. It took several minutes for Roswitha, who was slogging along behind her, to notice the unusual grooves in the snow in front of her. She raised her eyes from the snow immediately in front of her and looked up. Leofrun, hands still grimly grasping a stirrup, was being dragged through the tracks of the others by her horse. Roswitha ran through the deep snow in an awkward high-stepping gait and passed the word forward to stop, then returned to Leofrun and gently unclenched her hands from their clasp.

She laid her down in the snow as the others circled their horses to provide some protection from the snowstorm. Cei and Trevenna knelt down beside the prone and motionless Leofrun. Only her eyes were visible through a narrow strip in the wrappings about her face and they looked glazed and unfocussed. Clearly she could not go on. Cei looked around at the others and realised she was not the only one. Ethain was on his knees in the snow, sitting back on his heels with his head hung down, looking for all the world as if he were asleep.

They had been on the go for more than forty straight hours and they all looked as if they were at the limits of their endurance. Cei had no real sense of how far they had travelled during those hours but in all that time they had not passed any place likely to give them shelter, at least none that he had seen. He weighed up what options there were. They could secure Leofrun to her saddle and let her horse carry her but she would certainly die from the cold before they could find any place to shelter from the storm. Or they could wait here until the storm blew itself out but there was a fair chance they could all die from exposure before the storm died. He worried that they might not yet be far enough away from the Adren and was afraid that once the storm ended they might find their pursuers still within sight or still on their trail.

He turned his face to the flying snow and lowered the wraps from his face hoping the blast of ice on his bare skin might clear his mind to other options. He knew he could not send others onwards to hunt for shelter, they would never find each other again in the blizzard that raged across the plains.

He looked at Trevenna who leant across to him and shouted in his ear, 'If we carry on we'll die one by one!'

And if we stay, he thought, we'll die together. He reached a decision, better to die together than alone, if die they must. He fetched his heavy axe from his horse and shouted to the others to cut an ice cave. Swinging his axe into the snow he started to dig a hole with Trevenna shovelling the loosened snow with her shield to form a bank on one side of the excavation.

The others joined in and they dug down deeply and quickly so that within an hour they had formed an open sided cave facing east, just big enough for them all to crawl into. Their horses stood in the lee of the cave with the dugout snow now forming protective wings and a growing overhang developed as the storm drifted more snow onto the roof of the hastily built cavern.

Trevenna and Roswitha tried to revive Leofrun while the others wrestled their gaunt horses to the ground at the entrance to the shelter and they crowded together, man and beast sharing the heat that might keep them alive. Once they were out of the wind and free from the flying snow, Cuthwin rationed out some of the remaining feed for the horses. They had been weakened further by the journey through the storm and were already close to starvation.

The blizzard continued outside and the cavern threatened to close around them as the snow accumulated around the mouth, gradually narrowing it. Every now and then someone would leave the relative warmth of the group and taking an axe, cut back the encroaching snow. Cei lit a tallow candle and placed it in a dug-out hollow above him. If the flame went out then they'd know they would be dangerously low on fresh air.

Leofrun was still suffering from the cold despite those clustered around her attempting to warm her up. She had revived enough to be talking to those lying against her but she was doing so in a disjointed often incoherent way. Cei wondered if they were losing her but could think of nothing else to do that might help her.

With the horses and warriors crammed tightly into the ice cave the temperature had slowly risen, not by much but coupled with being beyond the grasp of the wind they began to feel less frozen and heavy fur gloves were thrown off as feeling was rubbed back into nerveless fingers. Ice began to melt from beards and rigid faces regained some expression as they began talking once more.

Despite this apparent revival Cei knew that they were all exhausted. Now that they had stopped he prayed that the storm would keep up so that they could rest for a few hours. Aelfhelm was reminding everyone to keep working their muscles to prevent them from stiffening but the response was desultory so he lumbered to his knees and went round them one by one forcing them to flex and straighten tired leg muscles.

Only Merdynn seemed to be in reasonable shape. His beard still held fingers of ice and his deeply lined, leathery face and long bony hands had taken on a patchy blue colour but his eyes were clear and his voice was free from any trembling. Cei had known Merdynn since he was a child and was not wholly surprised by how well the old man seemed to be coping. Even his warriors now seemed to accept that Merdynn was just utterly different. It seemed to them that he wore his years like a mountain does, scarred, cracked and worn yet likely to stand forever and that his energy was like that of a river, a ceaseless flowing of something as insubstantial as water and yet it would eventually carve out great valleys. Unable to understand how this could be they put it down to a clever cunning on Merdynn's behalf, a cunning that had cheated the gods and their weapon of Time and having explained it as such, thought no more about it. Even

Leah had mostly dropped her superstitions about him, regarding him, foolishly, as an aged father with the power to protect them.

They drifted into an exhausted, fitful sleep and Ethain repeatedly awoke thrashing about, convinced the Adren had found their cave and were pouring through its dark mouth. His fears proved groundless but Cei's fears for Leofrun were realised when Trevenna gently woke him to tell him that she had died. He felt guilty about her death; he could accept the deaths of those lost while fighting the enemy but he was unable to forgive himself for losing one of his riders to the winter. Trevenna told him that her death was painless and peaceful but Cei could not shake the conviction that it should have been avoidable, perhaps if they had stopped earlier, not pushed quite so far or quite so hard.

They laid her at the mouth of the cave and wrapped her in her cloak then divided out her supplies and weapons. The others insisted that Ethain take her sword, it was far superior to his with a better balance and much lighter. He took it feeling like a fraud and sat as far from the body as he could but his eyes kept returning to the prone form outlined on the floor of the entrance. He consoled himself with the thought that while there were only eleven of them left alive now, he was one of them and they were heading for safety.

The storm showed little sign of abating. Every time the wind dropped and the blizzard lessened Cei would go outside and gauge whether or not they could carry on but they were merely lulls and the wind would quickly renew its malicious scathing of the desolate winter landscape forcing Cei back inside to wait and fret.

Ethain tried talking to Leah to take his mind off the dead body guarding their cavern but she was uncommunicative and unusually sullen. He gave up and retreated back into himself, armed with one more anxiety to feed his unhappy mind.

Trevenna kept the restless Cerdic occupied with playing endless games of dice while Aelfhelm massaged his aching knee and talked quietly to Merdynn, asking him questions and trying to learn as much as he could from the old man. The others lay among the resting horses and slept as best they could. Cei drifted in and out of sleep as he waited for the storm to pass.

He waited for two days and then the wind suddenly stopped. The abrupt silence woke those sleeping and they looked at each other in confusion wondering what sudden noise woke them. Cei quickly left the cave, having to crouch to pass through the entrance, which had become more tunnel-like with the accumulation of snow.

Thick, heavy snow was still falling from the darkness above but the wind had died to a whisper. He clambered up onto the top of their cave and even in the poor visibility he could see that their tracks were unsurprisingly completely buried under a clean and undisturbed layer of fresh snow.

He returned to the others and they spent the next hour taking a meal and readying themselves and their horses for another long journey. Cei was once again hoping to be able to put more distance between themselves and the Adren while the falling snow could still cover their tracks.

They left Leofrun in the cave and collapsed it on top of her. The spring animals would find her but there was little they could do about that. Despite her death they resumed their journey in better heart than they had finished the previous one. They were fed, as were their horses, albeit lightly, and rested too but the fresh snowfall made travelling arduous as they led their strung-together horses beside them. The basket-like snowshoes they wore reduced the depth they sank at each step but the horses had no such luxury and they struggled as the group laboured on in a muffled silence broken only by their own strenuous breathing.

Hour by hour the snowfall lessened until it stopped altogether and the clouds drifted apart on a light wind that barely brushed those on the ground. The stars appeared in sporadic gaps above them and they congratulated themselves on having kept to their course through the storm though Cei knew they had just been fortunate the wind had not veered on them.

Ethain, standing up on a horse for a better elevation, searched the lightening landscape for signs of the Adren pursuit but with the sky still partly obscured by clouds he could not see far. For as far as he could see, there was no evidence of pursuit and they took heart from this and Merdynn led them on, changing direction slightly to make towards the northwest.

As the miles edged behind them the ground started to gently slope upwards until the plains were left behind and before them was once more a country of shallow, forested valleys and modest bare hills. From a vantage point on the first of these low hills Cei stopped and waited for the banked clouds to drift away from the moon, which Merdynn assured him would happen soon.

An hour passed and the moon was still obscured. Cei paced back and forth along the hilltop weighing up the need to see if they were still being tracked across the plain against the time they were losing whilst they waited. He told the others to wait beyond the brow of the hill to minimise the chance of them being seen from the plain. Merdynn was leaning against a lone, stunted tree and he smiled brightly at Cei as the Anglian Warlord paced by glowering at him.

Eventually Merdynn's promised moon shone from a winter sky that was still scattered with the last trailing vestiges of the snow clouds. Ethain was promptly summoned and he searched the plains that stretched out into the dim distance. The pale white landscape was patched by the cloud shadows that slowly slid across it. For a long while Ethain was still as he scanned the country below and Cei watched his face closely. He saw the sudden start of fear in Ethain's eyes and knew he had spotted them. Ethain took an automatic step forward as if the extra yard would show him that his sight had played him false.

Cei swore, demanding from the nearby Merdynn an explanation how the Adren could have followed them through the storm. Merdynn pointed out sharply that it was not his fault then fell silent as he remembered it probably was his fault that they were being pursued in the first place.

'Are they following our tracks?' Cei asked peering fruitlessly out across the plain in an effort to see what Ethain saw.

'I don't know! I can't see our tracks from here! They're a good day's travelling away,' he replied angrily. He had been sure that the plains would be clear and was clearly shocked to have found they were not. 'Besides, our tracks must still be covered where they are now. How can they hunt us if the snow's covered our tracks?'

Cei turned to Merdynn for an answer to Ethain's question but Merdynn just pursed his lips and raised his eyebrows as he shrugged.

'We'd, umm, better get moving though, don't you think?' Merdynn finally said to the staring Cei who turned and strode back to where the others were waiting. Ethain and Merdynn followed him.

The rest of the group were standing around their horses and gazing down into the valley.

'They're still following us,' Cei announced.

Several swore in disbelief.

'How near are they?' Aelfhelm asked.

'A days journey, perhaps less.'

They swore again, regretting now the time they had wasted waiting only to find out that they were still being shadowed.

'There's a fire down there,' Cuthwin said quietly.

Cei realised they had all been looking down into the valley below. He followed the direction of Cuthwin's outstretched arm. A few miles along the valley floor a thin pall of smoke trailed skywards in the moonlight.

'Looks like a small cluster of huts, difficult to tell, they look no more than mounds of snow,' Aelfhelm said.

'People live in these lands?' Cei asked Merdynn.

'There's some scattered villages, herders mostly. They trade with the Bretons.'

Without anything more being said they set off down the hillside, towards the smoke and away from the distant Adren.

As they approached the source of the rising smoke they saw that there had indeed been a village here, only five rudimentary round huts huddled closely together but a village nonetheless. Only the smoke rising listlessly above the central mound gave any sign that the dwellings were still inhabited.

The huts looked to have been turf roofed and they sat low on the ground but as they led their horses between the first two they could see that the roofs had collapsed and the winter snow had covered them completely. Whoever had lived here had clearly abandoned them and left. Except for the central one.

Cerdic left his horse with the others and approached the low door to the central hut. It was off its hinges and leant across the opening and it looked as if it had been smashed down and then poorly patched together again. Cerdic looked back at the rest of the group then bent down to enter.

There was a dull thud and he recoiled clutching his head. Another stone flew from the cover behind the hut opposite and smacked into his heavy cloak. He drew his sword and charged his attacker. The others drew their weapons and went to join him but before they rounded the side of the hut, Cerdic emerged holding up a struggling young boy who looked to be only nine or ten years old. From his hand dangled the offending weapon, a worn and well-used sling.

Trevenna burst out laughing and the others joined in.

'The little bastard could have had my eye out with that,' Cerdic said, still holding the child off the ground by the scruff of the neck.

'Oh, the songs they'll sing of brave Cerdic!' Trevenna called out to more laughter.

'I ought to skin the bugger,' Cerdic muttered, his pride far more hurt than his head.

'Don't worry, we'll tell them back home that it was a herd of ravenous wolves!'

'Pack. Not herd,' Merdynn corrected her.

'Oh a pack isn't big enough to tell of young Cerdic's bravery!' Trevenna added with glee, enjoying her revenge for the song Merdynn had taught them and which Cerdic had taken great delight in turning against her. It did not bother her that Cei was the chief culprit. His turn would come.

Cerdic put the boy down and he immediately tried to scamper away but he was firmly held by his ragged cloak. He looked terrified and Trevenna felt guilty for indulging herself whilst the child was plainly frightened out of his wits by these strangers. Cerdic's discomfort was not over yet. The door to the hut was flung outwards and another child raced at Cerdic and kicked him in the shins before he could grab hold of his new assailant.

'Don't stand there bloody laughing! Help me control the little animals!'

Trevenna, to her shame, sat down on the snow seized by her laughter. Only Aelfhelm was of any mind to help and he strode across to Cerdic and, bending his tall frame, lifted both children off the ground, one under each arm.

'Where do you want their skinned hides hung, Lord?' He asked Cerdic and Trevenna hooted with delight.

Cei indicated the hut and Aelfhelm carried them inside the dwelling they had clearly been using. Both the boy and the girl, who looked slightly older, were still struggling and Aelfhelm told them to both sit still in a tone of voice that struck them as one not to argue with. Merdynn went and sat beside them and told them not to worry, they meant them no harm and were only passing through their village.

Cei was going to kick out the fire when he noticed that the entire room was stacked to the low roof with piles of cut, smoked meat. The Adren were still the other side of the hill and too far away to see the thin smoke from this fire so he left it. He decided they would stop for an hour and eat a hot meal before the last long leg of their journey to the Breton villages.

He told Thruidred to strip the moss and mould from the logs stacked by the fire and told Godhelm to go outside and block the smoke-hole in the roof. It would get smoky in the hut but better that than a constant stream rising into the winter night, he reasoned. Thruidred threw the stripped logs onto the fire and they smoked less.

The two dark haired and unkempt children watched cautiously as the strangers began boiling water over the now roaring fire. When it burned down to charcoal they would cook some of the meat that these children had in abundance.

Merdynn started to gently ask the children questions. At first their answers were monosyllabic. They were in equal measure frightened and fascinated by the strangers who were largely ignoring them as they hurriedly went about preparing their meal. Occasionally one of them would pass by them and ruffle their already tousled hair, remarking on what scruffs they were. They were more than scruffy. The whites of their round, wide eyes contrasted sharply with the black, ingrained dirt on their faces. Cei's warriors looked no cleaner and were indeed a good deal dirtier but there was a feral quality about these two children who had been abandoned to fend for themselves in the winter darkness.

Merdynn's patient and gentle questioning began to bring results. The answers they had did nothing to reassure the adults around them and gradually the warriors became silent as they went about their tasks, listening to the children's tale.

The girl's name was Charljenka and her younger brother's was Nialgrada. One of the village's goat herds had strayed to a distant hill and the two children were sent to bring it back to the village. The unwelcome task had saved their lives. It was after the Lughnasa festival and the sun had already set. Most of the village's stock and supplies had already travelled to the Breton villages by the sea. The villagers were about to take the journey to the coast, where they spent the dark months, and had been seeing to the final necessary tasks before the onset of winter when the monsters had come.

Merdynn asked them who the monsters were and could they describe them? Nialgrada studied his fingers and fidgeted but Charljenka sensed the interest from the adults around her and described what had happened.

The two of them had been rounding up the goats in a wood on a hill a few miles away when the valley below them had filled with shadows. The shadows had made straight for the village and soon after they could see the smoke of the burning huts from where they hid on the hilltop.

Merdynn asked her to describe these shadows. One or two of the warriors suppressed a shudder as she sat staring in the dancing firelight while she solemnly described the monsters that had destroyed her home. It was not natural for a girl as young as this to talk with such a quiet intensity about such horrors.

Trevenna sat silently appalled at herself, that she could have had a laughing fit as these two children attacked Cerdic when only the gods knew what nightmares had persecuted them.

The young girl described the shadows as a horde, more numerous than flies on fresh dung in summer. Evil, shambling creatures with the armour of cockroaches. Their cloven hands carried great goats' horns, sickle-sharp. They had passed through the valley as silently as the wind through long grass. They were herded by moon-bright helmeted men on horseback.

Charljenka stopped and stared at the fire. The room was silent and everyone watched her through the thickening smoke.

Nialgrada spoke up in a quiet, small voice, finishing what his sister had started. He called them the Soul Stealers of the Shadow Lands. He had just about reached the age where he no longer believed the stories told to scare children into obedience but he knew the Soul Stealers were real now. He had seen them.

The warriors looked at each other. They knew that the children only described what they had seen in the familiar terms of their daily lives but none had heard the Adren described or explained so completely before.

More than one of them made the sign to ward off evil.

Merdynn and Cei looked at each other. They were thinking the same thing. If the Adren had passed through here then they would have gone on to the coastal villages of the Bretons. And that would mean that the Adren were both before and behind them.

Cei led his warriors from the small village of clustered hovels. He and Merdynn had agreed that they had little choice but to continue on towards the Breton coastal villages despite the news from the two children about the Adren. They had no doubt that the Adren would have attacked the Bretons but Merdynn hoped that at least the main village would have held out as it was perched high on a cliff top with its back to the sea and a narrow headland before it. It was in any case the only option they had.

The children had been keen to come with them and Cei didn't feel he could leave them alone in their deserted home. Doubtless the rest of the village's inhabitants would have been massacred and their bodies taken on by the Adren for meat. The warriors were careful not to speculate about the fate of the villagers in front of them but the two youngsters had sensed something was being kept back and they grew distrustful once more.

The village had been emptied of any supplies not already taken on to the coast and without winter feed for the goats, and not knowing the way to the coast, the children had slaughtered their small herd and smoked the meat. They may have been village children with little or no knowledge beyond their narrow lives but they knew everything that there was to know about goats it seemed. Cei's warriors now travelled with their horses' flanks adorned with haunches of smoked goat.

Charljenka and Nialgrada travelled with Ethain, sitting on his horse as he walked beside them, telling them tales and answering questions. Leah was surprised that their distrust for the warriors did not seem to extend to Ethain. Her affection for Ethain had been waning fast but this newly discovered talent for being able to make the children happy and perfectly at ease with him gave her pause for thought.

Trevenna had been hoping to become friends with them to make up for acting the way she had when they first met but they had rebuffed her efforts as they had Aelfhelm's and the others. Only Merdynn and Ethain enjoyed their trust. This side of Ethain surprised Trevenna too and as she slogged through the snow she wondered why it should surprise her so.

Only Leah and Trevenna were preoccupied with the young goat herders, the rest of the warriors dwelt upon the fact that a band of Adren was still remorselessly tracking them and that they were likely to be heading straight towards a larger contingent. They were not happy about either prospect but they clung to the hope that the Bretons were somehow still alive and holding out in their cliff top fortress.

If they were not then Cei was at loss about what to do next. He had been feeling increasingly unsure about his choice to abandon their quest east. During the storm it had seemed the only wise and sensible option but now that the travelling was easier, coupled with the fear of being bracketed by two Adren forces, he was not so sure he had made the right decision. It was not just Arthur depending upon the success of their journey east. The Wessex Warlord had made it clear that in the face of the overwhelming number of the enemy poised to invade, Britain's only chance of survival depended on Cei's success. Had he doomed the lands of Britain to defeat at the hands of the Adren? The questions circled in his thoughts like patient carrion.

Merdynn was more concerned with the immediate future and he studied the landscape as the miles passed by hoping to recognise a hill, wood or valley that would position the Breton village in his mind. The trouble was that he rarely visited the Bretons in winter and the land changed under the long darkness, deep snow hid the rivers while fields and hills took on a masked uniformity. He was becoming more and more concerned and was on the point of suggesting that the others lay up somewhere while he went ahead alone when a hill rose before them crowned by a single ancient oak tree. He was so relieved to see it that he felt like he was seeing an old friend, one he had begun to expect not to meet again.

They were about ten miles away from the Breton village and he nonchalantly informed the others. They were encouraged not to have seen either any evidence of the Adren that had attacked the children's home or any sign of those who pursued them. Merdynn suggested that they detour a few miles to the North where another spur of land jutted out into the sea and from where they might get some idea of whether the

Breton fortress was still inhabited without getting too close to any Adren that may be in the vicinity.

Cei agreed and they changed course to meet the coast to the East of the Breton headland. As they covered the last few miles Cei questioned Merdynn about the Breton village and why he hoped it might still have held out against the Adren.

The way Merdynn described it the village did indeed seem like a fortress. The original fortifications had been built many hundreds of years ago to keep the Bretons' stock and harvest safe in the winter from marauders who came from deep within the Shadow Lands. Over recent generations the raids had diminished and Merdynn speculated that it was probably because the raiders themselves had fallen to the growing might of the Adren overlords but the raids had been so devastating that the Bretons had continually repaired and replaced the fortifications.

The main village was set on the seaward edge of a headland. Devilishly windy and wet, and altogether a thoroughly miserable place to live, Merdynn added, remembering his various visits to the place. The headland narrowed as it joined the main coastal cliffs and a huge wall had been constructed of rocks and stone. It stood fifty-feet high and was at least twenty-feet deep at the top and deeper still at the base. It stretched from side to side across the narrow neck of land with sheer cliffs dropping down either side to the sea. As if the height alone was not enough, a broad, deep ditch had been dug in front of the wall making it appear taller yet.

In the centre of the wall were the gates and they were fashioned of ironbound oak. A bridge spanned the ditch and it could be tilted back by huge winches so that it stood in front of the gates as an extra protection. Behind the defensive wall lay the village with pens and folds for all the outlying villages' stock and covered barns for stored grain and crops.

Cei listened intently as Merdynn described the place, picturing in his mind the extensive walls and the hive of activity that must have existed in the village during the long winter months. He could see why Merdynn was hopeful that it might have held out against the Adren - if they had enough warning of their approach and if they had the time to get all their stores within the walls. What he could not see was how they could enter the fortress if the Adren were outside the walls. He put the question to

Merdynn who stopped dead in his tracks and just stared at him. Cei was not at all reassured by this reaction.

They followed a shallow, winding valley that led to the coast. Merdynn tried to picture it in the warmth of a summer day when it was a pleasant, green pastured vale with extravagant willows trailing their low canopies into the gentle stream of the small river that flowed by on the last leg of its long journey home. Hares would sit under the shade, their bodies twitching to their heart beats as dragonflies skimmed across the rippling water and butterflies danced endlessly above the buttercups among the long grasses. Under the cold stars of winter the land was robbed of colour and left for dead; nothing moved in the darkness and the silence lay on the land like a shroud.

Not for the first time the company felt as if they were little better than violating intruders as they stamped across the silence and left their scars on the pristine, dead land. Their anxiety increased as they started climbing the valley side to reach the headland from where they could see the Breton stronghold. Safety or despair rested on what they found and all that they had endured seemed to be coming to a conclusion, one way or the other, on the headland before them.

They struggled up to the lip of the valley and the salt air of the cold sea-breeze blew into their faces with the scent of salvation and home. The Breton village was still out of sight and they hurried through the snow towards the end of the long headland.

In the valley behind them the Adren Captain lifted his hand for the Adren band to halt. He could sense that the hunt was over. His quarry had nowhere left to run. The sea was before them and he was behind them. He turned to his soldiers and ordered them to take the old man alive but to kill the others. The tracks ahead were clear. He divided his force into three, one to follow the tracks and the other two to flank out on either side. He signalled his troop forward into the valley.

Cei had reached the end of the promontory and Ethain was inspecting the Breton village that jutted out into the frozen sea only a mile away.

The bay between the two capes was winter-locked and sea ice looked to extend for a mile or two out from the shore. Eddies of spiralling snow swept across the flat surface below them.

The others waited anxiously for his news. He could see signs of life on the Breton side of the huge wall that still looked intact. On the other side and about two hundred yards from the wall a ring of fires burned and they showed a large encampment gathered there. He reported what he saw. It could mean that the Bretons still held out and the Adren were camped before their walls or it could be that there simply was not enough room in the village for all the Adren and they had spread out beyond the walls. Ethain could not tell from where they were but observed that the village did not look to be overflowing with people.

Cei was standing on the cliff edge that sloped sharply down to the frozen sea below drawing his fingers up and down the scar on his face as he pondered whether or not the Bretons were still there and if they were, how he could get his company behind the safety of the walls when he heard the children squealing. He ignored it, irritated at being distracted. They had gone off to play in the snow, happy to be close to their winter home and eager to see their parents who they thought were in the sea village. The others ignored them too, thinking they were just squabbling, all except Ethain who thought their screaming held more than just sibling anger. He took his eyes from the opposing headland and walked back towards the rise that hid the children from sight. Before he could reach it they came sprinting back through the snow, falling and scrambling up as they thrashed in haste towards them.

Ethain held up his hands to calm them when he caught what they were screaming. It was one word over and over, 'Stealers!' He froze, his mind insisting it was not possible for the Adren to have caught up with them yet. The children reached him and clung to him as they sobbed in fear, still repeating the one word. Ethain grabbed each by the hand and dragged them back towards the group, shouting at the top of his voice that the Adren were coming.

His voice could not compete with the ceaseless roar of the wind whipping over the peninsula and they did not hear him until he was almost upon them. They turned at his frantic, incoherent shouting but they had no need to understand his words. The Adren were charging over the rise of the land only a hundred yards behind him. Ethain let go of the struggling children and fumbled for his sword with his heart racing and his mind screaming for him to run.

Charljenka and Nialgrada darted past the warriors and with a departing screech for them to follow they disappeared over the edge of the bluff. Trevenna started after them in horror, thinking they had leapt to their deaths rather than face their Soul Stealers but they were disappearing down a steep narrow track leading down through the undergrowth that clung to the cliff. She yelled to the others to follow and grabbed a horse's reins, starting off down the perilous path the children had taken. Although it hadn't been necessary over the last leg of the journey, the horses were still tied together, which made it possible for Trevenna to lead all the horses down from the headland by herself. It was the same rope that led them to their deaths. She had not gone more than ten yards when the second horse in line missed its footing on the treacherous track and slipped off the edge in a cloud of scrambled snow. It was a long drop to the small shingle beach on the side of the headland and one by one, in quick succession, the other horses in line were dragged panicking over the edge.

Those who were left at the top of the cliff ignored the cacophony below them as the Adren closed the distance at a mad, ragged charge, their swords raised high and howling in bloodlust at their cornered quarry.

Merdynn stepped forward and raised his staff, yelling for the others to follow Cei and Trevenna. Those nearest to the path immediately started to scramble down it. Cerdic and Roswitha stood by Merdynn while Aelfhelm hesitated at the head of the cliff trail, inadvertently blocking Ethain's way. Ethain turned back to face the charging Adren, cursing Aelfhelm, just as Merdynn stepped forward chanting in an ancient language. The wind seemed to shriek in response and the snow lifted and flew in a twisting funnel as the sudden whirlwind crashed into the leading ranks of the Adren. Dozens were flattened by the blast or lifted and flung aside.

Cerdic looked on in wonder and Roswitha howled a war cry in triumph but Aelfhelm had seen Merdynn sink to his knees in the snow. A second whirlwind followed the first but it was already dissipating when it hit the stunned Adren ranks. Whatever magic Merdynn had wrought had drained him of his strength. Ethain's sudden hope collapsed in ruins as he saw Aelfhelm stoop to lift the old man to his feet. Merdynn sagged lifelessly in his arms. The Adren charge had been stopped by the twisting, raging wind but they were beginning to re-marshal themselves and some were already advancing over the broken bodies of their companions.

'Get him to safety!' Cerdic roared at Aelfhelm.

Aelfhelm nodded and slung Merdynn unceremoniously over his shoulder and began his descent down the precarious path. Cerdic took his place at the head of the trail as the Adren screamed in rage at the departure of their tormentor. Ethain screamed in rage too that Cerdic had blocked his escape. Left with no choice, other than attacking Cerdic, he turned to face the Adren.

The Adren leapt over the remains of the smashed bodies and bore down on the three remaining warriors. Their onslaught was furious but ill-gauged and the tight ring guarding the cliff path caught the initial rain of blows on their shields and cut back at the enemy. Ethain only wounded his assailant but others fell dead before Roswitha and Cerdic. They were vastly outnumbered and the Adren threw themselves at the warriors in an uncontrolled fury. The sheer press of the numbers trying to get at them almost forced them flailing off the top of the bluff and would have done so if Cerdic had not relieved the press by swinging his sword in great sweeps and cutting down those before him leaving a swathe of bloody dead in the space between the defenders and the Adren.

The Adren hesitated and a crude but sharply edged spear flew from their midst. Roswitha had been momentarily wiping the sweat from her eyes with the back of her sword hand and did not see the spear until it thudded into her belly. She doubled over with a soft gasp and toppled forward, driving the spear deeper into her stomach as the end planted into the snow in front of her. She rested there for a second before collapsing sideways, her dead eyes staring at the reddened snow and fallen bodies around her.

The Adren howled in triumph and readied for a final charge. Cerdic took a step towards the fallen Roswitha and Ethain saw his chance. He bolted for the path down the cliff face.

Cerdic stared after him in disbelief, thinking it must be a feint or trick but the Adren's howling increased and in that moment he knew he would never be the Anglian Warlord or lead the war bands of Britain. He knew he would die in the snow with the smell of the sea air in his nostrils, and only the hard stars above him would witness it. There would be no songs to remember him by. He glared at the Adren before him, the muscles in his face twitching in a snarl. He screamed in despair and fury and charged into them. He died cursing the friend who had deserted him.

Ethain was careering down the precipitous path and at several points nearly finished the Adren's work for them. He was sobbing as he ran and kept repeating 'I'm sorry' over and over again as his vision blurred with tears of shame and fear. His feet flew from under him as he slipped on the icy path and he crashed his head against the ground.

He lay there for a moment, his body wracked by great gasps as he tried to breath. As he lay there for a second he looked out to the Breton village and could have screamed in frustration to be so close to safety. Then he saw the figures out on the ice, cloaks buffeting in the wind, halfway between the headlands and making towards the shingle beach below. Instinct took control again and he was up on his feet hurtling down the path, blood pouring from where he had cracked his head.

Halfway down the slope he saw two warriors barring the path. Thruidred and Godhelm recognised Ethain and made way for him as he tore past them, his face covered in blood, waving his arms madly and repeatedly shouting something incomprehensible. They stared after the departing figure then looked at each other and they both simultaneously made the sign to ward off evil. Clearly whatever was going to come down this path had turned the courageous Wessex warrior into a fleeing madman.

Ethain finally reached the bottom of the cliff and tumbled onto the shingle beach where he lay panting.

'Cerdic? Roswitha?' Aelfhelm shouted to him.

He lay on his back mumbling to himself and holding his head. Aelfhelm cursed and made to go back up the hill. Trevenna stopped him with a hand to his chest.

'They're dead. We're alive. They're going to stay dead and we're going to join them if we can't get across the ice!' she shouted at him. He cursed and thrashed at the stones about him in a rage but he did not go back up the path.

The small beach was a scene of frantic activity. They too had spotted the figures from the Breton headland and they were attempting to haul the dead horses, their gear and the goat meat from the surrounding icy rocks and onto the shingle. Cei kept glancing up the cliff face trying to spot his two warriors and how far down the path the Adren were. He could see neither and cursed continually.

They struggled to load as much of the supplies as they could carry and set off across the ice with the wind blowing the fallen snow all around them. They could not see or hear the desperate rearguard being fought out above them. The path was only wide enough for the Adren to attack singly but they were doing so ferociously and without regard to their own lives. When one was killed another leapt straight at the defenders as they gave ground and bought as much time as possible for those below.

Cuthwin picked up the two children and began heading towards the far headland. The others on the beach followed him, scrambling onto the sea ice. Cei stood on the shore looking back up at the path. He could not leave his two warriors behind. Trevenna turned and forced her way back to him and hauled on his arm.

'If Godhelm or Thruidred come down that path alive they'll have a hundred Adren right with them. They'll still die but without a reason. We're the reason they're dying up there! Don't waste it, come!' she shouted desperately and tugged him away from the cliff face that loomed above them.

A little way out onto the ice Aelfhelm was arguing with Merdynn.

'Why are you waiting?' Cei shouted as he neared them.

'We need to slow their pursuit or we'll never make it across the ice!' Merdynn answered, sagging with weariness.

Aelfhelm shrugged in desperation, clearly doubting that the old man was in any state to be able to do anything to slow down the Adren. Merdynn once more drew himself to an upright position and summoned his last reserves of strength. The strange language filled the air and he brought his staff down on the ice with a crash. Cracks spread out immediately from the point of impact, creating a crescent around the small beach they had left behind.

Merdynn collapsed in the snow and Aelfhelm bent down to hoist the crumpled, unconscious figure over his shoulder once more. Cei told him to make after the others and turned back to the beach. The cracks had widened through the ice leaving a band of seawater twenty-feet wide encircling the shingle strand, effectively cutting it off from the ice shelf. It would not stop the Adren pursuing them but it would gain the warriors time as their enemy searched for another route onto the sea ice.

The warriors, bent with loaded supplies, stumbled at a half run, desperately trying to put the beach behind them and reach those coming to meet them as the rearguard on the path finally fell beneath the Adren swords. They had done their task well and Cei did not see any Adren on the beach until after they had reached the Bretons.

No greetings were exchanged. It was enough for now that neither band was Adren. The Bretons took the burden of supplies from the gasping warriors, surprised to find them carrying two children and urged them to make haste. The Adren had reached the beach and were already searching for a way to get out onto the ice after them.

Free of their loads they stumbled on in silence each lost in their own thoughts of their dead companions. Leah was half supporting Ethain as he lurched through the snow and she glanced at the blood still trickling down Ethain's face. She could not stop the tears that started to run down her face over the loss of young, proud Cerdic. Everyone assumed Ethain had been wounded during his stand with Cerdic and Roswitha and he did nothing to dispel that assumption.

They reached the base of the Breton cliffs and scrambled around to the far side where a sweeping arm of tumbled rocks and boulders jutted out of the ice to form a sheltered anchorage during the summer months. There was evidence of previous attacks from the sea ice all around the base of the Breton cape where the bodies of dead Adren still lay, half covered in snow and grotesquely frozen.

Their rescuers hauled Cei's band up onto the stone quay. They recognised the inert form of Merdynn and stared with wonder at the worn, ragged and exhausted band before them. Two men picked up Merdynn and began carrying him up the steep steps to the top of the high cliff.

The two children stood uncertainly to one side, scared and wondering if they were safe yet or not. One of the Bretons called out their names, unsure if they were the two children he knew. They recognised the man as one of their uncles and ran to him.

Cei, still exhausted and breathing heavily, explained to Bran, the leader of the Bretons who had rescued them, that they had been travelling long and far through the Shadow Lands and reassured him their appearance belied their intent.

The Breton chieftain held up his hand to stop him, 'Enough. Companions of Merdynn are friends to us. Enemies of the Dea Arduinna are friends to us. Those who bring our children back to us are friends to us. You are all three and you bring with you food for the fires and weapons to meet our enemies. Welcome to the last foothold we have in our own land and you are welcome to stay for as long as we still hold it. Come.'

Bran turned and led the way up the steep steps to the top of the headland. His men carried the supplies salvaged from the dead horses and Cei's warriors laboured up the steps cut into the rock face.

When they eventually reached the top, Bran led them to his own roundhouse, barking out orders for others to redouble the watch on the cliffs and the wall. Merdynn had been led elsewhere and Bran had placated the concerned Cei, saying he would be treated for his exhaustion.

Once in the warmth of the roundhouse they collapsed into chairs and sank down on the furs lying on the floor. Cei thanked the Breton leader who grunted in reply as he told a young man to fetch hot food and drink. The Breton waved him to a seat by the table and Cei unbelted his winter cloak and sat with his back to the fire. He could feel it's warmth but could take no comfort from it, thinking about his companions who had died cold deaths in the snows between where he sat and the ruined city.

The Breton chieftain sat back and studied him as they waited for the food and hot drinks to be brought. He was extremely curious about where they had come from and how they had arrived here at his stronghold. He wanted to know why they travelled with the sorcerer, Merdynn. He wanted to know what was happening beyond his own lands and who this new enemy was that had swept out of the Shadow Lands with such fury. But he was a patient man. A lifetime spent on fishing boats at the unpredictable mercy of the masterless seas had taught him to be patient. The patient fisher always caught the fish. It was only a matter of time.

Cei finally raised his tired eyes from the table to meet the gaze of the Breton. Bran was about a head shorter than Cei and had a smaller frame too but something about the deeply lined, sea-worn face and hard, dark eyes marked this man out as tough and uncompromising. Cei had seen men like this before on the Anglian coast. Men who had spent their lives on cruelly capricious seas, fighting the elements every time they left their harbours and cheating death every time they were caught by a storm and made it safely home. They invariably made good warriors but were hard men to lead. Bran looked just such a man as he sat there absently stroking his drooping moustache and levelly gazing back at Cei.

The food and drinks arrived and were placed on the table. Bran poured a hot drink for the warriors and handed a cup to each in turn. The strong smell of mint suffused the room and mingled with the unwashed odour from the warriors.

'The sorcerer we know. A friend from the old days,' Bran finally said as he sat back down opposite Cei, inviting him to tell the rest of the tale.

So between mouthfuls of the scalding drink Cei told Bran the tale that had taken his warriors to this stronghold. Bran listened carefully, occasionally looking at the warriors sprawled about his roundhouse as they ate. He raised his eyebrows when Cei told him that they had been separated from Arthur's war band during a raid on the Adren, he mentioned nothing about the quest east. Bran did not believe that the sorcerer would have been unable to find his way back but he kept his peace as Cei continued. He nodded in acknowledgement of the service done to his people when Cei got towards the end and mentioned the young goat herders and their village. Cei brought the tale to a conclusion with a gesture around him as if to say 'and these are those that remain and this is where we are'.

'When we saw the whirlwind on the headland we knew the sorcerer was with you and that you were in trouble. So we ventured out on the sea ice to help, had the Dea Arduinna, or Adren as you name them, been half-awake they would have rushed from before the walls and caught us all. But the last while has been reasonably quiet.

'They swept upon us after the sun had set and the slaughter was merciless. Hundreds of my people died in the surrounding area here. Only half of us made it to the safety of the stronghold with only a half of our winter supplies before we closed the gate. For a time they attacked the wall and tried to scale the cliffs around us but recently they seem content with the occasional assault, preferring to wait until we run out of food. Perhaps your arrival here will spark them to renewed attacks?' Bran looked to Cei for an answer.

'Your sanctuary may cost you dear. I doubt that they have hunted us over so many leagues to leave us in peace now,' Cei said, regretting the extra danger they brought with them.

'I don't know of these Belgae tribes that you speak of but you say these Adren were there and slaughtered them. I haven't heard of Eald or Branque or such distant villages yet they too were hacked to death you say. They came here for the same reason and would stay to see it done whether or not you and the sorcerer were here. If Merdynn recovers perhaps he can advise us what is best to be done. You say that Arthur of Wessex defends the land across the sea?'

'You know of Arthur?' Cei asked surprised, and Trevenna looked across with interest.

'Dark haired lad, gray eyes? Though I suppose he would be about your age by now.'

'Yes. Warlord of Wessex. How do you know of him?'

'Merdynn brought such a boy with him on some of his journeys here many years ago. Introduced him to my father, the chieftain in those days. Didn't like him. He reminded me of the sea under a winter moon.'

'How do you mean?' Trevenna asked.

'Only the surface is lit. Everything underneath is dark. And the sea is wild and will do whatever it chooses with no regard for any man. He's a warlord now, eh? Can't say I'm surprised.'

'Trevenna, my wife, is Arthur's sister and I count Arthur as a friend,' Cei told him.

Bran looked at them both without any trace of contrition. 'It was many years ago,' Bran said by way of concession and then shrugged, giving the impression that he did not think Arthur would have changed much in the intervening years. 'Eat. Rest. The Dea Arduinna will soon be at the walls again and we'll need every warrior,' Bran said and left the roundhouse.

The others renewed their attack on the thick vegetable broth with Trevenna voicing her appreciation of the food and her distaste for the Breton leader. No one contradicted her but the Anglians silently agreed with the Breton. Cei left the roundhouse but did not follow Bran towards the wall. Instead he made for the end of the peninsula and stared out over the sea ice. He had noticed fishing boats that had been hauled up beyond the storm line at the base of the cliff but they would not float again until the sun returned to Middangeard. He and those that remained with him were not leaving this stronghold, not during the winter.

He stood and stared out across the sea towards the unseen lands of Britain. The cold wind blasted over the ice and buffeted around the cliff face and Cei lowered his head and ran a hand over his face. Four more of his warriors had died on the peninsula to the East. There were only seven of them left now and they would have to spend the rest of the dark winter helping to defend this fortress from the Adren.

He had failed in his quest east into the Shadow Lands, and now he was caught between the frozen sea and the Adren army.

Chapter Four

A rthur arrived at Caer Sulis to find that Cael had all the arrangements for the wedding feast in hand. The square before the Great Hall was cleared and cleaned and the hall itself had been scrubbed down and thoroughly swept out. Even the fire pits, that probably held decades' worth of ashes and embers, had been emptied and fresh cut cedar wood had been laid aside for the fires. As they passed through the streets of the town it seemed that the cleaning had spread like a fever and everywhere people were busy clearing away the debris of winter. A pre-dawn light glowed in the West and everyone was preparing for the coming of the sun.

Arthur sent Mar'h to Caer Cadarn on the pretext of organising further supplies for the Gates and to arrange for several more wains to be dispatched to the Veiled City to collect the food and weapons. Although there were more supplies to send on to the garrison at the Causeway the real reason was to make sure he was nowhere near Caer Sulis when the Uathach arrived, and word had reached him that they were only a day's march away. He had left Gereint and Elwyn to bring the Mercian warriors and the tribes' counsellors from the Haven. They were due to arrive at about the same time as the Uathach.

He settled himself in the Great Hall and idly watched the activity as newly cleaned tables and benches were brought back into the hall. Beasts had already been butchered and the smell of roasting meat filled the air as the lengthy process of cooking for the feast began. New torches were fixed into the walls and tall candles were brought in and lined along the trestle tables. The shutters on the windows were propped open and Arthur's thoughts inevitably turned to Branque and the slaughter that he could not stop. He had been unable stop it then and neither could he stop reliving it now. The memory was like a thief sneaking through his thoughts and dreams, returning unexpectedly at quiet moments to once again steal the lives of those he had sought to protect. The dreams and memories fed his hatred for the Adren and he longed for the battle ahead when he could begin again the slaughter of those who threatened his kingdom.

Ceinwen brought him some food but she stopped and stood to one side of the table and watched his face warily. She felt a chill go through her as she saw the hatred in his gray eyes. She placed the food quietly on the table deciding she would leave him to be alone but Arthur looked up at her and for a moment she felt that terrible hatred directed towards herself. He blinked and the intensity in his stare switched off immediately. He smiled at her and indicated to a chair for her to sit. She suppressed a shudder, suddenly scared that his mood could change so quickly and so easily.

'Everything appears to be ready,' she said for the want of something to say.

'Indeed it does. I hadn't realised that Cael had such a talent for organising.'

They both watched Cael as he effortlessly hauled another table into the hall. He was a big man both in height and in girth and the heavy table he carried pressed against his barrel of a stomach looked to be made of nothing heavier than wicker. His close-cut hair gave his head a slightly pointed look and his constantly flushed cheeks and wide-open eyes gave him a perpetually surprised and slightly embarrassed look. Even among the other warriors, whose minds were always turned to the next meal, his appetite was legendary and he eagerly awaited the feast.

'How did it go with the counsellors?' Ceinwen ventured turning her gaze away from the busy Cael. She still felt nervous despite Arthur's easy manner.

'They've accepted me as Warlord of Britain. I shall rule in the absence of a king and for as long as the Adren continue to threaten us. Once we have defeated them a new king will be elected and I shall return to being the Wessex Warlord.' Arthur spoke in a matter of fact manner as he toyed absently with his drinking cup but Ceinwen guessed there was far more behind his bland statement and wished she had been at the council meeting at the Haven.

'The Mercian warriors?'

'They too will follow me, under the command of Gereint who has been formally recognised as their warlord.'

'And they're happy about the treaty with the Uathach?'

Arthur stopped twirling the cup on the table and looked at her, 'They're happier with my proposal than they were with King Maldred's.'

Ceinwen nodded, hearing the edge in Arthur's voice and guessing that the council were not at all happy that Arthur had promised to give the Uathach lands to clear and farm in the South and safe passage to the Western Lands in return for support in the coming war. It was, however, far better than the king's proposal whereby the Wessex and Anglian lands would be forfeit entirely, to the king and the Uathach respectively.

'I've told the Anglians that they cannot return to their lands yet.'

Ceinwen shot Arthur a quick glance. This was a surprise. Arthur continued, 'It's too dangerous. If the Adren break through the Causeway Gates then Anglia would be quickly cut off. We wouldn't be able to defend them. So I've asked all the peoples to stay west of Caer Sulis for the summer months. It'll mean that much less of the land will be harvested but the Cithol supplies should more than make up for the shortfall. The first transport should arrive soon along with the first of the new crossbows.'

'And the Anglian chieftain has accepted this?' Ceinwen asked, still surprised by Arthur's decision.

'With Cei in the Shadow Lands, Aelle looked to Elwyn for advice and he's already agreed to move the families of the Anglian warriors to Whitehorse Hill for their safety.'

'Gods, they can't be happy about not returning to their homes.'

'They weren't but these aren't times to be happy in and I will not see any village in Britain destroyed like Branque or Eald or the Belgae villages.'

Arthur's voice had taken on a tone to match the look in his eyes when Ceinwen had approached the table. She stayed silent for a few minutes as the activity carried on in the hall below them.

'Every man, woman and child will be trained for some aspect of the war ahead, whether it be as warriors, messengers, riders, healers or cooks for the army. This will be done at Caer Sulis and Whitehorse Hill. I thought to put Mar'h in charge of the training whilst we go east with our band and the Mercians. Do you think he's capable of it?'

Ceinwen thought for a moment, remembering how much more like his old self Mar'h had seemed back at the Haven. He would be disappointed not to be at the Causeway when the Adren came but with his left hand now useless perhaps it was for the best. He would certainly make an excellent fighting instructor.

She nodded her agreement. 'How many do you hope to train as warriors?'

'Mar'h will decide that as he trains them. As many as possible and as quickly as possible for we'll have less than three hundred at the Causeway to meet the Adren invasion.'

'What about the Uathach and the Cithol? At least the Uathach will be there with us surely?'

'Perhaps. We shall see. If Ablach honours the agreement then we may have six or seven hundred with which to face the Adren.'

'He must do, why else would he present his daughter to marry you?' Ceinwen asked, suddenly afraid that they would have to stand against the Adren host alone.

'We shall see,' Arthur repeated, once more toying with the empty cup.

'What will you do if he doesn't?'

'As I said. Burn their lands and kill them all.'

Ceinwen watched Arthur as he spun the wine cup on the surface of the table and she knew by the way he had spoken so implacably that he meant it in absolute earnest. She recalled the tales she had heard about the campaign in the Green Isle and had no doubt Arthur would do as he said. She had no idea how he would carry out his retribution whilst still having to defeat the Adren and she had no intention of asking him either. She had approached him with the food thinking she would ask him how he felt about marrying the Uathach girl but she decided against it now and in an oblique way he had already answered her question.

The chieftains and counsellors of the southern tribes arrived with the Mercian warriors some time before Ablach led his Uathach band into Caer Sulis. When the arrival of the Uathach was announced in the Great Hall Arthur felt an immediate and acute sense of loss. In some deep recess within himself he had blindly hoped that Ablach would not come to Caer Sulis with his daughter, Gwyna. Even though that meant the Uathach would not stand with them against the Adren still some part of him had hoped for it, for that would mean he was free to be with Fin Seren. When their arrival was called out from the doors of the Great Hall he experienced a sudden assault of vertigo as if the whole world had abruptly fallen away from beneath his feet leaving him drifting, his true desires no longer able to anchor himself to the world.

Deep inside a voice cried out with the desperation of a plea from a grave being coldly filled by the events he could do nothing to stop. Except there was one last chance to do as he wanted; he could leave the hall and ride to the Veiled City, to Fin Seren. Once again he felt as if he werc suddenly at a great height, not because he had climbed upwards but because the ground he stood on had plummeted away from him. He physically felt the onslaught of the vertigo and his stomach lurched and his chest constricted around his heart. He put a hand on the table to steady himself as he watched Ablach enter the hall. The voice from the tomb within, where he had interred his love for Fin Seren, was already half buried but all the more desperate for it and it frantically screamed one word at him: no. He could feel the sweat on the palms of his hands, all he had to do was walk away from the hall. Walk away from Gwyna and the treaty with the Uathach. Walk away from Britain.

He slammed shut the door of the tomb and the voice inside died. He felt the firm wood of the floor beneath his feet and the Great Hall come back into focus again. He would not turn his back on Britain.

Ablach was walking up the hall towards him. He was flanked and followed by ten of his warriors who strode through the hall of their enemy with a swagger and arrogance born of a nervousness that their pride sought to conceal. Ablach looked unchanged from the last time that Arthur had seen him. His small black eyes shifted from side to side as if he was seeking someone but apart from those preparing the feast the hall was mostly empty. Morgund lounged in one corner with his feet propped up on a table as he chatted to Morveren but Ablach could see no others from Arthur's war band. He had indeed been searching for one face, Mar'h, the true father of Gwyna.

Ablach's warriors formed a protective ring about their chieftain as he stopped in front of the raised platform where Arthur was standing. Arthur noted that they all had their hands on their weapons as if expecting some kind of treachery. They had the look of hardened warriors, veterans from years of raiding the southern lands. They were tall men, strong and scarred from dozens of skirmishes and battles. They had a wild, barely restrained violence about them and they reminded Arthur of the warriors that had been in the Wessex war band when he had become the warlord; violent, brutal men constantly looking for the next fight and taking whatever they wanted whenever they wanted it and from whomever they chose.

Since becoming warlord almost twenty years ago Arthur had changed all that and he knew with certainty that the men and women in his war band could defeat these wild warriors whether it was in individual combat or on a battlefield. The Uathach warriors may well have looked more fearsome but their wildness was their weakness. The training, discipline and cohesive fighting ability of his warriors had transformed the Wessex war band into a formidable fighting force that was feared by its enemies and respected by those it sought to protect.

Under the leadership of Cei the Anglians had gone through a similar transformation and Gereint had remodelled the king's company, the Mercians, along the same lines although, curiously, there were no women in the Mercian war band.

Ablach stood looking up at Arthur. Like his warriors, he too was thinking of treachery but his thoughts were of perpetrating it. Arthur stood alone while he had ten of his bravest warriors behind him.

'I wager your lands that I win,' Arthur said conversationally.

Ablach beamed up at him and barked out his distinctive laugh. He climbed the steps to the dais and the wooden planks of the floor creaked under his massive frame. He stood before Arthur and held out a spade-like hand. Arthur took the hand and looked up into the dark eyes made smaller by the heavy jowls and fat-layered cheekbones of the Uathach chieftain. Ablach was one of the few men in Middangeard who stood taller than Arthur did and he was heavier too but neither doubted who would be the quicker in single combat.

'And I would probably lose my lands too but you can't blame me for considering the temptation, son.'

Arthur resisted the urge to recoil from being called 'son' by the monster before him. Ablach was monstrous, both in his physical size and in how he ruled his lands to the North of Anglia. Two other chieftains ruled the rest of the northern lands. Hund ruled the land to the North of Mercia and Benoc held the power in the far north. Unlike the southern tribes the Uathach had no rule of law and no war bands to enforce the laws of the land if necessary. There was relative wealth for the strongest and it was bought at the expense of everyone else who were consigned to lives of subsistent survival and to die deaths of lingering hunger or sudden violence. They were hard lands and hard lives and they were led by vicious men who knew nothing of restraint and who cared only for their own appetites and ambitions.

Ablach had offered this marriage for several reasons. He wanted land in the South, good land that he could farm and that would increase his wealth. He wanted passage on the ships from the Haven, not because this would help his people whom he saw as little more than tools to increase his power, but because it would offer him new lands and new opportunities to fortify his rule. He realised the Adren would attempt to invade Britain and he needed the southern tribes to help protect his own land. For all these reasons he had proposed the marriage of Gwyna to Arthur but what he really desired was to find a way by which he could rule the rich southern lands and this offered a route to that goal.

Arthur publicly claimed that the marriage would ensure that the Uathach stood alongside the southern warriors in the war against the Adren but he held a greater design too. Once they had defeated the Adren he would turn his attention to the North. He planned to use his marriage to Gwyna to justify taking complete control of the northern tribes and uniting Britain under one rule.

As they faced each other on the dais in Caer Sulis they both knew that whatever aims or plans the other had they would be in direct contradiction to each other. In a way they both understood, this marriage would mark the start of each of their plans to destroy the other. For his part, Arthur fully intended to offer land in the South and passage to the Western Lands for the northern tribes. Once the peoples of the North had seen how life can be different and how the rule of law can improve their lives then it will leave only the warriors of the North to deal with but for now he needed those warriors to help repel the Adren. Ablach had no such intention of honouring anything unless it best served his immediate personal ambitions.

The Uathach guard waited at the foot of the raised area while Arthur and Ablach sat down and settled the details for the wedding. It would take place in ten hours time once the Uathach had rested after their long journey. Ablach wanted his men to be able to carry their weapons into the hall and Arthur had no objection. He would make it clear that anyone who drew a weapon in the Great Hall, Uathach or southern, would answer immediately to his own sword. He told Ablach to keep his men in check and any of them that insulted or attacked any of the people of Caer Sulis would also answer to his sword. With that, Ablach and his guard retired to the quarters set aside for them and where Gwyna and the others were already preparing for the wedding.

Arthur sought out Ceinwen and told her to find Elwyn and Gereint and to make sure that all the warriors in Caer Sulis were ready to ride to the Causeway soon after the wedding feast. He had questioned Ablach why he had only brought fifty of his men with him and Ablach had replied that all the northern warriors were gathering at Dalchiaran, his own fortified village, and that he would return there to collect them after the wedding before heading to the Causeway.

Once the Uathach had retired Arthur walked down to the river that ran along the southern edge of the town. The scattered grey clouds to the West were under-painted in shades of red and pink and stood against a starless horizon. Arthur looked to the East where the last of the winter stars stubbornly shone from darker skies and he wondered about the fate of Cei, Trevenna and Merdynn. He had no way of knowing if their quest had failed or succeeded, if they were alive or lying dead in the Shadow Lands of the East. He could only trust in his feeling that they were still alive. He breathed deeply in the cold air. Their fate was out of his hands and all he could do now was defend the Causeway with as many warriors as he could gather together.

The sound of hammering rang across the fields from the town and echoed around the wide valley. Soon the whole town and surrounding area would be busy with the people coming from the Haven and these fields would ring to the sound of weapons training as Mar'h sought to turn people who had previously led rustic lives into an army capable of facing the Adren. Along with the warriors too old or maimed to stand at the Causeway, Arthur had decided to assign Mar'h ten others from the combined war bands of the South to help him turn men, women, youths, fishers and farmers, into disciplined fighters with the skill and courage to stand when the Adren charged. It would be a difficult and unenviable task but a crucial one and he wondered if he should undertake the training himself. Arthur knew he would be able to do it better than any other would and he was still far from sure whether Mar'h was up to the task.

He walked on along the riverbank, past the royal houses and with his back to the sunrise. He knew his place was on the Causeway and despite wishing to take the moulding of a new army upon himself he felt a deep unease that he was not already at the Gates. He turned away from the river and made his way back to his quarters to prepare himself for the ceremony. In the lightening skies to the West the first of the long diagonal lines of migrating birds were returning to inland Britain.

Caer Sulis would normally have been teeming with the returning people from the Western Lands at this time of year. This year's Imbolc festival for the Wakening of the Sun would be held earlier than usual to coincide with Arthur's marriage to Gwyna and most of the people from the southern tribes were still at the Haven. Arthur had determined that Caer Sulis would mark the furthest point east that the people could return to, which meant that the Anglians, among others, would have to find temporary homes in Wessex, Mercia and Caer Sulis itself. The town was designed as the gathering place for the journey across the Western Seas and was easily large enough to accommodate the Anglians who wished to remain there. It was Arthur's plan that many of the Wessex and Mercians would stay there too, at least until Mar'h had selected those whom he wished to form into an army.

If the town was unusually quiet for the time of year, the Great Hall was as full as it could be. The counsellors and chieftains of the three tribes were spread throughout the tables on the raised dais, while the forty warriors who had accompanied Arthur through the Shadow Lands were seated just below the raised area at the top of the hall. Ablach and ten of his men were also on the dais while the rest of the Uathach were in the main part of the hall with Gereint and his two hundred warriors. There were over four hundred people in the hall, three hundred of them were warriors and each of them carried their weapons.

Arthur stood outside in the square before the hall with Ceinwen by his side. They had changed from their heavy winter clothing for the ceremony and both felt the cold of the spring dawn as they patiently waited for Gwyna. She had chosen Ruraidh, the leader of the ill-fated

Uathach raiding party that Arthur had saved in the Shadow Lands, to stand beside her at the wedding. Arthur had chosen Ceinwen. Like many of his warriors, Arthur had shaved off his winter beard and he felt the cold wind on his face all the more keenly for it. Ceinwen's light cloak rippled about her as she stood with arms folded, her weight on one leg. She caught Arthur's eye and nodded to the edges of the square. The people who had wintered in the town were beginning to line up against the buildings that faced the open space outside the hall. Arthur spotted one of the elders of the town and strolled across to her. After exchanging a few words he rejoined Ceinwen at the steps to the hall.

'What did you say?' Ceinwen asked shifting her weight onto her other leg and glancing back at the woman Arthur had spoken to.

'I told them they could all enter the hall after we go in.'

'And join the feast?'

'Yes.'

'There won't be much room,' she pointed out.

'Then it will be crowded.'

Ceinwen frowned, 'Why tell them to come in then?'

'I want those inside to remember why we have to hold the Adren at the Causeway.'

Ceinwen paused again before she voiced her fears, 'Do you think the Uathach will come to the Causeway?'

Before Arthur could answer there was a commotion at one end of the square. Ruraidh was leading a large bay horse towards them. Gwyna sat upright on the horse as it plodded slowly across the mud of the courtyard.

Ruraidh helped her off the horse, gently lifting her down onto the steps. She stood there and looked up at Arthur. Ceinwen stared at her as she tried to equate the venomous warrior she had met in the Shadow Lands with the pretty young girl before her now. She found it hard to believe they were the same person. Arthur was having the same difficulty.

Gwyna wore a close-fitting, finely tailored dark blue dress. Ceinwen could still see the bandaging around her injured shoulder despite the long sleeves that covered her arms. It was a plain full-length dress, unadorned by frills or lace and its colour traditionally represented the purity of the bride. Ceinwen would later turn to Morveren and scoff at that idea but as she stood in front of the young woman the dark blue seemed fitting and appropriate to her. The dress flowed to her ankles that were adorned with gold rings and her small feet were bare. Her unruly tangle of dark red hair had been wrestled and tamed into one long braid that reached down her back to the single white cord that was tied about her narrow waist.

Ivy, signifying fidelity, was entwined around the cord that held a sheaf of wheat and a few sprigs of sage against her side as blessing for fertility and wisdom. A delicate gold torque encircled her throat with the open ends crafted into the shapes of two snakeheads. Ceinwen could not stop herself from thinking that the torque said more about Gwyna than anything else she was wearing.

Gwyna smiled as Arthur looked at her. The hard lines of winter had left her face and her lips were no longer blistered and cracked. Even her hazel eyes that had held such hardness before seemed softened and only the small creases around the corners of her eyes and to either side of her smiling lips belied her young age. Arthur had seen that look before and knew there was nothing innocent about the girl standing before him; nothing innocent at all. He returned the smile.

Taking his eyes from Gwyna he turned his attention to Ruraidh and held out his hand.

'We're a long way from the Adren and the Shadow Lands,' Ruraidh said as he clasped Arthur's extended hand.

'The Adren are looking to shorten that distance,' Arthur replied.

Gwyna stepped between them, 'Time for war later.'

They agreed and taking Gwyna's hand in his, Arthur climbed the steps to the Great Hall. Drawing his sword he banged the hilt on the door three times. The double doors swung open and the noise of the gathering inside stilled to silence within a few seconds.

Arthur and Gwyna stood side by side within the doorway with the other two just behind them and to one side. As the people of Caer Sulis filled the square a steady drumming of fists and dagger hilts began to spread throughout the hall. The shutters over the windows were closed and the noise increased as the hall gradually fell into darkness as the tallow candles were extinguished along the length of the tables until the only light was from the small fire that burned in a bowl by the doorway.

Elwyn and Gereint, as leaders of the Anglian and Mercian war bands, lit rush candles from the small fire and led the way up the centre of the hall. This was a Wessex custom and it signified the new light of a new union. It was a peculiarly evocative scene. The hall was echoing to the noise and in utter darkness save for the rush candles, held aloft and leading the procession to the head of the hall.

When they reached the dais the flame from the procession candles was passed from table to table until the soft blush of candlelight once again lit the whole hall. The townsfolk of Caer Sulis shuffled into the hall and along the shadows of the walls as they sought to make room for those filing in behind them.

Arthur and Gwyna stood at the front of the dais before all the gathered warriors and people as Ceinwen and Ruraidh bound the Uathach girl's right hand to the warlord's left in the Triquetra, a three-looped knot that symbolised the three layers of life – the body, the mind and the spirit. This too was a Wessex custom and once the knot was complete the bonded couple raised their arms to show the unification to all those before them. A great roar filled the hall and immediately the fire pits were re-lit and food and drink started to arrive along the tables.

Although the formal part of the ceremony was over, it would not be considered complete until the newly wed couple had received all who wished to present themselves after which they would leave the hall together and retire to their prepared quarters.

Arthur and Gwyna sat at the foremost table on the raised area of the hall with Ceinwen and Ruraidh by their side as the first of many supplicants, well-wishers and the simply curious lined up to speak to them. The Triquetra had been taken from their joined wrists and lay to one side of the table along with the herbs and flowers that had adorned Gwyna's waist. On the tables around them sat the counsellors and chieftains of the three southern tribes with Ablach and ten of the Uathach warriors.

This feast was serving as both the marriage celebration and the Imbolc festival and everyone in the hall seemed intent on doing justice to both. The wine and beer flowed freely and roasted carcass followed roasted carcass as every person put the fears and darkness of winter behind them. It seemed to them that Ablach was prepared to honour the treaty and stand with the southern warriors at the Causeway and they believed this signalled the end of the ceaseless raids and damaging border wars between the North and South. It was a time to celebrate and the fears of the forthcoming Adren war were washed aside in concerted drinking and drowned out by a carefree raucousness that some of the more experienced warriors recognised as little more than forced bravado.

Arthur felt it too. As he talked to the various warriors and villagers before him he sensed an underlying desperation to the frenetic feasting in the hall. He thought it felt like people were indulging themselves one last time in something soon to be denied to them. Perhaps it was because he was preoccupied by these thoughts that he did not notice two separate things in the hall below him; the Uathach warrior growing ever more impatient in the line before him and the two hooded figures who entered the hall unannounced and unnoticed. He would never know that the two uninvited guests had been at his marriage feast.

As Arthur was standing on the steps to the hall looking at the girl he was about to marry, Terrill had arrived in Caer Sulis with the first of the supply wains carrying food and the new weapons. He also brought Fin Seren. When he had given her Arthur's cryptic message she had insisted on accompanying him to Caer Sulis. Lord Venning would never have allowed his daughter to travel beyond the Winter Wood so she had not asked his permission. She had left her maids armed only with the poor cover story that she was walking the woods in the last of the winter starlight.

The first that Captain Terrill heard of the great wedding was when he left the wains with those still working in the storage barns. His suspicions that Arthur and Seren were closer than it seemed were partially confirmed when she had insisted on travelling with him but his deeper fears were not realised until those at the barn told them whose wedding it was. He had seen the first assault of bemused shock on Seren's face as she heard the news. When they were alone he had questioned her and her expressionless face and absolute denial had been betrayed by her trembling hands. She had refused to answer any of his questions and insisted instead on going straight to the Great Hall. He in turn was shocked that she could feel this way about someone from outside the Veiled City. The Cithol privately regarded those living above ground and beyond the borders of the Winter

Wood as simple barbarians at their best and as dangerous animals at their worst. That Fin Seren, Lord Venning's daughter, could be attracted to one of them was just astonishing to him. That someone as gentle as Seren could be attracted to Arthur, whose very nature seemed to seethe violence, was almost beyond his belief.

As he reluctantly led her towards the hall he cursed himself for not realising the significance of Seren's previous meetings with Arthur. He had been suspicious too that Seren had stopped wearing her Elk Stone pendant at about the same time as one of Arthur's visits. Only now was he certain that Seren had given it to Arthur as a token of her love. He still had no idea how far that love had gone; that Seren carried Arthur's child.

They stood close together in a shadowed recess between two burning brands near the entrance to the hall. No one noticed or paid them any attention and they kept the hoods of their cloaks pulled over their heads. Terrill was watching the drunken antics of those nearest to them with an increasing sense of distaste. The music he could hear from further up the hall sounded crude and rudimentary. There did not seem to be any kind of order to the proceedings at all and people were eating, swilling drink, shouting and falling over each other in a chaos that horrified him. The Cithol rarely hunted animals for food and the sight of so many half-torn and half-eaten haunches, ribs and legs of various animals made him feel distinctly unwell.

Fin Seren only had eyes for what was happening at the top table where she could see Arthur slouched back in his chair as a line of people inched past his table. Between the passing people she caught glimpses of the girl by his side. The realisation of what was happening was beginning to penetrate her shock. As she blinked away the denials her tears began to swell and track down her cheeks. She held her arms folded tightly against her chest trying to still the sobs that threatened to rob her dignity. She wanted to run to Arthur and tell him what she felt she should have told him before now, that she was bearing his child, that she loved him. She wanted to run from the hall and bury herself in the Veiled City. She wanted to be back in the Winter Garden with Arthur and at the same time she never wanted to see either again. As the conflicting emotions swept through her unchecked, her lips began to tremble and the tears spilled freely. More than anything she wanted to understand how all of this could have happened.

Terrill could stand the assault on his senses no longer and taking Seren by the arm led her from the hall. She did not resist and managed to hold back her desperation until they were once more seated on the lead wagon of the train returning to the Veiled City. As Terrill held the reins and looked ahead, Seren sat beside him and finally abandoned herself to her desolation. With her head hung down and her arms limp by her sides, palms upturned, she let the heart-rending sobs of despair shudder, catch and then break upon her.

As Captain Terrill and Fin Seren began their journey back to the Winter Wood the nervous Uathach warrior finally came before Arthur. Although his posture did not change, Arthur immediately sensed fear and the threat of violence from the man before him. He glanced at Gwyna and saw a look of surprise on her face then looked over his shoulder to where Ablach sat. The Uathach chieftain was draining another cup of wine with a good deal of it spilling down either side of his thick beard. Ablach was watching the Uathach warrior with avid interest and Arthur realised that Ablach had planned whatever was about to happen.

'I claim the right of challenge for this woman's hand,' the warrior said, staring at Arthur defiantly.

Arthur looked at Gwyna, 'Do you know this man?'

Gwyna looked nonplussed. The man before them was called Mador and they had been lovers before she had travelled to the Shadow Lands with Ruraidh's band. She nodded in answer to Arthur's question, her mouth still open in surprise. They had been lovers but no more than that and she did not understand why he should be issuing a challenge now.

Ruraidh stood up and walked around the table to the warrior. 'What are you doing Mador? Gwyna's not your woman and you know it!' Ruraidh said, but he was forcefully pushed away.

'We were together and this dog took her from me!'

Other people nearby had been following this interesting development with amusement but a quiet began to spread from the top tables when Mador insulted Arthur.

'Gwyna, do you wish to be with this man?' Arthur casually asked, still slumped back in his chair.

'No, of course not, and you know this Mador,' she replied, addressing the last part to the warrior whose hand was already resting on his sword hilt.

Arthur looked up at Mador. 'It appears you are mistaken. This is a peaceful feast, absent of enemies and much has been drunk. Rejoin your friends and boast that you called me a dog and lived.' Arthur waved a hand to dismiss the young warrior and reached for his wine cup.

Ablach leaned forward anticipating the moment when Mador would strike. He had planned this challenge during the journey to Caer Sulis. If Mador succeeded then the southern tribes would be in chaos without Arthur and he might well be able to benefit from that. If Mador failed then it would not reflect upon himself and Gwyna would still be with Arthur so he would be none the worse off.

Mador had put his right hand on his sword hilt as a feint. He was left handed and it was his left hand that plucked the dagger from his belt and sent it arrowing towards Arthur only six-feet away.

Ceinwen jumped to her feet, drawing her sword as Gwyna stared on in horror. Arthur remained seated and Ceinwen looked at his chest expecting to see the dagger buried there but Arthur had caught the blade in the bowl of his wine cup. Arthur smiled at Mador as he upturned the cup and emptied the knife onto the table.

Mador snarled half in fear, half in fury and clumsily drew his sword, which hung on his wrong side. Arthur stood up to face him and hurled the table aside. Gwyna was cursing Mador while all the warriors in the hall were trying to get towards the front so that they could get a better view of what was happening on the dais.

Mador rushed forward and slashed his sword downwards at Arthur's left shoulder. Arthur took a step backwards and sideways, and as the blade passed his chest he moved forward and struck Mador in the face with his fist. Mador's head snapped back and he stared at Arthur stunned by his speed. Arthur leapt back again as the sword sliced through the air in a backhand cut and again he stepped in and struck Mador in the face once the sword had swept harmlessly by. Mador staggered backwards, blood pouring from his nose and mouth. He wiped at the blood on his face, shocked that Arthur could evade his sword and strike so quickly. He was dimly aware of shouting and roars from the hall behind him but he was watching Arthur who still had not drawn his sword.

Arthur stood facing Mador with his arms casually by his sides as the Uathach warrior slowly circled him. The Wessex Warlord looked utterly calm and his breathing was unlaboured. Mador cursed him as he hefted his sword in his sweaty grip. Arthur smiled at him and Mador realised with a fresh wash of fear that Arthur was enjoying himself. He lunged forward desperately trying to drive the blade into Arthur's midriff but his unarmed opponent turned, swaying sideways, and the blade plunged past him. Arthur grasped the sword arm and snapped the wrist inwards, breaking it. The sword fell to the floor and Arthur twisted Mador's arm up behind his back and sent him crashing to the ground. Grabbing his hair he jerked his head back and drawing his own dagger he pressed the blade to Mador's exposed throat.

Arthur looked up to where Ablach had been screaming on his warrior and called out loudly for all to hear, 'In the spirit of our peaceful feast I let Ablach decide his man's fate.'

All eyes turned to the Uathach chieftain who stared from the prone Mador and back to Arthur. Ablach realised that if he asked Arthur to spare his warrior then he would be condoning the attack upon his host. If he let Arthur kill him then he would be seen to be abandoning his own warrior. He spat on the ground and said, 'I leave it to the mercy of the Warlord of Britain.'

Arthur shrugged and slit Mador's throat. 'I have no mercy,' he said standing up as Mador thrashed on the floor trying to stem the flood of blood.

Ceinwen looked to the Uathach warriors expecting them to launch an attack but it had been a single combat and Arthur had offered their chieftain a chance to spare Mador. In their eyes it had been fair. Eventually two of them climbed the steps up to the dais, stared warily at Arthur for a second then wrapped their dead comrade in his cloak and lifted him away.

Arthur dragged the table back into place and took his seat behind it once more but the queue of people had melted away. The feast resumed and the gathered warriors grabbed more wine and beer as the combat was relived and other famous challenges were recalled. This would become a renowned feast and they were here and witnessing it; for the warriors in the Great Hall it was already turning out to be an excellent marriage.

Five miles to the East of the town Terrill stared after a rider who had galloped past them racing towards Caer Sulis. The relay messenger was bringing word that the Adren were massing on the Causeway.

Chapter Five

C ei knelt by Merdynn's low bed. The old man had lain in a fitful dream state for several days, hovering between this world and the next as if his ancient spirit was undecided which one it belonged to. An hour ago he had finally regained consciousness and was now propped up by pillows and tentatively supping a light hot broth. The enchantments he had worked in an attempt to safeguard Cei's band had nearly been his last.

'How do you feel?' Cei felt a little foolish asking the question but tradition demanded that the ill be asked how they feel.

'Ill,' Merdynn replied between mouthfuls of the soup, 'Weak. And tired too, which is surprising as I'm told I've been asleep for days on end.'

'I wouldn't call it sleep. More like a disturbed death.'

'Well, that's comforting to know. I'm glad to have you around.'

Cei smiled in relief, Merdynn's reply told him all that he needed to know; he was recovering. Merdynn noticed his smile and snorted into his soup.

'If you must know, and I suppose you must, I've been somewhat lost in walking through my memories. And I have rather a lot of memories to get lost in.'

'Then you'll have to be more careful working your magic if that's the result of them.'

'Indeed. There was a time, ah well, but that was long ago. It seems that there's little left in the land now. The last Age sapped all the old enchantment from the land. In truth it's been waning for a long time, surprised there's anything left in the earth at all.' He put the half-empty bowl down by the side of the bed and closed his eyes.

'So the spells you worked came from the land?' Cei asked, unable to bridle his curiosity.

Merdynn opened his eyes again with an obvious effort, 'In a manner of speaking, yes, but it's far more complicated than that.' He drifted off again and his bearded chin settled on his chest once more.

'Merdynn?'

His eyes flashed open, 'Good grief! If an old, ill man closes his eyes it means he wishes to rest!'

'It's just that I didn't want you to...'

'Don't fret yourself, I'm not going to sink into a 'disturbed death' as you so reassuringly put it. I only wish to sleep.' He saw the look of reproach on Cei's face and noticed for the first time how tired the Anglian Warlord looked. His dark blue eyes were ringed black and his fair, red-tinged beard made his face look gaunt. Merdynn was quietly shocked by Cei's appearance.

'Does the fortress still hold?' he asked in a kinder voice.

'Yes. Yes it does.'

'And will you be able to hold it for the next few hours?'

'Yes.'

'Good. Until then, then.'

Cei watched as the old man slipped into an untroubled sleep and then wearily eased himself upright. Trevenna was standing in the doorway and Cei smiled at her.

'Is he all right?' she asked.

'Good as old.'

Trevenna massaged her arm where an Adren weapon had struck her some days ago then looked up tiredly into Cei's eyes, 'They're preparing to attack the main wall again.'

'The cliffs too?'

'Not this time.'

'Good. Come on, the others will think we've sidled off for a moment of passion.'

Trevenna laughed softly, 'Oh for that kind of energy. You realise that if we get out of this I'll sleep for longer than Merdynn did?'

'Not exactly the encouragement I was hoping for,' Cei answered laughing too.

'Come on then,' Trevenna said and led the way back to the sounds of battle. Behind them Merdynn opened his eyes, sighed and reached down for the unfinished bowl of broth.

On their way to the wall they passed Cuthwin who was striding off to the cliff edge followed by four of the Bretons' dogs that bounded through the snow relishing this new game that the whole village seemed prepared to play indefinitely. Along with Ethain, Leah and Aelfhelm he was one of the few of Cei's band who had survived the Shadow Lands. By the standards of the other warriors in Cei's spear riders he was a quiet young man, not yet twenty but despite his restrained demeanour he was popular among his companions. He was always ready to pass the time with anyone and usually ended up making them laugh. He had a likeable nature and a quiet confidence that was reflected in his steadfast ability to fight. His swordsmanship would never be dazzling or be imbued with the mad battle frenzy that took over some of the others but he was calm in a fight and knew exactly what he was doing. He was, as Cei had succinctly put it, reliable. None of the others were surprised that he had survived the Shadow Lands but he was puzzled that experienced and better warriors such as Herewulf, Wolfestan, Roswitha and Cerdic had all died and yet he had lived. He put it down to the chance of war but could not help wondering about it.

Cei called out a greeting to him and he waved his sword in return. He was on what had become known as the 'dog patrol'; a circuit around the unprotected edges of the headland. The dogs had become extremely adept in detecting any sign of the Adren trying to scale the cliffs from the frozen sea. When they simultaneously attacked the wall and the vertical sides of the promontory, the Bretons found themselves stretched far too thinly and several times they had found themselves on the brink of being overrun.

The Adren had been laying siege to the Breton fortress since the sun had set but the assault had found a new impetus when Cei's band had joined the defenders. Since then the Bretons had lost over a hundred people trying to keep the Adren at bay. Bran, the Breton leader, had managed to get just over five hundred of his people within the safety of the defensive wall, which stretched across the headland, when the Adren had first attacked. Everyone else had been slaughtered in the villages that lay around the fortress and now he was losing more of his people day by day and attack after attack.

Adren bodies lay in frozen heaps at the base of the wall and at the bottom of the cliffs but despite their casualties their numbers had increased as new contingents arrived from the North, and the Adren in the darkness beyond the fortress walls now numbered over five thousand. Bran had less than four hundred and that included the old and young but even those not able to wield a weapon still played what part they could; some prepared the food, some tended the wounded, and others watched the cliffs for Adren.

Bran kept almost a hundred of his force constantly on the wide ledge that ran across the inside length of the wall to repel the ladders and grappling hooks and to hurl down missiles upon the attackers. They manned the wall in shifts but the incessant attacks had sapped their strength and eroded their will to resist.

Cei's few warriors seemed to the Bretons to be everywhere. Trevenna or Leah would be fighting on the high wall, hurling back the Adren that had reached the top and encouraging those around them to carry on the fight against the enemy. Aelfhelm and Cuthwin would be in the thick of the desperate fighting when the Adren threatened to establish a foothold on the cliff tops. With nowhere to hide and nowhere left to run to, Ethain too played his part and stood his ground alongside his companions although he was more often seen working tirelessly among the wounded or inspiring the children to the bravery necessary to help their elders.

In the midst of all was the Anglian Warlord. The Bretons spoke quietly that he must be possessed for no one had seen him sleep or stop longer than a few minutes to eat and in the fighting he was like a wild spirit of the sea unleashed against their enemies.

Cei and his warriors had, of course, slept but they had rarely retired to do so and they had snatched what sleep they could between the attacks of the Adren. They were well aware that they could not do this indefinitely and they were already feeling the effects of sleep-deprived exhaustion. The few hours of rest they had accumulated during the lulls in the fighting were simply not enough and they knew that sooner or later fatigue would lead to a slip or mistake that would cost them their lives but with the Adren surrounding them and the coastal seas still frozen there was as yet no other alternative and they knew there was no possibility of help arriving either. It seemed that the Adren controlled all of Middangeard beyond the Causeway; everywhere but where they stood. All they could do was to keep fighting, keep defending the headland and to keep the Adren at bay for as long as possible.

The only access to the top of the wall was a single stone stair near the central gate and Cei climbed up the steeply cut steps. The Adren had been unable to force the gateway and the double protection of the withdrawn bridge against the ironbound oak of the gates still held firm.

Cei reached the top where Trevenna was waiting for him. Together they ran half-crouched along the ice-cleared ledge to where Leah was sheltering behind the solid stonework.

'Ladders again?'

Leah nodded and took off her iron-crossed leather cap to sweep her sweat-matted hair from her face. Arrows clattered against the other side of the stonework and fizzed over the top of the wall.

In the early days of the attacks they had stood at the wall and fired their own arrows down into the ranks below them but the Adren could put two or three hundred archers within range of the wall and the Bretons had lost too many people in that way. Their supply of arrows was limited too so now they waited for the Adren to reach the top when the hail of missiles from below would stop, and then engage the enemy as they tried to establish themselves on the wide parapet. Groups of children scurried across the ground on the Breton side of the wall, collecting the spent Adren arrows and distributing them among the bowmen.

'Where's Bran, and Aelfhelm?' Cei asked.

'Aelfhelm's on the left side. I think Bran's leading a dog-patrol along the cliff edge,' Leah replied.

They heard the deep twanging sound of catapults. At first the Adren had hurled stones and boulders at the high wall but the ancient masonry had held firm and the missiles had little effect. The Adren had changed their tactics and were now using the catapults to hurl heavy rocks that were chained to rough hewn ladders so that as the rock cleared the wall it brought the wooden ladder up against it and then acted as a counterbalance to stop the defenders from simply levering the ladders away. The chains were attached to the ladders by an iron bracket four rungs from the top and they were too thick to cut through quickly and any attempt to do so meant leaning out over the edge of the wall and courting the Adren arrows. It became a frantic battle to fight off the attackers and sever the chains attached to the boulders so that the ladders could be cast aside and the attack repelled.

'Here they come,' Leah said and secured her skullcap back on.

'Good hunting,' Trevenna said and put a hand on Leah's shoulder before she and Cei ran back to the centre of the wall, still crouching over to stay under cover.

As they passed along the Breton line the catapulted rocks sailed out of the darkness and over their heads trailing the chain links behind them before smashing against the inside of the wall and snapping taut as the counter-balanced ladders slapped into place all along the high wall. Immediately axes and hammers rang out as the defenders tried to cut through the chains.

They could hear the battle cries of the Adren as they started to climb the ladders and the Bretons tried to hurl stones, rocks and boulders down the length of the ladders without being hit by the hail of Adren arrows that filled the air above the lip of the protecting masonry. One of the Bretons managed to drop a heavy rock that crashed straight down one of the scaling ladders, clearing it entirely but as he did so he was hit by three arrows and flung from the parapet.

Each defender knew what they had to do and already some were trying to crack the chains that held the ladders in place. Others crouched waiting for the first Adren to appear over the wall, ready to thrust with spears or loose their arrows at the attackers. Others waited with hooked poles so that as soon as the links were broken they could haul the ladders sideways to crash back down to the ground or into adjacent ladders packed with the assailants.

Trevenna knelt and fitted an arrow to her bow that she held sideways and pointing at the top of the ladder only ten-feet away. To one side a heavyset Breton was swinging an axe down on the thick chain that effectively held the ladder in place. Cei stood opposite him alternately striking at the chain with his own war axe.

A shield appeared first and Trevenna held her aim, waiting for the right moment. As the Adren cleared the wall and leapt to the parapet he was hurled backwards by the force of the arrow that buried itself instantly in his chest. Another appeared and Cei, leaving the chain to the Breton, swung his axe into the Adren's shield and sent him flailing off the top of the wall. Trevenna sprung to her feet and brought her bow to the vertical as she loosed another arrow point-blank into the face of an attacker as he scrambled over the edge. Behind her sparks were flying from the chain as the Breton frantically hammered at it. Two girls, no more than fourteen

116

or fifteen years old, crouched to one side waiting with the hooked poles.

Two Adren hoisted themselves over and onto the parapet. Cei rammed his axe head into the face of one and kicked out at the other. Trevenna dropped her bow and in one movement pulled her sword free and ran it through the Adren that Cei had stunned with his axe. As she did so Cei bodily threw the other off the parapet. Behind her the chain finally snapped apart sending its attached boulder to crash down to the ground on the Breton side of the wall. The two girls immediately hooked the ladder and hauled it to one side. Cei joined them and the ladder slid sideways to crash into the next one in line.

All along the wall the same frantic battle raged as the Adren fought to gain the parapet. Cei took a second to scan the battle to see where they might be losing ground. The Breton and the two girls ran straight to the skirmish by the next ladder where the chain still held. Trevenna was shouting and Cei looked to where she was pointing. Further along the wall to their left ten Adren had gained the ledge and more were pouring up the ladder behind them.

Aelfhelm had seen the danger too and they both fought their way through the individual battles raging along the parapet to attack the Adren from either side. Trevenna had picked up her longbow and was following Cei. She did not have a clear line of fire into the Adren already on the ledge so she shot her arrows at those reaching the top of the ladder behind them in an effort to stop their numbers swelling.

She could see that Aelfhelm had reached the other side of the attackers and had halted their advance along his side of the wall but she was still unable to shoot directly at them. Cei was ahead of her. He knew that if the Adren could secure the parapet around three or four of the ladders then they would be in real danger of losing the wall.

He did not hesitate. Casting aside his shield he charged straight into them, swinging his war axe in a wide ferocious arc before him. Two of the Adren were cut down instantly and a third was knocked from the wall. At last Trevenna had a clear line of fire and without considering the danger of hitting Cei she sent four lightning fast arrows scything into the enemy midst.

Two Bretons, encouraged by Aelfhelm's attack, charged into the Adren with their shields held before them forcing the Adren backwards as they all stumbled over in an entangled mess. Their charge had taken them beyond Aelfhelm and he launched himself bodily into the confusion causing more of the close packed enemy to falter and fall. Cei swooped into the chaos with his axe hacking down with manic energy and brutal violence.

Trevenna shifted her aim back to the top of the ladder and more Bretons joined in the melee, wielding hand sickles and long knives. Suddenly she was out of arrows but Aelfhelm was already at the ladder and swinging at any Adren that gained the top. Behind him the last of the enemy was hacked to death and hurled from the wall. Cei was driving his axe through the chains and as they finally split apart the ladder was hauled sideways to crash to the ground.

Another assault had been repelled but as Trevenna looked along the length of the wall she could she that it had been dearly won. She walked back towards Leah as the dead and wounded Adren were stripped of their swords and shields and then thrown back over the wall. Their own wounded were carried back down the steps to the main hall where their injuries were treated as quickly as possible.

'Close this time,' Trevenna said and grimaced as she clasped Leah's hand.

'What's wrong? Are you hurt?'

'No. Just my shoulder, from the first Adren attack ages ago. I hadn't noticed it during the last one, yet just shaking your hand...' she shrugged.

'You've got time to notice it now.'

They made their way to the central stair and waited as the Bretons wearily climbed down in front of them. Others who had not been involved in the last defence immediately took their place on the wall as lookouts for the next attack.

When they descended the steps they both sat down heavily in the snow with their backs against the cold stone.

'They aren't going to stop are they?' Leah sat with her long legs stretched out before her and her bloody sword lying across her thighs. She looked exhausted. Her pale blue eyes were reddened and the skin below them was shadowed grey.

'Merdynn's back with us again now, perhaps he can come up with a plan,' Trevenna offered then added, 'Do I look as tired as you do?'

Leah smiled and studied Trevenna's face, 'Well, I don't know how I look but you certainly look as tired as I feel.'

'I'm too tired to work that out.'

Someone passed in front of them with a bucket of drinking water and they helped themselves to several cupfuls of the ice cold, refreshing water.

'Where's Ethain?'

Leah shrugged. Cei and Aelfhelm walked up to them and Cei gave Trevenna a gentle nudge with his foot, 'Come on you two, let's get some food before the bastards return for more.'

Trevenna accepted the offered hand and Cei hauled her to her feet with a grunt.

'You three did well to stop that breach. I thought it might have been over then,' Leah said as they made their way to the huts of the village.

The others did not reply, they knew how close it had been and they knew it was only a matter of time before there was a breach that they could not stop.

Two of the huts had been designated as food points and cauldrons of hot broth simmered constantly over low fires as bowlfuls were ladled out and more ingredients continuously added. Bran was standing by one of the fires with his feet planted firmly apart and doling out various orders to those around him. He spotted Cei and his companions and called them over. They were all taller than he was and he looked up at each of them in turn.

'You're all exhausted. Take a hut and sleep for six hours.'

Cei shrugged and leant wearily on the keel of an upturned boat. They all knew what the shrug meant. If they left the wall and slept for six hours the Adren would take the fortress. If they did not sleep, then sooner or later, they would die on the wall. They reasoned it was better to die on your feet and make it later rather than sooner. Bran nodded, understanding and reluctantly agreeing.

'I hear Merdynn's recovered and is awake. Let's see what he has to say.' Bran turned and led the way to the hut that Merdynn was lying in. The others took their hot meals with them and ate as they walked.

Ethain was standing at the end of the headland looking out through the winter darkness across the ice and to the open seas that led to Wessex. He shivered in the cold and wrapped his thick cloak tighter around himself. He too was exhausted; exhausted by the fear that constantly threatened to snap his brittle self-discipline. So far he had managed to avoid the worst of the fighting but not all of it by any means.

For sometime now he had felt trapped and not just in the sense that they were all trapped on the headland. He felt trapped inside as he relentlessly fought against the urgent pressing of panic that continuously threatened to wash over him. He felt as if he was on the verge of drowning and had been for weeks now, thrashing in desperation to keep his mouth above the water. He was not sure how long he could retain the vestiges of control that stopped him from just curling up in a corner, sleeping and waiting for death.

To avoid the pitched battles he had worked tirelessly carrying and tending to the wounded and he had spent long hours walking the cliffs or standing on the wall peering into the darkness to give warning of the approaching enemy. In the rare quiet moments he had turned his gaze inward, to the darkness within himself and it never took long for the image of Cerdic to surface accusingly. He could still see the shocked disbelief and bewildered despair etched clearly on Cerdic's face as he had deserted the young Anglian warrior to certain death at the hands of the Adren.

It was almost more than Ethain could bear. Only one thought kept him within the bounds of sanity. He was alive and Cerdic was dead. No matter how guilty he felt, he was alive to feel it and Cerdic would never feel anything ever again. During the lulls in the Adren attacks the others, particularly Leah, had asked him what had happened on the cliff tops of the headland across the bay. Ethain had told them that he had taken a blow to the head and stumbled to his knees. Roswitha had already fallen with a spear skewed through her stomach. Cerdic had shouted for him to escape down the cliff path while he held the Adren off. The others had believed it readily enough as it fitted with their image of the brave young warrior and they pictured his last stand as a suitably heroic one. Only Ethain knew that Cerdic had died in despair, betrayed by a friend, but even he found he was beginning to half believe his own false version of events and he withdrew more and more from his companions.

The attacks on the Breton fortress had been incessant and there had been no time for him to spend with Leah. He was surprised to find that her absence did not bother him in the least. It seemed his infatuation and lust ranked a long way below his own survival and yet he remembered how in the ruined city he had stood and fought by her side when he could have left her. As his mind teetered on the deep abyss of his guilt he thought his memory must be playing him false. Why would he do such a thing? How could he? He wondered if it was just another lie that he had told himself and which he now believed to be true. He began to worry that his reality was diverging from that of those around him.

He was still shivering and he started to walk along the trampled snow of the cliff edge, looking down and scanning the sea ice for danger. He saw the Adren snaking down from the mainland and onto the sea ice and he knew that another attack on the cliff paths was imminent. He hurried his pace and told a group of Bretons he passed that he thought he had seen Adren on the ice and to keep a sharp lookout. He made his way towards the main wall and away from the cliffs, gambling that they would not attack both at the same time and hating himself for being so craven.

When Cei and the others arrived at Merdynn's hut they crowded in and stood as near to the fire as possible. The sweat from the battle had dried on them and the cold air of the winter night had quickly settled into their bones once more.

Merdynn was sitting on the edge on the low bed, wrapped in his familiar brown cloak and looking more like his old self with each passing hour.

'How goes the defence then?' he asked, looking up at the figures crowding into the small home.

'Each attack brings them closer to breaking through. I don't think it will be long now,' Aelfhelm replied.

'Cheerful as ever I see, always managing to find the bright side. Something of a miracle you've lived to be so old really.'

Aelfhelm did not have the energy to defend himself even though he felt affronted at being labelled as defeatist. He also thought it was a bit rich that Merdynn of all people should call him old, but he just stood there, his lean frame stooped with weariness, determined to save his energy for fighting the enemy. His lack of response stopped Merdynn's levity instantly.

Cei squatted down by the fire and looked levelly at Merdynn, 'We're running out of time, Merdynn.'

Merdynn sighed, 'How are the supplies of food?'

'At the rate we're dying we'll run out of mouths to feed before we run out of food,' Bran stated.

'The dawn is not far away. The sea ice will break up. You have fishing boats drawn up beyond the storm line?'

'Yes,' Bran answered.

'Then we must wait for the ice to break then abandon the fortress and sail for Britain. I, at least, must do this for Arthur needs to be told the quest east failed.'

The others nodded. They had already agreed it was the only plan available to them but they had forgotten that Bran did not know the full reason behind their journey eastwards.

'What quest east?'

Merdynn looked up at him frowning, 'Arthur had sent us to destroy the Adren food supplies. We failed.'

Bran grunted, accepting the brief explanation for now but knowing there was a greater tale behind it. If they found themselves in a time and place safe enough for questions then he would seek out the truth of the matter but other more serious concerns occupied him now.

'How long until the sea ice breaks up?' Trevenna asked.

Bran shrugged, 'Perhaps a week, maybe longer if the storms come out of the East.'

Leah rubbed a hand across her cracked lips, thinking the same thoughts as the others. She noticed her hand was trembling from the fatigue of the muscles in her sword arm and she stared at the shaking hand in surprise. She did not think they could keep the Adren at bay for another week or two but she left it unsaid. There was no need to say it. Then in the heavy silence they all heard the frantic baying of the dogs. The Adren were attacking along the cliff paths.

They spilled out of the hut quickly and Bran started to shout to the lookouts to find out where the attack was coming from. Trevenna saw Charljenka and Nialgrada, the two young goat herders they had rescued from an abandoned Breton village, as they ran past. They were carrying quivers of collected arrows. She called out to them and she and Aelfhelm exchanged their empty quivers for full ones.

Bran had ascertained that the Adren were attacking at four points around the headland and he started to bark out orders to those around him. Someone shouted out that Ethain had already taken a few others and gone to the wall to keep watch for an attack there. Bran grunted his approval and struck out for the nearest attack.

Cei was told that Cuthwin had a group of Bretons covering one of the other attacks so he sent Aelfhelm to defend the fourth point and led the other two to the far end of the promontory. It was here that the stone steps led up from the Bretons' summer harbour and Cei knew the Adren attack would be fiercest at that point.

They sprinted through the snow to reach the Bretons who were already positioned on the headland overlooking the stone steps. Through the darkness they could see a hundred Adren or more gathered on the ice and quay at the foot of the cliff. The Bretons had a stockpile of rocks and boulders ready to be hurled down on the assailants once they started the climb. These missiles were more effective at first than arrows. The Adren would advance with their shields raised to protect them from the bowmen above and the force of a rock crashing down on them had a more damaging effect.

The Adren began the climb and immediately a spate of missiles rained down on them. As soon as a shield was turned or one of them stumbled an arrow would fly down from the headland to find its exposed target. The Adren pressed on upwards and the furious hail of rocks intensified as they passed the halfway point. Cei was watching nervously in case they went for the fishing boats but they were intent upon reaching the top and passed them by.

One by one they tumbled off the steep path as arrows or rocks found their mark but on they came, regardless of losses or life, until they were within twenty-feet of the top of the headland. Trevenna and Leah took wider positions now firing a constant stream of arrows into the single file below them. If any of the Adren dropped a shield to bring their bows to bear then they immediately became a target for the longbows above.

The Bretons had cut away the last five steps so that the Adren had to scramble over the steep, snow-covered grass to reach the top. Cei and the Bretons around him steadied themselves as the Adren finally made it to the ledge and began scrabbling to the top. Cei strode forward wielding his war axe double-handed as he swung it over his head and down onto the lead Adren. It hammered into the upraised shield and smashed the attacker into the ground. As the Adren raised himself Cei kicked him in the face and he fell backwards, his wheeling arms knocking aside another's shield and an arrow instantly buried itself in the suddenly exposed chest.

All around Cei the Adren were spreading out and trying to gain the last ridge. The Bretons thrashed at them with sledgehammers and swung at their heads with long handled harvest scythes. Trevenna and Leah ran out of arrows and joined the fray with sword and spear.

The Adren died by the dozen but they would not give up. There would be no flight back down the steps, they would press their attack onwards until they succeeded or until each one was dead. Two of the Bretons had fallen and a third was rolling in the snow, screaming and holding her leg that had been sliced through to the bone. Someone dragged her backwards out of the melee and Cei caught a glimpse of Charljenka and her brother as they tried to bind a tourniquet above her wound.

On the right two Adren at last managed to reach the level ground of the headland. Leah dropped her spear and her sword whirled as she forced them both away from the edge before others could join them. Trevenna leapt towards the danger to beat back those clambering to join the two Adren. Leah never saw the spear that thrust upwards from the ledge below her but she felt it as it tore a deep groove up the front of her thigh. She crumpled to one side and clutched at the searing pain. The Adren pounced at her and she took one blow on her sword and twisted away from the other but she ended up sprawled in the blood-splattered snow, defenceless. She passed out as snow flew into her face, knowing she was about to die but the kicked up snow was not from her attacker.

Trevenna had seen her fall and had jumped across her to stand between the Adren and her fallen friend. She parried their attack and suddenly

Cuthwin was by her side with more Bretons. They had beaten off the attack from the other side of the headland and raced across to help Cei's band. Together they quickly dispatched the two Adren and Cuthwin joined the last of the battle at the top of the steps. Trevenna knelt by Leah and examined the deep bloody tear along her thigh. She packed snow around the wound then tore a wide strip from the cloth shirt under her battle jerkin. She bundled it up and pressed it against the bloody tear, fixing it tightly with her belt.

Cei joined her and they lifted Leah onto her outspread cloak and with the help of Cuthwin they bore her quickly back to the main hall. The fighting around the headland had ceased and as the Bretons carried their wounded back to the hall, others took their place to renew the watch on the cliffs and sea ice. Another attack had been repelled but they had taken further casualties.

Once in the hall they laid Leah down on one of the pre-prepared tables. It had been freshly scrubbed but the wood was dyed dark with the blood of those injured over the last few weeks. Trevenna took out her long knife and cut the trousers away from the injured leg.

'Gods, I wish we had Ceinwen here,' she muttered as she began washing away some of the blood from the ugly wound. The spear had sliced deeply up into the muscle and blood was flowing freely onto the table. Leah had regained consciousness and was groaning and swearing with the effort to stop from crying out.

An old woman appeared at Trevenna's elbow and with surprising strength pushed her to one side. 'Go and do your work outside and leave me to do my work here.'

The three of them took a step away from the table as the old woman examined the torn flesh.

'I'll stay a while but you two best check what's going on outside,' Trevenna said.

Cei brushed the filthy hair from Leah's face and cupped the back of her neck. 'Stay with us Leah,' he said and she clasped his forearm fiercely as the old woman probed the agonising wound.

'Tell Ethain I'm here,' she replied through clenched teeth before passing out once again.

Cei nodded and he and Cuthwin left. Trevenna watched as the old woman fished out the bleeding artery from the mess of ruptured flesh. Blood jetted in thin streams from the severed artery and splashed across Leah's thighs and quickly pooled on the table. The old woman called out and a man turned from an adjacent table and quickly crossed to her side. He delicately twisted a thin twine around the end of the artery that she held and pulled it taut. The blood stopped immediately and the old woman washed the long tear again then quickly sewed the sides together with a thicker strand of twine. She rubbed an ointment into the wound and wrapped the whole of Leah's upper leg in firm bandaging then washed her hands in a bowl of hot water. Leah was lifted off the table and taken to one side of the hall where furs and cloaks were laid out as makeshift beds. The table was scrubbed with a stiff brush and more water, and the next casualty was laid out before her.

Trevenna watched Leah being carried away and turned to the old woman, 'Will she live?'

'Do I look like a god? Do I look like a seer? She'll live or die, I've done what I can.'

Trevenna looked at her wretchedly and the old woman's hard eyes softened a little, 'I've seen those with worse wounds recover.'

Trevenna nodded thankfully and went to Leah. When she was out of earshot the old woman turned her attention to her new patient and muttered under her breath, 'And I've seen those with less die.'

Outside the wind strengthened. It blew from the West and it brought rain.

Above the Breton fortress heavy grey clouds blanked out the last of the winter stars and hid the first signs of the spring dawn. Aelfhelm was crouched on the parapet that ran along the length of the high wall with his cloak wrapped tightly around him and his hood pulled up over his head. He looked down on the last village of the Bretons as the cold, stinging rain swayed in opaque veils, drifting over the headland and lashing down on the huddled buildings. He watched as figures ran from cover to cover and as another patrol set out along the cliff paths. Visibility was limited but any warning of an impending Adren attack could mean the difference between either surviving for a while longer or finally falling before the incessant assaults.

Next to him stood Cuthwin. He was looking the other way searching the darkness before the walls, waiting and watching for the Adren to launch the next attack. They really needed Ethain on the wall, he was invariably able to see the Adren readying to attack before anyone else could, but he was with Leah who still lay in the hall with the other wounded.

In the lulls between the attacks the Adren would use their catapults to hurl boulders over the wall and into the Breton compound. Usually they fell harmlessly onto empty ground but occasionally one would crash down on a roundhouse or barn, smashing through the thatch roofing and killing anyone in its path. The Bretons had built temporary lean-to shelters against the base of the high wall where the projectiles could not fall and many slept there when they were not guarding against the attacks.

Cuthwin knelt down beside Aelfhelm and cursed as another catapulted boulder crashed down somewhere in the village below them.

'See anything?' Aelfhelm asked.

'No, not that you can see much out there with this rain but it won't be long before they come again. The rain certainly won't deter them,' Cuthwin replied.

The sweeping downpour stung exposed flesh and made them feel miserable and uncomfortable. It soaked their thick winter cloaks making them heavy and cumbersome but despite all the discomfort the rain was a blessing. A wind from the West bringing rain at this time of year was unusual, normally the winter fought to keep the land in its grip by hurling defiant snowstorms from the Shadow Lands. The deep snow lying on the headland was already being washed away by the driving rain and it would not be long before the sea ice melted too. This would reduce the points of attack available to the Adren and, more importantly, free the seas for the Breton fishing boats.

'Perhaps we'll escape back to Britain after all,' Cuthwin said voicing what they were both thinking.

'Perhaps,' Aelfhelm answered, not wanting to openly tempt the fates.

'Have you seen Leah? Do you think she will she live?' Cuthwin asked.

Aelfhelm shrugged, 'The spear sliced the artery in her thigh. She's lucky to be alive. If there's no infection then perhaps.'

Cuthwin smiled at him and slapped the flat of his sword on Aelfhelm's shin. 'You're getting a bit cautious in your old age. Perhaps this, perhaps that, you should be more confident old man.'

'Perhaps,' Aelfhelm answered and Cuthwin laughed.

'Your turn to stare into the dark,' Cuthwin said and Aelfhelm stood and peered out to where the Adren were preparing their next attack.

'Here they come!' Someone shouted out and all along the wall defenders drew their weapons and waited for the ladders.

Ethain sat crossed-leg on the floor by Leah. She was lying on three layers of fur that served as a mattress and she was asleep while all around her villagers moved between the wounded and dying, tending to them as best as they could. He stared at her drawn, pale face. The grey shadows under her wide-set eyes and her cracked lips stood as testament to the winter they had spent in the Shadow Lands, alternatively fighting and fleeing and now finally trapped in this coastal village. Ethain knew she was about thirty years old but as he looked at her lying on her fur pallaise he thought she looked more like forty or even older. No fever had set in yet but she looked ill. Ill and so tired. He dabbed a damp cloth against her cold-blistered lips and her eyes flickered as she moved through her own private dream world.

He felt ill too. He was sick and tired of everything and everyone. He was sick of his fear, sick of feeling guilty and sick of trying to conceal it all from everyone. More than anything he wanted to be back in Wessex, far away from the Adren and far away from any warriors. He felt he would do or give anything to be able to spend the summer months living peacefully by some riverbank deep in Wessex. He looked down at the heavy strapping on Leah's thigh and wondered if she would want to spend the summer idly passing time in the warm sunlight of a green land. He looked away sourly. He knew that if she survived she would want to rejoin the fight. She would want to stand by her friends, and not let them down.

He stood up and crossed to the doorway, stepping over the prone bodies of the others who had been wounded. He could hear the sounds of battle over the clattering rain and his heart jumped in fear once more. He was afraid of being killed or ending up in this hall with the other wounded but he was also afraid of failing those around him, as he had failed Cerdic. He turned away from the doorway and busied himself with helping the injured. It would not be long before more joined them.

The attack on the wall was furious. Thirty ladders were catapulted into place and the Adren swarmed up them as the defenders desperately hacked at the chains to enable the ladders to be hauled aside. For both sides it was as much a fight against time as it was against each other. The Adren threw as many into the attack as they possibly could and once again they established a foothold on the parapet before two of the ladders. The Bretons lost over twenty people as they fought to retake the lost ground and secure the wall. Twelve more were badly injured and they were rushed to the hall where Leah lay. But for all the ferociousness of the attack it was only a diversion.

It was Bran who spotted the real danger. Whoever was leading the Adren assault on the fortress had seen what the Bretons had seen. The sea ice would soon thaw. At the height of the onslaught on the wall an Adren Captain led a thousand Adren onto the ice to attack the village via the cliff paths. He spilt his group into four and sent three troops of a hundred each to scale the cliffs at different points. He directed the remaining seven hundred to the Bretons' summer harbour where the steps led up into the village. It was the same place where Leah had been injured in the fight for the cliff top.

Bran shouted out orders to those defenders not already on the wall and they tracked the Adren force from the top of the headland. Cei joined him at the top of the steps above the small harbour.

'How many are down there?' Cei asked.

'A thousand or more. They've sent some on around the headland,' Bran answered.

'You have people tracking them?'

Bran pointed out to the end of the headland with the sword he had taken from the fallen Leah and Cei saw others moving through the teeming rain as they followed the progress of the Adren below them.

'The main body is down here. Looks like they'll come up the steps again,' Bran added, turning his attention to the army readying themselves on the ice.

'We'll need everyone to defend this time,' Cei said. Bran nodded and

Cei sent two of the nearby Bretons to gather everyone from the village who was still able to stand and fight.

As the battle continued on the wall Cei marshalled the defenders to the various points of the Adren attack. He stayed at the top of the steps along with Bran and Trevenna. He looked around at the fifty defenders who stood about him. They were a mixture of men and women, ranging from the aged to mere children. All of them were soaked by the drenching rain and clutched an assortment of recently sharpened ancient weapons and their more familiar farm implements. Young and old hands gripped sickles, scythes, hoes, hammers, axes and hastily fashioned spears. Some of the Bretons wielded the curved swords taken from dead Adren.

Cei looked back down to the seven hundred well-armed Adren on the sea ice and found his throat was to too dry for him to swallow. He and Trevenna were the only ones with longbows and they only had about fifty arrows between them. He glanced across to her to find she was already watching his face. She smiled at him and he looked into her calm, turquoise-blue eyes and found the strength to smile grimly back at her.

He walked amongst the Bretons talking to them as they lined up on the edge where piles of rocks, which had been fetched from the foot of the cliff between attacks, were stacked to be hurled down once more. They were scared but they were fighting for their homes, their families, their lives, and each of them was now experienced in facing the Adren attacks.

Cei told them that they were veterans; that they were warriors and if they held firm then they would repulse this assault as they had the others. He did not shout or exhort them to fight heroically. These were farmers, midwives, fishermen and net-menders not warriors and he spoke to them quietly and confidently. They believed that if the Anglian Warlord thought they could win then they only had to follow his instructions to make it so. They trusted him.

Cei thought they were all about to die.

He and Trevenna would take position at opposite ends of the line to maximise their angle of fire down onto the Adren when they ascended the steps but he did not see how they could stop them this time.

'Make sure they don't take me alive,' Trevenna said softly as she passed him to take up her station on the far end. Cei stared after her as she encouraged those she passed. He wiped the rain from his eyes and fished out the string for his longbow from inside the thick sheepskin fleece he wore under his cloak.

The seagulls had returned to the headland over the past few days and Cei could hear their cries from the base of the cliff as they attacked the carcasses left from previous attacks. The rain began to drive down harder and the Adren swarmed over the ice-bound harbour and started to climb the steps, their shields raised in readiness for the hail of rocks and boulders about to descend upon them.

Cei turned at the sound of more defenders arriving behind him. Sixteen more had come from the village, among them Merdynn and Ethain. The only people now left in the buildings of the village were those too injured to walk. Merdynn was leading a bedraggled donkey, which pulled a small narrow cart behind it. Alongside the covered cart walked Ethain carrying an oil-soaked brand that spluttered and hissed in the hammering rain.

'Out for a winter stroll you two?' Cei asked, relieved to see them.

'We thought your brawn could use a little help on the tactical side,' Merdynn replied.

Cei quickly looked under the cover of the cart and saw it was stacked with dry logs, the sort used in the main fires of the Breton hall. They were about two-feet long and between six and ten inches across. Cei looked at Merdynn thinking they were just extra missiles to hurl down upon their attackers but the old man pointed to a large bucket of oil that two children struggled to carry between them and to a long trough that others had placed on the ground. Cei grinned at Merdynn and told him to set it up.

The Breton villagers had already begun to rain down stones and rocks upon the advancing Adren. Trevenna stood on the edge of the drop and swept her drawn bow back and forth along the line below her, waiting for a shield to be knocked to one side or for one of the attackers to slip on the steep, wet path. Cei took his place at the opposite end of the line and every few seconds their longbows would twang and an arrow would speed down to its target.

Behind them Merdynn and Ethain soaked the logs in the oil while others held the cover over the cart to keep it as dry as possible. They carried the trough to the most precipitous edge above the advancing Adren and one end of it was knocked out with an axe. The two children, Charljenka and Nialgrada, hurried back to the village to fetch more oil while Ethain handed the brand to Merdynn and joined Trevenna adding his longbow to the defence of the cliff path.

The arrows were finding their mark and the crashing rocks were taking their toll on the Adren line as the attackers sought to gain the higher ground. Most of them were still on the sea ice waiting for those ahead of them to make progress up the narrow cliff path. The children came back with another bucket of oil full to the brim and slopping over the edges. The trough was jutted out over the steepest drop and the logs in the cart were doused once more in the oil.

One of the Bretons took the first log and placed it in the trough. Merdynn held the burning torch to it until it was thoroughly alight and the trough was tilted up. The burning log rolled down the length of walled channel and disappeared over the edge.

Cei watched from his place where the steps led up onto the headland. The falling log stayed alight but hit an outcropping ledge and bounced harmlessly over the Adren line. The trough was not long enough for a direct drop onto the enemy. He shouted instructions to a Breton next to him and handed him his shield. The Breton ran across to where Merdynn and the others were preparing to light another missile.

They hauled the trough in and lit the next one in the upturned shield, then taking one side of the shield each they used it to sling the burning wood over the edge. They repeated the action and after five attempts they found their range and the flaming missiles began to fall among the Adren. Their weight alone would have caused damage to those below but the effect of the flames resulted in further confusion among the Adren and each time one smashed into the line the archers above would fire arrows into their midst.

Despite the number of Adren falling they kept advancing. In all the attacks on the Breton fortress, no one had ever seen the Adren retreat. They kept attacking the wall until all the ladders were cut from their anchors and cast aside, and the groups that attacked the cliff paths did so until each one of them had fallen. Cei was under no illusion about the several hundred strong force now struggling up the path below them.

They would simply keep on coming.

So he was amazed when he saw the lead group break away from the path. He realised why a second before Bran began shouting, 'The boats! They're going for the boats!'

Wielding the sword he had taken from Leah, Bran started for the steps.

'No! Come back!' Merdynn shouted.

Bran hesitated and Merdynn ran to the group above the path.

'If they destroy the fishing boats we have no way of escaping!' Bran shouted to him.

'And if you and sixty others go down there to fight several hundred Adren then you'll not need an escape route! You'll die there!' Merdynn shouted back.

Bran looked up at him and then back to where the Adren were approaching the boats that had been hauled above the stone harbour and beyond the reach of the winter seas. The other Adren paused in their advance and the Adren and Bretons alike watched as heavy tree-cutting axes were taken to the fishing boats. Those around Cei stood silently in the rain and looked down as the Adren cut away the wooden stanchions holding the boats in place. They watched as one by one the boats were slid and tumbled over the short drop to the iced harbour and then hauled out onto the sea ice where they lay like beached whales, their deaths inevitable. They watched as others began methodically smashing holes in the hulls until all the Breton boats lay keeled over on the ice with gaping holes from stem to stern. Their only hope of escape from the enemy lay broken on the ice to be claimed by the sea when winter turned to spring.

When the last boat was gutted the Adren roared and renewed their assault up the steps. The Bretons were grim-faced and heavy-hearted. Each knew what the destruction of the boats meant. Cei helped Bran back up over the edge of the headland and looked across to Merdynn who stood with his arms folded across his chest and his head bowed in the pouring rain.

The Bretons restarted their assault on the enemy with a renewed fury. Cei sent the children on a mission to collect as many spent arrows as they could find from the battle at the wall while Bran ordered his runners to go to the wall and all the points around the headland where the Adren attacked and report back on how each defence was holding.

The Adren gradually crept up the steep slope despite the devastation caused by the hail of rocks, flaming logs and arrows from above. The children returned to the frantic scene with another fifty spent Adren arrows that they had collected from the wall that was still under a concerted attack.

Cei grabbed the arrows from them and sprinted the short distance to where Trevenna and Ethain were placed. He handed them some of the crude arrows and explained what he was going to do then repeated his explanation to Bran as he made his way back to the head of the steps. With the help of Bran and two other Bretons they manhandled the now empty cart over the lip of the headland. The last few steps had been cut away making the final approach steep and treacherous and they took care positioning the cart at the top of the remaining steps and then pushed it over onto its side.

Cei and Bran stayed behind the upturned cart as the Adren drew nearer under the continuing hail of missiles. When they were only twenty yards away Cei sent his first arrow into the chest of the lead Adren. He tumbled to one side and lay still in the pouring rain on the verge of the drop. The next one took his place and Cei sent his second arrow to find its mark. Realising where the new attack was coming from the third Adren brought his shield down to protect himself from Cei's longbow and was immediately hit by Trevenna's arrow from above and to his left. The next Adren in line stepped over the bodies in front of him and suffered the same fate. They began to realise that they were caught in a crossfire and the foremost could not protect himself from the two points of fire.

The certain death at the front of the line would have stopped most advances but the Adren came on, trying to increase their pace and close the distance to the upturned cart. They huddled closer together trying to share the protection of their shields but Trevenna and Ethain shifted their aim and sent their arrows into exposed legs and the inevitable gaps in the black shields.

Still the Adren came on, always climbing and gaining another yard each time they stepped over a dead body in front of them. They picked up the shields of the dead and used them to form a defensive shell. They were almost at the cart. Bran cursed and sheathed his sword as he yelled at the Bretons behind him. Two of them picked up the long trough they had tried to roll the logs from and slid it over the edge of the higher ground and down to Bran.

Together Cei and Bran lifted the trough onto the cart and clambered over to the other side. The Adren were only yards away advancing blindly behind their wall of shields and still being bombarded from those above them. With a roar of effort Bran swung the trough off the cart and holding it laterally across his chest he charged down into the Adren line.

Bran was no taller than the Adren he charged into but his rage was fuelled by what they had done to his people and it leant him strength beyond his frame. He smashed into the unsuspecting line sending the first five Adren sprawling before he too fell. Cei was right behind him and jumped over his prone form windmilling his battle axe with both hands and battering the Adren before him over the edge of the stone stairs.

Behind him the two archers on the headland finished off those still left alive by Bran's charge and two other Bretons leapt down to the cart to upright it once more. Merdynn had sent the children for more oil and this was now slopped into the cart.

Bran regained his feet and drew Leah's sword rushing after the advancing Anglian Warlord. The shocked Adren were beginning to recover from the unexpected attack and one of them managed to catch Cei's axe on his shield without being sent flying over the edge. Immediately Bran lunged forward, his sword passing by Cei's side and into the Adren's stomach. Cei kicked the dying Adren into those behind him and Bran edged by Cei to press on the attack and sustain the impetus of their downward charge.

Behind them and further up the slope Merdynn was setting the brand to the oil in the cart. Once the fire took it was impervious to the rain and two Bretons began to push the cart down the steps. Ahead of them Bran was embroiled in a sword fight with the leading Adren. Bran's attack had been furious but he had no shield and as the Adren parried his thrust on his own black shield he cut at Bran and caught him below the ribs. Bran stumbled and the Adren pressed his attack catching the Breton's right shoulder with another blow. Bran dropped his sword and Cei scrambled past him to ram his axe head into the Adren's face. Bran staggered to his left and clutching the deep cut to his side slowly toppled over the edge of the stone stairs. Cei reached out a despairing hand but Bran had gone.

He saw the blazing cart being pushed down the steps, the two Bretons still guiding it by the two long poles used for harnessing it to a donkey or pony. He raced back up the steps towards it and found a ledge below the stairs to stand on as it passed by. The two Bretons increased their pace and the cart bumped and jolted over the steps as they sent it crashing into the Adren line.

They sprinted back up the slope to join Cei. One of them stooped to pick up Bran's fallen sword and they raced on up to the top of the headland where others hauled them over the edge and back into the Breton line. The Adren had been pushed halfway down the cliff and they had only just managed to lever the burning cart over the edge.

The Bretons were dismayed to have seen Bran fall but it quickly turned to rage and once again the fist-sized stones and larger rocks were hurled down into the Adren file. Cei had collected his longbow from his original defensive position and he tucked the long handle of his axe into his belt as he crossed to Trevenna and Ethain.

'How many arrows do you have left?' he asked them.

Ethain shook his head and Trevenna upturned her empty quiver by way of an answer. He looked back down at the Adren. He estimated that there was still over four hundred on the cliff path and below in the harbour.

'Any ideas?' he asked them.

'Hide?' Trevenna said with a smile.

There were two things they could not do and if the other two were just realising it then Ethain had been aware of it for some weeks now. They had nowhere to hide and they could not run. Merdynn joined them.

'Any ideas?' Cei repeated the question to him.

'Not really. I quite liked the last one though, burning cart, ensuing chaos and all.'

'Can you summon any of your sorcery? Like you did before? Bring the cliff down on them?' Cei asked.

Merdynn pursed his lips and shook his head. Below them the Adren were gaining ground once more on the cliff path.

'Trevenna, check on Bran's messengers and see if any of the other attacks have been repulsed. If so then send word for those who can to come here – and to bring any arrows they can find. If it's possible I want Aelfhelm and Cuthwin to come here – but only if they've beaten off their own assault. It looks like we'll have to defend the steps one at a time.'

Trevenna dashed off to organise the older children who were acting as the runners. Cei turned back to the other two and pointed to the last part of the slope where the steps had been cut away.

'If we level out the ground there then four or five of us can block the top of the steps. When one of us tires another can take their place.'

Ethain could see what he meant. The stone stairs were three to four-feet wide and there was only enough room for the Adren to advance in single file. Cei's warriors could meet the head of the advancing file and try to hold them one at a time before they could spread out and use their greater numbers to overwhelm the defenders. The Bretons could continue their missile assault on the Adren line while the others held the top of the stone stair.

Merdynn could think of no better plan and nodded in agreement. Ethain was shifting from foot to foot and could not stop his voice quavering as he said, 'But there's hundreds down there. We'll each have to kill scores of them!'

'You only have to kill the one in front of you,' Cei replied, echoing Arthur's words.

Ethain wished he could swap places with Leah knowing that everyone would be better off if he could. He was appalled at the prospect of taking his turn at the top of the path and he doubted he could kill two or three of them let alone scores. Cei watched the advancing Adren but Merdynn was watching Ethain's gaze jump from place to place as he sought an escape route.

Trevenna returned with the news that the fighting continued on the wall and around the headland. The Adren had not broken through anywhere yet and the enemy were resorting to scaling the wall with unsecured ladders that the defenders were easily repelling. Aelfhelm and Cuthwin would join them as soon as they could safely leave the wall. The attacks elsewhere on the headland were being overcome and the runners said that others could join them here soon. The two young goat herders, Charljenka and Nialgrada, had managed to scavenge another ten arrows some of which were covered in blood. Trevenna realised that they must have been pulled from the bodies of the injured or dead and looked at the two silent children wondering what scars they would carry if they lived through this.

Cei told her to keep the arrows for last-ditch cover and set about clearing a level patch of ground just below the lip of the headland. Some of the Bretons helped him while others kept up their barrage on the advancing Adren line. Cei ordered the Bretons back up as Trevenna jumped down to join him. Merdynn joined them and brought Ethain with him, clasping his upper arm firmly.

The level ground they stood on was about fifteen-feet wide and eight-feet deep. The steep path from the harbour climbed up to them from the right and it turned into the level space from that direction. In front of the clearing was a precipitous slope and behind them a three-foot ledge up to where the Bretons stood in defiance.

The Adren were almost upon them. Cei took his position to meet the first one and the other three readied themselves behind him. Merdynn stood by Ethain and he held Leah's sword that he had taken from one of the Bretons.

Cei hefted his war-axe, one hand at the end of the handle, the other halfway up the shaft. He had discarded his winter cloak and stood in the easing rain with his feet planted firmly apart and as the first Adren gained the last step the fight began again.

He swung his axe and the Adren took it on his shield and staggered but avoided going over the edge then cut back at Cei with his curved sword. Cei blocked it and reversed his swing to send the axe head into the side of the Adren's face. The next one came straight at him but was stunned by a slingshot stone from above and Cei barged him over the edge. Brutal duel followed brutal duel and all the time the Adren line was bombarded by the Bretons. In their fury to reach the defenders some attempted to scramble around the almost vertical wall to one side of the steps and others tried to reach the small clearing from the ground that dropped sharply away to the other side of the stair but the only way up onto the headland was through the maniacal Anglian Warlord.

When Cei was eventually forced back Trevenna and Merdynn immediately sprang forward to engage those spilling into the clearing and they tried to force the fighting back to the narrow stair. Ethain joined them but the momentum was with the Adren and more gained the clearing.

The Bretons grouped themselves around the ledge above the fighting and hurled whatever they could at the attackers. Trevenna managed to haul herself up over the ledge and snatched up her longbow. She fired arrows into those attacking the other three and the Bretons quickly hoisted the defenders up over the edge in a mad scramble to reach the relative safety of the higher ground.

They fought desperately to keep the Adren from gaining the headland but they were tiring and outnumbered and the Adren were relentless. As one of their number was cut down by a scythe another would grab at the handle or blade and attempt to pull the defender back down towards them. It seemed as if two were prepared to sacrifice themselves if it meant a third could get at one of the defenders. The Bretons could not stop the Adren from finally gaining the level ground of the headland.

The attacks elsewhere on the Breton fortress had been repulsed and from other points on the headland and from the direction of the wall exhausted defenders rushed towards the Adren breakthrough. The defence turned into a scattered battle that raged across the top part of the headland but these villagers were no longer like those slaughtered at Eald or Branque. For months now they had fought the Adren on the cliff tops or on the wall and unlike the other villages to fall to the Adren the Bretons had the chance to defend themselves and fight back.

There were no battle lines or defensive positions on the headland just an intermingled chaotic confusion of individual fights to the death. The only exceptions were the Anglians. Cei and the other three stayed close together fighting as a band as they cut their way across the battlefield. Aelfhelm and Cuthwin did the same and held together a group of ten defenders from the wall as they advanced into the battle attacking the scattered knots of Adren.

The battle lasted an exhausting twenty minutes and the fate of the fortress hung in the balance for most of that time. Had the Adren gained the headland from the harbour with fewer casualties then the Bretons would have lost. Had only fifty Adren breached the wall then they would have taken the fortress there and then but the Bretons had done just enough to hold this attack.

As Cei squatted among the dead, exhausted and bloody, Merdynn tapped him on the shoulder and pointed to the West. Below the rain clouds that stretched out to the western horizon they could see the pale light of dawn. Cei stood up and stumbled forward a step. Merdynn held out a hand to steady him and Cei looked at the old man. His thinning white hair was bedraggled and hung lankly down to his shoulders, soaked by the persistent rain and the sweat of battle, but only his eyes betrayed any signs of the extreme weariness that Cei was feeling. The sword in his hand was bloody and he had fought skilfully.

'Where did you learn to use a sword like that?' Cei asked.

'You pick things up,' Merdynn answered, shrugging as he surveyed the battle scene and then added, 'You'd better take charge of this mess now that Bran's gone.'

Cei bent down and wiped the gore from his axe on a dead Adren. People were standing where they had finished fighting, leaning on weapons or searching among the dead for family or friends. Cei called Ethain over and sent him to the wall to keep a lookout for the next attack. The villagers were gradually making their way across to him, looking for direction on what to do next. He recognised one of Bran's companions approaching him, a grey haired middle-aged woman called Cardell. Her husband had not made it to the safety of the headland when the Adren initially attacked and she had seen her children die one by one during the defence of the fortress. Despite this, or perhaps because of it, she had proved increasingly capable of leading the villagers in the fighting against the Adren and Cei was glad that she had survived the latest attack.

'What do we do next, Cei? They've destroyed the boats, haven't they?' she asked.

'Yes, the fishing boats are gone but we're still alive and we can still escape from here. First task is to set watchers. I've sent Ethain to the wall but I want two or three more up there and we need some lookouts in case they try the cliff paths again. Second, we need to get the injured to the main hall and find out if we still have any healers left among us. Third, get some food going. We need meals and rest.' Cei looked round for Aelfhelm and Cuthwin. They were nearby and he called them over.

'Help get the wounded into the hall and kill the Adren wounded. Collect all the useful weapons and distribute them among the villagers then throw the Adren dead over the cliffs and build a pyre for our own dead. And I need to know how many we have left who can still fight. Get it all done quickly, we may not have much time before they come again.'

Cardell started to organise her people while the two Anglians started to search the strewn Breton bodies for those still alive. Cei turned to Merdynn, 'Where's Trevenna?' he asked.

'I think she's already gone to see to the wounded in the hall.'

'Good. Come with me,' Cei said and led the way to the end of the promontory.

The rain seemed to have exhausted itself too and all that was left of the driving downpour was a swirling drizzle that drifted in patches over the coast like a fine sea mist. They reached the far end of the headland and Cei gazed out over the sea. His limbs ached with fatigue and he gripped his upper arm to still a twitching muscle as he pointed out over the sea ice. 'It's cracking and thawing.'

Merdynn saw that Cei was right. He could see long channels of dark water snaking through the ice, and to the West he could see the rippling effect of waves under the breaking frozen surface.

'Just a bit sooner and we could have just sailed away from here,' Merdynn commented without any trace of bitterness.

'How many do you think we have left?' Cei asked.

'Perhaps a hundred. Maybe less.'

The Breton villagers may have been armed and able to defend themselves against the Adren but they were still only villagers and not trained warriors. The Adren that had made the top of the headland had taken a fearful toll among the defenders and more Bretons than Adren lay dead on the puddled and soaked ground of the headland.

'The Adren won't know that. One good thing about their refusal to retreat is that information doesn't get back to their commanders. We'll have to put as many people on the wall as we can to make it look like we can still defend the fortress and then hope the sea ice cracks before they decide to attack the cliff paths again.'

Merdynn agreed. He was looking to the West. The drifting mist now hid the horizons and closed the world around them but it was definitely lighter in that direction and his thoughts turned to the Causeway. Cei read his mind.

'They'll be invading Britain soon. How do we escape from here, Merdynn?'

'Oh, I was looking forward to hearing your plan. I thought you told Cardell that we'd escape, must have misheard you.'

'We could try cutting our way through their lines and disappear into the Shadow Lands,' Cei suggested but without any conviction.

'Hmm. A hundred of us against four thousand Adren, in the open too. No, even if we did manage to surprise them and get through, remember that they tracked us across hundreds of miles through the Shadow Lands. They'd just hunt us down.'

'Is dying here our only option then?'

'No, no there is another option.'

'What?'

'There is a boat. One boat, more of a skiff really, probably only able to hold three people.'

'Where?'

'It's on blocks behind the wood cutters' hut.'

Cei turned to him, 'That's right! I remember seeing it. It must have been hauled up here to be repaired over the winter. A few of us could sail it across the sea to Wessex.'

'And bring back two or three Wessex fishing boats.'

'If we could hold the wall for, what? Three or four more days? With the sea ice thawed we could get everyone off the headland without the Adren being able to stop us.'

'If some were left holding the wall against them.'

'Or perhaps we can just melt away without them realising.' Cei clapped the old man on the shoulder and strode off to inspect the skiff leaving Merdynn to marvel, not for the first time, how even a splinter of hope can rekindle a person's faith even in the darkest despair.

Chapter Six

Gwyna watched as first Mador was carried out of the hall and then as his blood was washed away with a bucket of hot water. She was furious. Murderously furious. She kept her expression neutral and smiled at those nearby but her knuckles were white as she gripped the seat of her chair. Her anger was not directed at Arthur or indeed Mador but towards her father who had told her nothing about this attempt on Arthur's life.

Behind the bland expression her thoughts were raging against Ablach. How dare he jeopardise her new position by the side of the warlord? Had Mador succeeded then she would have lost everything and been cast back into the life of relative obscurity where the limitations of her future would only serve to mock her newfound aspirations. As she had grown up in her father's village of Dalchiaran she had come to resent the smallness of her life. Her youthful ambitions had felt suffocated by the imprisoning horizons that had restricted all that she might accomplish. She had increasingly viewed those around her as weak with no desire or aim to achieve anything more than being able to stand on the tallest pile of dung and throw it at those below them. For as long as she could remember she wanted a better life, a richer life, something more than what she saw as the tallest dung pile and she did not care how she achieved it. She would have willingly plotted, deceived, stolen or murdered to haul herself up and away from the endless and pointless scrabbling that constituted the lives of even the rulers of the northern tribes. She had never imagined that marriage could be the means to realise her ambitions.

When the opportunity presented itself to sneak into Arthur's tent and kill him she had grabbed at it as a way to exorcise her burning resentments. She resented the ordered, comfortable life of those from the southern tribes. She resented the possibilities open to them. She resented Arthur's power and his easy command of those around him, and her resentment was matched only by her envy. If she could not attain that power herself then the next best thing in her estimation was to deny it to the hated southern tribes and so she had tried to kill Arthur. When he had effortlessly denied her that satisfaction she had been more than willing to satisfy another of her needs. She had been surprised that her outward antipathy towards Arthur had masked something deeper and quite contrary. She had certainly not considered or thought that it might eventually lead to an escape from her hated life. Instead she had just abandoned herself to a more primal, driving desire that needed no calculating deviousness and which was not fed by bitterness.

Arthur was not the first man she had slept with but no previous union had unleashed the pure, violent passion she had experienced that night. She had been under no illusions that it may lead to a more permanent bond between them. Arthur was over twenty years her senior and the Warlord of the Wessex while she was merely a girl from the lawless northern tribes. Even being the daughter of Ablach counted for little outside of her hemmed horizons. As she had rode away from the Causeway Gates after that night with Arthur she had questioned Mar'h about him, trying to find out more of the warlord's true history and life and what kind of man he really was. Mar'h didn't know that they had spent the night together and thought her previous venom towards Arthur had transformed itself to a girlish crush so he smiled and indulged her with stories about him. At the time he had no idea that she was his daughter.

Despite her injured shoulder, Gwyna had been in an unusually good mood on that journey back to Dalchiaran. Somehow the release and satisfaction of her passion had dissipated her bitterness and temporarily freed her from the suffocation of her normal life. She had joked and laughed with Mar'h and over the course of their long journey they had grown to like each other in spite of the many reasons they had to hate each other's peoples. He thought the change in her was because she was returning home after the nightmare of the Shadow Lands but he could hardly have been more wrong. As soon as she rode into her village she felt the walls of her small life closing inevitably around her once more like an obscuring fog bank rolling in from the coast and she lost sight of the distant horizons that her raised spirits had shown her. The light in her eyes dimmed as they adjusted to the grey reality of her life.

She had been thrown into complete confusion when Mar'h had been accused of raping her mother so many years ago, long before Ablach married her and, she thought, long before she was born. She liked Mar'h and she associated him with Arthur, one of the few people she privately admired and who represented so much of everything that she wanted for herself. She had begun to harbour hopes that a friendship with Mar'h might lead to further contact with Arthur and perhaps the chieftains of the South, yet now he was accused of raping her mother.

She had refused to confront the deep and conflicting emotions that events around her were igniting and she had shut herself away from them, unsure what to believe or what to think. Then came the astonishing news that her father was offering her in marriage to Arthur. When Ablach had told her about the proposal she had selfishly and fervently prayed to her gods that the whole issue of Mar'h and Esa would just disappear. She had reasoned that it had been long ago; her mother had got on with her life and married well so why go and endanger the future of her daughter now?

Suddenly all her ambitions and hopes seemed possible. She could leave behind the dunghills of her home and marry the Warlord of Wessex, a man who in her eyes represented power; a power that she could share. She had known that Arthur would only accept the offer as a way of guaranteeing that the Uathach warriors would stand with him against the Adren but that had not diminished the arrangement in her eyes at all. Gwyna had no naïve notions of love and felt no particular bond with Arthur; as a husband he would do as well as any other man but as a means to achieve all she wanted then she could hardly have hoped to do better. She realised that her father was using her as a pawn in his own personal ambitions but once married to Arthur she would be far more powerful than a pawn. She had her aim set at being Queen.

Gwyna was furious that her father had jeopardised everything she wanted and was so close to getting. As she stared at the last of Mador's blood being washed away she found herself wishing it were her father's. Mador had not been a bad man to her but she knew he was weak; a good fighter but easily led. She turned to look at Arthur beside her. He was talking with Ceinwen who was laughing at something he was saying. She felt a small stab of jealousy and it surprised her for she certainly did not love Arthur. Neither did she have any expectations of loving him but that did not concern her because she was already in love with the possibilities this marriage offered. Perhaps, she thought still watching Arthur and Ceinwen, the two of them had been lovers in the past and she was surprised once again that this thought troubled her. She put her uneasiness to one side telling herself that if he had enough of an appetite to want other women besides herself then good luck to him, just so long as he and everyone else knew that she was his wife and just so long as no one threatened her new found power.

She studied his face as he talked to Ceinwen thinking that by the time she was his age he may well be dead and if the gods blessed her then she might have a son old enough to take his inheritance but still young enough to need a mother's guidance. She doubted that the southern council would let her take Arthur's position when he died but if he could become king then their son would take the reins in due course and then she could make herself the power in the land. She said a quick and fervent prayer to her gods that she would bear a son and the sooner the better. There was no guarantee that Arthur would survive the coming war so she promised herself that she would do as much as she could to become pregnant as soon as possible. Knowing that the majority of women never conceived she muttered another hurried and intense prayer that she would be one of the blessed ones. She had heard the rumours of the various bastards that Arthur was said to have sired so she felt confident that he could father offspring but she resolved to carefully seek out alternative fathers. She needed a child; preferably a son, and it wasn't important who fathered it.

The din of the feast in the hall suddenly increased and Gwyna searched the gathering below her to see what had caused it. A brawl had broken out between some drunken Mercians and a group of equally drunken Uathach warriors. She watched as Arthur strode quickly down the hall and into the heart of the melee. Morgund and Ruraidh had followed him and together they heaved the opponents apart before any real damage could be done. Gwyna noted how both sets of brawlers quickly stepped away when they saw who had broken up the fight and she recalled how easily Arthur had defeated Mador. Clearly the tales and stories were true about him. He was a dangerous man and she reminded herself to be careful around him and keep her deeper desires for control and power well hidden from him. She felt Ceinwen staring at her and she turned to her with a smile on her lips that never touched her eyes.

Ceinwen suppressed a shudder and smiled back. She felt there was something about the Uathach woman, and despite her age she had to admit that Gwyna was a woman and not a girl, something she could not quite define. Whatever quality it was, it made her feel uneasy. The celebrations were reminding her of the last fateful night at Branque too and the memories of Andala and her daughter were haunting her once again. Ceinwen poured herself another cup of wine and left the dais, passing Arthur as he made his way back to Gwyna. She remembered how Arthur was making her feel increasingly uneasy too and shrugged, thinking that perhaps they were well matched after all. She pushed her way through the people thronged about the tables as she looked for Morveren and Morgund. She wanted to forget her past life, forget Arthur, Gwyna, the Uathach and the Adren. If only for a brief time she wanted to forget everything that she had been dwelling on and join her friends in whatever foolishness they were undoubtedly engaged in. When she found them she was not disappointed.

The feast was due to last for days, not that a bystander could have seen any signs of anyone doing anything other than heading for oblivion by the fastest route possible, but it only lasted for seven hours. The last in the relay of messengers from the Causeway fought his way through the carousing crowd and made his way towards the dais.

Gwyna saw him before Arthur did and she felt an instant jab of apprehension. The man was heading straight for them and he looked completely sober but clearly exerted. She knew the man was carrying urgent news and it could only be about one thing. The Adren were moving on the Causeway. She cursed quietly to herself and drew Arthur's attention to the approaching messenger. She asked the gods why this had to happen now and not a few days later, nonetheless she felt a thrill of excitement. This is what it was like to be at the centre of power in the land. News of outside events took ages to reach the villages, if it ever arrived at all, and could rarely be trusted to be accurate yet here she would be among the first to know and she would be right where the decisions were made.

As the warrior spoke in Arthur's ear she cast a glance at Ablach and wondered again why he had not brought all the northern warriors to Caer Sulis as he had promised. For a fearful moment she allowed herself to think that he may be planning to renege on the treaty but she told herself that the Adren were as much a threat to Ablach's lands as they were to Arthur's and she breathed more easily again. She knew that he had nothing to gain and everything to lose by abandoning the treaty, so surely he knew that too. Gwyna took another gulp from her wine as the panicked moment of uncertainty passed, besides, she reassured herself, not even her father would be mad enough to blatantly betray Arthur.

The messenger had delivered his news and Arthur leant across and briefly told her what she had already guessed then he beckoned Elwyn and Gereint over to him. He told them to let the chieftains and counsellors know and then to start gathering their warriors from the drunken chaos below. Arthur walked across to Ablach and took him to one side away from the noise and throng of people.

'The Adren are gathering on the far side of the Causeway. The attack will come soon. I'm ending the feast and taking the war bands east. Meet me there with every warrior you can muster. And don't delay. Remember that your lands depend on it too.'

Ablach swayed slightly, his eyes glassy with the drink he had consumed. He put a huge hand on Arthur's shoulder to steady himself and turned his face away as he belched loudly.

'I'll head for Dalchiaran straight away. That's where my men are waiting. I'll gather them and ride for the Causeway. Straight away,' Ablach replied, slurring his words. He reeled away and started to roar orders to the nearest of his warriors. Arthur returned to Gwyna, his expression cold and his teeth clenched tightly.

'Will you ride with us to the Causeway, stay here or go with your father?' he asked her.

'I'll ride with you of course,' she replied, genuinely surprised by the question.

Ruraidh approached them and stood before their table swaying slightly. 'Ablach's taking most of the warriors back to Dalchiaran but me and some of the others want to ride straight to the Causeway with you,' he said to them both.

'The same warriors who were with you in the Shadow Lands?' Arthur asked.

'Yes. We have some scores to settle with the Adren.'

'Ruraidh, I can trust you to take a message north. I want you to take your band and tell the northern tribes just what's at stake here. Any tribe, clan or village that doesn't help us at the Causeway I'll hold to what I promised Ablach.'

Ruraidh stared at Arthur before replying, 'What did you promise Ablach?'

'That if he broke the treaty and left us to stand alone against the Adren then I'd destroy the northern tribes.'

'I'll take the message because if we don't all defend the Causeway then the Adren will destroy both our lands.' Ruraidh then turned to Gwyna and added, 'I'll see you at the Causeway.'

All through the hall the word was spreading as the various captains tried to organise their drunken warriors. It was another four hours before they were ready to ride out of Caer Sulis. By then the Uathach had already departed for Ablach's base at Dalchiaran where he claimed the rest of his warriors were already gathering. The Wessex warriors were still unsure whether or not the Uathach would honour the treaty and even Arthur had no definite sense about Ablach's intentions. It seemed to him that Ablach had not yet chosen which course best served his own purposes and he was right; Ablach had indeed not yet decided if he and his warriors should make for the Causeway or leave the southern tribes to their fate and make instead for the North. As Ablach rode for Dalchiaran pondering his options and weighing the alternatives, Arthur led two hundred and fifty warriors out of Caer Sulis and onto the Westway, once again riding east.

The relay messengers had gone via Whitehorse Hill where Mar'h was collecting the latest production of weapons for his new army. He and the others at the hilltop fort knew that Arthur would soon be coming east and they rode down to the Westway to wait for them.

The rolling hills of Wessex were cast in the unique quality of light that exists just before sunrise. It always seemed to Mar'h that the dawn light was somehow colder and clearer than its counterpart was in autumn when the sun would eventually set in the East. With the spring sun still below the western horizon, the shadowless hills, valleys and woods were lit only by the indirect sunlight that was reflected down from the pale blue sky. The wind from the West was keen and cold but lacked the freezing grasp of the gales that usually blew from the still ice-locked Shadow Lands of the East. Isolated grey clouds hurried eastward as if fleeing the sunrise.

They were too low to be lit by the coming sun and they looked heavy and purposeful. They reminded him of the dark smoke that pillared the skies in the aftermath of Uathach raids.

Mar'h waited with the ten other warriors who had been chosen to help him with the training. They were all a good fifteen or twenty years older than him, old enough to be beyond their fighting prime but each with the experience brought by decades of battling the Uathach, experience they would now use to help turn villagers and farmers into an army capable of facing the Adren.

Eventually they could make out the approaching line of horsemen on the Westway. They were still several miles away but Mar'h could see the three flags of the southern tribes flying at the front of the column. They watched and waited as the mounted warriors of Britain closed the distance at a steady canter. When they drew level Arthur stopped briefly and passed on some last orders to him and Mar'h exchanged a few words with his friends who rode behind Arthur and then he pulled his horse back off the track-way and watched as the combined war bands of the South rode by. The older warriors around him were all thinking the same thing; two hundred and fifty were riding to reinforce the eighty already at the Gates and there was reputed to be over twenty thousand Adren across the Causeway. When the warriors had passed they rode back to Caer Cadarn in silence.

Several hours ahead of Arthur's war band Captain Terrill and Fin Seren were approaching the Winter Wood. They also rode in silence. Although neither knew it they were both wondering what they would say to Lord Venning. When Seren's immediate anguish had exhausted itself she had forced herself to confide in Terrill that she was pregnant with Arthur's child. He was appalled by the revelation for many different reasons but he instinctively realised the enormous effort it must have taken for Seren to reveal her burden to him and he hid his shock and revulsion as best as he could. How she could have kept it secret from everyone for so long amazed him. Either she had been blindly optimistic about the future or supremely confident in her ability to control it. In either case her world had clearly come crashing down in ruins about her. He recognised the extent of her desperation by her decision to tell him about the child. The implications were overwhelming. Despite having known her all his life and having been her childhood friend he was at a loss to understand how she could have formed a union with an outsider and how she could have managed to conceal the result from everyone for so long.

Children were a rare blessing for the Cithol. It was one of the few things they still had in common with the outsiders. For centuries they had been so removed from those outside the Veiled City that they did not even have a collective name for them. Recently they had taken to referring to them as the 'barbarians', 'outsiders' or simply as 'the others' and they used the terms as Arthur's people used 'Uathach' to describe the northern tribes. To the Cithol those that lived above ground and beyond the Winter Wood were simply barbaric and Terrill was struggling with Seren's revelation and its implications. He had thought the two peoples so different that a childbearing union would not be possible. Apparently he was wrong and he was having great difficulty coming to terms with that fact. It certainly explained why not a single one of his people had sensed that Seren was pregnant. Usually they would be able to discern it simply by meeting the expecting mother, even at the early stages of pregnancy, but this unborn child was a product of something entirely different and it confused and scared him. Seren had entrusted him with an enormous confidence and he was debating within himself whether or not to tell Lord Venning as soon as they arrived in the Veiled City.

Seren was debating the same issue but for her it was a well-rehearsed debate. She knew the arguments for and against telling her father. She had rehashed and replayed them over and over until they had first robbed her of her sleep and then her appetite. No matter how much she thought the argument through she could see no way in which it could end well. Her final conclusion to herself had always been that she had Arthur's love and that was all that mattered to her in the end. Now, it seemed to her, all she had was his unborn child and that conclusion was far less comforting.

She had adjusted her clothing to conceal the outward signs of her pregnancy but the time was fast approaching when no amount of concealment would hide what would soon be apparent to everyone.

She had thought about refusing to name the father but that was only a short-term plan for she felt sure that her child would be clear evidence that the father was not Cithol. Nothing was working out as she had foreseen it. With Arthur to stand beside her she would have proudly faced her father and mother and anyone else in the Veiled City, even Commander Kane who was responsible for the security of the city and for ensuring that the population followed its laws. Either they would have accepted the unchangeable or she would have left with Arthur to live among his people but without Arthur her confidence and surety had vanished. She was utterly miserable and completely lost. Her tears began to flow freely again.

Captain Terrill had no idea what to say to her so he just took her hand and held it. They rode on in silence with the horse drawn cart they travelled on rocking from side to side as they left the Westway and made for the Winter Wood.

They made their way through the well-spaced trees on the western fringes of the Wood with the pale dawn sky growing lighter above them until they came to a newly constructed stabling area. It was from here that the Cithol supplies were loaded onto the carts and wains and taken west to Caer Cadarn or on to Caer Sulis.

They climbed stiffly off the cart and Terrill exchanged a few words with those who had journeyed in the wains behind them before leading Seren down the paths that led deeper into the Winter Wood and to the Veiled City. He escorted her all the way down to the lakeshore Palace of her father and neither said a word until they stood by the entrance to her home. Seren turned to him and rested a hand on his chest, her eyes imploring him.

'Please don't say anything to anyone yet. Give me a chance to tell my father first.'

Captain Terrill nodded and left her at the entrance. He was still undecided and she knew it. Whatever she decided to do she realised she best do it quickly. Terrill had been a good friend to her for as long as she could remember but his obedience to Lord Venning and Commander Kane was beyond question. It was only a matter of time until he told one or the other, if not both, and however badly they reacted it would be worse if it did not come from her.

She entered her room and saw that a fire had been lit by one of her maids and some food put to one side for her on a small table. All her short life everything had been done for her and she was only just beginning to realise it. She had never had to worry about anything either great or small so nothing had prepared her for the agonising indecision she now felt and she sat by the fire without taking off her winter cloak and ignoring the food laid out for her. Her mind darted from choice to choice and settled on none. She realised she was twisting her hands together and that she still wore her fur gloves. She peeled them off and cast them to one side then brushed her wet cheeks with the palm of her hand.

For the next hour she paced across the floor of her room, alternating between the pain and humiliation of seeing Arthur with the Uathach girl and the fear of telling her father that she carried Arthur's child. All the time she was keenly conscious that Terrill would be holding his own private debate and she knew that his innate loyalty would soon force him to do what she could not bring herself to do.

She crossed to the door and rested a hand on the metal ring trying to force herself to open it and leave the room but her hand slipped away and fell limply by her side. She hung her head and cried with her forehead resting against the cold door. Her tears fell on the stone floor until the back of her throat stung with the taste of salt and she had to wipe her dripping nose with the back of her hand.

Behind her a side door opened into her room and one of her maids came into the room. It was Hannah. The woman who had tended to her every need all of her life. The woman who had been more of a mother to her than her real mother had been. Seren turned away from her as if she could conceal her distress simply by turning her back to her.

Hannah put down the clothes she had been carrying and walked across to the stricken girl and took her in her arms. Seren buried her face in the old woman's shoulder and blurted out her problems as shuddering sobs racked her. Hannah could understand nothing of what the girl was saying but soothed her as if she were her child. She sat Seren on the bed and sat beside her with a comforting arm around her.

When her tears had abated Seren looked into the old woman's face and took her wrinkled but strong hands in her own.

'You won't abandon me will you, Hannah?'

'Of course not, child.'

'No matter what happens?'

'There is nothing that could make me leave you. What's the matter? Why all the tears?' Hannah had been alarmed by Seren's crying, she had not seen her weep like this since she was a young child but it was more the tone of her voice, the desperate need to know that she was not alone that truly frightened her. Seren did not answer her but gradually regained her composure in silence, swallowing back the taste of her tears and blowing her nose on one of the clean shirts Hannah had brought in.

'That will look nice on you when you wear it,' Hannah said, shaking her head.

Seren burst out laughing and the tears threatened to overwhelm her again but she held them at bay and stood up.

'I'm sorry Hannah. Sorry for everything I've put you through over the years.'

'You make it sound like decades girl. And you make it sound like a goodbye. What's wrong? Tell me.' There was an urgency to Hannah's voice that betrayed her concern.

Seren shook her head and managed what she thought was a brave and reassuring smile. It was neither and it made the old woman's heart constrict in fear and love for the young girl before her.

'Where's my father?'

'He's in some meeting or other but what is it, Seren? Who's upset you this much? Is it Captain Terrill?' Or worse, she thought, Commander Kane.

'Is he in the council room?'

'No. I think he's in the smaller chamber up at the back of the valley. Must you see him now?'

'Yes. Yes, I think I must,' Seren answered and going to the basin in the far corner of the room she splashed water over her face in an effort to erase the evidence of her tears. She changed from her travelling clothes and turned to Hannah before leaving, 'Wait for me here Hannah, please. I don't think I will be long.' But she would never again see the old woman who had raised her.

Terrill watched her leave the Palace by a side gate and took a deep breath of relief. He had not wanted to betray her confidence but he had been on the point of going to Lord Venning himself with the terrible information. As he watched her make her way up the steeply sloping stone path he studied her trying to see any sign of her already advanced pregnancy. He thought how ironic it was that the pregnancy of Lord Venning's daughter should be such bad news. Normally being with child was a cause for celebration especially if it was one of the ruling family who was going to have a child, but this child was in direct contradiction of the strict rules of the Cithol society.

They had lived for centuries in this underground valley and while their city was large it was still enclosed. They had needed rules and customs to keep their society running smoothly and without problems and so it had; trouble was rare and never serious. For Fin Seren to have lain with anyone outside of a formal union would have been unthinkable to Terrill; unthinkable but ultimately forgivable. For her to have been with an outsider, a barbarian, stupefied him. For it to have been Arthur, a leader of the outsiders, and for the union to have borne a child was just plainly disastrous in Terrill's estimation. Not for the first time he asked himself if that would make Arthur the protector of the future ruler of the Veiled City, and yet Arthur had married one of his own kind so where did that leave Seren and her child? His thoughts and questions echoed back and forth and as he watched the young girl trudge up the pathway between the stone dwellings; he did not envy her the task ahead.

Seren felt more confident now that she was committed to a course of action. Her actions, decisions and emotions had led her to this current situation and she was prepared to stand by them. She realised that in truth she had little other option but having finally accepted her situation she had found a new determination and courage.

The narrow path wound its way up the steep side of the underground valley as it turned and twisted between the terraced dwellings and Seren felt herself tiring. She wondered if it was because of her condition and stopped to regain her breath. She turned and looked out on the section of the lake that she could see between the stone houses that lined the path and that fell away below her. The lake was completely still and its dark smooth surface reflected the lights from the houses on the far shore. Seren did not think of it as a cavern with a rock-hewn ceiling somewhere above her in the darkness. It was her home, her people, her Veiled City and she felt a momentary panic that events might force her to leave it forever behind.

She sighed heavily and gathered up her long grey dress at the knees to start the final climb to Lord Venning's lesser council chamber. It was the last house on the valley side and was situated where the slope met the almost vertical wall of the cavern. Indeed half of it was built into the rock of the wall so that only a portion of the whole house was visible from the outside.

As Seren approached she could see that more of Commander Kane's guards were stationed at the front gate than was usual and this puzzled her. The only person from outside who could possibly be here was Brunroth, Merdynn as Arthur called him. She quickened her pace despite the steep steps feeling that in Merdynn she may well have an ally or at least a friend who could intercede on her behalf with her father.

To her amazement the guards barred her way at the gates to the small house. She stared at them in bewilderment and they looked at her uncomfortably. Lord Venning only had a few dozen guards because safety in the Veiled City was hardly an issue and Seren knew both of those who barred her way.

'Rowse? Lowry?' She said looking from one to the other.

'I'm sorry, Seren. Commander Kane's orders. Absolutely no one is to enter. I'm sure he had no idea that you would come this way but, well, there you are. Orders I'm afraid,' Rowse answered her and he did indeed look apologetic.

Seren could see that they meant to follow their orders. Clearly her displeasure was a lot more bearable than the displeasure of Commander Kane. She shrugged as if it was not important one way or the other and smiled at them both.

'Strange days indeed that a daughter cannot enter her father's house. Perhaps I should insist on you both having to escort the next supply train to the barbarian town of Caer Sulis?'

She laughed at their sudden discomfort and told them she was merely teasing. She smiled brightly at them both again and turned to take the path that ran away from the house and along the smooth rock of the cavern wall. Once her back was turned she allowed the puzzlement and anger to show on her face. Surely the gates would not be barred if it was just Brunroth visiting her father, she thought to herself. It crossed her mind that perhaps Arthur was here too and her heart leapt at the thought before the likelihood of his never returning to the Veiled City settled over her with a depressing certainty.

Like most of the children of the city she had played and explored throughout the whole valley but few children had such friends as Terrill. His father had been the captain before him and so the young Terrill had known about the lesser trodden passageways and tunnels of the Veiled City and together the two children had delved into all the known tunnels and even discovered more ancient ones known only to themselves.

It was one of the official yet secretive passageways that Seren was now thinking about taking. Her father's second council chamber had been built into the rock face for a good reason; a passage led up from there to the Winter Wood above. Seren knew a series of tunnels that could take her onto the one that led down to the house. She had waited there numerous times when Brunroth had visited always hoping to catch another glance of the warrior who sometimes accompanied him. The warrior whose child she now carried.

She stopped by the entrance to a passageway that led up into the semi-darkness and tried to remember the route she would have to take. It was not a quick route but it might lead her to the house in time to discover who might be meeting with her father and she was growing more curious about that the more she thought about it. She was concentrating so hard on remembering the right route through the underground labyrinth that she had no idea that someone was behind her until she felt a hand on her shoulder.

She jumped and whirled around expecting to see one of the guards or Commander Kane himself but it was Terrill and he looked as surprised by her reaction as she was by his sudden appearance behind her. She put a hand over her heart as if physically trying to calm its runaway beating. She thought wryly to herself that it had been through quite enough already.

'What are you doing creeping up on me like that?'

'I was going to ask you what you were doing creeping around the top of the valley.'

'Well, I asked first,' Seren said and Terrill thought he heard a trace of her former childish petulance. He was a year or two older than Seren and all through their childhood he had acted as if he were her older brother. With the recent revelations he had forgotten just how young she still was and his attitude towards to her softened.

'I was concerned about you going to see your father.'

'More concerned that I might not go and see him you mean.'

'Both are true, Fin.'

He had not used her name like that since they were children and her defiance melted away instantly.

'I went to see him but the guards turned me away. The guards! Me!' She did not feign the feeling of outrage that had been growing steadily since being denied entrance to the house.

'Why? Is he in council?'

'Yes, but who would they want to keep me away from? That's what I want to know.'

Terrill looked curious despite himself as Seren continued, 'And I want to find out. And what's more, I am going to find out. You remember the old tunnels? The ones that can take us back to the one that leads into the house?'

Terrill did remember them but it was not his place to question whom Lord Venning might or might not be meeting. Still, he was the Cithol Captain and the guardian of the Winter Wood and he had been excluded from this council. He was more than curious; he felt affronted.

'Will you come with me?' Seren asked.

Perhaps it was his childhood memories of the games they had played when they explored the tunnels that prompted him or perhaps he felt bad about the high-handed way he had been judging his friend but whatever his private reasoning Terrill agreed to go with her. She took his hand and together they stepped into the half-darkness of the tunnels.

The first tunnel climbed steeply upwards. It was more than wide enough for them to walk side by side and the floor, while not as smooth as the paths around the houses on the lakeside, was still even and easy to walk along. The in-set crystals that lit the underground city were spaced along the tunnel roof as well but here they were set apart at wide intervals and there were long stretches of darkness between the dim pools of light.

Seren felt the years slipping away and imagined that they were children once more exploring the endless tunnels that honeycombed the Veiled

City. She cast a glance at Terrill to see if he was feeling the same way but the dimness of the passageway hid the features of his dark-skinned face and she suddenly felt alone. Her happy memories of childhood were instantly stripped away. She was not the child and the child in her womb would not tolerate the child in her heart. She realised that she had to banish any temptation to wallow in her own childhood now that she was soon to be a parent herself. Inevitably her thoughts turned to Arthur and as Terrill led her along the increasingly ill-lit tunnels the tears began to silently spill through her eyelashes again. She desperately wanted to see Arthur, to somehow explain everything and to somehow recapture the expectations she had held. Once again she found herself hoping that it would be Arthur who was secretly meeting with Lord Venning.

Even as Seren was hoping that he would be with Lord Venning, Arthur was arriving at the grove that looked down on the Winter Wood. He had decided to rest the horses for a few hours before making for the Causeway. As Seren and Terrill felt their way along the darkest of the tunnels, Arthur and the warriors of the South stood on the hillside and watched as the first of the sun's rays radiated across the land from the western horizon.

Seren and Terrill knew nothing about the beginning of the spring sunrise above them but ahead of them, at the end of the last tunnel, they too could see a growing light. The narrow passageway that they were inching along led directly onto the tunnel that descended from the Winter Wood and down to Lord Venning's more private council chambers. Ahead of them they could see the flickering light of burning torches from around a curve in the tunnel. Terrill realised that the brands must have been used to light the tunnels for the unknown visitors and he put a gentle hand on Seren's arm to stop her.

Suddenly the sound of voices carried to them. They could make out Lord Venning speaking to Commander Kane but then a third person spoke and something in that voice immediately chilled their souls and they stood rigidly still. Long shadows stretched across the tunnel floor and bent obliquely upright against the wall ahead of them. One of the shadows stopped and turned. It seemed to be staring directly at them. Neither of them breathed and then the shadows were gone. The torchlight faded as the group moved on upwards to the Winter Wood.

Seren realised she had stopped breathing and took in a long breath. Terrill wiped his palms dry on the sleeves of his tunic and clenched his fists to stop his hands shaking. They stood in silence both trying to understand the sense of dread and foreboding that had momentarily stole upon them. Whoever it was who had been with Lord Venning and Commander Kane was clearly very powerful and very dangerous. They were both scared by what they had sensed and it was nothing like the childhood frights that they had shared before in these tunnels. This was a fear that pierced deeply and touched their hearts. The stranger's will had a malign elemental force to it and both of them were pathetically grateful that only a fraction of it had turned their way.

They stayed standing silently in the cold tunnel until they heard the returning voices. Terrill put a finger against Seren's lips then whispered quietly to her. She nodded her understanding. Ahead of them and to their left was a small channel that they could crawl along and which would lead them into one of the top rooms of the chamber. They were relieved now to have missed the visitor to their city but they were even keener to learn what they could about him.

Neither of them were sure if they would be able to fit into the tight channel. As children they had had no problem scampering along it but neither of them were children now. After some minutes of quiet frustration and doubt Seren finally found the opening and crawled into it.

It was only about thirty-feet long but it seemed to take an age for them to scrape and wriggle their way to the end where it opened up into the room. Seren had a panicked moment of claustrophobia when she thought the end had been blocked up but it was only the detritus of disused furniture that had been stacked against the wall and she pushed it to one side. She scrambled out and began to help Terrill, understanding now why her knees and elbows had always been scraped or grazed when she was a child.

They both stood in the semi-darkness of the storeroom brushing the dust and dirt from their clothes. As Seren softly walked to the doorway to listen for the voices below, Terrill stood caught in indecision. His sense of duty and obedience fought with both his loyalty to Seren and his anger at being excluded from whatever had been said in the chamber below them. He would have claimed that it was his loyalty to Seren that won through but in truth it was his fear of the stranger and the need to learn more about him that ultimately led him to join Seren by the doorway.

They could hear voices. Seren strained to hear what was being said but could not make out any of the conversation taking place in the room below. To Terrill's increasing anxiety she softly crossed to the top of the stairway. She knelt there concentrating on the sound of the voices then turned to Terrill and beckoned him over. Despite his misgivings he crossed to the stairwell to join Seren who unnecessarily put a finger to her lips. He knelt by her side and tried to still the sound of the blood thumping in his ears. Finally he too could hear what was being said below. It was a moment he would spend the rest of his life regretting.

Chapter Seven

L eah was dying. Ethain knew this and was surprised how little he cared. He had more important things on his mind. Right now Cei was deciding who should go on the small boat back to Wessex to bring back the larger fishing boats that could rescue the trapped Bretons. Leah may be dying from an infected wound but he could still be safe if only he could convince Cei to choose him as one of the three to make the crossing to Wessex.

He was squatting down by Leah's side and she stirred again, her head rolling from side to side on the bundled cloak that served as a pillow. Her face was sheened with sweat and her hair clung wetly across her forehead and cheeks. She looked, and was, desperately ill and Ethain wondered what it was about her that had attracted him so much. Whatever it had been it was gone now and gone for good. He knew for certain that she would not be among those who might escape from the fortress. He was beyond caring who did. All that mattered to him was that he should make it back to Wessex. He had made the point to Cei that he was the only one amongst them who came from Wessex and he might be best positioned to persuade the fishermen to make the journey across to the Breton coast.

At the time he had understated the point, sure that Cei would be unwilling to risk failure by not including him, but as the deliberations had continued he fretted and worried that perhaps he had not made his point strongly enough. He occupied himself by thinking how he could effect his escape from the current nightmare if Cei did decide to send him across on the skiff.

So far he had come up with two plans. The first would mirror Cei's plan up to the point where he would be expected to return with the fishing boats, supposing they could actually find a village willing to help them. He had no intention of returning to the Breton coast, quite the opposite. He would wave off the fishing boats, wishing them good fortune, under the pretext of immediately returning to Arthur's war band that would undoubtedly be at the Causeway. He could argue that his duty lay with his warlord and the defence of Britain. It might work. There was no real reason why they would disbelieve him. Once the boats were gone he would travel west, not east, and hide on the moors or go even further west, to the ends of Wessex if necessary. The problem with this plan was that should Cei and the others eventually make it back to Arthur then his absence would be questioned and unexplained, which is why he was leaning towards his second plan.

Ethain had not yet openly thought through the details, or examined the implications, of the second option and it remained unrefined and gnawing away in some dark corner of his thoughts. It would guarantee his safety but only at the expense of condemning everyone else and he would also have to silence those who travelled with him on the skiff. In the same dark corner of his mind the voice of the scared youth who had escaped from the Adren attack on Eald cried out in horror at contemplating the betrayal of so many. As he squatted by the fevered Leah he wondered how he could have changed so much in so short a time.

Cei and Merdynn were in agreement that they had to despatch the boat soon or it would be too late. What they could not decide upon was who should make the crossing. Ethain was wrong when he claimed he was the only one there who was from Wessex. Trevenna too was from Wessex but she had lived in Anglia with Cei for the last twenty years so it was questionable who would recognise her among the coastal villages and Cei did not want to appear as if he were just getting her away to safety. Cei thought that Ethain should go. Merdynn thought it should be Trevenna and argued that as the sister of Arthur and wife of the Anglian Warlord she would be recognised and that she would be more convincing than some young unknown warrior would. Cei thought that Ethain would be better placed as he had previously accompanied Morveren back to her home among the Wessex fishers.

They had already decided that Cuthwin should go as he was by far the best able to handle the small boat. Merdynn too would go, as he had to get word to Arthur that their quest east had failed and that the Adren would still be getting their supplies from the Shadow Land City. There was no doubt that Merdynn would be recognised in Wessex but most of the villagers held him in deep suspicion and they would be unlikely to sail across the sea at his request.

There were obvious merits to either argument but they realised it was more important to leave quickly than it was to dwell on whether Trevenna or Ethain should go so Merdynn picked up a stone and hid it in one hand allowing Cei to choose and for fate to decide. Fate decided that it should be Ethain.

Once that had been settled they went to inspect the rushed preparations of the boat. It was indeed small with only just enough room for three people and the supplies they would need. Although the boat had a small mast and canvas sail Cei thought the crossing would still take the best part of three days. The larger fishing boats would take perhaps half that time to return, which meant that they would have to hold the Adren at bay for five or six days.

There had been no more attacks since the previous large-scale assault on the cliff paths and the sea ice was now too broken and unstable for the Adren to risk any further attacks from around the base of the cliffs. Their only point of attack now was over the high wall and Cei had put three quarters of the remaining Bretons there in an attempt to fool the Adren that they still had more than enough people left to defend the fortress.

There were just a hundred of them left now and Cei had decided that only twenty-five could rest, sleep and tend the wounded at one time, the others were on the wall to defend against any attacks. Cei was surprised that the Adren had not pressed their attacks after so nearly overwhelming them during the last one. The only explanation he could think of was that they did not know just how close they had come to victory.

As he neared the boat he saw that Cuthwin was standing back and surveying his work.

'Is it ready?'

'It's as good as when it was first made. Better even.' Something in Cuthwin's voice told Cei that the young man's usual confidence was faltering.

'Is that good enough to get you across the sea to Wessex?'

Cuthwin looked at him before replying, 'It's a small boat, Cei. It depends which way the winds blow and how strongly.' He shrugged then grinned, 'It'll be exciting if a storm blows up.'

Cei clapped him on the shoulder, 'You'll be fine. You've sailed out storms before and you'll have Merdynn and Ethain to help you.'

'Ethain, eh?'

'He might know some of the villagers you come across. It'll help to have a friendly face among you. Merdynn could scare them into putting out to sea but he won't be with them on the return journey and they might just turn back once he's gone. You know the Wessex lot, unreliable at the best of times.'

Cuthwin smiled but he was wondering how reliable Ethain would prove to be. He had his doubts about the young Wessex warrior. 'When do we leave?' he asked.

'Now. It will take about five or six days for you to get back here and if the Adren attack in force, well, the sooner you get back the sooner we all get away from here.'

For the first time Cuthwin truly realised what was being asked of him and he felt the responsibility weigh heavily on him. If he could not bring back the fishing boats then everyone left in the fortress would die. He looked at the boat once again and wondered if it really was up to the journey. He wondered if he was.

Cei saw the doubt and said, 'You'll be fine. Just do your best and that will be more than enough to get you there and back. Get some of the Bretons to give you a hand with this down the cliff path and I'll go and tell Ethain he's going.'

Cuthwin gathered some help and they put the boat on a cart and wheeled it off to the steps that led down to the harbour. Cei made his way to the hall where the wounded were tended to. He found Ethain by Leah's side.

'How is she?'

'The old woman says that it isn't good. She doesn't expect her to live,' he replied and looked back down at her desperately trying to calm himself. Inside he was screaming to know if he was going or not but he fought to keep his expression disinterested.

'There's nothing you can do here Ethain. Let the old woman look after her. The best thing you can do for her is bring the fishing boats back quickly.'

Ethain's heartbeat quickened further. 'You want me to go to Wessex?'

'Yes. With Merdynn and Cuthwin. And it's time to leave now.'

He did not trust his voice or eyes so he simply looked down at Leah and silently nodded. Cei misread his actions and put a hand on his shoulder to comfort him, thinking he was loathe to leave the girl he had become so close to and who was balanced on the edge of life. Ethain bent down and kissed Leah's hot forehead and then left the hall struggling to keep the spring from his steps and the smile from his face.

Cei watched from the headland as they rowed the small boat out from the harbour along a dark channel between the broken ice sheets and on out towards the open sea. They were lost to sight in the sea mist before they even cleared the ice floes. He hoped that the drizzle and mist hid them from the Adren too.

He turned to head back to the hall to ask the healer how the wounded were. He tried to put the small boat and the three who sailed in her from his mind. There was no more he could do other than wait and hold the Adren at bay. Halfway to the hall he changed his mind and walked to the wall instead. The fatigue from the battle was taking its toll and he wearily climbed the steps up to the top of the wall. Aelfhelm and Trevenna were at the top of the stairs.

'Any sign of them?' he asked leaning against the stonework for support.

'No. Strange but good. Perhaps they've had enough,' Aelfhelm said and Trevenna snorted to show what she thought of that particular hope and then added, 'But it sounds like they've begun working on something out there.'

Cei listened and soon heard the sound of hammering.

'What do you think they're up to?' he asked.

The other two shrugged in unison.

'Building something to breach the wall I suppose,' Aelfhelm said and turned his gaze out into the swirling rain to search for signs of the enemy approaching.

Cei watched him and saw how exhausted he looked. He looked thinner, older and immensely tired. He supposed they all did. He looked at the others who were nearby and none of them seemed to be simply villagers any longer. They looked like a strange group; hybrid warriors with the outward appearance of the normal people they had once been but with the taut expressions of those who had been forced to fight and who were now determined to fight on to the death. Their determination was grim but brittle and Cei wondered how long they would be able to carry on this new alien role that had been thrust upon them. Just a few more days, he thought. Just a few more days were all he needed from them.

He called over to Cardell to select twenty-five of those who most needed rest and to send them down to get out of the rain, eat and find a place to sleep for a few hours. It only left about fifty on the wall but no attack seemed imminent and they needed time away from the tension of keeping watch from the wall. He sent Trevenna to find the two children, Charljenka and Nialgrada, and to get them to start ferrying food up to those still on the wall. More than anything he wanted to sleep but he forced himself to slowly walk back and forth along the length of the wall and to talk to each of the Bretons who stood guard. Over the next few hours their spirits rose. The Adren were not attacking, they had hot food, help was on the way and as Cei pointed out to them, they had held an Adren army at bay for months and they were just peaceful villagers. They warmed to the thought of what the warriors of Britain would do to the Adren when they returned to take back their land and when that time came they would be right by the warriors' sides to take their own revenge. They passed whetstones from one to another and sharpened their weapons almost wanting the Adren to come again so that they could kill some more of them. Cei felt proud of them, fifty villagers standing at the wall in the rain with the Adren before them and their own dead behind them. He told them so and told them that Bran too would have been proud of them. He told them that they would sing of this defence in the halls of warriors. For generations to come they would sing the song about how the villagers had held the last Breton fortress against the Adren host and that song would be about them. As he made his way down to the hall to see the wounded he silently prayed that the defenders could hold out for another few days and that Cuthwin would return with the fishing boats of Wessex.

Cuthwin was having problems. A vicious squall had swept across them a few miles out from shore and his lodestone had been washed overboard in the sudden and turbulent waves that had assaulted the boat. He would have to make for the Wessex coast by dead reckoning alone. Merdynn had drawn a map back at the village to show where they were and where the fishing villages were. They had lost the map too so it was all guesswork from now on but none of that really worried him. He was confident he could guide the boat to anywhere he wanted to. What worried him was that they had lost their food and water. He privately blamed Ethain as he had been the one who had secured their stores and equipment in the boat while Cuthwin had been busy making his final checks on the boat itself. Had it been Trevenna with them and not Ethain then she would have stowed their gear properly and they would still have had their supplies. It had quickly become clear to him that Ethain was more of a danger than a help on the boat. With Merdynn's assistance he had righted the boat and they were back on course and making good speed towards Wessex but he knew it would be a long journey without food and water.

The Bretons had given them the oiled capes that they wore when they put to sea and the waterproof layer protected them from the worst of the cold spray that the wind was whipping from the tops of the waves. The last of the seagulls that had followed them had already wheeled away to skim the waves back to the shore. They had left the coastal mists behind but the clouds that were beginning to break up still vented spiteful showers across the expanse of the rolling sea. A few miles ahead of them they could see the slanting, grey columns of rain falling seawards as if they were an extension of the clouds from which they fell. The wind was from the southwest and pushed fiercely at their small sail, which was stretched taut and straining against the crude rigging that held it in place. Cuthwin let the boat run with the wind and he kept one hand on the tiller to direct them ever northwards. He had told Merdynn to join Ethain on one side of the boat to counter the tilt and the bows cut through the water that foamed down either side and which left a widening wake trailing behind them across the undulating waves.

While Cuthwin considered the implications of losing their supplies and while Ethain refined the second and more drastic of his plans for salvation, Merdynn was thinking about greater issues. He let the motion of the boat and the sounds of the sea lull him to the point where they all became part of the same sensation so that they were no more than a distant background to his thoughts.

He pondered on what King Maldred might have done in Arthur's absence and whether or not he had agreed to the Mercians helping to defend the Causeway. He weighed the possibilities of the Uathach helping Arthur and whether the Cithol had provided help or if they still remained to be convinced. He thought that perhaps the king had gone to the West after all in which case he would soon be returning with the tribes of Britain. He asked himself so many questions without realising that some of them had already been answered while he had been in the Shadow Lands and that others no longer required an answer.

Suddenly the thought struck him that if the peoples had not returned yet from the West then the fishing villages would more than likely be empty so there would be no problem in requisitioning at least one of the larger vessels but that raised the question of whether or not the other two could get the boat into the sea and sail it back by themselves. He decided to keep that thought to himself for now. One problem at a time and the first problem was to get there. The one question he kept returning to was that of the Adren and he brooded over his suspicions on who might be leading them and what his purpose may be. They did not seem to be interested in taking slaves or gaining land that they could use to grow crops or for supporting their herds. He considered how the Adren had seemed to slaughter everything and everyone in their path with the exception of the Irrades in the ruined city. Merdynn could only guess that the Adren had formed some kind of alliance with the deformed and poisoned inhabitants of the ruins. As the boat edged northwards and as the first nudges of hunger and thirst reminded him of the loss of their supplies he turned his thoughts solely towards the commander of the vast Adren armies. Merdynn at last confronted the fear that had been growing since the first Adren attack at Lughnasa. The Shadow Land City had closed its gates to outsiders hundreds of years ago but the last news he had received from there was that the city's ruler had appointed a new counsellor. The brief description he had heard of the new counsellor had set him thinking of those from his Order who had gone into the East a long time ago. At first Merdynn had hoped it was impossible but as the many years passed and as the tales that he heard when he travelled beyond Middangeard grew, his hope had turned to fear. He feared that

the Shadow Land City and its Adren armies were commanded by one
of his brothers who had disappeared into the East and he feared that
Lazure was merely the lieutenant of the more powerful eastern Khan,
and his greatest fear was that the Khan of the eastern plains was the most
powerful of those that remained from the ancient Order.

As Arthur's war band stood on the hill overlooking the Winter Wood
and as Seren and Terrill made their way through the dark tunnels under
it, the first sunlight in six months fell across the waves as the small boat
neared the mid-way point between the Breton and Wessex coasts. The
three seafarers momentarily forgot their thirst and hunger and stared to
the West. Wherever the peoples were, whether it was at the Causeway
or on the wall of the Breton fortress, everyone who had wintered in
Middangeard stopped and stared to the West when the rim of the sun
edged over the horizon. Those who could see the sunrise turned their
faces to the weak warmth and closed their eyes thankful to have survived
another winter. Many of them wondered if they would live to see it set in
the autumn or rise once more in a year's time. Many would not.

Three days after leaving the Breton fortress they finally saw the dark
strip of land before them and they watched it grow as Cuthwin sailed
the boat ever closer. Merdynn studied the coastline trying to match the
unfamiliar view before him with what he remembered about the shores
of Wessex. He thought that they were off the Cornish coast and told
Cuthwin to parallel the shore and turn to the East. With the wind behind
them they sailed east and scoured the coast for any signs of habitation.
Cuthwin took the boat closer to the shore afraid that they might miss one
of the small fishing villages and he asked Ethain to scan the bays ahead.

Ethain did as he was told and used his better eyesight to search the
land ahead of them but his thoughts were fixed on the knife by his side.
He had decided that if the first village they came across was deserted
then he need not do anything too hasty. If that were the case he would
have plenty of time to decide what to do but if he spotted an inhabited
village first then he would have to decide before the others saw it or,
more importantly, before the villagers saw them.

For the last three days he had struggled to find it within himself to either return to the fortress or to go on with Merdynn to the Causeway. He could do neither. He wanted no more part of it. Any lingering thoughts of loyalty to his friends or his people had been finally stripped away during the journey across the cold sea. He felt that perhaps he was capable of one last act of courage; the courage to kill his two companions and then run. He quailed at the thought of facing either Cuthwin or Merdynn and so he had decided that he would wait until their backs were turned. He thought that if could despatch them both while at sea then he could just take the boat into the shore and head deep into Wessex. Word would never reach Britain about Cei and the fortress. The Adren would soon overrun the Bretons and there would be no one left to reveal his part in it all. He could find refuge in some remote part of Wessex and, he thought, never have to face either the Adren or his conscience again. He would be safe at last. He refused to call it treachery. He reasoned that he was being true to himself so how could that be treachery? If by some misfortune he was discovered and brought before Arthur then he could just claim that the others died in the Shadow Lands and he had only just returned and was still too horrified by all that had happened to be able to act rationally. Had he been thinking more coherently then he might have asked himself how such a meeting with Arthur would end and what his actions might mean for the safety of Britain but he had left such thoughts of consequences far behind.

His heart jumped and adrenaline pumped through his body. He thought he had seen signs of a village a few miles ahead of them. He waited as the boat rose on the next wave and he casually studied the cove ahead. It was definitely a village but he could not be sure if its population had returned yet. He waited impatiently while the boat wallowed between two waves then stood up as it climbed the shallow trough.

'What is it? Do you see a fishing village?' Cuthwin asked. He did not bother to follow Ethain's gaze but studied his face instead.

Ethain's thoughts raced. 'Yes. A few miles further on. Definitely a fishing village and it looks like it's inhabited too.'

Merdynn clapped his chaffed hands in delight and performed a little jig which nearly sent him crashing overboard as he lost his balance on the rolling boat. Undeterred he beamed at the other two and congratulated them on their joint achievement.

'Will we sail in? Or row?' Ethain asked.

'We'll sail a bit closer then row in,' Cuthwin answered and grinned at him thinking that with luck they could be back at the Breton village within a day.

Ethain was thinking that if he could take the tiller and get Cuthwin to take down the sail then he would be behind both Merdynn and the Anglian.

'It'll be quicker if we beach the boat this side of the breakwater rather than have to sail around it and tack back,' Ethain suggested. He did not want them to get too close to the village as they might be spotted and it would be more difficult for him to hide the bodies. For a moment the realisation of what he was planning struck him with a cold shock. A voice inside quickly soothed him saying that these two and the Bretons were all going to be killed by the Adren anyway and that this was the only way he would survive the massacres ahead.

'Good plan,' Merdynn said and Ethain stared wildly at him thinking he had read his thoughts but Merdynn was pointing to a place where Cuthwin could land the boat a few hundred yards this side of the breakwater.

'I'll take the tiller, you get the sail,' Ethain said to Cuthwin.

'Look who's taking charge now that we're safely here!' Cuthwin laughed and stood to make room for Ethain.

Ethain edged past him as the boat rocked from side to side. Cuthwin started to furl the sail. He was facing away from Ethain as he worked the sail loose. Cuthwin's legs automatically absorbed the rolling of the boat and Ethain's fear increased as he realised that the young Anglian's natural balance on the boat would give him a distinct advantage if he didn't strike cleanly. Merdynn was kneeling in the water that slopped about the bottom of the boat as he struggled to free the oars. They both had their backs to Ethain and he drew the knife from his belt.

'So, what are you going to do now?' Merdynn asked, still on his knees and fighting the long oars.

'What?' Ethain stared at the old man's back, again shaken by his words.

'On to the Causeway with me or head back with Cuthwin?'

Ethain steadied his balance and took an uncertain step towards Cuthwin. 'Neither,' Ethain replied and rammed his knife upwards into Cuthwin's back.

Cuthwin fell forward into the sail and tore it free as he fell. The sail wrapped around him as he half turned to face his attacker. He tried to free his sword but the sail pinned his arm to his side. Ethain fell on him with a maddened howl and the knife flew back and forth in arcs of blood as he struck repeatedly at Cuthwin's chest. The canvas sail was drenched in blood and Cuthwin stared lifelessly at the sky.

Merdynn was scrambling to his feet and about to draw Leah's sword that still hung at his side. Ethain turned to him with tears running through the blood that had splashed his face. As Ethain came at him Merdynn saw that all sanity had left his eyes and then he felt the thump of the knife as it punctured his stomach. Ethain struck again and the pain registered in a piercing agony that doubled him over and paralysed his limbs as he slumped down over Cuthwin. With his hands clutched to the wounds in his stomach he stared up at Ethain and muttered through teeth clenched in pain, 'Cei? The others? Arthur? Why? Gods, why?'

But it was unlikely that Ethain even heard the questions. He was gibbering uncontrollably and the only words that Merdynn could make out were 'no more' repeated over and over. Suddenly Ethain flung the knife into the waves, grabbed Merdynn's staff and leapt from the boat. Merdynn could hear him thrashing towards the shore as he struggled to remain conscious.

He forced himself to his knees with both hands still tightly pressing his stomach and his face sliding along the rough wood of the boat. He looked at Cuthwin and knew immediately that the Anglian was dead. He cursed and slid his face upwards against the side of the rocking boat until he could see over the edge. Ethain was already nearing the shore and Merdynn stretched out a shaking hand towards him. He uttered a string of words in an ancient language that ended in a groan of pain as he felt consciousness slipping away. He forced himself to breathe deeply and the enveloping blackness abated for a moment. He took his eyes away from the figure crawling onto the shore on all fours and looked towards the breakwater that was only a hundred yards away and the village that lay just beyond the rocky outcrop. He knew he had to reach it. Tentatively he took one bloody hand away from his midriff and stretched out for one of the oars. Agony flashed through him and he cried out and collapsed once more into the swilling blood-mixed water at the bottom of the boat. He had to get to the village. He had to get help for Cei and the others. He tried to move again but his strength was draining rapidly.

A young girl from the village was standing on the breakwater watching the small boat bobbing on the waves when she heard a thin wail of rage and despair that caused the seagulls around her to take to the air in raucous alarm. She turned and fled back to the village.

Cei was in the hall with the wounded. He was sitting by Leah and holding her hand. On the other side of her sat Aelfhelm and Trevenna. They had been talking quietly when Leah stirred into wakefulness. Cei bent over her and spoke to her softly.

Leah turned her reddened eyes up to him. 'Is Herewulf safe?' she asked weakly.

Cei looked across to the other two and was about to reply when Leah spoke again.

'No. No, he's dead isn't he? They're all dead aren't they?'

Cei reached for a cup of water and brought it to her lips. Trevenna raised Leah's head a little from the pillow so that she could drink. More spilled from the corners of her mouth than she actually drank but she nodded gratefully. The fever seemed to have abated a little and she was lucid but the others had seen what was happening a dozen times before. Most of the warriors feared two kinds of death and this was one of them, a slow lingering death from an infected wound. The other kind was to die screaming on a battlefield for hours or days on end long after all help had left you behind. They held firmly to the belief that if you had to die then do it quickly and have done with it. Leah was not so lucky.

'Ethain? Cuthwin?' she asked.

'They've gone to get help from Wessex with Merdynn,' Trevenna answered.

'How long have they been gone?'

'Four days now. They'll be here soon.'

Leah turned her face to Cei and gripped his hand. 'Don't let them take me. And burn my body too, I don't want them bastards feeding on me.'

'Oh the Wessex lot aren't that bad. Ugly but not that bad.'

Leah smiled. 'Just you make sure, Cei. Promise me.'

Cei bowed his head and nodded.

'Promise me,' she insisted.

'I promise you, Leah. I promise to get you back to Wessex and I promise the Adren won't get you.'

The intensity left her pale blue eyes and she rested her head back down. 'Good,' she muttered faintly and drifted back down to her tortured dreams.

Cei put his head in his hands.

'She's not going to live is she?' Aelfhelm asked wearily.

'No,' Trevenna answered.

Aelfhelm sighed, depressed as much by Trevenna's lack of hope as he was by Leah's dying.

'Gods I'm tired. If I get back to Wessex I'm going to sleep for a month,' Aelfhelm said.

Cei looked up at him. 'You'll get back to Wessex. The boats will be here soon now. They're probably already on the way.' He stood up and looked around for the old woman who had been tending the wounded and called her across.

'I want you to sort the wounded into three groups. Those that can walk to the boats and those that need to be carried.'

'And the third?' she asked. Cei just looked at her and she dropped her eyes.

They left the hall and stood outside in the cold air. The drizzle and mist were clearing away. They all automatically glanced at the wall to make sure there were no signs of an imminent attack.

'Four days and no attacks,' Aelfhelm stated what they all knew and what none of them could explain. Cei led them towards the cliff edge and as he did so the last shreds of the mist blew past them like thin smoke. To the West the sun had already broken over the horizon and shafts of sunlight stretched across the coastline.

'Aelfhelm, build a beacon at the end of the headland and make sure it smokes. The Wessex boats may need guiding here,' Cei said.

Trevenna touched his arm and drew his attention to the wall. Cardell was signalling to them.

'One more day. A few more hours. That's all we need,' Cei said as they strode back to the wall.

When they were standing at the top of the wall they saw why Cardell had been signalling them. The sea mists had hid what the Adren had been working on for the last two days but now everyone on the wall could see across to the Adren lines. They all stared and no one said a word.

About a mile away they could see ten tall wooden towers. They were easily as high as the wall and each one seemed to have a platform or roof running around the base about ten-feet off the ground and some type of tunnel at the base of each tower which projected out in their direction. At the top of each tower was a drawbridge that was clearly intended to be lowered once the towers were near enough for them to bridge the ditch that ran in front of the wall. As they watched they saw figures entering each tunnel and swarming around the bases of the towers. They were gradually moving forwards. Behind the towers there were thousands of Adren lined in ranks and advancing slowly as the towers inched towards the fortress. Leading them was a blue robed figure on a white horse.

'Looks like some bastard got them organised,' Cei said and spat over the wall. He looked along the length of the parapet. All the Bretons were looking at him. Everyone knew that as soon as the towers reached the wall then dozens of Adren would spill out at ten different points to be followed by hundreds more and then by thousands. Cei looked back over what was left of the Breton village and on out over the sea towards Wessex. It was simply a matter of whether the boats or the towers arrived first. At the end of the headland the beacon sent smoke spiralling to the sky.

Merdynn surfaced to consciousness through waves of pain that knotted his stomach and brought beads of sweat to his lined forehead. He kept his eyes closed as he tried to quell the pain inside and listened to the sounds around him. The memory of the events on the boat flooded back to him and he opened his eyes in horror. He was in a darkened hut with a small fire burning in a hearth somewhere nearby. He could smell the scent of medicine leaves being boiled and he turned his head to one side. A man in his fifties was sitting on a low stool watching a young boy stir the pot over the fire. Neither had realised he was awake and the man spoke to the boy instructing him what to add next and how long to leave it boiling.

Merdynn tried to speak but no sound came out. He tried to lift himself off the bed but found that his arms did not have the strength and his stomach erupted in agony at the merest tightening of the muscles around it. He gasped in pain and frustration. The man appeared at his side.

'Are you awake?'

Merdynn nodded and opened his eyes once more. With a great effort and speaking slowly he asked the man where he was. The man had to bend close to his mouth to hear what he said.

'We found you in your boat against the breakwater. Your companion was beyond help and we're doing what we can for you. You're Merdynn, the counsellor, aren't you?'

'How long have I lain here?'

'A day or so. You should rest, your injury is very bad.'

'Listen. Bring your elders here. I came here for help. You must sail for the Breton coast. Adren are attacking there. The Anglian Warlord and the Bretons need you to take them back across the sea.' Merdynn closed his eyes in exhaustion. The man stayed at his bedside staring uncertainly at Merdynn who summoned his strength and said as forcibly as he could, 'Bring them now, fool! Every hour could cost them their lives!' The man was spurred to action more by the desperation in Merdynn's eyes than by his words.

'I'll fetch my brothers.'

'Not your brothers, fool, the elders!'

'The elders aren't in the village. There's only a few families here. The warlord's decree said that the people should be near Caer Sulis. Don't know why, not much of a place to be near if you ask me. He wants the fishing boats all gathered at the Haven. Don't know why he wants that either. He needs to explain things a bit more if you ask me.'

'I'm not bloody asking you!' Merdynn cried half rising in his bed before falling back with a grunt of pain.

'I'll fetch my brothers then,' the man said as he slowly stood up.

His brothers arrived shortly after and Merdynn painstakingly explained the situation to them. Whether it was by Cuthwin's skill, Merdynn's directions or just blind chance they had arrived at Morveren's village and they were her brothers who were gathered around Merdynn's bed. They were not convinced by his tale and Merdynn would have cursed and raged at them if he had anything of his old strength but he harboured what strength he had left and used it to patiently explain the situation again. The brothers still looked unconvinced and Merdynn finally threatened to curse all the men and women of the village so that no children would ever be born to them again.

The small group withdrew to discuss the matter. Most of the villagers had stayed at the Haven and were being trained for war so only a few had returned to the fishing village and they had been told to sail the boats around the Wessex peninsula to the Haven, not to some distant coastline. The old man lying on the cot certainly seemed to be Merdynn and none of them wanted to cross either him or the newly appointed Warlord of Britain. The old man appeared to be mortally wounded but, as one of the brothers pointed out, if he was Merdynn then who was to say if a knife wound could kill him or not, and even if he was dying he could still curse the village.

Morveren's brothers remembered Arthur coming to their village when they were young men and they had eventually heard the rumours about him and their mother so they had little love for the Wessex Warlord but they reasoned that if Arthur was to be the next king, as people were saying, then it would do them no harm at all to have rescued his sister and Cei from the Adren army. They decided to take one boat and sail for the Breton coast.

Merdynn insisted on accompanying them and they carried him out to the boat on the small cot he lay on and placed him below deck in a corner of the hold where their catch was usually kept. As they got under way Merdynn drew them a rough map of the Breton coast and told them what course to take before he subsided once again into unconsciousness.

The towers crept ever closer. As they neared Cei could see that the tunnel-like extrusions they had seen were acting as shelter for those that hauled the tall wooden structures. The roof flanging around the base provided cover for the Adren that were re-feeding the rounded trunks that the towers were rolling on. It may have taken the Adren three days to construct these siege towers but they had produced a faultless weapon.

Cei could see no way of stopping them. If they still had their horses and dozens of warriors then they could risk riding out to topple and fire them but with just the villagers and on foot it would only shorten the fight.

Cei had done what he could. He had smashed away the stone steps that led down from the wall so that the only way to get down now was to use one of the three ropes that hung from the parapet. Those of the injured that could be moved had been taken to the end of the headland where the steps descended to the harbour. The old healer woman had a sharp knife put to one side for those who could not be moved and the hall was ready to be burned should the Adren break through. Leah had regained consciousness once more but the others were on the wall and she had died alone and uncertain of what was happening around her.

The beacon was being fed by the remaining children and smoke still wrapped its way upward and trailed eastwards with the wind. Two watchers stood on the cliff looking out to sea waiting for the first sighting of the boats that would rescue them and as soon as they saw them all that remained of the Bretons would retreat back to the steps and down to the harbour. There they would defend the cliff path while the boats from Wessex lifted off the others. Aelfhelm had already agreed to take charge of a detail of ten Bretons who would act as the last defenders on either the wall or the steps when the boats arrived.

Everyone who could still fight was on the wall and they alternatively switched their gaze from the towers that crawled closer and the still empty sea behind them.

The towers were only five hundred yards away now and they could hear the chanting from the massed Adren ranks behind them. Cei and Trevenna stood together on the wall and they looked at each other.

'Now would be a good time to come up with a great plan,' Cei said lightly.

'Now would be a good time for Merdynn and Cuthwin to turn up with the Wessex boats,' she replied.

They both looked behind them and out to sea. There was no sign of the boats from Wessex.

'Well, the Adren will take the wall before the boats get here. It looks like we'll be defending the steps again but from below this time,' Cei said.

'It's over isn't it, Cei? This time there's no escape is there?'

'Merdynn will bring the boats here. We'll just have to defend the harbour. He's never let us down. Remember that time on the moors when we were lost in the mist wandering around with that cow we stole?'

'Borrowed you mean!'

They both laughed at the shared memory and those around them took heart from it. The towers were almost upon them and Cei issued his final commands for the last defence of the Breton fortress.

They brought Merdynn up on deck as the fishing boat rounded the headland and as he lay there he heard Morveren's brothers talking about the bodies of two children they had seen broken against the rocks at the base of the cliffs just above the waves that pounded in from the sea. He wondered if they were the bodies of Charljenka and Nialgrada the two young goat herders who they had come across at the abandoned village during their flight through the Shadow Lands. Perhaps, at the last moment, they had leapt to their deaths rather than face their soul stealers.

Two of the brothers lifted Merdynn on his cot and carried him up the steep steps to the top of the headland. The beacon had burned low but it still sent grey smoke billowing upwards and eastwards. It had served its purpose and guided them into the coastal Breton fortress but they were too late. The fortress had finally fallen and Merdynn's soul screamed in anguish that the day he had lost after being stabbed by Ethain had been the difference between saving Cei and the Bretons and their deaths at the hands of the Adren.

They raised him up so that he could see across the headland to the wall that had protected them all for so long. Above the edge of the wall he could see the tops of several tall wooden towers and knew how the Adren had finally broken through. The gates were torn from their iron brackets and lay askew to either side of the gaping entrance. Merdynn thought that they had been broken after the Adren had gotten in. The hall where the wounded had been tended was just a smoking ruin with only a few of its timber struts still standing upright. Merdynn wondered if Leah had died before they broke through.

The pain that consumed him seemed to subside as he imagined the pain of those who had died here during the last hours of their long defence. To have lasted the six months of winter only to have died hours from salvation struck him as cruel beyond fate, and the tears welled in his old eyes.

The brothers were searching among the ruins of the village and along the base of the wall but Merdynn knew they would find no one, either alive or dead. He could feel something inside him twist in despair that he should have failed them. He could not shake the image of Trevenna's turquoise blue eyes and Cei's easy smile and neither could he shake the certainty that he would never see either again. He tortured himself by trying to guess if they had fallen defending the wall or if Aelfhelm had tried to hold the wall while Cei and the others raced for the harbour, desperately trying to buy another hour or two from their destiny in the hope that he would return in time. All the long years he had lived and he was a too late by a few hours. He gripped the grass in his clenched fists as he dwelt on how his friends had died. Perhaps they had been separated from each other in their headlong race for the steps to the harbour and been cut down one by one. Perhaps they had died in desperate, small groups surrounded and overwhelmed by the enemy.

Morveren's brothers returned and shook their heads. They made to lift Merdynn and take him back to the boat but Merdynn directed them to the western side of the headland and asked to be placed there. At first they were unwilling to leave him and protested that he should return with them as there was nothing he could do here now. Merdynn let them insist then cajole and finally plead but when they were silent he just gave them a message to take to Arthur who would be at the Causeway.

'Just tell him that I did what I could and it wasn't enough. Arthur must stand against the Adren, he must stand against the tide. My task is unfinished and we shall not meet again. We died. We all died. Ethain betrayed us but the blame is mine. Tell Arthur to look for him. Arthur must find him. Now go.'

They left Merdynn leaning against a rock so that he faced the rising sun in the West. Seagulls effortlessly rode the currents along the cliff face below him. His sight gradually dimmed as despair and regret weighed down his soul. His hands opened lifelessly on either side, resting on the ground where the long tussock grass was tugged by the cold wind.

181

Chapter Eight

Yes, but can we trust him?' Lord Venning was pacing the small room without looking at Commander Kane who sat at a table near the fire.

'The alternative is Arthur and we both know we can trust him to do as he says and that course would only lead to complete disaster,' Kane replied.

He knew his Commander was right, that Arthur would lead the Cithol to disaster, but he was still fearful of the choices he had just made. The fire had been lit for the visitor who had just left and its flickering light caused their shadows to leap and stutter in the otherwise dark room. Commander Kane kept his eyes on Lord Venning as he paced back and forth.

'You know that Arthur and his savages won't keep the Adren at bay for long. And you know that Arthur would rather destroy the Veiled City than see it fall into the hands of his enemies.' Kane could see that Lord Venning was still unconvinced about the course they had chosen and he inwardly cursed him for his weakness. *It's too late now to have doubts you old fool*, he thought to himself.

'This is the only way that we can keep what has been ours ever since we made this our home. Any other course would have scattered us to the outside world to live among the barbarians and even that would have been short lived for the Adren will kill everyone who oppose them. This was the only way,' Kane said, trying to mollify the other's conscience.

Lord Venning remained silent as he crossed and re-crossed the small chamber. Kane wanted to scream at him to stand still but instead added gently, 'Any other choice would have condemned your people to death.'

Lord Venning finally stopped pacing and looked at Kane. 'I've condemned everyone outside the Winter Wood to certain death at the hands of the Adren.'

'Could you have saved them? No. But you could save your people and you have. Let the kings and chieftains of the savages worry about Britain. Your responsibility is to your people and what you've done tonight saves them from the savages' fate.'

'But can we trust *him* to keep his word to let us continue here as we always have?'

Kane thought he detected a whining quality to Lord Venning's voice and he worked hard to keep the sneer from his face.

'All he wants from us is our allegiance and the extra food we can produce to feed his armies. Which is the same as Arthur wanted. They're no different except that Arthur will lose. Why ally ourselves to the side doomed to defeat when for the same price we can ally ourselves to the victors?'

Lord Venning listened to his Commander and then he turned his back and stared at the hurtful glare of the fire. 'But is it the same price? I've betrayed Brunroth.'

'Nonsense. Arthur betrayed him when he sent him on that fool's errand to the Shadow Land City.'

'True. I was undecided until *he* told us that Brunroth had fallen on the Breton coast. While there was still a chance that he might have succeeded I would have stayed with his plan.'

Liar, Kane thought but said, 'Of course you would have but that hope is dead and Arthur is to blame. You owe him nothing. If, by some work of their gods, they manage to defeat the Adren then we are no worse off. We have what we've always had – the Veiled City. And if they are defeated, as they surely must be, then we have not stood in *his* way and the only change here will be to produce more food in the caverns for the Adren instead of the barbarians. Besides, according to our histories we have far more in common with the inhabitants of the Shadow Land City than we do with the savages that Arthur leads. They are our natural allies not the barbarians.'

Lord Venning nodded and sat down at the table. Kane studied his black eyes that were staring sightlessly at the table surface. He saw guilt and remorse in the expression opposite him and he despised the feebleness it demonstrated but he still needed Lord Venning to lead the Cithol. He may not command his respect but Lord Venning still commanded the respect of the Cithol Council so he decided to play to his Lord's vanity in an effort to bolster his self-confidence.

'What do the ancient histories say of *him* and the Shadow Land City?' Kane asked even though he knew the histories better than anyone other than Merdynn. Lord Venning steepled his fingers and began to speak.

'It is written...'

Pompous fool, thought Kane but he feigned a keen interest and nodded his head even as his thoughts turned elsewhere.

'...that those of the Shadow Land City escaped the end of the last Age the same way as we did and possess something like the power we have here, some legacy from the last age that, like us, they can maintain and use but not replicate. The outsiders used to travel to that city. Brunroth used to travel that way before the road was barred to them.' At the mention of Merdynn the Cithol Lord's eyes lost their focus and his head seemed to droop towards the table.

'Who closed the way East?' Kane prompted, irritated that his train of thought had been interrupted by Venning's falter.

'What? Oh, their ruler did but Brunroth always suspected that it was at the bidding of his new counsellor who had come out of the East. The last time I spoke to Brunroth in private he confided that he thought the counsellor had gradually taken control of the city. At first he only advised the ruler but as the generations passed and each ruler was replaced by the next he became more powerful until the city reached a point where the counsellor was the ruler. For decades the barbarians still had contact and trade with some of the lands between here and the Shadow Land City. Brunroth thought that when the counsellor took full control of the city he then brought across his Adren army from the Eastern Lands and one by one the other lands fell silent. But it happened over such a long time and so gradually that the rulers of Middangeard barely realised their world was becoming smaller and it was of no concern to us. But now, at long last, it is our turn.'

Kane had returned his attention to Lord Venning when he mentioned that Merdynn had spoken to him privately. 'So the counsellor who took control of the Shadow Land City centuries ago is the one who now leads the Adren?'

'Yes.'

'Then he is the same as, or the equivalent to, Brunroth?'

'Yes, though neither Brunroth nor I were sure of this. I am now.'

'I thought it was Brunroth when *he* came down the passageway. The same and yet somehow different, more powerful, more sure.'

'Lazure Ulan. The one from the East who commands the Shadow Land

City and the Adren army. The one who pledges we can stay in the Veiled City as long as we agree to supply his armies with food. The one who has conquered all the Shadow Lands from here to the distant East and who, thanks to us, will now defeat Arthur at the Causeway. And yet Merdynn suspects he is only an emissary from an even more powerful ruler in the distant east.' Lord Venning turned to face the fire again even though the bright flames hurt his eyes.

'You had no choice. You were wise to tell him of the ancient tunnel that runs under the Channel Marshes. Now he knows we are not his enemies and now he can destroy those that do stand against him. Arthur would have destroyed our city, *he* will protect it for it's part of the old world, the old world that *he* wants to recreate once more. A world with no place for Arthur and his peasants.'

'What have I done?' Lord Venning asked rising to his feet.

'Saved us and saved our city! You've secured a future unimaginable in its grandeur!' Kane answered and guided the Cithol Lord from the room and back to the path that led down to the Palace and the lake.

An hour later Seren and Terrill stood looking at each other in the glade where the tunnel opened up into the Winter Wood. The first slither of the sun had risen above the unseen western horizon and the woods were alive with the piping calls of the spring birdsong. The tops of the still bare trees were beginning to creak and crack at the first caress of the sun's warmth and the rushing chatter of the growing streams echoed throughout the Winter Wood but neither of them heard any of the woodland sounds. They just stared at each other.

It had been a steep climb up through the tunnels from Lord Venning's private council chamber and Seren was breathing heavily. Her breath clouded in the cold air and beads of sweat lined her forehead and tracked down across her temples as she rested with her hands on her knees. Terrill leant against a huge block of moss-pitted stone. He needed to steady himself, not from weariness or the cold that was beginning to make him shiver but from the shock of what they had heard only an hour ago.

There were very good reasons why he had been chosen to be the Captain of the Winter Wood and not least among them was his ability to assess

situations and make clear decisions when it was necessary but these traits
had temporarily abandoned him. He tried to gather his thoughts which
had become a confused jumble of random recollections. Too much had
happened too quickly for him to be able to untangle one reaction from
another. He felt Seren's hand on his arm and she beckoned him to follow
her further into the woods and away from the tunnel entrance.

He trailed after her along the lesser-used paths and all the time his
mind was in turmoil. Everything that he had taken as constant in his life
had been shattered and he was trying desperately to fit the pieces back
together again. He tried to recall the exact time when everything began
to unravel but could go no further back than the feast in Caer Sulis where
his senses had been assaulted to the point of nausea. Then his faith and
loyalties had been thrown into confusion by Seren's revelation that she
was carrying Arthur's child. He still felt revolted by the fact that Seren
had desecrated herself in such a way and he still felt that somehow he had
betrayed his Lord and his Commander by not taking the appalling news
to them immediately. Finally there was the conversation between Lord
Venning and Kane that they had just overheard. It was just too much for
him to be able to grasp.

He thought to himself that just a few months ago his life was so simple
and straightforward. The outsiders were where they belonged, outside
the Veiled City, and everything was as it should be. Since then it had all
gone quickly downhill until it reached a speed he could no longer match
and events were now turning in on themselves with consequences he
could no longer control or predict.

He realised they had stopped once again as Seren put both hands on
his shoulders.

'Calm yourself, Terrill, you need to calm yourself.'

He heard Seren's voice and she was relieved to see the wild stare leave
his eyes. He looked around but did not recognise his surroundings.

'Where are we?'

'Deep in the Winter Wood,' Seren replied, 'A secret place known only
to Brunroth and myself. We're safe here for now.'

She disappeared into a cave and Terrill took stock of his surroundings.
He thought he knew the Winter Wood better than anyone else but this
particular place looked entirely unfamiliar to him. Judging by the

terraced nature of the ground he guessed that he must be standing on a broad expanse of ancient stone steps. To his left a tall oak had thrust aside the buried stonework and he could see its still frozen roots trailing down the terracing before him. He shook his head and took a couple of deep breaths and his heart rate dropped as he forced himself to be calm.

He could see that Seren had not disappeared into a cave, at least not a natural cave. The entrance was arched and in one or two places he could see the fashioned stonework beneath the deep winter-stiff moss and sprouting fungi that covered the sides of what must have once been a wide doorway. He climbed up to the entrance and looked back through the wood. The rising sun was still hidden by the woods and would remain so for weeks but the brightness already stung his eyes. He turned his back on the West and followed after Seren.

He waited at the mouth of the cavern and stared into the darkness until his eyes adjusted to the more familiar dimness. He sensed that there was a large space before him and that there were rough steps leading downwards. He heard Seren moving about on the floor somewhere below him and gradually the darkness began to take on differing shades and shapes. He descended to where Seren was kneeling on the floor.

'What you doing? And what is this place?'

'I'm making a fire,' she answered and looked up at him sensing his puzzlement. 'Merdynn taught me how to.'

'Merdynn?'

'Brunroth. It's what the outsiders call him.'

'It's what Arthur calls him.'

'Yes,' she answered quietly.

She returned her attention to the fire and using a small bow looped around a trimmed piece of hard wood she resumed the rapid sawing motion until eventually a thin curl of smoke twisted upwards. She picked up the softer wooden base and gently tapped the embers onto some kindling. Bending lower she blew gently and a flame flickered briefly among the dried straw. She breathed on the embers again until the flame took and she gradually fed the fire with dry twigs and then larger pieces of wood. Once the fire was alight she went to one corner of the cavern and brought back two crudely fashioned stools, placing them by the fire. They both sat in silence for a while.

'What is this place, Seren?'

'Merdynn said it might have been a place of worship for the people who once lived here but how he knew that or what they worshipped he would not say. He did say that it was a new religion but then what is new to Merdynn may be ancient to us.'

Terrill looked around and saw that the ceiling of the cavern was hung with the roots from the trees above and that the stone walls were similarly cracked and trellised. There was an edging of stone around the walls at the height of the entrance and he guessed that the floor had given way a long time ago and they were standing in the cellars or basement of the ancient building.

'What are you going to do now?' she asked gently as she fed another log into the fire.

Terrill shook his head. 'I hardly know what's happened recently let alone know what I'm going to do next.'

'I'm not going back.'

'Back where?'

'To the city.'

'You must! Where will you go? You certainly can't stay here, not as you're... I mean considering that...'

'That I'm pregnant?'

'Yes.'

She heard the undertone of anger and disgust in that one word and frowned at him. 'Is it so hard for you to believe and accept that I laid with Arthur? That I love him?'

He turned away from her and she reached out a hand to place on his knee in an instinctive attempt to connect with the only friend that she had in the Veiled City. He swept her hand away and she saw the look of repugnance on his face. She felt her heart grow heavier. 'Terrill, I love Arthur. Whatever you think of that won't change either it or the fact that I carry his child.'

'Was it here? Did you meet him here secretly?'

'No! And why should that matter to you?'

'How could you? He's a barbarian, everything about him screams violence! You saw him at the council! I thought he was going to strike Lord Venning!'

'He was trying to spur us into the action we need to take! Besides, you thought he was right!'

'I thought the Adren were our enemy and that they would seek to destroy us too but I didn't know then that your father and Commander Kane were going to meet with, with *him*!'

'And you'd choose to deal with someone like that over Arthur!'

'You heard your father – *his* people are more like us than the outsiders are! The Britons are just savage barbarians!'

'How dare you! What gives you the right to condemn them like they were beneath us?'

'Because I saw them at that feast! They're no better than animals, they act just like animals. They disgust me. You saw them too! Can you imagine those scenes in the halls of the Veiled City?'

'They're different from us but that doesn't make them less than us! We can't begin to imagine how hard their lives are and it was a celebration! Just a celebration!'

'It was Arthur's wedding feast you stupid, foolish girl! He was marrying one of his own kind, another barbarian!'

Seren physically flinched at the words. Suddenly they were aware that they had both stood at some point in the argument and were now shouting into each other's faces. Terrill's own words sunk in and he realised what he had just said. He reached out a hand but it was her turn to swipe it angrily aside.

'So you think that we Cithol are decent, civilised people do you? After what you heard my father and Kane say, you still think we are the better people? Our Lord makes a deal with the leader of the Adren – that enlightened troop of learned troubadours who have been busy teaching the high arts to the villages of Middangeard, yes those Adren! A deal that condemns and betrays everyone but ourselves! And that's how we mighty Cithol show our decency and tender civilisation? Is it? Well? Is it? We're the barbarians!'

'You're upset, you don't mean that!'

'Of course I'm upset you fool! My father has just betrayed everyone in Britain and as if that wasn't enough he's condemned us along with every one of them!'

'No! He's saved us!'

'Oh Terrill, think about it. You know what the Adren have done and we now know what *he* wants. If the Cithol have any part to play in *his* plans then the best we can hope for is to be slaves. I'd rather die with Arthur and his warriors trying to stop that. At least I'd die among people who valued their freedom and didn't barter it away. At least then I could die with decency and not see my people enslaved. Lord Venning hasn't saved us, he's condemned us. Our only hope lay with Arthur and now that too is gone.' Seren finished quietly and sat back down.

She thought back to the shadow in the tunnel that had seemed to turn and look at them, realising now that it must have been the shadow of Lazure Ulan, and whatever else she might be conjecturing about, she was certain that the Adren Master was as evil as Merdynn was good. They had both sensed it and she could not understand why Terrill was arguing the case for Lord Venning and Commander Kane. She was at a loss to understand how either of them could have agreed a treaty with someone who felt so terribly wrong. She wondered what measure of desperation could have driven her father to deal with Lazure. She stared into the semi-darkness of their cavern and did not notice when Terrill too resumed his seat. She frowned as she asked herself the questions she had no answers for. Did they think that *he* would honour any agreement or treaty? Did they really think Lazure could bring back the wonders of the last Age and did they really want that? Was this the first meeting between Lazure and Lord Venning and if not then how many times had they met? Could Lazure, like Merdynn, wander the land unseen by his enemies? What was driving her father to betray Arthur and deal with the Adren Master?

Terrill watched her and wondered when it was that she had grown up and changed into the woman now sitting beside him. He was so used to the likeable but petulant and spoilt young girl that this new determined young woman, who held such twisted principles, was almost a stranger to him. For the first time he fully realised that Fin Seren was destined to be the next leader of the Cithol and for the first time he also sensed the mettle inside her that came with such a responsibility.

He mulled over her arguments and despite himself he found that he agreed with most of what she had said but he could not shake either his natural revulsion of the barbaric Britons or his innate loyalty to his masters who were, after all, the leaders of the Cithol. He was convinced that they would only do what was in the best interests of their people or at least what they thought was in the best interests of their people. He asked himself if they could be wrong. He was quite shocked to realise that Seren had raised points that led him to question the wisdom if not the motives of his leaders.

He turned to her and spoke quietly, 'If Lord Venning meant to betray Arthur why would he be sending him food and weapons?'

'I don't know. It's puzzling. Perhaps he's only just decided to turn his back on the Britons. Perhaps he's supporting both sides to keep his options open, but whatever his reasoning - there's only one side that can win now.'

'Did you know about this tunnel under the Causeway?'

Seren snorted dismissively, 'Until recently I didn't know about Caer Sulis, the Causeway or anything else outside the Winter Wood for that matter. I'm beginning to realise that I knew very little about anything of any importance. I'm certain that Arthur doesn't know about the tunnel.'

'They'll be slaughtered then, won't they?'

'Yes.' Seren spoke the word with such wretched despair that Terrill could not bear to look at her.

'Then we best hope that Lazure keeps his word with Lord Venning.'

'He won't! Surely we can warn Arthur somehow?' Seren said.

'How?'

'I don't know!'

'Well, we can't.'

'Then Merdynn!'

'But he's trapped or fallen somewhere on the Breton Coast, wherever that is.'

'Then we'll make for the Causeway and hope we are in time.'

'On foot! And in summer light?'

'We'll take one of the wagons used for carrying food to Caer Sulis!'

'*We*? You want me to go against Lord Venning and the Veiled City?'

Seren stared at Terrill incredulously. 'It's Lord Venning who's abandoned the Veiled City. Perhaps Arthur can save it. It's time to decide where your loyalties lie, Terrill. Are you loyal to Lord Venning or to the Cithol? Merdynn or Lazure Ulan? The Britons or the Adren? Make no mistake, these are the choices now.'

Terrill sat in the flickering light of the stone cellar with his head in his

hands Seren watched him, waiting to see which way he would choose.
Arthur's war band rode two or three abreast and the column of two
hundred and fifty warriors lined the Westway for half a mile as they
crossed the South Downs and cantered towards the Causeway but the
land was empty and there was no one to witness the sight of the southern
war bands riding to war.

The frozen ground had spilled the recent rains and melting snow
into fast flowing rills and turbulent streams that cut garrulously across
a landscape newly released from the silence of winter. The Westway
bridged the swollen rivers and followed the higher ground wherever
possible to avoid the perennial flooding of low-lying land and they made
good time on their journey from Caer Sulis.

Their shadows stretched out before them across the rolling grasslands
as the sun crept its way over the western horizon behind them. As they
approached the white cliffs they saw more and more makeshift huts and
roundhouses where the families of the Anglian war band had set up their
temporary home before moving on once again for the safety of Whitehorse
Hill. A few of the Anglians remained to tend to the livestock that had
already been loosed to pasture as best they could on the still frozen grass.
The Anglians had kept a small part of their herds on these pastures to
supply the warriors on the Causeway with fresh meat and milk. The mix
of cattle, sheep and goats stood in the cold light and waited patiently
for the last of the winter feed to be rolled out to them. They ignored the
horsemen and faced the West as if paying homage to the sunrise.

Despite the rising sun and the westerly wind it was a cold and bitter
dawn. The first hints of the coming summer were all around the riders
but they only served to emphasise how short a time they had before the
eastern armies unleashed their onslaught.

When Arthur reached the cliffs above the Causeway he saw that a
palisade had been built along the entire length of the headland. He reined
his horse in and surveyed the land below. The warriors fanned out to
either side of him along the cliff top. Although they could not hear it
from where they were a loud cheer went up from the eighty Anglian
and Wessex warriors who had guarded the Causeway during the dark
winter months when they saw Arthur's war band outlined on the sea
cliffs behind them.

The dawn sunlight had not yet reached the Causeway below them and the Channel Marshes were still in shadowed twilight and snaked by mists. The line of the elevated Causeway could be seen between the twisting curls of vapour as it led straight across the marshes and on to the distant shores that were already bathed in sunlight. Those on the cliff top could see the haze of smoke from thousands of fires that burned on the far land where the Adren waited. Arthur turned his horse and started down the steep path that led into the shadowed expanse below.

He had left the defence of the Causeway in the hands of Ruadan, his second in command, and Hengest who was the son of Aelfhelm and who led the Anglians in Cei's absence. As they made their way down the side of the towering white chalk cliffs they studied and approved of the defensive positions that had been added over the winter months. They hoped that they would be redundant for if they had to use them it would mean that the Causeway had fallen and they would be retreating back into the mainland. They knew that if they could not halt the Adren host at the Gates then they had little chance of holding them elsewhere.

Despite these sobering thoughts the warriors began the descent down the cliffs without heavy hearts. They were riding to battle and to defend their land and people. These were the reasons why they had chosen warriors' lives and many of them looked forward to the coming battle with a blend of anticipation, resolution and confidence.

Wide patches of snow still clung to the shadowed cliff face and the path was slippery with ice. The path downwards grew steeper so Arthur dismounted and those following him did likewise. It was clear that the defenders stationed at the Causeway had re-cut the path to make it steeper and the broader road to the North that had switched back and forth down the cliff side had been cut away altogether. Arthur thought bitterly that with the Eald and Branque villagers massacred there would no longer be any need for the broader road. Like his warriors he was relishing the prospect of fighting the enemy again after so many months of waiting.

When he reached the foot of the cliff he found that Ruadan and Hengest were waiting for him and he led his horse to one side to talk to them as Gwyna and the others passed by and on towards the Causeway Gates.

'You've made the path steeper,' he said, looking back up at the line of warriors still leading their horses down the track.

The other two exchanged a quick glance. They had not seen Arthur since he had passed through on his way back from the raid on the Shadow Lands but they had heard that since then he had slain the king, forged a treaty with the Uathach, married the daughter of one of the northern chieftains and attempted to bring the Cithol into the alliance against the Adren, yet the first thing he said to them concerned the steeper path. Ruadan smiled. He had known Arthur since the time when Merdynn had brought him to the Wessex war band as a young child and realised that the simple comment on the path said much about what had passed and what concerned the warlord now. Ruadan knew that Arthur would be content that he had done all that he could have done over the winter and while it remained to be seen if it would all come to fruition there was no more he could do to influence the events behind him. His place now was on the Causeway and he was only concerned with how the defences had been organised.

The much younger Hengest was far less familiar with Arthur and the lack of greeting coupled with the immediate focus on their defensive work stopped his many questions dead in their tracks.

'And we've taken away the roadway the villagers used,' Ruadan replied.

'I saw that. Good. Do you plan to stable the horses down at the Causeway or on the cliff top?' Arthur asked and started walking his horse across the flats towards the Gates as he spoke. Ruadan fell in step as he answered and Hengest followed behind feeling resentful that the months of backbreaking work digging up the frozen ground seemed to be going unacknowledged. He found himself wishing Cei was there.

'No Adren attacks yet?' Arthur asked turning slightly to put the question to Hengest.

'Not yet. We thought they were waiting for the dawn but...' he shrugged.

They passed a series of low wooden walls about three-feet high and spaced a hundred yards apart and to either side of the pathway that led from the foot of the cliffs to the Causeway. Arthur did not need to ask what they were for and he nodded his approval. To one side of the pathway ran a wide wooden trough fashioned from the lengths of hollowed-out tree trunks and raised above the flat ground by small stone cairns set every twenty-feet or so. The trough channelled fresh water down from the higher land to the Gates and they followed the line of the waterway as they made their way across the flat ground. The aqueduct was probably as old as the Causeway itself and despite numerous attempts to bore wells throughout the half-mile wide stretch of land below the cliffs it was still the only consistent source of fresh drinking water.

During heavy rains and the spring thaw the cliffs offered short-lived springs and waterfalls and the flat land was riddled by pools of water during the early dawn days but the summer sun would soon evaporate the standing water and parch the land turning the spiny grasses brown. It was about half a mile from the base of the cliffs to the beginning of the Causeway and another half a mile from there to the Gates. The marshes crept up to the shores and spread out to either side of the Causeway and for as far as the eye could see the marsh mists wreathed and coiled close to the ground and lingered over the waterways and stagnant pools. The distant seas would soon push their rising spring tides into the wetlands and the early spring sun would attempt to burn it away and the yearly battle would inevitably become obscured in the resulting fog.

Those familiar with the Causeway at this time of year knew the dense fogs of early spring were not far away with their impenetrable banks of ground-hugging clouds that would roll across the marshes and suffocate the senses. The Causeway ran a straight course so it was impossible to go astray but travellers in the marsh fogs would be desperate to reach either end and leave behind the eerie world where vision was limited to the few feet around them and the silence hung like a pestilence depriving them of the ability to see, hear or breathe easily. The sudden piercing cry of an unseen marsh creature had been known to send lone travellers blundering off the Causeway in panic. Those that managed to rein in their fear scrambled back up the banks onto the road once again and lived to tell of their nightmares but those that crashed further into the marshes never came back. The more superstitious of the Anglians said the piercing cries were the echoes of despair from those souls lost in the mists and anyone caught out in the Causeway fog and who heard those cries could not bring themselves to ridicule the superstition.

Eventually the scorching summer sun would burn away the mists and the shimmering air would become filled with the reek from rotting vegetation and the stench from stagnant pools. Clouds of ubiquitous mosquitoes would infest the entire heat-hazed valley and those stationed at the Gates dreaded the still days when the insects would torment them. Standing on the banked earth of the Causeway under the sweltering sun of high summer and swotting at the biting mosquitoes it was almost impossible to believe that only a few months previously it had been the cold, hateful wind that bit as it swept off the frozen marshes layering ice and deep rime over every exposed surface. In the unforgiving days of the dark winter depths it was just as hard to imagine the baked and cracked earth beneath the remorseless sun of summer. Whether an Adren army faced you or not the Causeway was not a good place to be stationed.

No one knew when or how exactly the Causeway had been built. Merdynn had insisted that it was not an undertaking of the previous Age but many doubted that such a feat could be achieved by people like themselves. It ran in an unwavering line for over twelve miles and was the only land link between Britain and the rest of Middangeard and the only way across the Channel Marshes that spread for hundreds of miles to either side of the raised earth bank. Whatever its origins may have been it had certainly stood there since before the Anglians had arrived from the lands north of the Belgae over a thousand years ago. For centuries it had served as a trading and migratory route but the kingdoms of Middangeard had fallen one by one until only the Britons remained and now the Causeway threatened to betray them as a means to convey the Adren to their shores.

As they crossed the flats Arthur sensed Hengest's resentment. He would normally have ignored it but he realised that with Cei in the Shadow Lands the young warrior carried the responsibilities of the Anglian Warlord and it was, after all, Arthur who had sent Cei east along with Hengest's father, Aelfhelm.

Hengest knew the real aim of Cei's journey to the East and how much depended upon it. He also knew how slim the chances of success were and how much slimmer the chances were of their returning home. He was content with that in the knowledge that his father and the others would have gone willingly on such a journey. They were all skilled and experienced warriors and he only wished he was with them, wherever they may be, but he knew his task was to hold the Causeway until Cei and his father destroyed the Adren's ability to feed their Shadow Land army. Perhaps, he thought, they had succeeded already and that soon the Adren supplies would be running low.

They passed another of the short wooden walls and his resentment towards Arthur's lack of praise for all their hard work returned. He also felt irked that Arthur had not felt it necessary to explain to either of them anything of what had happened over the winter in Caer Sulis but despite his antipathy towards Arthur he made sure his expression gave nothing away to him. He had seen his anger before and had no desire to ever see it turned towards himself.

Arthur glanced at the young warrior's hands as they approached the beginning of the Causeway. Despite the wrappings of cloth and thick mittens that Hengest would have worn during the winter Arthur could still see that his hands were raw and blistered. He stopped and inspected the defensive works that had been constructed at the end of the Causeway before it opened up onto the flat land below the cliffs.

'Did you have to light fires to thaw the earth before you could dig into it?' he asked the question directly to Hengest giving him the chance to explain what they had done and to give him an opportunity to sing his own praises. Hengest did not need a second invitation and spoke enthusiastically and at length about the winter work on the defences. Arthur did not listen to a word of it. He was not concerned about how the defences had been built only about how they would be employed. As they approached the narrow neck of land that led onto the Causeway Arthur could see that a wooden wall had built across its width. It stood fifteen-feet high with a ramp of earth that sloped up to a rough line about four-feet from the top. It was the last defensive position on the Causeway before it opened up onto the flat land below the cliffs. Two crudely fashioned but stout gates stood open in the centre where the sloping earth had been cut away to allow easy passage for horsemen and carts carrying supplies. Off to the right the aqueduct ran through a gap that had been cut into the wall of upright tree trunks.

Arthur climbed up the ramp and gazed out towards the Gates but the mist that hung above the marshes to either side had begun to wrap itself over the raised Causeway in drifting tendrils and he could no longer see the fortification that was only half a mile away. The other two had joined him and Arthur turned his attention back to the way they had come.

'So this is the last line of defence on the Causeway?' he asked them.

'Yes and between here and the Gates we've cut a gap in the Causeway. It's bridged at the moment but once the attack starts we can replace the bridge with simple planking that we can haul back once we've crossed it. If we have to cross it that is.' Hengest realised that he had perhaps been talking a bit too avidly about the plans for retreating and he glanced to Ruadan for reassurance before continuing, 'Then it's the shorter walls for alternated cover until the defences on the cliff path.'

They automatically looked to the white cliffs that towered above the gloomy mists spreading out across the flats. The cliffs seemed as if they were suspended above the ground and Arthur gazed for a moment at the borders of the land he had sworn to protect. The air was still and the mist clung damply to their clothing and chilled their faces. The occasional crying screech carried to them from the hidden marshes with a disembodied quality that made it impossible to tell which direction it had come from and leaving them with the feeling that they were intruders in an unfamiliar land.

'There's three more walls like this one between the Gates and the far end of the Causeway, with smaller barricades between each one of them,' Ruadan said, breaking the silence.

'The real defence will be at the Gates but we can make them pay for every yard they advance along the Causeway,' Hengest added.

'Good,' Arthur replied and walked back down the earth ramp to collect his horse.

When they arrived at the West Gate Arthur told Hengest to gather the warriors who had wintered on the Causeway as he wanted to tell them personally what had happened in Caer Sulis. The war band had ridden on ahead of them and were already inside the Gates greeting those they had not seen in months. When Arthur walked through the gateway the noise died down and the three hundred warriors of the southern tribes turned to him. He stood facing them in silence and then a great roar went up as they hailed the Warlord of Britain. The clamour was echoed beyond the walls as hundreds of marsh birds rose through the surrounding mists in fright at the sudden shouting.

The last of Hengest's short-lived resentment washed away as he stood proudly by the warlord and basked in the clamouring acclamation. When the shouting died down Arthur told Hengest to take thirty of the newly arrived warriors and replace those manning the defences further along the Causeway. As he rode off Arthur looked around the compound noting the changes and seeing how the recent arrivals were already familiarising themselves with their new surroundings. First on their agenda would be the kitchens, then where they were to sleep and finally where the smithy and weapon supplies were. Arthur glanced after the departing Hengest and Ruadan saw the look.

'He's a good man. Young but very talented at constructing defensive works.'

'You've both done an excellent job here,' Arthur replied, still studying the walls and the staked ground beneath them.

'Well, we'll soon see won't we?'

'Yes, we will.'

'I don't understand why they haven't already come at us.'

'The longer they wait the better. We'll be busy enough soon enough.'

'Perhaps Cei's already cut their supplies?'

'Perhaps. Perhaps they don't think there's any need to rush. Perhaps they don't think we'll hold them here for long. Perhaps they're just waiting for the fog.'

Hengest had spread the word for the Causeway warriors to gather for Arthur to speak to them and Arthur strode over to where they were congregating. Ruadan knew he would wait until Hengest brought back the others before he started to recount the events of winter so he gazed around the compound looking for Ceinwen. He saw her near the West Gate laughing with the usual group that now included Balor and Tamsyn and he made his way over to them. He could hear Balor's laugh from a hundred yards away. Balor was still laughing when he joined them.

'Ruadan!' Morgund shouted when he saw him and grasped his extended hand. Ceinwen turned quickly and threw her arms around him. The others grinned at them as the embrace continued. Ceinwen looked tiny beside her brother as he lifted her easily off her feet.

'That was Hengest haring off through the gates wasn't it?' Morgund asked.

'Certainly was. Why?' Tamsyn asked.

'Well, he'll be taking over Elwyn's responsibilities now won't he?' Morgund said and glanced across at Morveren with a smile. She looked back at him sourly.

Tamsyn watched the interchange. 'What? Are you and Elwyn together now?' she asked the blushing Morveren.

'No! Don't take any notice of this idiot,' she replied quickly, gesturing to Morgund.

'I just meant that Hengest's going to take charge of the Anglians from Caer Sulis, Elwyn's lot. I didn't mean to imply that anything was going on between our Morveren and the straw head. But I like the way your minds work,' he finished grinning at Morveren and Tamsyn.

'Bit young to be commanding the Anglians isn't he?' Ceinwen asked.

'You call thirty-odd young? Oh, I see, I suppose you would,' Tamsyn said and put a hand to her back as she bent her tall, strongly built frame and took a few faltering steps forward. Like Morgund her dark limbs were muscled and well toned and seeing her feign the frailty of old age made the others laugh. Ceinwen swore at her and despite the obvious mismatch in their respective strengths she landed a firm kick on her backside.

Ruadan turned to Balor but his beady blue eyes were watching Tamsyn rub her backside and so he said to no one in particular, 'I see nothing whatsoever has changed in the least bit.'

Tamsyn led them off to show them properly around the new fortifications but in the backs of each of their minds was the thought that things had indeed changed. Ceinwen's thoughts inevitably turned to her family while the others considered their own losses: Tamsyn had lost her brother, Talan. Elowen and Tomas lay dead in the Belgae villages. Mar'h was back in Caer Sulis with a crippled arm and Ethain and Trevenna were travelling deep into the Shadow Lands. They were conscious that already there were fewer of them to stand around and laugh with each other. None of them wanted to contemplate who among them might not live to take the Westway back home.

Once Arthur had addressed those who had wintered at the Gates he met up with Hengest and Ruadan again. He wanted to see the changes they had made to the Gates and the defences that had been built along the length of the Causeway. Ruadan quietly told Hengest to leave out the mechanics of how they had achieved things and concentrate instead on what was the purpose of each of the works.

Inside the compound of the Gates a second smaller wall had been constructed that paralleled the higher East, North and South walls before funnelling back to the gate they had entered by. There was a gap of over thirty-feet between the two walls and most of that ground was already prepared for the sharpened stakes. Ruadan led the way to the South side of this inner wall where the gate had been placed and they walked around the perimeter until they came to the East Gate. The outer walls stood between twenty and thirty-feet high and Arthur could see that firing slits had been cut every two yards along the base of the wall facing the Causeway.

As they approached the East Gate Arthur looked up at a wooden scaffolding structure that had been erected above the gateway. He gestured towards it and Hengest grinned.

'I based it upon the designs of the crossbows that the Cithol delivered to us.'

'You've already received supplies from the Cithol?' Arthur asked.

'Oh yes, food, crossbows and bolts. Strange lot though. They arrived and unloaded their carts then turned around and left. Hardly said a word to anyone and they always had their hoods close about their faces too. They caused quite a stir so it's as well that you sent us warning of their arrival,' Ruadan answered.

'Will they be sending us people to help with the defence?' Hengest asked, momentarily sidetracked from the desire to explain his invention that was poised above the East Gate.

'Perhaps. Tell me what this is.'

Hengest led them up the ladder to the platform that ran around the inside of the walls.

'I took the principles of the Cithol crossbow and, well, made it bigger really. Merdynn talked to me about something like this a few years ago but I couldn't see how it would work until I saw the Cithol weapons. It's like a huge crossbow but with a few extras too.'

'I saw something similar out on the flats,' Arthur said, remembering a strange wooden frame that stood near the last wall.

'Yes, we'll be bringing that up here soon – I just need to finish ranging it on the flats first. It can hurl a boulder up to two hundred yards and with good accuracy too.'

'Is this what this does then?'

'Same principle with winches, gears and rope but this one fires more directly – like a crossbow but the bolt is the size of a log and we can put some effective attachments on it too.'

'Can you aim it?'

'It's fixed on the Causeway but it can be elevated and lowered to fire upon different points between here and the next wall – about two hundred yards away.'

Arthur examined the contraption while Hengest looked on proudly. Bracketed planks either side of the central groove provided cover for those working the mechanism.

'And it takes three people to fire it?' Arthur asked.

'Yes, that's right. One either side to work the gearing to bring back the rope and the firing block which catches here,' Hengest leant across to point to the place he meant and Ruadan gave him a warning cough. 'And one to load and release it,' he finished quickly.

'You have boulders stockpiled for the other one? And logs or whatever it is you fire from this one?'

'Yes, most of it is still on the flats.'

'Good. Bring them up as soon as possible. Ruadan was right. You have a gift for this kind of defence. If these work then they'll slaughter the Adren.'

'Don't worry, they work. I've tested them already.'

'Let's just hope the Adren don't have anything similar,' Ruadan added.

'Even if they do at least we have strong walls to protect us,' Hengest replied.

Arthur nodded and looked out to the Causeway. Almost immediately in front of the gate the Causeway had been cut away to leave a gap of fifty-feet that was spanned by a retractable bridge. Water from the marshes swirled about the muddy ground below the bridge. A lone figure stood on the far side looking out over the mists to the North. Arthur recognised the long, red hair.

'I'll ride to the watch tower at the far end of the Causeway and look at the defences between here and there. Hengest, finish ranging your new weapon and bring up all the stockpiles from the flats. Ruadan, I want every defensive point on this Causeway manned constantly from now on.'

Arthur was about to leave the wall when he turned back and peered into the mists either side of the gap in front of the gates.

'Did you build the walkways to provide fire positions on the gap?'

Ruadan looked at Hengest before replying. 'No, we couldn't. The sands are unbelievably treacherous. Everything we laid down just sank under its own weight.'

'Even bushels bundled together?'

Ruadan shrugged, 'We tried that but as soon as anyone attempted to walk on them they too started to get sucked under.'

'Good.'

'Good?' Hengest asked incredulously.

'Yes, good.'

'I had to be dragged out with ropes twice!' Hengest spluttered.

'You lived. If you couldn't build walkways then neither can they. And that means you can live longer.'

Arthur left them to their tasks and collected his and Gwyna's horses before riding out the East Gate to meet his new wife.

They rode the two hundred yards to the next wall and ditch in silence. Arthur spent a few minutes talking to those stationed there before they resumed their journey along the Causeway. Gwyna guided her horse across to Arthur's until their knees were close enough to occasionally touch. Their pace was unhurried and the mists closed around them until it seemed that the whole world only consisted of the Causeway just before them and just behind them. They could feel the moisture in the air on their faces as they gently made their way forward. Somewhere overhead and off to their left they heard the slow beating of wings as a flight of geese unerringly sought their home through the marsh mists.

'It's so peaceful,' Gwyna said quietly, almost more to herself than to Arthur. He looked at her face and she felt his eyes on her but she gazed straight ahead. She had changed back into her war gear before leaving Caer Sulis and she looked to Arthur once more like the wild Uathach girl he had met near the slaughtered Belgae villages. The harshness of the winter she had spent in the Shadow Lands had left its evidence in the lines on her face but the gaunt hue of hunger had left her cheeks and she looked well and healthy once more. From the way she held the reins he could tell that her shoulder was as good as healed and he attributed that to her youth. The arrow wound he had received at Branque still ached and the damp air of the marshes seemed to be making it worse. He was easily old enough to be her father and their respective recoveries showed that as clearly as any other indicator. She finally returned his gaze and smiled at him.

'It is,' he said.

'What?'

'Peaceful.'

'Oh. Yes. It's hard to imagine the blood that will be spilt here soon.'

'Soon it will be hard to imagine peace.' As Arthur spoke an unbidden image of Fin Seren in the Winter Garden came back to him. He tried to dispel it but his thoughts turned back to the time just before Ablach entered the Great Hall at Caer Sulis. For a moment then he had considered abandoning everything just to be with her. To be with Seren and to be at peace. Such a decision would probably have alienated the Cithol as potential allies and certainly would have wrecked any chance of an alliance with the Uathach yet still he had considered it. He had chosen to agree to Ablach's offer of the marriage to his daughter because it increased the chances of defending Britain successfully but even now there were no guarantees that either the Uathach or the Cithol would stand with the southern tribes.

Gwyna felt him distancing himself once more from her and mistook the silence.

'I knew nothing about Mador's challenge back at the feast, Arthur.'

'I know. Your father planned it.'

'Then he was foolish.'

'He was,' Arthur said then looked directly at her, 'Will he come to the Causeway with his warriors?'

Gwyna turned to look out towards the white blanket that shrouded the marshes debating what to tell him. Wisely she decided to tell the truth.

'I don't know. I think he's unsure what best serves his purposes but he would be a fool if he thinks he can stand alone against the Adren.'

'And we've already agreed he's a fool.'

'His ambitions aren't mine anymore. Mine changed when I was wed to you. Now mine are the same as yours.'

Another defensive wall was materialising from the mists ahead of them and they both stopped their horses to finish the conversation in private.

'And what are my ambitions?' Arthur asked, his gray eyes staring at her.

'To defeat the Adren and to unify the tribes of Britain,' she answered holding his stare and then added, 'And then to rule it all.'

He smiled at her and turned his horse to continue along the Causeway.

Chapter Nine

Seren paced the cavern. Terrill had left several hours before with the promise to bring back food and warmer clothing. He had left without resolving the conflicting loyalties he was torn by and Seren was deeply worried that he might go to Lord Venning or Commander Kane and tell them that they had overheard the meeting with Lazure Ulan. She knew that Terrill would only be loyal to her to a certain extent and she feared that his years of obedience to his Lord would ultimately overrule any allegiance he felt towards her. He had a strong sense of loyalty but that sense was defined more by the custom and dictate of others than it was by himself. Now that his personal definitions of loyalty were in contradiction to those he had previously followed he had to decide for himself which he should adhere to, and Seren feared he did not have the strength to overcome the simple rules he had always lived by.

She had already decided that she had to face her father. She had to tell him that she carried Arthur's child and she felt she had to confront him about why he had decided to support Lazure, but more important than either of these dreaded tasks she first had to warn Arthur somehow of the tunnel that would lead the Adren under the Gates. If Arthur and the Britons died on the Causeway then everything else would be pointless. It would mean going against her father, something Terrill was plainly unwilling to do, but she was convinced her father was wrong. She was convinced that only Arthur could preserve the Veiled City in the face of the Adren onslaught and that Lazure had no intention of honouring his promise to let the Cithol live in peace. It was not a light matter to go against Lord Venning but she only had to remember how she had felt in the tunnels when the shadow of Lazure had turned towards them to know instinctively that she was right.

She suddenly stopped her pacing as it struck her that her father must also feel he was instinctively right about his deal with Lazure. Perhaps a strong conviction in one's own instincts ran in the family; convictions that were strong enough to stake your peoples' entire future on. It occurred to her that this was what it meant to lead a people. In time it would be her convictions and strength, her will, that would lead the Cithol. The prospect daunted her and she suddenly felt very young and alone but at the same time her sense of outrage at her father's betrayal grew and strengthened. She realised that it was Arthur's implacable will that would lead the Britons into war against the Adren and she acknowledged that she lacked the ability to do likewise with her own people but she knew what was right and what was wrong, and she was convinced that dealing with Lazure was utterly wrong.

The fire was dying down so she fetched another armful of logs from the pile that had been stacked against one wall of the underground chamber and placed a couple on the fire. She stood the others upright as close to the flames as she could and watched as the moisture began to sizzle and fizz from them. Her stomach rumbled as if echoing the drying logs and she clasped her arms tightly about herself. She was hungry and thirsty, and despite the fire she was cold too. In their flight from the Veiled City neither she nor Terrill had stopped to equip themselves for the world above. What they had overheard at the meeting between Lord Venning and Lazure had made them both feel like outlaws and they had acted instinctively like fugitives and ran from the place of the crime.

Seren sat as close to the fire as she could and extended her hands over the flames thinking bitterly that it was her father and Kane who were the criminals not her or Terrill. For the first time since returning to the Veiled City she had nothing to do but wait and her thoughts inevitably turned once more to her own misery. She wished that Merdynn would magically appear before her and explain how everything had so suddenly gone wrong and then, somehow, make it right again. She relived her encounters with Arthur and the disastrous sequence of events that had unfolded since she travelled to Caer Sulis. Tears slipped down her cheeks and she absently wondered how she had any left to cry. A stupor crept over her and without realising it she sat staring at her memories as the hours were silently stolen from her. The fire crackled, burnt and finally died unheeded.

She had no idea that a figure stood by the entrance above her until he addressed her. She leapt to her feet and nearly stumbled as her numb legs threatened to betray her balance. She thought wildly that perhaps Merdynn had answered her earlier prayers but then the voice spoke again.

'Fin Seren, you are to come back with us to the Veiled City.'

The figure was outlined against the light of the entrance and she could not see who it was but the voice was unmistakable. It was Commander Kane and she automatically looked for a way to escape, but she knew the entrance was also the only exit and so she turned to face him.

'You have no authority over me,' she replied with surprising resolve.

'You have broken the laws of the city and I am bound to enforce those laws but it is your father, Lord Venning, who demands your presence.'

She stared up at the Commander realising that Terrill must have told them everything and then led them to her hiding place. Cursing silently to herself she crossed the cavern and climbed up to the doorway.

Commander Kane stood blocking the entrance and Seren had to stop a step or two below him.

'And what laws, exactly, have I broken?' As she spoke she looked up at him and she could now see the self-satisfied expression on his face as his gaze dropped to her abdomen. For a moment she was on the verge of striking him but she mastered her sudden anger and climbed the last steps forcing Kane to step aside.

The light outside already seemed brighter and she had to draw her hood over her head to shield her eyes. Behind her Commander Kane mistook her action and laughed derisively. 'Well might you hide your face, girl.'

Seren spun around to face him, 'I have nothing to hide and nothing to be ashamed of, unlike you.'

A flash of hatred crossed Kane's expression before his insolent smile spread once more into place and he extended his hand to suggest that she walk in front of him. She looked around at the ten guards and saw Terrill's face among them. He could not meet her eyes and he looked as miserable as she felt.

'So many brave guards for one girl? No wonder you won't face the Adren or stand against their master.'

'That's quite enough. Now move,' Kane replied as if he was admonishing a small child.

'You know that from now on the names Kane and Cithol will mean traitor to the people of Britain?'

Kane's contemptuous sneer slipped immediately from his face and he snarled at her, 'Traitor to the people of Britain? You mean those barbaric peasants scratching at the earth and squabbling among each other? That noble race of lice ridden rats? What should I care for the folly of savages?' And his eyes once more dropped to her lower stomach leaving her in no doubt what he meant.

'They're standing in front of us, fighting to protect us and you take the opportunity to stab them while their backs are turned. Noble Commander Kane! How your name will ring through the histories!'

Kane's temper threatened to break and he shoved her viciously forward. She stumbled to one knee and Kane raised his hand to strike her but Terrill stepped in quickly placing himself between them and helping her to her feet. She shrugged herself free from his grip and to his horror she turned and spat on him.

'You're the same as him, he echoes your words. Do they still sound as pretty to you?'

Seren was led away by the others leaving Terrill to stare after her appalled at what he had done.

The journey back to the Veiled City was hurried and silent. Commander Kane had quickly regained his composure while Seren, flanked by the city guards, seethed in silent anger. Had she been more aware of those around her she would have realised that the guards were distinctly uncomfortable about having to escort the Cithol Lord's daughter against her will but she walked with head bowed and her hood pulled tightly around her face and she saw nothing of their discomfort.

The Winter Wood, when it was shrouded in darkness, was as much a home to her as the city itself but with the rising of the sun it had become an unfamiliar and hostile environment. The buried ruins of a previous age became more noticeable in the spring light and seemed to her to be an ugly scar that covered the entire forest floor, visible in relief and evident wherever one looked. The soft calling of owls as they hunted for winter prey had been replaced by the harsh chatter of starlings and sparrows and the cold air was filled with the raucous cries of skirmishing crows as they noisily acclaimed their return to their summer territories. Her woods were coming alive with the racket of alien invaders and she resented the intrusion.

The pathway was muddy and cloying as she trudged along it. Even the trees were showing the first signs of surrendering their uncluttered elegance and sharply defined beauty as buds of green spread across their limbs like an infestation. She longed for the deep stillness of the dark months and ached for the joy that she had felt in the Winter Garden with the snow and ice surrounding her and the hard stars slowly wheeling over the bare branches of the stark trees. She drew her light cloak more tightly about her and hurried on between her guards as quickly as she could.

Just when Seren was sure they were going to make for the main entrance in the centre of the Winter Garden Kane barked out an order and they took a narrower path that led to one of the less frequented entrances. She recognised it as the one that she and Terrill had fled from after hearing about the deal with Lazure.

Kane led them downwards until they reached the far end of the tunnel where it opened up onto the valley of the Veiled City and where Lord Venning's smaller council chambers were. Kane took Seren by the arm and steered her into the house and up to a small, windowless room that was furnished only with a low bed and a small table.

She looked around the bare room as the door closed behind her. She heard a bolt slide into place as she was locked in. The room that she and Terrill had made their escape from was just across the corridor and she smiled humourlessly at the irony. She assumed that the passageway leading into the other room would be blocked up by now and that a guard would be standing outside her door in case anyone tried to see her or in case she tried anything as futile and foolish as trying to break down the door.

She sat on the edge of the bed and chided herself on her immediate thoughts about how uncomfortable it felt. She poured herself a cup of water from the stone jar on the table and hungrily attacked the bread that had been left on the plate beside it thinking that her privileged life as the daughter of Lord Venning was well and truly behind her. Once she had chewed her way through the heavy bread she lay back on the bed and wondered idly how much her father knew about her imprisonment and how long she would have to wait to face his wrath and that of the council.

Her thoughts turned to what Lazure had said about Merdynn having fallen on the Breton coast but she dismissed the prospect as too unlikely thinking that Merdynn would never be trapped by the likes of Lazure; he was far too old and far too cunning for that. She speculated that perhaps Lazure had only said that to tip her father's allegiance towards him and away from Merdynn. She made a point to remember to put that obvious fact to her father when he eventually called for her but, try as she might, she was unable to dismiss the implications of her father revealing the information about the tunnel under the Causeway. She felt a tightening knot of anxiety and frustration that she was unable to get this news to Arthur. She prayed silently that the tunnel had collapsed entirely some time over the ages since it was built. She tried to comfort herself with the thought that the tunnel must at least be in a serious state of disrepair and would require months of work before Lazure could use it, but still the suspicion that every hour was crucial fretted away at her and it was a long time before she finally drifted into a fitful sleep where she dreamed that Merdynn had died alone on a cold headland far from home.

Arthur awoke from a similar dream and lay where he was staring up at the canvas roof of his sleeping quarters. He tried to dismiss it as just a dream but it contained too many details and the events he had seen were too consistent and too sequential for it to be easily waved aside as just a dream. He looked across at Gwyna who lay asleep beside him and he studied her face letting the fabric of the dream fray and drift apart until only one or two images remained. She appeared to be frowning in her sleep and her eyes were flicking back and forth beneath her closed eyelids as if she too were dreaming. He had been surprised by her honesty about her ambitions when they had talked on the Causeway and he felt that perhaps up until that point he had misjudged her.

Casting aside the furs that were still necessary to keep out the cold he climbed up off the floor and started to strap on his battle gear. Gwyna, now awake, lay there and watched him as he immersed his head in a bucket of cold water. He wiped the water from his eyes and saw her staring at him. 'You were dreaming.'

'Was I? I never remember them,' she replied, then cast aside the blankets covering her and added, 'Come back to bed.'

He smiled at her naked invitation and threw a pile of clothes at her.

'Get dressed. I want you at the war council and I want you to suggest that we put kegs of oil at every defensive wall along the Causeway.'

'Why?'

'So that we can set the walls alight to buy us time as we retreat to the next wall.'

'I realise that but why ask me to suggest it?'

'I need the others to trust and respect you.'

Gwyna paused as she was dressing, 'I'm one of the 'Uathach', they'll never trust me.'

'You've made a habit of trying to kill me. That's why they don't trust you.'

'You weren't complaining a few hours ago,' she pointed out with a smile.

'And I'm not complaining now.'

As Arthur left the tent Gwyna smiled to herself and hurried to buckle her sword on and follow after Arthur. When she stepped outside their makeshift quarters she was momentarily disoriented. A dense fog had descended while they slept and she could barely see the walls of the compound. When she caught up with him he was already with a group who were leaning over a map of the Causeway defences that was spread across a table. Their breaths were clouding over their heads as they spoke and seemed to add to the pervading fog. They shifted to make room for her and she glanced around at them trying to remember who was who. She recognised the shortest of them with the close-cropped hair and iron-grey beard as the Mercian Warlord, Gereint, and guessed that the younger man standing by his side was his brother Glore. She had already met Ruadan, Arthur's second-in-command, and Hengest who was now the Anglian leader and she recognised the man next to him, Elwyn, whom she recognised from the Shadow Lands. There were two each from Mercia, Anglia and Wessex and she wondered awkwardly whether she had any place at this war council.

Arthur was pointing to the crude map and making it clear how he expected the Causeway to be defended. There were few questions and no mention of either the Uathach or the Cithol joining them. When Arthur spoke about defending the wooden walls that were spaced along the Causeway Gwyna added the suggestion about the kegs of oil and Hengest nodded and said that he would see to it.

When Arthur finished he looked at the commanders and asked if there was anything else. Ruadan pointed out that the Adren seemed to have given up on an attempt to build a parallel Causeway about a mile to the North. No one doubted that they had the manpower to eventually achieve such a feat but it would take months if not years and clearly the Adren had no intention of waiting that long.

Arthur ended the council and the others left to relay the respective tasks to their warriors. Arthur remained standing where he was and staring at the map that depicted the Causeway defences. Gwyna watched him for a minute or two before speaking. 'Can we hold them here?'

Arthur looked up at her and replied simply, 'We have to hold them here.'

'What, forever?'

'No, just until they're all dead,' he replied smiling at her.

'Arthur, I was in the Shadow Lands. I saw how many there were of them. There's less than three hundred and fifty of us and there must be twenty to thirty thousand of them. I saw what happened to the Belgae. How long do you think we can hold them here?'

'Long enough for Cei and Merdynn to destroy their supplies. Then the size of their army will be their undoing.'

'But what if they fail? What if they've failed already? What do we do then?'

No one had so far dared to suggest to Arthur that his sister and closest friends had already died and that the venture east might have failed and Gwyna recoiled at the venom in Arthur's reply.

'Whether they're alive or dead, whether they succeed or fail, the Adren are here now before us. I want to see these marshes drenched in their blood. For every mile they advance I want to see a thousand of their corpses left behind. And if they cross the Causeway into Britain then I'll hunt them down and kill each one of them. And when I've killed all their soldiers I will seek out wherever it is they call home. And I will slaughter their families and children. I will annihilate their entire race and that destruction will begin here on this Causeway today!'

He turned and strode off towards the East Gate leaving her standing by the table. She was shocked by the pure hatred and cold rage she had just witnessed. For a moment she had been convinced he was about to strike her and her hands shook as she folded the map berating herself for having courted Arthur's anger. She looked around the compound trying to find a familiar face but the fog had thickened even further and the few warriors that she could make out were only vague figures and she recognised none of them. With most of the warriors spread out along the Causeway the Gates seemed half-deserted and eerily quiet. She stood holding the folded map limply in one hand and feeling heavy hearted. It was not so long ago that she would have counted every single person on the Causeway as a bitter enemy and while they were no longer enemies they certainly were not her friends and she knew the reverse was true too. She put the map down and leant against the edge of the table with her arms folded across her chest and watched as a group of Mercian warriors appeared out of the fog some distance away. They were heading towards her but in the few seconds before they became more distinct she thought they looked like marsh wraiths and she wondered how many more ghosts would be left by the coming war. One of them called out something to her but she could not understand the accent.

'What?'

'Where's the rest of Ablach's bastards?'

She stared at the bearded Mercian warrior who had asked the question but said nothing in reply and they passed by without stopping. One of them made some suggestion about Ablach just sending some Uathach girls for their entertainment and their laughter faded as the fog closed about them once more. Gwyna stared after them stony-faced before striding off towards the blacksmiths to sharpen the edge on her sword.

Arthur walked the length of the Causeway stopping at each manned defensive position to talk to the warriors stationed there. The main topic of conversation seemed to revolve around why the Adren had not yet attacked. A popular theory, particularly among the Anglians, was that Cei and Merdynn might have already cut their supplies and the Adren army was already in disarray. Others thought that they were determined to build their own road across the marshes and so bypass the Britons' defences altogether. Many of the defenders asked Arthur what he thought the Adren were waiting for and he just gestured around them at the dense fog that had cut visibility down to about thirty yards. He was partly correct, the Adren were waiting for two things; the spring fogs and Lazure Ulan. The mists curling above the waterways of the marshes had already thickened and spread with the rising of the sun and Lazure had just returned from the Breton coast.

When Arthur reached the watchtower at the far end of the Causeway he saw that the defences were already garrisoned by most of the warriors who had travelled into the Shadow Lands with him. He had told Ruadan to organise it that way so that the first to face the Adren would be the ones who had already fought against them. The defences consisted of a single wall, fifteen-feet high, and a central tower that stood a further ten-feet above the wall. The tower's upper reaches were partially obscured by the fog that lay clamped around them in the still, cold air and the two flags of Wessex and Anglia that Arthur knew were raised from the top of the tower were lost in the whiteness.

There were no shelters built here and most of the warriors were standing around the fires that burned brightly at the base of the wall. Even the glow from the fires failed to penetrate the mists and Arthur had not seen them until he was almost upon the outpost.

Arthur could sense the nervous boredom of the warriors as he joined them by the fires. He looked around to see who was where and saw Morgund chatting to Cael who was, unsurprisingly, slowly turning some cooked meat over one of the fires. Ceinwen was off to one side and laughing with Morveren as she checked the shoes on her borrowed Anglian horse. Arthur had previously decided that Morveren would act as the relay messenger between the different groups strung out along the Causeway. Balor and Tamsyn were up on the wall hotly debating the advantages and disadvantages of using a heavy axe in battle. Elwyn was up in the watchtower with Berwyn and Sacwulf, the two Anglians who had been rescued from the Belgae villages.

The talk and silences of those around Arthur all added to the familiar atmosphere generated by warriors who knew that they would soon be involved in the frantic uncertainty of battle but not knowing when exactly that would be. They were bored and yet also on edge with anticipation but he sensed no more fear than was usual before the fighting started.

Some of them were going through their pre-battle routines; sharpening weapons on small whetstones, testing the string on their bows, re-checking to make sure a good-fortune charm was secured in a pocket. Everyone had their own way of preparing themselves for battle. He was surrounded by experienced warriors who knew what to do and when to do it. He felt proud of those around him and they in turn felt proud to be in the first line of defence against the Adren and just as he strolled to the nearest fire the Adren finally unleashed their onslaught upon Britain.

Elwyn shouted a brief warning from the tower and then the air was thick with arrows. The Adren had brought over a thousand archers unseen and unheard to within a hundred yards of the wall. They fired blindly but the Causeway was straight and they only had to aim directly into the fog before them. The fifteen-foot wall, which consisted of bound tree trunks sunk upright into the earth of the Causeway, took the brunt of most of the first volley but the attack was deafening as the arrows slammed into the wall and tore overheard like a flock of demented birds.

Balor had been crouching with his back against the ramparts but the taller Tamsyn had been standing as she chatted to him and he watched as she was flung aside to crash into the warriors below. He leaned over to look at her spread-eagled body on the ground and saw the cluster of arrows embedded in her back and then he quickly thrust himself back against the ramparts as another Adren volley rocked the wall and slashed through the air above him. He looked around trying to see who else had been hit and saw another warrior being dragged from the middle of one of the fires where he had fallen. Most of the other warriors had been standing against the base of the wall so they had been protected from the initial volleys. Then he saw Ceinwen lying flat out on her back some way from the wall. Morveren was trying to drag her behind her horse which lay on its side with one leg kicking pathetically in the air.

Balor hauled his axe free from his belt and gripped it tightly trying to make sense of what was happening around him. He felt removed from the unfolding events and he was mildly curious about what would happen next but not overly anxious about it as it did not seem to really involve him. Arthur was already yelling out orders and Balor struggled to make out what he was saying. Then he suddenly seemed to jolt back to reality as he heard Arthur shouting out for raised shields. He automatically unslung his shield and raised it over his head just as the third volley rained directly down on the compound. Either Adren archers further back had unleashed the volley or the initial archers had elevated their aim to send their arrows arcing up to come crashing straight down onto the defenders. Balor swore as his shield was slammed back onto his head with two arrows buried into the thick hide and wood. He cursed to himself and tried to listen as Arthur's voice was raised above the chaos again.

He was shouting to Elwyn and those in the tower trying to find out if the Adren were attempting to charge the wall yet. Balor risked a quick glance over the edge of the wall and saw hundreds of figures charging out from the fog about fifty yards away. Most of them were carrying short scaling ladders.

'They're coming!' he yelled down to Arthur and the warriors started to scramble up the inset wooden rungs on the wall. Everyone expected the deadly hail of arrows to cease once the Adren reached the wall but if anything it intensified. The unseen Adren archers were no longer firing in organised unison but independently and the arrows were now scything through the air constantly.

The Adren were almost at the wall. Arthur realised that if the Adren archers kept up their deadly fire then there was no way that he could defend the ramparts without exposing his warriors to their arrows. It was a measure of the enemy that they were prepared to kill their own soldiers in greater quantities than the Britons just so long as the Britons died. Arthur jumped back down from the wall.

'Back! Get Back! Longbows! To me!' Arthur's voice roared above the noise of the charging Adren and the warriors abandoned the defences and ran to form a line twenty yards from the wall where Arthur stood.

Balor joined the line and rammed his axe back into his belt then fumbled to release his longbow from where it was slung on his back. Someone released it for him and he turned to see Morgund already fitting an arrow to his own bow.

'I'd sling your shield on your back if I were you – you'll be needing it soon.'

Balor did as Morgund suggested and cursed him for his calmness.

'Fire!' Arthur roared.

217

Balor realised that he was slower than everyone else as the longbows snapped all along the line and the first of the Adren to reach the top of the wall were flung backwards. It suddenly became clear to him why Arthur had ordered them off the wall. The attacking Adren were now caught in a crossfire between Arthur's longbows and their own archers who could not see that they were only killing their own soldiers.

As the slaughter continued Balor realised that he had left his arrow bag back at the wall and the quiver hanging from his belt was nearly empty. Morgund seemed to have seen this despite not taking his eyes from the targets ahead of him and he kicked his own half-empty bag towards Balor who gratefully bent down and swooped up enough to refill his quiver. He was a strong man and fit for his forty-five years but his arms and back were already aching and they had only been in battle for a few minutes. As he sent another arrow flying into the growing massacre at the wall he wondered, belatedly, if you really needed to be a warrior almost from childhood instead of becoming one later in life as he had.

Arthur was walking behind the line steadying those that needed it and checking on the overall supply of arrows. The Adren were beginning to make some headway despite the deadly crossfire and more were now making it over the wall to the Briton side of the Causeway. Arthur stopped behind Morveren who was using a shorter bow. It took enormous strength and stamina to keep firing the six-foot longbows but at this range the shorter bow was just as effective and she was firing at the same rate as the others around her.

'Did Ceinwen get hit?' Arthur asked her as he sent an arrow into an Adren who was clambering down the side of the wall.

Morveren carried on firing and tried to steady her breathing enough to reply. 'The horse reared up. Got hit in the first hail. Its hoof caught her flush on the chin. Out cold.'

Arthur glanced behind him to where Ceinwen had been dragged. She was still dead to the world.

'Arthur!'

Arthur looked down the line to see Elwyn leaning back and shouting to him again. Arthur returned his attention to the wall and saw that more and more of the Adren were gaining the top.

'Cover me!' Arthur shouted and made his way back to Balor.

'And make sure you don't hit me,' he said quietly to Balor as he edged past him and then sprinted for the wall.

The rate of fire behind him increased as the warriors forced their tiring muscles to work harder. As he reached the base of the wall two Adren jumped to the ground beside him and he kicked out at one and cut his sword at the other who fell back clutching his bloody face. He swept his sword at the first and nearly decapitated him. He picked up a burning branch from the fire and raced to one of the oil kegs set against the wall. Arrows were flying in both directions above his head and Adren were falling all around him as he set the first keg alight and kicked it over against the wall. He sprinted to the next one, as the first roared into flames, and put the burning branch to that one as well. He saw a full arrow bag lying on the ground and picked it up but he abandoned any attempt to reach the third keg and dashed back half-crouching to his own line. He dropped the bag at Balor's feet and turned to see the flames taking hold along the wall.

'Every second person back to the next wall!' he shouted out and half the line picked up their discarded weapons and spare arrows and sprinted back into the fog. The others inched closer together and continued firing at the Adren who were struggling over the top of the burning wall. One had made it to the Briton side and he stood facing the line of bowmen and then without hesitating or checking to see if he had any support he charged the twenty warriors. Someone to Arthur's left swore in disbelief. Balor stepped forward and ended the lone Adren's charge with a bloody downward swing of his axe and then he kicked the dead body swearing at it. Every one of the warriors in the line was thinking the same thing; would they have charged twenty archers alone?

'Back to the next wall!' Arthur called out and the remaining warriors gathered their weapons and ran back down the Causeway. Morgund stayed behind with Arthur and they stared at the burning wall which had temporarily stalled the Adren attack.

'Take these,' Arthur said and handed him his longbow and arrows. Their eyes met and held for a second.

'Less than half an hour and the first wall's fallen already,' Morgund said.

'Half an hour and already a few hundred Adren are dead.'

'It's going to be difficult to convince them when they're beaten,' Morgund said shrugging and turned away without waiting for a reply. Arthur stooped down and lifted the still lifeless Ceinwen and unceremoniously slung her over his shoulder. Leaning against her weight he started off after Morgund and left the first line of defence burning behind him.

The second wall was little more than a barricade designed to offer some cover from the Adren archers and act as a firing position during a retreat back from the initial defences. Arthur was the last to arrive there and he called out to his warriors that there were only Adren behind him.

He propped Ceinwen up in a sitting position with her back against the barricade. She was beginning to regain consciousness and an ugly looking bruise was already blooming across the lower part of her bloody face. She shook her head drunkenly and spat out a mouthful of blood and a couple of teeth. Arthur took her face in both hands and tilted her head up to look into her eyes. She was mumbling incoherently through her cracked mouth and her eyes were glazed and unfocused. He told her to be quiet and called across to Elwyn for a warrior to carry her back to safety. Elwyn pointed to Saewulf, who stood out as a big man even among the other warriors, and he strolled across to see what was required of him.

Arthur told him to take Ceinwen back to the next main line of defence and warn them that the Adren attack was underway. A minute later Saewulf was disappearing into the fog carrying Ceinwen in his arms like a small child.

Arthur took stock of their position. They had lost five warriors in the defence of the first line, four of which had died in the initial onslaught of Adren arrows. He passed among his warriors gauging how they had fared after the first encounter with the enemy on the Causeway and seeing how depleted their arrow stores were.

Balor was bent over with his hands on his knees as he tried to regain his breath. He looked up and saw Morgund walking across to him.

'It's foggy enough old man without you blowing out great clouds.'

'What are you grinning about?' Balor replied, still short of breath.

'Just the pleasure of thrashing the bastards. We've waited far too long not to enjoy it now it's here. You're grinning too.'

Balor realised he was. Even though he was still breathing hard from the sprint back from the first wall he no longer felt any tiredness in his arms or any pain in the small of his back. In fact, he realised with his grin broadening, that he had never felt more alive in his life.

'Does it always feel this good to be in a proper battle?'

Morgund laughed and replied, 'It does if you're still alive, and if you're dead then you don't feel anything. Beats breaking your back behind a plough all day.'

'We must have killed scores back their.'

'Hundreds.'

They both looked to Arthur who had just corrected Balor as he passed them.

'Hundreds?' Balor asked.

'Yes and there's plenty more waiting to join them,' Arthur replied as he took stock of their remaining arrows.

'It would be more if it wasn't for this fog. We can't see them coming until they're almost on us,' Morgund said, needlessly gesturing at the impenetrable mist that limited visibility to a circular thirty yards.

'That works both ways, as the Adren are about to find out. Get yourselves ready, we're going to take back the first wall,' Arthur said and left them staring at each other as he called the others together to organise the counter-attack.

'You and your bloody 'can't see them coming'!' Balor said mimicking Morgund's deep voice.

'Thought you were enjoying the battle?'

'That was the defending bit, I've seen what happens to the attackers!'

'Don't worry, you'll be in and out before they know it. Just pretend it's one of your women.' Morgund jumped back a step as Balor swung at him and before Balor could think of an appropriate reply Arthur was calling for the forty-odd warriors to gather around him.

'Who are the fastest ten bowmen here?' The warriors looked around at each other and quickly agreed who were the quickest. 'Good. I want you to hang back twenty yards when the rest of us attack. We'll advance quickly and quietly and when we charge them I want you to do it silently and to keep silent. No war cries. I want to smash into them hard and without warning. Is that understood? I want confusion in their ranks and as many dead Adren as quickly as possible. Listen for my call. When you hear it get out and get out quickly. I'll give the word for the bowmen to start firing and after you loose fifteen arrows each then run for it. Questions? Good. The bowmen can leave behind their other weapons. Speed will be all you need. The rest of you leave your longbows and arrows here.'

The warriors discarded unnecessary weapons and followed Arthur as he disappeared into the thick mists. Morveren was among the last to set off after Arthur and she cast a glance backwards at the pile of her discarded weapons. She was to be one of the bowmen whose task it was to provide cover for the warriors once Arthur ordered them to disengage. She gripped her bow tightly but she felt naked advancing towards the Adren without her sword and shield. She knew they would be just a hindrance once the retreat was called and she trusted Arthur's judgement implicitly but she was still uneasy about leaving them so far behind her.

Most of the warriors were ahead of her, indistinct figures moving silently through the fog with their swords and axes held by their sides and their shields held before them. She re-checked the quiver hanging from her belt again and worried whether the wet mist would foul her bowstring.

'Still full?'

The sudden and quiet question from her side caused her to start. It was Morgund.

'What are you doing back here? You should be up with Arthur and the others,' she hissed back at him, embarrassed to have jumped at his unexpected presence.

'Plenty of time to catch up. Just thought I'd drop back and see if you were all right.'

'I'm perfectly fine. Get forward,' she snapped back at him.

'Just make sure you watch out for me and any Adren creeping up on me - that'll be your priority,' he replied grinning at her.

As he made to catch up with the others she put a hand on his arm. He looked at her but neither said a word and he strode off to regain his place at the front.

Morveren envied him his nerveless ease and tried to compose herself. She brushed her wet hair from her face and tried to wipe her hand dry on the thigh of her trousers but the thick fog had layered everything with a sheen of dampness. Dew beaded her bow and her wet clothes clung to her limbs uncomfortably. The warriors ahead of her had stopped with Arthur standing some ten yards further on with his back to them. Someone's weapon clanked dully against wood and Arthur immediately pointed towards the offender without turning around and the noise died instantly.

Morveren's heart was thudding rapidly and the roar of blood in her ears initially prevented her from hearing the sounds in the fog ahead. Gradually she could make out the shouts of command and the heavy noise of tree trunks being hauled aside. Somewhere ahead the Adren were dismantling the remnants of the wall they had recently taken.

Arthur signalled for the warriors to form into their two groups and he led them silently on towards the clamour ahead. Morveren's nerves stretched tauter as they advanced ever closer to the unseen Adren. Finally Arthur raised his sword high above his head and then, without looking around, he started to sprint towards the enemy. The warriors followed at a dead run, quelling their automatic urge to yell their battle cries.

Morveren and the other bowmen followed. They would form a line once they got close enough to see the wall. She watched as the warriors ahead of her sprinted onwards, their weapons drawn and held ready as they raced in silence through the last shielding of the fog and she felt a surge of excitement as the adrenaline pumped the fear from her body.

Suddenly the half-wrecked wall appeared out of the mist and she understood exactly why Arthur had ordered the charge to be silent. The Adren were busy throwing their dead over the steep sides of the Causeway while others were trying to tear down the parts of the wall that still stood. The wall was still burning in places and the thick smoke from the oil hung above the scene in the still air. Some of the Adren looked up at the sudden appearance of the charging warriors and Morveren felt the battle joy course through her as she realised how terrifying Arthur's attack must be for the totally unprepared Adren.

The warriors stormed beyond the wall leaving a swathe of slaughtered Adren behind them. Their onward rush meant that for long minutes they were continually attacking Adren who were confused, disoriented and unable to form a line of defence quick enough to check Arthur's murderous advance.

Morveren realised that someone was shouting to her left. She looked across and saw the stocky and very familiar figure of Elwyn frantically waving for the line of bowmen to advance. The Anglian warrior had been put in charge of the archers by Arthur and Morveren finally understood that he was yelling for them to press on up to the wall. The brutal, hacking progress of Arthur's warriors had carried them well beyond the wall and the bowmen were now too far behind them. The line sprinted up to the wall and took up firing positions as Arthur's advance into the Adren ranks began to falter due to the sheer number of the enemy that had been pressed together.

Morveren could see that Arthur was beginning to lose the advantage as the Adren further back on the Causeway began to realise what was happening and started to organise themselves. She slotted her first arrow into place and readied herself to draw her bow. All along the ruins of the wall the others were doing the same. Just when she thought that Arthur was leaving it too late she heard his voice rise above the din of fighting and almost as one the warriors turned and sprinted back to the wall.

The first flight of arrows flew into the Adren as the warriors sped past the line of bowmen. Morveren did as she was trained to do and ignored the Adren to her left and right and picked her targets directly ahead of her. The Adren were taken by surprise for a second time as their savage attackers were replaced by hammering close-range volleys of deadly arrows. The foremost Adren were flung back into others who in turn were scythed down immediately in the next merciless hail. Confusion reigned in their ranks once more as the assault ended as suddenly as it had begun.

Morveren had fired her last arrow and was racing back through the fog on the Causeway with the others all around her and ahead of her. She wanted to scream aloud her relief and joy but she saved her breath and channelled her bursting energy into sprinting even harder. She glanced at the figures running near her hoping to see Morgund or Balor but she saw neither and concentrated instead on covering the distance ahead of her.

Chapter Ten

Seren had lost track of how long she had been confined to her cell. The windowless room blocked almost all the sounds from the city outside and without the reference of the lakeside bell tolling the hours she had no way of gauging the passing of time. She had tried to keep track of the number of bland meals that had been passed to her but she had become convinced that the guards were altering the intervals to disorient her further. Sometimes it seemed to her that at least a day must have passed since her last meal then at other times it seemed as if one had directly followed another.

At first she had thought that her father would be unable to contain his anger at her union with Arthur and that he would summon her quickly to deny or explain what was being said by Terrill and Commander Kane but no summons had arrived. She was unable to think of Terrill without wanting to break something in the spartan room and she was unable to think of Kane without wanting to slowly strangle him. As she was unable to do either she forced away the thoughts of them by concentrating on other matters. There was much to ponder on but without any outside input her thoughts and feelings chased themselves in ever tightening and fruitless circles. Her moods swung from anger, at being locked away, to fear, for her unborn child, and underlying each waking moment was the burning frustration that she could get no word to Arthur and the Britons about the peril they unknowingly faced.

In solitude she fretted, cried and raged at the betrayals surrounding her. She felt betrayed by Arthur's marriage to the barbarian red-haired girl whose name she did not even know. She felt betrayed by her father's choice to ally himself with Lazure and the Adren over Merdynn and the Britons. She felt betrayed by Terrill who had told Kane that she was pregnant with Arthur's child and who had led him to her hiding place. She even felt that time was betraying her as it remorselessly slid from hour to hour as she paced the room powerless to affect anything that was happening in the world outside her cell. If Commander Kane had thought to torture her he could not have devised a better rack with which to stretch her emotions but for every painstaking minute she spent locked in her timeless purgatory a resolve began to grow deep inside her. It centred on her child and every question she put to herself became subject to the same simple query; what was best for her child? Once she could answer that question then each course would become clear and absolute.

When two guards finally came to bring her to the council room she just turned her back, mistakenly thinking that they had come to bring her more tasteless food and to empty the pail, which she had to humiliatingly use to relieve herself. When they just stood in the doorway she turned to them, 'Well?' she demanded.

'Lord Venning wishes to see you,' one of the guards answered, clearly uncomfortable about the whole situation.

Seren snorted in sarcasm, 'My father sends an invitation for dinner does he? How convivial. Perhaps I'll wear the clothes I've had to use for the last eternity. Do you think these will please him?' And she twirled once in front of them.

The guards could not look her in the eye and they stepped aside as she walked between them.

'You'd both better pray I never come to power in this city,' she said quietly to them and with no trace of levity as she left her cell.

She made her way to the main council rooms with the two guards trailing along in her wake. They looked and felt more like an escort than guards as they hurried to catch up with her. Seren entered the lakeside Palace and swept into the council chamber and stopped dead.

She had been expecting her father, Lord Venning, and Commander Kane to be there with perhaps Terrill present to give his treacherous testament but the long table was full with every member of the Cithol High Council. They were already seated and they stared at her as she came to a stop before them. She immediately became conscious of both her dishevelled appearance and the ever-increasing visual evidence of her pregnancy. She clasped her hands instinctively over the slight swelling and many eyes in the room followed the movement of her hands.

One end of the table had been left unoccupied and Commander Kane stood and indicated that she should sit there. Her green eyes flashed hatred at him as she took her seat and she took the initiative by launching an attack on her father seated at the far end of the table, 'Why have you kept me confined in a bare room?'

The table was silent as daughter glared at father. Lord Venning cleared his throat and his deep voice filled the room, 'Do you carry the child of Arthur of the Britons?'

'How long have you kept me confined?'

'Answer your Lord's question!' Kane commanded her.

'Answer mine!' she spat back at him but her mind was reeling. She had not expected her father to make her pregnancy known so publicly before she had the chance to deny or confirm the accusations. But he had and that could only mean that he believed Kane and Terrill. It also meant that he had already decided what was to be done with her. She was suddenly certain that the council had already discussed her actions and reached an agreement before she even had the chance to defend herself. Her ignorance of what had already passed made her feel more vulnerable and she fought to keep her face impassive and her hands from shaking. Lord Venning's voice carried through the room again. 'Do you carry Arthur's child?'

'I carry my child and your grandchild. How long have you kept me imprisoned?'

'You must answer the Lord's question!' Kane shot from his chair as he shouted at her.

'Quiet, dog. Remember your place and whom you address. Sit.' Seren pointed for him to retake his seat and one or two around the table lowered their heads and smiled. A twitch flicked across Kane's face as he slowly sat back down with his malevolent eyes fixed upon her.

'I am with child. And how does my father greet this joyous news? Throws me in a prison for days on end. The mother and the unborn future leader of the Cithol imprisoned and brought before a High Council who have already judged and decreed punishment before any defence is brought before them. Is this our justice then?'

'Neither you nor your child will have any place at the Cithol Council if Arthur is the father. Indeed, neither you nor your child will have any place in the Veiled City if Arthur is the father of your child.'

Seren stared in disbelief at her father and did not see the small smile of triumph on Kane's face. Her mind raced as this judgement sunk in. Her father was prepared to exile her if she admitted that she had lain with Arthur. She could refute the claim but it would be obvious once the child was born that the father was not Cithol so even if she denied it now it would only delay the inevitable. If the exile was to take effect immediately then she would accept it and flee to the Causeway to warn Arthur but she knew that Lord Venning would keep her here until she could no longer endanger the new alliance with Lazure Ulan. She could see that denial was pointless now that Terrill had revealed her secret to them.

All in the room were silently watching her and she lifted her chin in defiance as she spoke.

'Yes. Arthur is the father of the child I carry. I am proud of my child and I am proud of the father.'

Those in the room who had not believed the accusation looked on Seren with horror and disgust.

'Proud of the barbarian warrior who would bring down the Veiled City?' Kane asked, wanting her to damn herself entirely in front of the council.

'Proud of the Briton who defends his land and seeks to protect his people. Yes, I am proud, for Arthur stands against the Adren and their master. I could wish for no better father. Who here is prepared to defend our city and way of life? I'll tell you who, no one! Not a single one of you! Arthur defends the Causeway even as you squabble amongst yourselves like gossipmongers about who is or is not the father of my child. The fate of our future lies balanced on the fortunes of a battle that you hide away from like spineless worms burrowing deeper underground!'

'Curb your tongue girl, this is the High Council,' Kane retorted, delighting in her self-damnation.

Seren stood up in disgust her ivory pale cheeks now flushed in anger. 'High Council! High treason more like! You've betrayed Merdynn, you've betrayed the Britons and you've betrayed your own people. How could you treat with Lazure Ulan? With the Adren Master? How stupid can you possibly be? He'll enslave and destroy us once your treachery leads to the Britons' defeat!' She looked at the faces around the table before continuing, 'They've made a deal with the Adren Master, the Britons' destruction in exchange for assurances of safety for the Veiled City!'

Many of those around the table refused to look at her but none of them looked surprised and Seren realised with a sickening feeling that the council already knew about, and had agreed to, the betrayal of Arthur's warriors.

'What? All of you? You've agreed to this? Was our friendship with Merdynn so shallow? He and Arthur are the only ones who can defend us from the Adren, why betray them?'

It was Lord Venning who rose to answer her. 'Arthur and Merdynn are doomed. The Adren army was always going to defeat them. They and their people never stood any chance of resisting the Adren for long. To have supported them in this war would only have led to our own downfall. Lazure promises us safety. The people of his Shadow Land City are the same as us and he only wants to unite the power that each city has. Together we can truly begin to bring back into the world some of the glory of the last Age. With our power united we can one day resurrect the civilisation that once crowned this world.'

'You fools. Lazure won't unite our power with his, he'll take it for himself and you'll be no more than his slaves!'

'Fin Seren. You have broken the codes and laws of our city. You have formed a union with an outsider. By doing so you have negated any authority you have as my daughter and heir. You are no longer my daughter and no longer my heir. You shall be confined here in the Veiled City until you give birth. Your off-spring will be taken from you and then you shall be exiled from here.'

Having delivered the council's verdict Lord Venning sat back down looking both frail and weary. He raised his eyes from the table and watched with great sadness as his daughter was led back to her cell.

Seren left the room in shocked silence. She paid no heed to the guards flanking her and she was oblivious to her surroundings until she found herself once more in her hateful cell. She sat down heavily on the small bed feeling numb as the guards closed and locked the door behind them. Of all the possible outcomes that she had played out in her mind before the meeting she had never once considered that her father would take her child away from her. She had expected exile or imprisonment but always with her child, never without. It seemed impossible and for one unreal moment she thought she must be in the grip of some terrible but truly realistic nightmare.

The moment passed and she felt empty and sick. Her heart pumped a slow painful tattoo inside her chest and she suddenly dropped to her knees scrabbling for the empty basin by the bed. She vomited in great heaving retches until there was no more left in her stomach. She spat into the basin attempting to take the acidic taste from her mouth and sat back on her heels wiping the cold sweat from her pale face.

She climbed back onto the bed and sat on the edge with her head in her hands not at all sure that she was not going to be sick again. Her mind was replaying the brief and uncompromising meeting over and over as she tried to explain to herself how her father could be so cold and cruel. For a moment her bewilderment turned to anger at Commander Kane, thinking that he must have somehow poisoned her father's mind against her, but she knew that Lord Venning was too strong to be so easily led. He was the leader of the Cithol and no one could sway his opinion or guide his judgement against what he thought was best for his people. Kane could only have presented a face to reflect and reinforce her father's own arguments and beliefs.

She leaned over and spat once more into the basin thinking that she may not be able to save the Britons from Lazure's trap or the Cithol from their inevitable enslavement; ultimately she might not even be able to save herself but she had to find a way to save her child. If nothing else could be salvaged from the wreckage, she had to save her child, no matter what it took and no matter what it cost.

Ceinwen had so far taken no part in the battle for the Causeway. She could remember nothing about the first couple of days after being knocked out by the horse that had reared up in its death throes. She had finally come to her senses back in the main fortification of the Gates and had spent the weeks since tending to the steady stream of wounded who were carried in or who had made their own way back from the fighting further along the Causeway.

She had treated her own injuries as best she could and although she still found speaking or eating painful her jaw was already healing. Her smile would be missing a few teeth from now on but any sense of feeling sorry for herself was soon put into perspective by tending to the more seriously wounded. She found her injured pride harder to treat; she had thought to be standing alongside the warriors in their defence of the Causeway and to have been so stupidly injured before the first attack had even properly begun made her feel foolish and inadequate. It wasn't long before she realised that while she was not the hardiest of warriors she was the most skilled healer on the Causeway. Clearly her strength lay in treating injuries rather than creating them and she threw herself wholeheartedly into doing just that.

The fog was still clamped over the marshland and the sun rising over the cliffs to the West was only evidenced by a brighter whiteness in the surrounding mists. The days passed with the distant sounds of battle gradually drawing closer as the Adren fought their way ever nearer to the Gates and Ceinwen watched as exhausted Wessex, Anglian and Mercian warriors returned in alternating bands to collapse and sleep within the safety of the fort. She found herself organising the groups of warriors making sure that there was food available for them and then letting them sleep for a few hours before sending them back up the Causeway to rejoin the battle and relieve others on the defensive lines.

Each band had its own tales to tell; strident tales of heroic acts and the quieter stories of how friends and comrades had fallen. Each tale told of the same dogged defence and the same fighting retreats. The warriors from the three tribes would leapfrog each other as they gradually gave ground before the Adren onslaught. Mercian warriors would cover the retreat of an Anglian band while a Wessex contingent would prepare for a counter-attack and then their roles would be reversed as the battle surged back and forth along the Causeway. Ceinwen listened to the different reports from the nearing frontline and while each told a separate tale they all held to the same story of retreat and defence and retreat again. The warriors of Briton were doing exactly as Arthur asked of them; making the Adren pay an appallingly high price for every yard they gained but still they came on, throwing themselves at every defended line until the Britons had no choice but to retreat or be overwhelmed.

It seemed to Ceinwen that every group of warriors who stood around a table eating a hurried meal had fought with Arthur on the frontline. Ceinwen doubted that Arthur could have been in every single fight as the battle for the Causeway had been raging now for weeks but in all that time he had not returned to the Gates. She assumed and hoped that he took his rest never far from where the battle was concentrated; even in the summer daylight everyone still needed some sleep and fatigue would only lead to a mistake and death.

She had sent a handful of badly injured warriors back to Caer Sulis in the hope that they would recover and be able to rejoin the war at a later stage but some of the injured had refused to go. As she watched another shattered band enter through the main gate she remembered one particular Mercian who Glore, Gereint's brother, had brought in a few days ago. His lower leg had been mangled by an Adren weapon and her only option had been to amputate it below the knee. Once her coma-inducing drugs had worn off he had refused to return to Caer Sulis 'to wait, maimed, for the Adren to turn up there too,' as he had put it. Instead he had insisted on being allowed to defend the Gates should the Adren get this far. His only compromise was to exchange his longbow for a shorter one and he stumped around the compound berating any of the wounded he thought were able to return to the fighting.

Ceinwen had just finished bandaging an Anglian warrior's arm when she looked up to see the last of the current group of warriors coming in through the main gate. Morgund was at the head of the band and with him were Balor, Morveren, Cael and Gwyna. It had been a few days since they had returned to the Gates and she was relieved to see them again. They all looked desperately tired and many of them had minor injuries that needed treating. She went to meet the recently arrived group and after a quick greeting she directed the more seriously wounded to the dressing station before joining the others as they slumped around a fire.

'It's good to see you all,' she said trying to keep her teeth clenched.

'How's your jaw?' Morveren asked as she massaged her arm and shoulder.

'It'll heal. Fewer teeth.' She shrugged then asked, 'Have you seen Ruadan?'

'He's at the front now with Hengest and the Anglians,' Morgund answered.

'What's happening out there?' Ceinwen asked through her clamped teeth.

'We're killing thousands of them,' Gwyna replied tiredly.

'And thousands more of the bastards keep coming at us,' Balor added.

They stopped speaking as wooden trays of food were laid around the fire. They reached hungrily for the fresh bread, roasted meat and pitchers of goat milk.

'Fresh bread?' Morveren asked, staring at the loaf in her hand.

'Yes. They make it over there,' Ceinwen said, pointing to where the makeshift kitchens were set up.

'Just seems strange. It's like coming out of the fog into another world. A world where fresh bread is baked.' She shook her head and bit off a mouthful quickly following it with a long swig of milk.

'Arthur?' Ceinwen asked.

'Still commanding at the front.'

'I think he wants to kill every Adren himself.'

'He's having a good go at it then. Did you hear about the last counter attack...'

Ceinwen watched as they began recounting the most recent battle. She had seen it dozens of times. The first thing a group did when they came back from the front of the battle was to see to their wounded and then their own injuries. Then it was food, relive the battle and sleep where they sat. Always in that order and it was never long before sleep overcame them. The only exception was before her now and that was Cael who, as ever, put food as his first and last priority.

She often found herself cleaning out the cuts and wounds of warriors who had fallen asleep as she treated them, dead to the world and oblivious to what she was doing. Many of the lighter injuries just needed disinfecting and dressing but she knew from experience that to delay treating such wounds would inevitably lead to the far more serious problems of infections and fever. She had five others working with her, young sons and daughters of Anglian warriors who, like those who staffed the kitchens, had refused to leave for Caer Sulis when the others had. Each was invaluable and they worked their way through each returning group of warriors and rarely had time enough to rest or eat.

The oldest and leader of these children was a young sandy-haired Anglian boy called Aelfric and Ceinwen called him over. He stood before them and reported on who among the new arrivals needed her attention saying that he would deal with the others.

Morgund looked up at the boy as he delivered his verdicts with a serious face and complete confidence in his own judgements. Ceinwen was used to both his manner and his seriousness which seemed so out of place in one so young but Morgund watched fascinated then burst out laughing.

'I see the Anglians have found a young Cei to organise them!'

The others, finishing off the last of the food as they sat around the fire, grinned at the boy but he just looked them over and nodded to them before telling them where they could find dry blankets if they wished to sleep. He made to go then turned back to them and told them that if they wanted any weapons sharpened whilst they slept then to leave them there by the fire where they could pick them up after they had rested. He strode off purposefully to organise the other children with the good-natured laughter of the warriors following him but inside he was swelling with pride at being likened to his warlord.

They were not diverted long by the young Anglian and they heaved themselves to their feet and trudged off to collect dry blankets and steal as much sleep as they could. Ceinwen noticed that they all left their weapons behind to be sharpened.

Normally she would have let them sleep for six hours but everyone who was asleep in the compound was woken four hours later when ten warriors burst through the main gate dragging and carrying wounded. The largest of them was shouting to rouse everyone and Ceinwen dropped what she was doing and sprinted across to him. She recognised Saewulf, the towering Anglian they had come across in the Shadow Lands raid, although she had no recollection of having been carried by him all the way from the first wall back to the Gates. She also recognised the man he was half-carrying as Berwyn, the second Anglian they had rescued from the forests outside the Belgae villages.

Berwyn was moaning and clutching his bloody stomach and it was all Saewulf could do to hold him in an upright position. Other warriors were streaming in through the gate and suddenly the camp was in chaos. Ceinwen looked up at Saewulf and shouted to make herself heard above the growing confusion.

'What's happening?'

'The Adren have broken through!'

'Where's Arthur?'

'Don't know! Last I saw he was trying to hold the rearguard together. There's just too many of them, they overran the first ditch position. Arthur tried to hold them in the ground before the last ditch!'

Ceinwen quickly looked around the mayhem at the main gate and saw Morgund and the others running towards her with their newly sharpened weapons. Despite the pain she forced her jaw to work and screamed out above the noise of the chaos to get everyone's attention.

'Get Berwyn and the other wounded to those fires over there! I want ten of you on the wheel to retract the bridge but wait for the order! Who knows how to fire that contraption above the gates? You four get up there! The rest of you follow me!'

With Morgund and the other Wessex warriors by her side and the rest of them following her she raced out of the main gate and into the fog of the Causeway.

Within a few paces they were crossing the bridge that spanned the fifty-yard gap that had been cut in the Causeway. Below them the swollen melt waters of the marshes swirled and eddied. Ceinwen could already hear the frantic sounds of battle ahead of her. There was only about two hundred yards between the bridge they had just crossed and the first ditch that Saewulf said had been overrun but the fog made it impossible to judge how far ahead the battle was. Bloodied warriors were streaming past them as they ran back towards the Gates then without any warning at all they ran straight into the charging Adren.

There was no time to form battle lines or a shield wall and the fighting erupted in a vicious uncontrolled melee. The warriors of Briton instinctively tried to form small fighting units and Ceinwen found herself back to back with Morgund as they both hacked at their frenzied Adren opponents. Morgund was roaring with all his might for the Britons to keep advancing. Somewhere ahead of them Arthur was making a stand and with the Adren now behind him there was no way he could retreat back to the Gates.

The fifty warriors who had followed Ceinwen from the compound had checked the Adren charge but it was still chaotic with individual duels and small groups interspersed and fighting each other. More Adren were joining the battle and the Britons were too enmeshed in fighting for their lives to be able to put any order to the anarchy. Their own charge towards

Arthur had been checked too and a bloody stalemate was developing as the furious fighting continued.

Ceinwen took a blow on the shoulder and was knocked to the ground. Morgund swung at her attacker as she scrambled back to her feet to block a blow aimed at Morgund's back. They had swapped opponents and the speed and unexpectedness of the switch distracted the Adren she was facing long enough for her to slip her sword under his guard. She glanced at her shoulder and saw the iron strip, which had been fixed into her battle jerkin, bent into a ninety-degree angle. She only had a moment to think that without that strip she would have certainly lost her arm before two more Adren threw themselves at her. She struggled to take one blow on her shield but her arm was already deadening from the previous blow and she barely managed to deflect the Adren's weapon. She twisted to avoid the second attack and swung around slashing with her own sword but the Adren caught the blow on his shield while her second attacker swung below her limp shield at her legs. She saw it just in time and leapt clear. Then suddenly Balor was crashing into her assailants with his heavy war axe smashing one aside and disembowelling the other.

'We have to retreat!' he shouted.

But before she could answer more Adren were upon them and they were once again fighting for their lives and trying to hold their ground. Above the furious racket surrounding her Ceinwen heard a new source of battle further along the Causeway and unseen in the fog. Then she heard Arthur's voice roaring out commands. She hammered away the sword thrust at her and risked a glance towards the growing din of the new battle and saw about thirty warriors emerging from the mist coming towards them in a tight square with their shields raised and interlocking. Adren were swarming all around the square like wasps; throwing themselves at the wall as the Britons hacked down over their shields and gradually, yard by yard, fought their way back towards the Gates.

Morgund had seen it too and was shouting himself hoarse for the warriors entangled in the melee to make their way to either side of the square. Ceinwen immediately saw what he intended to do. If they could get enough warriors to the sides of the square then they could form a shield wall across the Causeway and stop any further Adren getting beyond them. They could retreat back to the bridge and, once they were across, it could be retracted leaving the Adren on the far side of the gap in the Causeway.

They battled their way to one side of the retreating square and Arthur's voice could be heard giving the command for the two sides facing the marshes to open and form a line across the Causeway. Those warriors previously facing the Gates now rushed out to attack the Adren caught behind the shield wall.

Ceinwen found herself fighting alongside the Anglian commander, Hengest. As they locked shields she shouted out to him if Ruadan was with the square. He nodded frantically before staggering under a blow and returning it with a thrust back over the top of his battered shield.

The Adren loose behind the Britons were quickly slaughtered and under Arthur's command the shield wall began inching its way back to the bridge again. When they were thirty yards from the gap Ceinwen heard Arthur behind her shouting to those in the wall to prepare to form a square again. Then he was gone to the other end of the line to give them the same instruction. Ceinwen realised that the bridge was narrower than the Causeway and they had to reform in order for the ends of the line not to be caught with the gap at their backs.

Arthur bellowed out his orders and the shield wall broke at right angles one third in from each end of the line. The Adren attack increased in ferocity as the warriors began crossing the bridge and two more of the Britons fell in the centre of the wall. Arthur was at the breach instantly and met the Adren with his own raging attack. They fell back before him and the wall held.

Most of the Britons were inside the compound now and Arthur was holding the open main gate with a double line of warriors while the Adren crammed on to the bridge as they fought to get past the narrowed shield wall. There was no way to retract the bridge with the Adren still on it and with Arthur's warriors blocking the gateway. Those already inside the fort were lined up on the wall and sending volleys of arrows down onto the bridge but more and more Adren were pressing on from the Causeway and instantly taking the places of those that fell. With the open Gates before them the Adren were sensing victory and so great was their desire to annihilate the Britons that many were forced off the edges of the bridge and the sides of the gap and fell to their deaths in the sucking marsh.

Ceinwen left the second line of shields and raced up to the parapet above the main gate yelling as she went.

'Aim it at the bridge! Now!'

As she reached Hengest's monstrous crossbow it finally fired. She flinched involuntarily at the crashing sound then stared at the havoc of destruction it had caused on the bridge. She continued staring even as the bridge was jerked away from the far bank stranding the Adren on the other side of the fifty-yard gap. The bridge was littered with dead and dying Adren. Limbs and bodies were scattered everywhere in horrendous bloody heaps. Some of the unrecognisably mutilated bodies were crawling and screaming through the wreckage as the bridge was withdrawn into the fort and the gates swung shut.

Ceinwen stared at the weapon in front of her and at the ruined bodies below as Arthur raced up to the parapet to join her. She turned her blank gaze towards him; Arthur was covered in sweat-streaked blood and gripping the top edge of the wall with both hands as he surveyed the ruination below. He was smiling.

Captain Terrill stared out across the underground lake. Its dark, still surface reflected the lights from the dwellings on the far bank in a perfect mirror image and he tried in vain to discern where the demarcation was between reality and reflection. He gave up the fruitless task and gazed along the shores of the Veiled City. Everywhere the pathways and roads were thronged with people heading towards the Great Hall and the last meal of the day. They were his people. This was his city. This was his home and he had always done whatever he thought was in its best interests. Over the last few days he had told himself this again and again as if repeating it would somehow take away the suffocating feeling of guilt he had felt since Lord Venning had pronounced his judgement.

Both Commander Kane and Lord Venning had praised him for his loyalty and sense of duty in telling them about Fin Seren and the child she carried and at first he had accepted the praise as rightfully his. A hard duty but one he had fulfilled as was expected of a captain of the Cithol but as the comforting words and praise of others continued they began to sound more and more hollow to him.

He looked up towards the unseen roof of the cavern and thought to himself that everything was beginning to feel hollow. Even the city itself was built in an underground hollow and nothing inside it rang true any longer. He asked himself why, if everything he had done was right, did he feel like a traitor? Did these feelings spring from wanting to put Seren before the good of the Cithol people or was there something deeper and more fundamentally wrong in what was happening? The sense of guilt and remorse haunted him and his thoughts kept returning to the near encounter with the Adren Master and he knew deep down that he had done something terribly wrong.

His loyalty and duty to his office and Lord were at complete odds to his own sense of right and wrong, and try as he might he could not quieten the inner voice that drilled away at his conscience. He looked around at his city again and marvelled at its beauty, at how it blended so naturally with its surroundings. No wonder, he thought, that the barbarians who had visited it looked upon it in awe. No wonder that they thought it was powered by some magic of their gods because it was a truly wonderful city. In all the world there was only one other like it and that was the Shadow Land City commanded by Lazure Ulan; the Adren Master who was so like Merdynn and yet so opposite.

Terrill gazed into the lake once more, ignoring the people who stared at him as they passed by. The questions that had been hunting him finally caught up and cornered his conscience demanding answers so that they could finally find rest. What was best for the Veiled City? Would Lazure remain true to his alliance and join with the Cithol in recreating the glory of the old world or would he enslave them for his own purposes? If Arthur escaped the trap on the Causeway could and would he defend the Veiled City against the Adren? Was Fin Seren right and her father wrong or were her emotional allegiances warped and untrustworthy? Where did his loyalty ultimately lie; with his superiors or with his people?

Terrill started to walk aimlessly along the smooth stone pathways that wound around the fringes of the lake. He was sure that Merdynn was completely trustworthy and although he thought of Arthur as a violent barbarian he nonetheless believed him to be a man of his word. He also put a lot of faith in Seren's judgement and she too was adamant that Arthur was the city's only hope. His answers were swaying away from the Cithol leadership and he stopped by a small stone bridge that arced gently alongside the path as it carried water off from the lake in a fashioned channel. By chance he had arrived at the point where the water was siphoned off and re-directed to the deeper chambers under the lake where the ancient source generated the power for the Veiled City.

Terrill knew that this was at the centre of it all. The city and its people lived only because of its hidden power. Lazure wanted to harness that power for greater purposes than just keeping a city alive and Merdynn was desperate to keep the Adren from reaching it. To follow Lord Venning's course was perhaps the best way to keep his people alive and his city intact but Terrill wondered at what cost. To follow Merdynn's course and side with the Britons would mean to win everything or lose everything.

He suddenly saw the answer as quite simple. If they threw their lot in with Lazure then they would surely be slaves to his design. If they backed the Britons then at worst they would end up as slaves to Lazure but at best they would keep the Veiled City as it had ever been and with it their safety and seclusion. It was not a case of whether he should be loyal to Merdynn or Lord Venning; he should hold true to what he thought was ultimately right.

He retraced his footsteps along the lakeshore knowing now what he had to do and knowing that he had little time to do it in.

Seren lay on her hard bed counting out the days in her head until her child was due. She had done the same thing numerous times but it calmed her mind and shut out the worst of the frustrations that burned inside her. She came to the same conclusion she always came to; the child would be born in late autumn as the sun set in the East. It would be born to the winter and she was delighted that it should be so. Locked in her cell she longed even harder to be in the Winter Garden with the cold stars overhead and the ice around her. Her thoughts were straying once more to the night she had spent with Arthur in the Garden when she heard a scuffling outside her room and a muffled cry.

She sat up on her bed and stared anxiously at the door hearing the rattle of keys from the other side. It swung open abruptly and Terrill burst in.

'Terrill?'

'Quick. There's no time to explain we only have seconds!'

Seren sat staring at him completely nonplussed and he dashed across to her and dragged her from the bed. He handed her a cloak and a pair of stout leather boots.

'Put these on. Hurry!' He spoke with such a desperate urgency that Seren did as he asked despite not understanding what was happening around her.

He took her by the arm and pulled her out of the room and across the corridor. She stared briefly at the two guards who were crumpled on the floor to either side of the doorway. She did not know if they were alive or dead and she had no time to find out as Terrill hauled her into the room opposite her vacated cell. He was throwing aside the various furniture that covered the narrow tunnel they had previously used to sneak near enough to overhear the aftermath of the meeting with Lazure.

'Surely they've blocked it off?' she said as it belatedly dawned on her that Terrill was helping her to escape.

'No. I never told them it was how we got in. Help me!'

She joined him in casting aside the detritus.

'You first. Hurry! If we don't get into the wood before they discover you're gone we'll never make it!'

She looked at him warily still suspecting some kind of trap.

'Please!' he hissed at her and she finally wriggled into the passage with Terrill following close behind her.

They crawled through the tunnel with frantic haste and once they were in the main larger tunnels they sprinted upwards fearing that at any second they would hear the sounds of pursuit.

They burst out into the harsh spring sunshine of the Winter Wood and immediately flinched and covered their eyes. For a moment they stood there recovering from their flight and letting their eyes grow more accustomed to the blinding daylight.

'Why? After all you've done, why?' Seren asked, still fighting for breath.

'Because Lord Venning is wrong. Lazure will enslave us. Only Arthur is prepared to protect us from the Adren.'

'They'll be dead already if Lazure's used the tunnel under the Causeway!'

'Don't accuse me now, Seren. Now's not the time. I've already put some supplies in the copse where the Britons go. We have to get there quickly.'

'And then?'

'As you said. We have to get to the Causeway and warn Arthur.'

'What changed your mind?'

Seren still looked at him with deep suspicion and he threw his hands out in a gesture of exasperation.

'Not now, Seren. You're free. You're in the Winter Wood. We're heading for the Causeway and Arthur. Take this for now and follow me.'

Captain Terrill turned without saying more and started off for the copse on the hill. Seren looked around once and clenched her hands in joy at being free and then followed quickly after the departing Terrill.

Chapter Eleven

T he Adren attack on the Causeway had stalled at the gap before the Gates giving Arthur's warriors a few days of respite from the constant fighting. During those days a battery of fifty bowmen manned the wall firing intermittent volleys of arrows into the fog on the far side of the Causeway and every thirty minutes or so the large catapult sent its missiles arcing over the main gate of the fort and up into the mist.

There was no way of knowing how much damage either assault was causing but they had generous stockpiles of supplies for both the catapult and the longbows and they knew where the Adren were on the far side. The Adren were maintaining their own intermittent fire and the Britons in the compound hurried across open spaces and only put down their shields when they were sheltered from the Adren arrows by the wall or the two long houses in the centre of the fort.

The fog still lay thickly about them clinging wetly to clothes and sending a penetrating cold deep to the bone. Groups of warriors tried to ease their aching muscles and tired limbs as they huddled around numerous fires that had been lit in the shelter of the East Wall. Many of the Britons had revived their winter habit of laying large stones beside or under the fires and then retrieving them when it came to their turn to sleep; wrapped in cloth the stones would keep warm and radiate heat for hours afterwards.

One of the buildings in the middle of the compound was used to treat and house the wounded while the kitchens had been set up in the other. A constant stream of warriors hurried across to the latter to have their eating bowls refilled with the hot, meaty broth that was kept simmering over the cooking fires.

From where Morgund sat with his back to the East Wall he could see neither of the two buildings, only the warriors hurrying into the fog and returning later trying not to spill their steaming bowls. He stood up and stamped the life back into his legs before picking up his longbow and staring out through one of the nearby firing slits in the wall. He fitted an arrow to the bow and sighted into the mist to where he judged the far side of the gap to be and sent the arrow flying into the fog. After staring for a while longer into the blank whiteness he returned to the group by the fire.

'Hit anything?' Morveren asked as he sat back down.

'Two Adren captains.'

'Not bad with one arrow.'

They lapsed back into silence enjoying the heat from the fire on their faces while trying to ignore the coldness settling on their backs. An hour or two passed during which Cael helped himself to another meal from the kitchens while the others derided him with their customary taunts and jibes.

Ruadan and Hengest joined them for a while and Morveren asked Hengest again how the huge crossbow mounted above the gate worked. Hengest explained patiently how the mechanism wound the entwined hemp back before the firing pin unleashed the hollow wooden tube filled with arrowheads, broken knife blades and large iron nails. He went on to explain how the wooden canister was caught by two upright iron stays at the end of the crossbow while the deadly contents splayed out to rake through the air decimating anything in its path for up to fifty or so feet but Morveren had stopped following him when he had attempted to explain how the winding mechanism had produced the extraordinary tension necessary to unleash such a force. As before she ended up nodding wisely at his enthusiastic explanation without having understood much of it at all.

'Have you seen Ceinwen?' Ruadan asked when Hengest had finished.

'Treating the injured as ever. Including Balor. And good luck to her,' Morgund answered.

'How is he?'

'Another nasty scalp wound, lots of blood but he'll be fine which is more than you can say for his temper.'

'Ugly?'

'About as ugly as the scar will be on his shiny head.'

'We'd better see about rescuing her then.'

As Ruadan and Hengest hurried off into the fog the catapult near the gates crashed into action once again causing the three warriors by the fire to jump in unison.

'Bloody thing! You'd have thought we'd have got used to it by now,' Cael said, eyeing his spilt food ruefully.

'Imagine what affect it's having on the Adren, a massive great boulder dropping out of the fog on your head,' Morveren pointed out.

'You didn't understand a word of Hengest's explanation did you?' Morgund asked her.

She grinned and shook her head, 'No. And that's the third time I've asked him too. I understand the basic principle, same as a longbow really, but I can't see how it works in practice.'

'Does it matter?' Morgund asked.

'No. I saw the mess it made on the bridge. I don't care how it works just so long as it does. And just so long as the Adren don't have anything like it. It's no way for a warrior to die.'

'Perfect way to kill Adren though.'

'Right. I'm off to get some food,' Cael said, and the other two stared at him.

'All this talk of slaughter making you hungry is it?' Morveren asked.

'Well, I spilled my last lot when that bloody catapult fired again.'

'But that was your third helping anyway,' Morveren said exasperated.

'Still spilled it,' Cael said and left to redress the injustice.

'Nothing stops him, does it?' Morveren said as they watched him disappear into the fog.

'Eating?'

'Yes.'

'No. He's the perfect example of a warrior. Nothing puts him off his food. The only time I've ever seen him concerned was in the Shadow Lands and then it wasn't the Adren armies but the fact that we were getting very low on supplies,' Morgund said, smiling at the memory.

'I saw him eyeing our horses at one stage, and there wasn't much meat on them.'

Once again they lapsed back into silence and listened to the noise of the Adren as they worked away on the far side of the Causeway.

'I wonder what they're up to,' Morveren said after a while.

'Trying to bridge the gap somehow. We'll probably find out soon enough.'

'Yes, I suppose we will. I wish this fog would burn off.'

Morgund looked into her eyes as she spoke and thought he saw uncertainty there. 'Are you all right?'

She looked up surprised by the question, 'How do you mean?'

'Talan, Tamsyn, Elowen, Tomas – you were close to them all and well, even Ethain is off somewhere in the Shadow Lands.'

'I can't help any of them now, they're gone and that's that. I can't change anything that has happened so I just try not to think too much about the past, or the future come to that. It's all about now really isn't it? I mean if we can't stop the Adren then we'll be joining them, won't we? And if we do beat the Adren then I'll have time to think about them later, won't I?'

Morgund smiled at her nodding in agreement and she wished that she had just answered with a simple 'Yes, I'm fine,' but now that she had started she found that she wanted to tell him the truth of how she felt, how she had to fight down her fear before each Adren attack. Once the fighting started her anxiety vanished but the waiting always saw it creep back to her carrying with it the reminder that many of her friends had died already and if death could take them then it could take her too. Each time she had hid her fear from the others until she had been able to master it and stand before the enemy with courage. Her courage did not spring from some noble idea that she was defending her land and people but from her absolute faith in their warlord who she would follow anywhere and from the utter conviction that she must never let down the friends and warriors standing with her. Death was preferable to failing her friends. She wondered if the joy she felt during and after a battle was partly due to having overcome the fear she had felt before it.

She wanted to tell these things to the man sitting opposite her but she feared that he would not understand her feelings or worse, ridicule them. She was mildly surprised to find that she cared so much about what Morgund thought of her. Over the last few weeks she had come to value his company more and more, both as a friend and a warrior, and she wanted him to think well of her too. She wondered if perhaps Morgund just hid his fear better than she did but he seemed to be fearless before battle and a natural warrior who relished the fighting and revelled in killing the enemy.

They both looked at each other as another rumbling crash came from the Adren side of the gap in the Causeway.

'I wish this fog would lift then we'd be able to see what they were doing across there,' Morveren said.

'I think it is. A bit at least. You can make out the kitchens.' He pointed across the compound to where the two central buildings could now be vaguely seen.

'We're just in a lighter patch. It'll close in again,' she answered and paused before continuing, 'You don't feel any fear before battle do you?'

Morgund snorted in disagreement, 'Of course I do. Everyone does but it's how you use and control it that matters. The first few times in battle, especially when you're young, you only really feel the excitement and exhilaration but after a while you begin to wonder if you actually are invincible then you start worrying about how many times you can cheat death before it catches up with you. That's a dangerous time because when you start thinking like that you start acting differently which only makes it more likely that you will be killed.'

'So what do you do then?'

'Stop thinking like that straight away. Look, everyone dies at sometime. There's nothing you can do about an arrow flying out of nowhere and taking your life so there's no point in worrying about that. Just fight the battle before you, trust to your skill and luck and make sure you kill the bastard in front of you. Just make sure it isn't your turn to die.'

She laughed, 'Simple as that?'

'Simple as that,' he grinned back at her.

'You really think everyone feels fear?'

'Yes. Well, I suppose some don't. Occasionally you get a complete madman who doesn't but they don't last long usually. You just need to accept the fear when it surfaces, ride it to its crest then let it spill into anger and violence and then it's a wonderful feeling and nothing can match it.'

'Nothing?' she asked, smiling innocently at him.

He laughed before replying, 'I've seen it grip you, Balor, Mar'h, even Ceinwen, everyone.'

'Arthur too?'

'He's different.'

'How?'

'He just is. He's the best warrior and best commander you'll ever see. The best any of us will ever see. It's impossible to imagine him afraid of anything.'

'Maybe it's easy not to be afraid when you're as strong, fast, skilled and ruthless as he is.'

'True, but there's far more to it than that. Few can command a battle like he can. He's always in exactly the right place and right in the thick of it too. And more importantly he somehow sees the whole battle and knows how to control it.'

'He nearly got caught on the Causeway.'

'But that's the point. Even then he held those around him together and fought his way back to the Gates. If he hadn't done that then they would have broken through there and then.' As Morgund finished speaking another thunderous crashing sound came from the gap and they both shot to their feet.

'Let's see if we can make out anything from the wall,' Morveren said and led the way up to the already crowded parapet. As she climbed the ladder she wondered if he was looking up at her. He was.

The fog had thinned and the visibility had increased to about a hundred yards. Everyone on the wall could see what the Adren were doing. Great tree trunks, cut from the far shores, had been rolled and carried the length of the Causeway and were being tipped down into the gap before the Gates. The Adren clearly meant to fill the cutting with hundreds of felled trees and already the floor of the gap was covered by the trunks that had been rolled down the far side.

The watching warriors were brought back to life by Arthur shouting for bowmen to line the walls and commence firing. As he strode below where Morgund and Morveren stood they saw him look to the fog-obscured west and heard him ask Gwyna where Ablach's Uathach were.

Ablach's warriors were already on the headland. Seren and Terrill could see their camp from over a mile away. Dozens of fires sent their white smoke directly upwards in the still air and strands of mist crept over the edge of the cliffs beyond the camp. Their journey to the Causeway had been unhindered and if they were being pursued then they had seen no sign of it. Their eyes had become more accustomed to what, for them, was the blinding sunlight of early spring but they still travelled with their hoods drawn closely around their faces. In truth it was a watery sun filtered through the haze created by a land returning to life after the long winter. The sun was still low on the western horizon and throughout their journey it had been to their backs but still they had struggled with the unfamiliar brightness that bathed the landscape.

They had stopped by a strand of trees to eat the last of their bread and take a mouthful of water before crossing the last stretch of land to the cliffs. Neither of them had been this way before but the Westway was a broad and levelled road and it was easy to follow as it wound its way southeast across the rolling countryside on its way to the Causeway.

The journey from the copse above the Winter Wood had taken them much longer than they had expected and they both felt sore and weary from travelling so many miles on the cart that Terrill had prepared for their flight. Seren had spent the early part of the journey bitterly accusing Terrill of betrayal but she had soon realised the pointlessness of her recriminations and they had made their peace at the start of the second day of travelling. As they rested in the thin shade offered by the trees Seren pointed to the camp, 'Is that Arthur's camp?'

'It must be. At least part of it. The rest must be down on the Causeway,' Terrill answered and handed her the last of the water.

She swigged it gratefully and wiped the back of her hand across her mouth. 'Then we must be in time. Lazure can't have used the tunnel yet!'

'Ready for one last push then?' Terrill asked, standing up and stretching out his hand to her. Seren ignored the proffered hand and stared past him. He turned to follow her gaze and saw what had caught her eye. A group of horsemen were approaching fast and the drumming sound of their hooves on the hard earth grew rapidly as they drew nearer. Seren finally stood and together they stepped out of the shelter of the trees to meet the horsemen.

Terrill looked around at their faces as they encircled them hoping to see a familiar face from Caer Sulis but he recognised none of them. Some of the riders had drawn weapons and the two Cithol immediately felt threatened. They instinctively edged closer to each other as the horsemen shifted around them. Terrill thought that even by Briton standards they looked unkempt and wild.

One of the mounted warriors barked a question at them. They looked at each other but neither had understood what the warrior had said.

'We're looking for Arthur. We have important news for him,' Terrill said to the ring of warriors with his earlier misgivings about the Britons resurfacing strongly.

The one who had questioned them before spoke again. Terrill thought he made out most of what was said but the accent was unlike any he had heard before and the words were spoken too quickly for him to catch it all.

'Arthur of the Britons?' Seren tried and pointed to the settlement of tents and fires on the headland.

On hearing her voice and realising that the smaller of the two cloaked strangers before them was a woman the horsemen focused their attention on her. One of them nudged his horse closer to her and tried to flip back the hood covering her face with the tip of his sword. She ducked and quickly stepped backwards. Their apparent leader spoke harshly to him and he pulled his horse back with a curse and a final leer at the cloaked and hooded Seren. The one with the ruddy complexion and braided beard, who seemed to be their leader, beckoned for them to follow him and he turned his horse away. Seren and Terrill exchanged a nervous glance but realised they had little choice and followed after the departing horseman with the others falling in to either side and behind them.

'I could hardly understand anything they said,' Seren said quietly leaning her head towards Terrill.

'I understood some of it. It's the same language as Arthur's but spoken differently, I think, at least they reacted when we spoke his name.'

'Perhaps they're from one of the other tribes?'

'We don't know much about these people do we?'

'No. Let's just hope they take us to Arthur quickly.'

They carried on surrounded by the horsemen and Terrill wondered if he really could spend his life around people like these. He realised it was far too late to be having second thoughts about the choices he had made but he still could not imagine a life among these people. He fervently hoped it would not come to that.

They were led towards a large tent that stood in the middle of the encampment and the warrior with the braided beard dismounted and gestured for them to wait as he swept aside the hanging animal skins that covered the entrance and disappeared inside.

A small crowd of warriors gathered to stare at the two newcomers and Seren and Terrill felt increasingly more uncomfortable as the long minutes passed. Finally they were told to go inside and they entered into the gloominess of the makeshift pavilion.

The stench hit them like a slap in the face and they both struggled to hide the nausea they instantly felt. It was a mixture of uncooked meat, animal dung and human odour and it filled the tent as thickly as the smoke that billowed from the central fire, but at least they were out of the sunlight and they were both grateful for that.

It was obvious to them who was the leader of these warriors; he was sitting on a broad stout chair that seemed to serve him as a throne and several servants were bringing plates of food to him. He looked over at the two who had just entered and he stared at them with his calculating small black eyes. He raised a thick-scarred hand dripping in animal fat and beckoned them closer. When they were standing before him he made a gesture for them to pull back their hoods and they did so.

Cries and curses rang through the tent and several warriors drew weapons as the Cithol revealed themselves. None of those present had seen a Cithol before and their white hair, translucent skin and strange eyes that showed no white at all immediately struck fear into them. They had all heard the legends of the southern Winter Wood and the ghosts that haunted those feared forests but none had ever thought to actually see or meet such apparitions.

Only Ablach did not react with surprise or terror and it was only his sudden barking laugh that stayed his warriors' hands. The warriors looked at each other uncertainly but as Ablach's laughter filled the room they sheathed their weapons keeping a wary eye on the two ghosts before their leader.

Finally his laughter ebbed away and he returned to eating the haunch of meat that he held in his hand as he flicked his eyes from Seren to Terrill and then back to Seren again. Minutes passed as he scrutinised them both and Terrill feared his stomach would rebel at the sight of this monstrous barbarian tearing meat from the bone with blood and juices flowing freely into his beard. Ablach sensed this and offered the half-devoured haunch to Terrill who just shook his head. Ablach's laugh barked out again at his reaction and food flew from his mouth. Some of it landed on Seren's cloak but she resisted the impulse to brush it off and steadfastly returned the Uathach's stare.

'Cithol by the gods,' Ablach said into his food. 'Cithol walk among us!' he exclaimed more loudly to those inside the pavilion. He seemed amused by the reaction this caused among his warriors as their suspicions were confirmed. Terrill could make out the word 'Cithol' but the rest was lost to him then Ablach turned his attention back towards them and when he spoke it was slower and more like the accents they had heard from other Britons.

'Are you the mighty Cithol army come to relieve Arthur?'

Seren was entirely confused by everything that she had seen and heard since sighting this encampment. She knew nothing about the politics and divisions of the Britons and had assumed that Arthur was the warlord of all the Britons but this monster before her seemed to be a chieftain in his own right. She decided to be cautious.

'The Cithol army is to follow us. We are but messengers and we carry a message for Arthur of the Britons.'

'It seems to me you carry more than just a message. Do the Cithol send their child-carriers to battle?'

'Is Arthur among you or should we look for him on the Causeway?'

Ablach stood up and towered over the two Cithol. He gave a curt order to those gathered in the tent and immediately they filed out, many with a last glance at the two ghosts dwarfed by their chieftain. Ruraidh remained standing just inside the doorway with his arms folded and his gaze locked on the two Cithol.

Ablach frowned at his captain's presence then chose to ignore it and gestured for the Cithol to sit down at a table littered with food and spilt drink. He saw Terrill's brief look of distaste and he swept the debris of the half-finished meals from the table with the back of his hand. He grinned reassuringly at them both, revealing his stained and yellow teeth, and held back a chair for Seren to sit. Seren nodded her thanks and took the offered seat. Terrill sat beside her and Ablach slowly walked around the table to sit opposite them.

He stared at Terrill for a long minute then switched his gaze to Seren, all the while picking absently at his greasy beard. Seren, uncomfortable under his scrutiny, shifted in her chair but she held his stare with her head tilted upward in defiance. Ablach just continued plucking his filthy beard and staring at her. The only sound inside the tent came from a guttering torch, which caused the shadows to shift suddenly and disconcertingly.

'Have your guards gone to fetch Arthur?' Seren asked in an even tone while continuing to look into his eyes. She thought her voice sounded intrusive and harsh in the oppressive silence.

'Arthur is on the Causeway. Fighting.'

Seren considered this and waited for Ablach to say more but he just continued to stare at her.

'This is Captain Terrill and I am Fin Seren. Who may you be?'

'Ablach.'

Clearly he considered this to be enough information and he offered no more. Terrill leant forward on the table and spoke for the first time since entering the tent. 'Why aren't you and your men down on the Causeway fighting with Arthur against the Adren?'

Ablach's eyes never left Seren as he answered, 'Why isn't your Cithol army down on the Causeway fighting with Arthur against the Adren?'

Terrill half rose from his seat angered both by Ablach's sneering tone and at being ignored by him but Seren put out a hand to restrain him and he sank back into his seat. Ablach had noticed the flicker in Seren's eyes when he had asked his question and he guessed that she was asking herself the same question and that perhaps there was no Cithol army. Having got the information he needed he took his gaze away from Seren and poured himself a cup of wine.

'I'm a chieftain from the northern lands. One of Arthur's captains. He's ordered me to hold the cliff tops to cover his retreat should it become necessary. We await his orders to join him in the battle below.'

Seren watched as he swilled the wine in his cup letting it slop over the sides and onto the table.

'And who are you, Fin Seren?' Ablach asked once again ignoring Terrill.

'I am Lord Venning's daughter.'

'Lord Venning?'

'The Lord of the Veiled City.'

'And he sent you as his messenger?'

'The message is important and we need to get it to Arthur as quickly as possible.'

Ablach noted the evasion and returned his attention to the wine swirling in his cup.

'The Causeway is no place for either of you. It's certainly no place for a woman carrying a child. Aren't child bearing woman precious to your people?'

'We must see him. The message is urgent.'

'You can't go to the Causeway while the battle is raging. No message from you could be important enough to take into the heart of battle.' He waived a dismissive hand at them and then smiled as he added, 'He can wait to hear he's sired another bastard!' Ablach was already laughing at his own joke when he saw the look of shock cross both faces opposite him. He quickly raised his wine cup to his lips to hide his own shock at their reaction.

Ablach's mind was racing with the possibilities that this new information offered him but he kept his eyes away from them both and reached down to the floor to retrieve the roasted goat leg that he had previously swept from the table. He noticed that Seren recovered the quicker and that she was watching him closely to see if he realised that he had stumbled across an uncomfortable truth. Intentionally misreading her scrutiny he offered her the roasted goat meat. She shook her head.

'Are you sure? You must have had a tiring journey.' He inspected the meat that was now covered in dirt from the floor of the tent. He brushed some of it off with his greasy hands and offered it once more.

'I'm not hungry. Thank you.'

'Please yourself,' Ablach replied and tore a chunk from the meat with his filthy hands. Seren could not prevent herself from staring at his fingernails which were long and black with engrained dirt.

'We must take the message to Arthur immediately,' Terrill said and again Ablach kept his eyes on Seren infuriating Terrill even further.

'I'll take the message to him.'

Seren and Terrill exchanged a quick glance.

'If Arthur trusts me as one of his chieftains then you too can trust me.'

Seren looked at the table wondering if Arthur did indeed trust this man.

'Tell me or not, either way I can't allow you to go down to the Causeway. Arthur wouldn't thank me for putting the daughter of his Cithol ally into the danger of battle.' Ablach shrugged then gestured to the food lying around and beneath the table. 'Are you sure you won't have something to eat?'

'I'm not hungry,' she repeated.

Ablach stood up and said, 'You can stay with us and if you do become hungry then you can join us here to eat. I'll get one of my men to find a spare tent for you.'

'The message is urgent!' Seren said as she stood up.

'Then you'd better tell me sooner rather than later.'

Seren hesitated a final time then committed herself, 'The Adren will use an ancient tunnel that runs under the Causeway. They'll surface behind Arthur between the Gates and the cliffs.'

Ablach considered this in silence keeping his face impassive despite the developing plans that this new information brought crowding to his mind. In the space of a few short minutes he had learned that the Cithol Lord's daughter probably carried Arthur's child, that Arthur was certainly doomed on the Causeway and it was unlikely that the Cithol were preparing an army. He needed time alone to think through the implications of these revelations.

'This is grave news. I'll send word to Arthur immediately. You should both rest now.'

He nodded to Ruraidh who called out to one of the guards and the two Cithol were led away to a spare tent. He sat back down at the table and threw away the dirt-encrusted meat he held. He spat out the remains of the mouthful he had taken and washed the grit from his mouth with a fresh cup of wine as he thought about how best to use what he had learnt. Ruraidh still stood inside the doorway and he too pondered what he had seen and heard.

Inch by inch and yard by yard the fog on the Causeway was gradually lifting. Morgund could clearly see the far bank now where the Adren were sheltering behind a wooden wall that acted as a moveable shield. As it advanced they rolled the next tree trunk behind it until they reached the lip of the gap and then they would tip the felled tree down the slope and retreat behind the wall to fetch the next one. The gap was steadily filling and the trunks were now halfway up to the level of the Causeway.

Morgund kept an arrow strung to his bow and whenever a target presented itself he would let fly and quickly string another. The Adren wall offered them effective but not total protection and arrows flew from the Briton side constantly as they sought exposed legs and arms.

All the warriors at the Causeway Gates were now either on the wall, firing from the arrow slits at its base or manning the two catapults. The one that lobbed the large boulders had been moved towards the far end of the Gates so that it could range on the Adren side of the gap.

Morgund flinched as he heard the crash of it firing behind him and lowered his head slightly when the resulting boulder tore through the air above his head.

'Ducking won't help if they get the range wrong!' Ceinwen laughed beside him.

'Bloody thing! At least they could hit that shield they're using!' he replied then stopped and stared as the last boulder crashed straight into the wooden wall the Adren were sheltering behind. It splintered and broke in two and every longbow on the Britons' side of the gap fired in unison. The shafts cut through into the exposed Adren ranks and row after row fell as their captains tried to get them back beyond the longbows' range and into the safety of the fog once more. It had only taken seconds but every Adren in sight had been slaughtered. Occasionally one would stir from the mounds of dead and four or five arrows would immediately speed across the gap to the new target.

'I think they hit the shield,' Ceinwen said and Morgund laughed.

Fresh bags of arrows were being thrown up to the wall by the warriors on the ground and buckets of water were being passed along the lines so that they could quench their thirst during the lull in the Adren attack.

Morgund was looking back into the compound. 'Are Aelfric and the others still here somewhere?'

'No. Arthur's already sent everyone who isn't a warrior back up the cliffs.'

'I don't suppose the boy was happy about that.'

'I don't suppose he argued with Arthur about it.'

'True.'

Someone shouted a warning and everyone immediately ducked down behind the wall as a flight of Adren arrows thumped into the wood and sailed overhead. Morgund risked a quick glance over the top and swore.

'That didn't take them long did it?'

Ceinwen bobbed her head over the edge and saw that the Adren were slowly advancing through the fog behind a new wall.

'They must have had another one ready.'

Another boulder from the catapult soared overhead and smashed into the Adren ranks behind the new shield as another trunk was rolled down into the gap. The trees had been cut to a more or less uniform length and every warrior at the Gates knew that before long the Adren would bridge the gap and be able to attack the East Gate and a fifty-yard section of the walls to either side.

As the level of the felled trees rose and the Adren shield began to cross the gap the hail of arrows from the Britons intensified until the constantly lifting mist between the two armies was thick with them. The Adren were no more than fifty yards away and at this range the arrows were punching blindly through the wooden wall killing those in their path, but as soon as one Adren fell another immediately discarded their own shield and stepped up to take their place helping to carry the wooden wall nearer to the fort. Behind them level pathways were laid on top of the trunks by the massed Adren who followed crouched behind their shields.

As the wall approached the Briton side of the gap it offered less and less protection to those following behind and the longbows killed hundreds of the advancing Adren. When it came into range the catapult above the East Gate finally fired its lethal storm straight into the centre of the wall and smashed it in two. One side toppled back on those carrying it and the other wavered before dipping forward. There were over two hundred warriors manning the fort each with either a short or longbow and within a span of twenty seconds a thousand arrows tore into the confused Adren ranks but even as the warriors above the gate struggled to reload the catapult, the next protective wall was already crossing the bridged gap and behind it sheltered two of the Adren's own war machines.

Arthur stood on the parapet his sword in one hand and his shield raised against the Adren arrows that still flew from the ranks beyond the gap. More of the enemy could be seen with each passing minute as the mist began to shred and he saw the two knots of Adren surrounding the catapults as they lumbered onto the bridge. He ran along the length of the Wessex and Anglian line that was positioned to the right of the East Gate and pointed out the threat to the best of his bowmen. Arrows flew to their new target but the catapults and their operators were well protected.

They both fired at the same time sending chain-linked grappling hooks sailing over the East Gate. As soon as they hit the ground they jerked backwards as a dozen Adren on each catapult started to reel them back in. Hengest saw the threat immediately and managed to deflect one of the hooks so it slid harmlessly off his crossbow catapult but the second hook embedded itself it the framework and the whole contraption creaked as the chain snapped taut. The Adren hauled on the spoked wheel attached to their machine and the snared catapult lifted and jerked sideways. Hengest scrambled to lever the hook free of the woodwork but there was nothing he could do to prevent the inevitable and with a final screech of protest the catapult was torn free of its moorings and wrenched over the side of the wall to crash in a tangled wreckage before the East Gate.

Hengest was still staring at the ruin of his machine when Arthur crashed into him and sent him careening backwards into the cover of the protective wall just as a flight of Adren arrows seethed through the air where he had stood.

'Hengest!' Arthur shouted into his face.

'It's gone,' Hengest replied blankly.

Arthur grabbed his tunic below the throat and slammed the Anglian back against the wall.

'Get to the other one and keep it firing at the Causeway for as long as you can! If they come over the wall then destroy it utterly!'

Hengest's gaze came back into focus and he nodded. Arthur dragged him to his feet and shoved him towards one of the ladders then looked out across the Adren bridge to see that the new wall was nearly upon them. He sprinted across to Gereint on the North side of the fort and told him to place ten bowmen in the compound behind his defensive line to help stop any Adren breach then did the same on the Anglian and Wessex line.

Now that the deadly weapon above the gate had been destroyed the

Adren came on with renewed purpose. The wooden wall they advanced behind was divided into manageable sections and had a latticework of planks and steps attached to the side facing the Adren so that once they reached the fort it could act as one large scaling ladder.

Under a ferocious hail of arrows the Adren raced across the last few paces and the combined wall crashed into place against a hundred yard section of the fort. Hundreds more died as they clambered desperately up to the top but there were hundreds more to take their place and the first wave of the enemy finally crashed over the top of the wall and into the Britons. The Britons held the wall against the first fury of the assault but the Adren were crossing the gap in their hundreds, racing to scale the wall and engage the hated enemy. The fighting at the top of the wall was desperate, the Britons had the advantage of position but the Adren kept throwing themselves into the battle and their numbers seemed limitless. There was no possible respite for the Britons and after a few hours of the raging battle Arthur knew he could not hold the wall indefinitely – not against such a continuous attack.

He shouted to Gwyna who stood in the shield wall. She ran back to him her longbow still held in her hand.

'Take one of the horses and find Ablach! We need his warriors. If they can't make it here in time then head for the Winter Woods! Do whatever you have to but get me those warriors! Go, now!'

Gwyna took a last look around her then sprinted across to one of the few remaining horses.

Ablach was standing on the cliffs overlooking the Causeway when he heard the clash as the two armies met on the wall of the Gates. Below him the fog still stretched out across the Channel Marshes in a white blanket that was lit brightly by the spring sun rising gradually behind him. In the distance he could make out patches of water and marsh grasses where the fog had began to drift apart. For the thousandth time he turned his eyes to the coral where the Britons of the southern tribes had stabled their horses. There were over three hundred fine horses and the only guards seemed to be children; all he had to do was ride away with them. He could take the horses and then sack Caer Sulis, Caer Cadarn and even the Haven and there would only be a handful of warriors to stand in his way. Britain was his for the taking. Once the Adren came up into the flats behind Arthur then those on the Causeway would be doomed so Arthur would never be able to exact revenge or retribution for the betrayal. Ablach's only doubt was whether or not the Adren would leave him alone in the northern lands. He may be able to take the South's wealth but how long could he keep it? He pondered the question as he stared at the horses.

Ruraidh, his captain who had seen the Adren host in the Shadow Lands, advised against it. He was convinced that only with the southern tribes could they hope to withstand the Adren army but Ablach was not so sure about that and the apparent news that the Cithol seemed unwilling to support Arthur diminished Ruraidh's argument further in his opinion. Ablach maintained that if the Cithol thought the Adren might leave them alone then it was even more likely they would leave his own people alone. In Ruraidh's opinion the likelihood that there would be no Cithol army only made it more important that they join with Arthur's forces immediately.

The frantic noise of battle rolled through the mist below and echoed against the cliffs drawing most of the Uathach from their camp and to the edge where they stared down to the shrouded Causeway. A light breeze was feeling its way down from the North and the desperate clash of weapons grew and fell on the wind. Many of the warriors cast glances at their chieftain wondering if he had chosen to leave the southern tribes to their fate. The Uathach were evenly divided in their opinion about what was the best course to follow. Some trusted Ruraidh's judgement and felt their best chance of survival lay with fighting alongside Arthur's warriors. Many of these had formed friendships with the southern warriors while they had been at Caer Sulis. Others hated the southerners so much that they would rather risk annihilation than lend Arthur any support whatsoever but if Ablach ordered them down into the fog then they would go; not to go would be seen as a craven refusal to join in battle.

They lined the cliff top and stood and stared for hours and never once did the sound of battle diminish in the valley below. More of the silent Uathach joined Ruraidh's side. The Britons were holding back an invading horde and the Uathach were restless as they stood idly by while the battle raged on the Causeway without them.

Ablach remained unmoved. Seren and Terrill had left their tent and enquired of him if the message had been sent and Seren had bluntly asked why the surrounding warriors were not going to Arthur's aide. Ablach ordered them both to be escorted back to their tent but the nearby warriors felt shamed by her words.

Before the two protesting Cithol had reached their quarters a cry went up from along the cliff top. Through the clearing mist one of them had seen a rider tearing across the flat land below them and making for the cliff paths. Many recognised her by the long red hair and the shield she still had strapped to her arm and they waited for her at the top of the cliff path as she led her horse up the last hundred yards.

She made her way straight to Ablach and the Uathach gathered closely around to hear the exchange between daughter and father.

'Thank the gods you've arrived!' Gwyna said still struggling for breath. Her face was sweat-streaked and her clothes were drenched in blood.

'We haven't just arrived,' Ruraidh said.

'What?' Gwyna asked turning to him.

'We arrived some time ago.'

'Then why are you still here?' Gwyna looked from Ruraidh to her silent father.

'Is Arthur still alive?' Ablach finally spoke up.

'Yes! You should see him and the others fight, everything we've heard about him is true but we're hard pressed. The Adren can keep putting fresh attackers into the battle while we can only tire. They'll soon take the East Wall. Why haven't you joined us?' She looked around the quiet circle of warriors and many could not meet her eyes.

Ablach was cursing to himself. Ideally he had wanted Arthur to die early so that he could ride down and rescue the rest of the southern warriors and then merge them into his own army. It was all a question of timing; he needed Arthur dead before the invaders sprang their trap because once the Adren were behind the Britons it would be too late to save any of the southern warriors. If Ruraidh was right then he would need as many of them as possible if he had to defend his land from the Adren.

'Why!' Gwyna was standing directly before her father and had screamed the question at him. She was thinking about the attack on Arthur that he had engineered at her wedding feast and wondering if he intended to finish now what he had started then. She knew that if he succeeded then her hopes and ambitions would die along with Arthur and the southern warriors. 'Why!' she screamed at him again.

'Perhaps he's waiting for the Adren to spring their trap.'

Everyone turned to look at the woman who had spoken.

'Who are you?' Gwyna asked looking at the hooded stranger who had pushed her way forward to join them at the centre of the circle.

Seren returned her stare. Despite the difference in appearance something about the sweat and bloodstained warrior before her reminded her of the young girl by Arthur's side in Caer Sulis. Seren had only seen her at a distance and then through a smoke filled hall but she was suddenly sure that the red headed warrior before her was the same girl that had sat by Arthur's side during his marriage feast. She pulled her hood back and narrowed her eyes against the hurtful brightness of the day.

Many of the warriors who had not been in Ablach's tent earlier took a step backwards and cursed at the sight of Seren but Gwyna looked at her levelly.

'I am Fin Seren, daughter of Lord Venning, and I have come from the Veiled City of the Cithol to warn Arthur that the Adren plan to use an ancient tunnel to get behind the Causeway Gates. If they succeed then Arthur will fall, the Veiled City will fall, and wherever you call home will fall too.'

Gwyna stared at the strange apparition who stood so proudly before them. She found it impossible to gauge the truth of what the girl before had said. She stared at her; the white hair, the perfectly smooth pale skin of her face and the green eyes that showed no trace of white all made it difficult to judge her by any normal standards but her voice carried conviction and defiance and Gwyna believed her. She turned to Ablach, 'Is what she says true?'

'Who can say with a Cithol witch? And how would the Cithol know of Adren plans?' Ablach replied but he could feel that the warriors around them were siding with Gwyna. He turned to face them, 'The rich lands of the South can be ours. Leave Arthur and his rats to die in the trap set for them. Let the Cithol ghosts fend for themselves. Take the southern horses and ride for Caer Sulis! We can steal the Adren plunder long before they can claim it!'

As he finished another shout went up from those who still watched from the cliff top. The mist had finally relinquished its fight against the sun and wind to leave only an indistinct haze in the distance and patches above the wider waterways. Ablach and the others went close to the edge to look out over the Marshes and what they saw took their voices away.

Their eyes were first drawn to the ferocious battle that raged over a mile away at the Causeway Gates but it was the Causeway itself that commanded their attention. It stretched out in a straight line for miles until it disappeared into the far haze and for as far as the eye could see it was packed from edge to edge with the Adren host. Thousands upon thousands of Adren were advancing upon the beleaguered Gates.

'You're a fool Ablach! Do you not see yet?' Gwyna shouted at him, then turned to the Uathach warriors, 'I've hated the southern warriors as much as any one here. But they are warriors with honour and they stand below against that horde, and they stand alone! They defend our lands as much as their own! Would you have it said that they defended this land unaided while we bickered and spent our time mending clothes or playing dice? Who here thinks that we can stand alone against that horde once the southern warriors are dead?'

'Why go down there to die with those you despise when you can take their wealth and return home with glory!' Ablach's voice drowned out Gwyna as he roared at his men belatedly realising his adopted daughter was threatening to take control of his warriors.

'What glory is there in running for home like beaten dogs trailing behind them what they could steal from the aged and infants?'

'It's too late! The Adren are on the flats!' Ruraidh cried out pointing to where the Adren were emerging from a wide subsidence half a mile from the cliff base.

Seren could only understand the gist of these exchanges and she watched warily as Gwyna turned to her father with a look of murderous hatred twisting her face. Every plan, every hope for the future, every ambition that Gwyna harboured rested upon her life and position with Arthur. If the warriors followed Ablach's course then Arthur and the South would fall and she would slip back into being nothing and no one. Seren watched in frozen horror as Gwyna slipped her knife from her belt and rammed it up to the hilt in the pit of Ablach's stomach. As he bent over and staggered forwards she leapt back, drew her sword and with a furious overhead swing she brought it down on the back of her father's head. Ablach continued his stumble forward and crashed to the ground with the back of his head split open and pouring blood.

Gwyna drew a shuddering breath and turned to face the Uathach with her sword still dripping her father's gore. 'Those of you who wish to flee home do so now but leave behind your swords for those who will fight to protect our lands! The rest of you mount up and take a spare horse. We ride to war!'

To a warrior they raised their weapons to their new chieftain and roared out, 'To war!'

Chapter Twelve

Seren watched as Gwyna led the Uathach warriors down the cliff path. Each took two horses with them, their own and one from the corral.

Below them Arthur fought to keep the Adren from breaching the East Wall of the Causeway Gates but, like the Uathach before her, it was the sight on the Causeway that held her eyes. Between the Gates and the distant haze it was covered by the advancing Adren. It looked to her like a black serpent ponderously heaving its way closer to its trapped prey.

The wind was from the North and it was still raw and cold. She pulled her cloak closer about her and clutched the hood together below her chin to stop the breeze from lifting it back and exposing her eyes to Terrill. There were so few Britons standing against the hordes of the eastern army and her own people, led by her father, had abandoned them to their fate. Seen from their vantage point it seemed such a hopeless resistance and she felt ashamed. Merdynn had said that every kingdom in Middangeard and those further to the East had fallen to the Adren army and now the Britons too would be overwhelmed and fall before the black serpent that now crawled upon their shores.

'There's so many of them.' Terrill echoed her thoughts aloud and his voice was filled with fear and awe as he stared at the endless black column.

'Lazure's army. And they've come for the Veiled City.'

'Perhaps your father was right to treaty with him. There can be no army that could stand against so many!'

Seren turned to him but her voice was more sad than angry, 'Would you rather be one of his slaves?'

'Would you rather die?' he replied, just as heavy-hearted. They briefly looked at each other both unwilling to rehash the argument now that they had seen the reality before them.

Seren sighed and turned away. 'Life is worth dying for. Slavery is a death not worth living for.'

'Certainly the Britons thought so. Arthur thought so.'

'Thinks so,' Seren angrily corrected him.

Terrill did not think that any of the Britons would make it back to the cliffs but he had no wish to provoke or upset her further. 'Where do you think they'll go now, if they escape?'

'Arthur will go to the Veiled City and defend it until the last.'

'Surely it would better if Arthur came nowhere near the city? If he defends the Veiled City then Lazure will think that Lord Venning has betrayed his treaty. He'll destroy us too!'

'Better that my father betrays his treaty than his people.'

'Didn't you hear me? Lazure will destroy us!'

'Perhaps not. If we can raise enough of our people then we can stand with the Britons in the Winter Wood. Arthur won't let Lazure destroy the Veiled City. We must return there and talk to those who would resist Lazure.'

'Go back? We've just fled from there!'

'Where else would you suggest we go? We've done all that we can here. We've delivered the message.'

Seren had just watched Gwyna kill her own father and then lead the Uathach warriors on their charge to relieve Arthur and she had begun to realise just how inadequately equipped she was to play any useful role in the brutal world that the Britons inhabited. The message that Arthur had sent to her via Terrill said that he 'did what he must rather than what he wished' but it seemed to her that the wish must belong to another lifetime now.

It had been that cryptic message that had spurred her to join Terrill on his journey to Caer Sulis where she had inadvertently witnessed the feast to celebrate Arthur's marriage to Gwyna, who seemed to her to be a ferocious creature with her wild hair and stone-hard eyes so unlike her own; a creature capable of slaughtering her own father in a fit of rage, a creature capable of leading vicious warriors, a creature capable of being Arthur's wife.

Seren realised with a cold and depressing certainty that Gwyna could offer Arthur far more than she ever could. She had delivered the information for Gwyna to act upon and there was now nothing more she could do. She did not belong to this world and she suddenly yearned to be back in the Veiled City, the very place she was due to be exiled from. Accepting the irony she acknowledged that the safest place for her and her unborn child was the Veiled City, for that was where Arthur would go next. If he escaped the trap below.

'But how?' Terrill asked interrupting her thoughts.

'What?'

'How do we get back to the city?'

Seren shrugged as she looked around the encampment. She saw one of the empty supply carts with its horses still harnessed and pointed to it.

'We'll take that cart and leave now. If we travel without stopping then we might make the Winter Wood before Arthur does.'

Seren led the way to the cart and Terrill followed. He did not think there was any possibility of Arthur ever following them to the Winter Wood and berated himself for the thought that immediately followed; perhaps it was best if he did not.

The fighting was at its fiercest on the walls to either side of the East Gate. Company after company of Adren seethed across the makeshift bridge and around the base of the East Wall pushing those ahead of them up the broad scaling trellis and into the line of defenders above.

Arthur had withdrawn most of his warriors from the further extremes of the fort and concentrated them where the onslaught heaved around the East Gate in an attempt to have some reserve to replace those killed or too exhausted to continue. He had left only a few bowmen further along the walls and they kept up the volleys of arrows that flew into the massed ranks of Adren as they crowded onto the bridge but he knew now that the battle for the Causeway would be won or lost in the bitter close fighting at the East Gate.

He never stayed long at any one point but continually fought along the whole breadth of the attack as he sought out the places where the Adren were pressing the hardest. It seemed to each of his warriors that he was never far away from them and just when they thought they must give way before the weight of numbers opposing them he would appear at their side and help to drive the Adren back. They took strength from his presence and fought all the harder but as each hour passed their exhaustion grew and always there were fresh companies of Adren surging forward like an inexorable tide crashing its waves against the wall in a relentless fury.

Below the wall stood the reserve force, itself tired and bloody, and a constant trickle of warriors scrambled up the ladders to join in the fighting on the parapet as wounded or exhausted warriors stumbled away from the immediate battle.

Just behind the reserve force and in the shelter of the inner wall Ceinwen worked almost alone in tending to the wounded. There was no more time or facility available other than to cauterise wounds with a searing iron and the smell of blood and burnt flesh hung sickeningly in the air. The screaming of the wounded was lost in the hammering roar of the battle. Those who were too badly injured to be helped were given vials of liquid to quell the pain and left to die while Ceinwen loaded carts with those not fatally maimed and directed those who were still capable to lead the carts back towards the cliffs. She kept a constant eye on the raging battle and saw Arthur leap down from the wall and start to shout orders to the reserve group. Almost as one they raced back towards her and the inner wall where spare longbows and bags of arrows awaited them. She watched as Arthur turned back to the wall and saw Gereint racing across to him.

Arthur saw him too and turned to cut the distance between them.

'Arthur! We have to pull back to the cliffs! There's too many of them and we can't fight them here! We have to abandon the Gates now!'

Arthur's hand shot out and grabbed the collar of Gereint's battle jerkin and he almost lifted him off the ground as he hauled him closer.

'You will stand your ground along with your warriors and defend this fort until I tell you otherwise!' Arthur dragged him closer until their faces were only inches apart. 'Is that clear?'

Gereint looked up into Arthur's eyes and his protest fell immediately silent. Arthur still held his sword in his other hand and for a moment Gereint thought he was going to use it. Suddenly the East Gates shuddered under a tremendous blow. The Adren had built a hinged doorway in the centre of their wooden shield so that they could access the gates and they were attempting to batter down the iron-bound wood with a massive tree trunk.

Arthur turned back to Gereint, 'Get you bowmen back to the inner wall now then wait for my next orders!'

Gereint sprinted back to the ladders to get word to his bowmen who were strung out along the North end of the wall. Arthur looked from the jarring gates back to the furious melee on the wall above and knew that if the Adren broke through the gates then his warriors would be slaughtered quickly. He too sprinted to his bowmen lined on the parapet over to his right. As he passed behind his warriors he roared above the din of the battle for them to prepare to fall back to the inner wall.

When he reached the far end of the wall beyond the section under direct Adren attack he saw Morveren among the bowmen and yelled out to her.

'Fall back to the inner wall! As the others disengage by section from right to left cover the wall with as many volleys as can! Do you understand?'

She nodded vigorously and picking up her arrow bag informed the others of the plan. They left their positions and raced back to the second wall.

Once Arthur could see that his and Gereint's bowmen had reached their place he strode back to the desperate fighting along the wall. He broke into a run as he approached them.

'Back! Back to the second wall! Now!'

He repeated the orders as he ran behind the struggling line and behind him the Wessex and Anglian warriors leapt from the parapet in a rolling wave and ran for the next line of defence. As they dropped from the wall flights of arrows sped over their heads and into the Adren who were at last claiming the ramparts.

Arthur continued running along the line, leaping over the strewn bodies and swerving to avoid those locked in combat. He was roaring out the same instruction and all along the wall behind him the Mercian warriors were peeling off and racing for the safety of the second wall. The volleys of arrows swept the wall behind the departing warriors but the Adren were too great in number and many were already jumping down into the compound.

Finally Arthur reached the end of the Mercian line and he leapt down along with the last of the warriors and once again the arrows flew in a flat trajectory over their heads and into the Adren ranks clambering over the wall and onto the parapet. Dozens were plucked from the wall and sent flying backwards by the force of the arrows that were being fired from less than fifty yards away but the Adren were determined to get to their enemy and the longbows could not cover the entire wall and nor could they hope to match the numbers that were spilling from the ramparts and into the compound.

As Arthur leapt to the ground and rolled forward to lessen the impact of the jump the East Gate finally splintered and broke inwards. Arthur scrambled to his feet and quickly looked around. Adren were pouring through the shattered gates and scores were now jumping down from the breached East Wall. The last of his warriors were trying to reach the second wall but they were already intermixed with the Adren and there were chaotic running battles everywhere.

In that moment Arthur knew the battle for the Causeway was lost. The Gates would fall to the Adren just like everything else that had tried to stand in the way of their inevitable tide. He could hold the second wall for a while longer but it was now a question of reaching the cliffs with as many warriors as could be saved from the doomed fort. A bitter rage gripped him at the thought that he could no longer keep the Adren hordes from reaching Britain and he sought out each running battle between him and the second wall and flung himself in a hacking fury at the Adren as he pushed his isolated warriors to the safety of the forming line at the inner wall.

He reached the second line as the last of the warriors he could not reach were cut down by the Adren. Two Anglians reached over the five-foot high wall and helped to haul him over the top. He recognised Hengest as one of them.

'Destroy the catapult by the West Gate. Completely!' he shouted as he regained his feet and looked around to assess the shield wall which was already coming under attack from the advancing Adren. About a third of his force stood some way behind the front line and they continued to fire devastating volleys into the Adren as they poured through the East Gate. One of the Adren captains was trying to group some of his own archers on the wall from where they could fire down into the southern warriors. Arthur saw what he was doing and shouted commands to his bowmen to kill him and those he already had around him. The next storm of arrows tore through them and left no one standing and their aim returned to the breached gate, but for every fifty that fell to the longbows twenty more surged through the gate and raced to join the attack on the inner wall.

Arthur could see that it was only a matter of time before the second line would be overwhelmed and knew that he had to start the retreat now if anyone was to be saved from the ruin of the Causeway Gates.

He glanced towards the empty flats where the mist was already in tattered retreat before the North wind and then joined the surging struggle around the inner wall and fought once again along the line of defence.

Even as he fought Arthur was recalling the defensive constructions between the Gates and the cliffs and planning how best to get to the sanctuary of the higher ground.

Beyond the West Gate the Causeway stretched for half a mile before it reached another ramped wall. Between the Gates and the ramped wall another bridged gap had been cut in the Causeway and beyond the last wall lay the flats below the cliffs with interspersed firing walls to cover any retreat.

Arthur sought behind the shield wall for the Mercian Warlord, Gereint. He saw the shorter figure with his close-cropped grey hair further along and line and he ran towards him.

'Gereint! Get your warriors on the West Wall with longbows! I'm going to retreat the shield wall back through the West Gate and then back down the Causeway. Cover us from the wall until we near the gate then use the ladders to get down the other side ahead of us and prepare to defend the next gap!'

Gereint raised his sword in understanding and began shouting orders to his men until those covering the broken East Gate were all Mercian bowmen and then he pulled them back to the West Wall. Once on top they hauled up the ladders and placed them on the other side of the wall. Gereint looked around for his brother Glore and was relieved to see him still amongst his warriors then he cast a glance back towards the flats below the cliffs. He stopped breathing as he stared out across the flats and gripped the edge of the wall with his free hand. There were three or four hundred Adren on the flats behind them making for the Causeway and more seemed to be joining them as he watched.

'Glore!'

Glore turned to see his brother shouting at him and lowered his longbow as he made his way across to him. Gereint just pointed to the West and Glore looked out towards the flats.

271

'Oh gods, how did they get behind us?'

Gereint just shook his head by way of an answer then said, 'Get Arthur. Quickly.'

Glore squatted down at the edge of the parapet and gripped the edge as he swung himself off and dropped to the ground below. He sprinted to Arthur who still stood behind the shield wall.

'Arthur! Arthur, you need to see this!'

Arthur turned at the shout and joined Glore as he began running back to the West Gate. A ladder was lowered for them and they both quickly climbed to the top.

'What is it?' Arthur asked.

'The Adren are on the flats. Gods know how they got there but they're behind us now.'

Arthur looked out beyond the Causeway and could see the figures making for the last wall but he could not tell how many of them there were. He asked Glore.

'Four, five hundred. There seem to be more each time I look.'

'Can we make it to the gap before they do?'

'Yes. I think so.'

Arthur wondered if Gwyna had made it to the cliffs in time. He looked around the fortification and weighed up what options remained to him. If they made their stand here then the Adren would eventually line the walls and finish them off with arrows. If they could make the far side of the gap and take down the bridge behind them then that would buy them time to deal with the new threat and they might yet be able to fight their way across the flats.

'Take your warriors and hold the far side of the gap. Wait for us there and once we're across the bridge we'll hold the last wall against the bastards on the flats. Then it'll be a charge for the cliffs before the others bridge the gap again!'

Gereint shouted out his orders to his warriors and they prepared for the race to the gap.

'And Gereint?'

'Yes?'

'Hold that bridge for us.'

'We will, Arthur.'

272

They looked at each other for a second and Gereint held out his hand. Arthur gripped his shoulder instead, 'I'll shake your hand when we're on the cliffs. Leave the ladders in place for my bowmen, now go!'

Arthur returned to the growing battle at the inner wall while Gereint led his exhausted warriors down the Causeway at a stumbling run. Arthur sought out Morveren among the bowmen and told her to get them all up on the West Wall to cover his retreat towards the gate.

Once she and the others were on the way to replace Gereint's bowmen Arthur stalked behind the two-deep shield wall shouting for them to prepare to give way holding the line. On his order the warriors began to retreat yard by yard towards the West Gate. The funnelling inner wall narrowed as it approached the gate and the shield wall grew in depth until it was five deep and the first of the warriors began to back out through the open gate. The longbows on the wall fired their last volley and the bowmen scrambled back over the wall and cast aside the ladders before regrouping on the Causeway to cover the wall they had just left. The Adren had no immediate way of accessing the West Wall and by the time they had found a way Arthur planned to have his warriors well beyond their bow range.

The Adren tore through the fort searching for any Britons that had been left behind and looking for any plunder that they could lay their hands on while their captains bellowed orders at them to join those who had continued the attack upon the retreating Britons. By the time their captains had organised archers to get up onto the West Wall the fighting around the rearguard was already three hundred yards away and well beyond the effective range of their less powerful bows.

The Mercian warriors had gone on ahead to secure the last bridge on the Causeway against the Adren emerging on the flats, which left the rearguard entirely composed of the remaining Wessex and Anglian warriors. They formed a double line, shield to shield, across the breadth of the Causeway with only five groups of four interspersed behind them ready to plug any breach that the Adren made in the line. The ragged line was continually giving ground against the Adren that were swarming from the abandoned Gates. Those who fell injured or exhausted before the advancing Adren were left behind by the retreating shield wall and were either trampled to death or butchered in a frenzied hacking.

As they neared the bridge Arthur's commands brought the two sides of the shield wall swinging back so that they were fighting on three sides as group by group they sprinted across the bridge to the side held by the Mercians. Gereint had placed half his own warriors in a line fifty yards from the bridge and facing towards the threat from the Adren on the flats. The other half were lined to either side of the bridge and were now firing volleys into the exposed Adren as more and more of Arthur's warriors raced back across the narrow bridge. Those who still had their longbows joined the Mercians and the hail of arrows flying into the Adren ranks doubled.

Arthur was one of the last across and he cast around for the wheel mechanism to draw the bridge back to their side. He found it but saw that they were unlikely to be able to haul the bridge back with so many still on it and without sacrificing the last few warriors who were holding back the unrelenting Adren. He was about to order its withdrawal nonetheless when he saw the rope lying coiled to one side of the wheel. He started to pay it out and cut four lengths off with his bloody sword. Seeing Morgund nearby with Balor and Cael he called them over.

'Tie one end around your waists, the other to the wheel! We're going to clear the bridge!'

As they started to do so he looked around for Hengest.

'Hengest! Over here! We're going to clear the bridge then I want you to drag it away from the far bank and haul us back in! We'll use the bridge as a wall to cover this side from their arrows. Can you do it?'

Hengest saw what they were doing and understood Arthur's plan immediately. He nodded but said, 'It shouldn't be you. Send another instead.'

Arthur just carried on and said, 'Get ready.' He looked at the others who had finished their preparations. 'Charge into them. Don't stop. Once we've cleared enough Hengest will pull the bridge and haul us back up the slope.'

With that he turned and sprinted to where the last of the rearguard were still holding the Adren at bay. The others followed trailing the ropes behind them.

As Arthur reached the line of defenders on the bridge he yelled for them to retreat then flung himself into the Adren ranks. He heaved two of them aside with his shield and swung his sword into those to his right. Balor was cutting a swathe through the enemy with his axe as he swept it from side to side while Morgund and Cael were charging into the Adren on the right of the bridge cutting, pulling and pushing as many of them off the edge as they could.

Suddenly the bridge jerked backwards and dipped before crashing off the edge of the far bank. Arthur and the others were pitched forwards as the far end of the bridge crashed into the marsh water. Morgund managed to clamber up the forty-five degree angle as the bridge was gradually reeled backwards and sprinted back to the Briton line as the bridge tilted back to its former level. The few Adren who had managed to stay on it were immediately picked off by the Mercian longbows. The gap in the Causeway had taken the Adren by surprise and their own archers were still well behind the point of battle.

Arthur and the other two were piled in with a mass of struggling Adren as they all flayed about in the sucking marsh water still desperately locked in combat. Arthur felt the rope tighten around his waist then suddenly he was torn backwards through the mud and away from the enemy. He thrashed about trying to keep his head above the putrid water and saw Balor being likewise dragged backwards. The next moment they were both being tugged up the earth bank. He looked back at the chaos below the far bank and briefly glimpsed two Adren clasped around Cael as his rope stretched out taut behind him. One of the Adren managed to free his knife hand and slash at the rope which sprang away and fell slackly into the water. Cael was thrashing around in the water and trying to free himself from the two Adren's grasp when he realised his rope had been cut. He threw his sword away and locked both arms around his attackers' necks and kicked away from the treacherous bank. He slipped under the swirling muddy water and took the two Adren with him as he disappeared into the blackness.

Cael went under as Arthur and Balor scrabbled up the last of the slope. Arthur knelt on all fours besides Balor coughing out the stinking water he had swallowed and wiping the thick mud from his eyes. He looked up at Hengest, 'Cael?'

Hengest shook his head.

'Morgund?'

Hengest pointed to Morgund who had already recovered his longbow and was firing into the Adren ranks. He helped Arthur to his feet and they both heard Gereint's shouting at the same time. The Adren from the flats had reached his line of defence.

'Prop this bridge up as a shield!' Arthur shouted.

Hengest immediately set about organising those warriors nearby to help him stand the bridge length ways on their side of the gap while Arthur dragged the still spluttering Balor to his feet and propelled him towards the next source of battle before rushing to Gereint's side.

Balor was still trying to claw the mud from his hands and face and he looked up to see Morgund smiling at him.

'Enjoy your swim?'

'How did you manage to stay dry?' Balor asked staring at the dry and mud-free figure before him.

'Used the bridge. It's what they're for.'

'You always were a lucky bastard. Did Cael make it as well?'

'He wasn't so lucky.'

'Are the others still with us? Morveren? Ceinwen? Ruadan?'

'Don't know where they are. Probably with Gereint holding the new line.'

'How did the bastards get behind us?'

'No idea. We'll be lucky to get out of this one now though; they have us on both sides. You ready for some more?'

Balor finished scraping the mud from his hands and gripped his war axe firmly once more before replying, 'Bloody right I am! This is what I call a fight, none of your prancing through forests loosing off a few arrows.'

Morgund laughed and made for Gereint's line of Mercians. As they neared the fighting they could hear Arthur shouting out the order to advance. Arthur wanted to push the Adren back to the last defensive wall on the Causeway and get his warriors away from the gap before the enemy could line the far bank with their archers. There was only one way to safety now and that relied upon breaking through the Adren who had outflanked them before the gap behind them was bridged. The ruins of the Gates had already been torn down for just that purpose.

Arthur knew that if his warriors were trapped on the Causeway with the enemy on either side or caught on the open flats by their greater numbers then the defence of Britain would effectively be over so he roared at them to advance and forced his way to the front of the battle to take the fight to those who sought to trap them. Once again the ragged line of Britons pressed onwards. They were exhausted by the constant days of battling and they were dangerously close to the end of their strength. At first they had fought to hold the Adren at bay on the Causeway. Then they had fought at the Gates to save their lives and to save what little hope of defending Britain remained. Now they fought on instinct, numb to everything other than Arthur roaring them on to kill.

Gwyna had been surveying the flats during the descent from the cliffs and when she reached the base she reined in the Uathach warriors' instincts to charge headlong into the battle and called Ruraidh over to her.

'Take half the warriors and all the spare horses and ride for the tunnel entrance. Collapse it, block it, do what you can but stop the Adren reaching the flats and hold the horses there!'

Ruraidh called out for various clan chiefs and together with their warriors they rode for the gaping subsidence from where more Adren were constantly emerging. Gwyna turned to the remaining warriors who were now freed from the burden of leading the spare horses and stood in her stirrups so that they could all see her.

'Charge in a line abreast and ride straight for the Causeway! We'll clear a line for Arthur's warriors to make it to their horses! Ride down everything in your path and don't stop until we reach them!'

With her sword raised she kicked back into her horse's flanks and led the charge across the flats. Ruraidh's contingent reached the tunnel first and the fierce fighting around the entrance drew the attention of the Adren already on the flats and making for the Causeway. They turned to deal with the enemy who had launched a surprise attack to their rear only to be faced with Gwyna's charge of over a hundred mounted warriors riding down on them at a full gallop.

The unexpectedness of that sight and the ferocity of the noise of such a charge should have caused them to take flight but the scattered Adren turned and held the ground where they stood. The thundering wave crashed straight through them and on towards the Causeway leaving a swathe of broken bodies in its wake.

Arthur kept moving forward and dragged the line with him. Morgund and Balor had fought their way to his side and carried the fight to his right. To his left Gereint and his brother Glore slashed and hacked their way towards the last rampart. They were all beyond the normal endurance of their strength and only desperation kept them going. Behind them the Adren were already constructing a makeshift bridge from the West Wall of the fort and although the Britons could not see this they nonetheless knew their time was running out. Every yard gained here was a yard nearer to the cliffs and a yard further from the Adren host behind them but to gain each yard they had to kill the Adren facing them and there were hundreds still between them and the flats.

They knew they would not make it and they fought all the harder at the bitter knowledge of their fate. They fought without their war cries and without cursing their enemy. They fought in a silent determination to kill whoever was in front of them and to gain another precious yard. Then through the din of battle they felt the ground underneath their feet echo to the drum of hooves and above the frantic clashing of weapons they heard the war cries of the Uathach. Suddenly the Adren in front of them were caught in confusion as Gwyna's charging warriors surged over the ramparts behind them and tore into the ranks facing the Britons. Cries went up along the advancing shield wall that the Uathach had come and they pressed home their attack with renewed hope. Caught between the fury of the two onslaughts the remaining Adren on the Causeway were themselves doomed to slaughter.

Gwyna searched among the southern warriors for Arthur and watched as he cut down one of the few Adren still standing. She urged her horse over to him.

'Arthur! There's more on the flats. Ruraidh's stopping more joining them but we have to hurry!'

'Our horses?'

'With Ruraidh, about half a mile away.'

Arthur looked back towards the gap and the main body of the Adren army. They were already hauling a bridge into place to span the cutting.

'We'll make for the horses. Destroy that bridge and then ride to cover our flanks!'

Gwyna wheeled her horse away and started crying out orders to the other riders around her. Arthur strode through his warriors who were in various stages of collapse. Some were leaning on weapons; others were half kneeling on the ground. All of them were exhausted.

'Half a mile! Just half a mile to our horses!' He started to drag warriors to their feet, 'Cover that half a mile and you stay alive!' Arthur picked up dropped weapons and put them back into hands too tired to grip them, 'Stay alive and you can kill more of the bastards in Britain!' He stood before them and roared at them. 'Get up you bastards! You're warriors of Britain! Do you want the Uathach to carry you? You haven't fought this long to die here now! Get up! Get the wounded to the centre!' He physically hauled up those who thought they were unable to go on and bullied them into the close order formation he wanted. He put Gereint and Morgund at the front and the southern warriors left the Causeway at a shambling run. He alternated between the flanks and rear shouting encouragement and threatening to hack to death anyone who floundered and all the time he counted down the distance to their horses.

There were still Adren on the flats and they banded together to attack the warriors as they made towards Ruraidh's force. As each band charged towards them Arthur shouted out the names of those who looked less likely to collapse and each time ten or so warriors would peel away from the formation and launch themselves at the Adren then run to catch up with the main body once again. What should have taken them only two to three minutes took them ten but they finally reached Ruraidh's warriors and their own horses.

Arthur looked down into the pit and saw the Uathach warriors blocking the exit of the tunnel. He gazed back towards the Causeway and saw Gwyna's riders heading back towards them. She had led a charge over the Adren bridge once it had fallen into place and cleared the far side of the gap for over a hundred yards before racing back over the bridge and collapsing it behind them. His warriors were mounting their horses all around him and he shouted out to Ruraidh to pull back from the tunnel. As the Uathach turned from the Adren they began to pour out from the gaping blackness and Arthur led his own warriors charging into their flank to give Ruraidh and the others enough time to mount up and ride clear.

They halted a few hundred yards from the tunnel and Gwyna's riders joined them. For a moment Arthur considered leading a charge back towards the Adren and starting the whole bloody slaughter once more but Morgund saw what he was thinking and catching his eye slowly shook his head. Arthur saw the message and saw that his warriors were unable to give any more. He knew that if they fought now they would all die cheaply. He turned his horse and without a word pointed to the cliffs.

Balor laboured up the last stretch of the steep slope leading his horse behind him. When he finally reached the top the sunlight fell on his face and he closed his eyes as an overwhelming mixture of relief and tiredness washed over him. He forced himself to lead his horse a little way from the path to make room for those following him and he gazed around the headland.

Someone was passing by with a bucket of water and Balor called out to him. He altered his path and offered Balor a ladle of water. Balor gave him a disgusted look and taking the bucket in both hands tipped it up to his mouth. He closed his eyes and gulped the water down his parched throat letting the excess flow freely down the sides of his face to run down his neck and onto his chest. He handed the bucket back and saw the red tunic, which showed the warrior to be one of the Mercians.

This was the first time he had fought alongside the Mercians and he had been surprised by how well drilled they were. He thanked the man and sat down heavily once again closing his eyes in weariness. He felt himself slipping immediately to sleep and forced his eyes back open with a slight jerk of his head. He stretched his legs out before him and pressed down on his knees to stretch them further all the time resisting the compulsion to lie back on the grass and fade into unconsciousness. Instead he looked about him at the warriors who were still being joined by those making their way up the cliff.

Many of them seemed to be injured and all of them seemed to be covered in blood but whether or not it was their own blood he could not tell. They were plainly exhausted. Most of them stood or sat alone and Balor could see no one talking. They had been fighting the Adren for weeks on the Causeway and the last few days had been one long constant battle and despite knowing that they were lucky to be alive and to have escaped the Adren trap they all had the same shattered look of defeat. They had fought beyond their endurance and now sat or stood in silence with glazed expressionless faces. Balor realised he must look the same and once again fought the temptation to lie back on the grass. He heard someone sit down behind him but he did not have the energy or inclination to turn around and see who it was.

'We're never going to live it down.'

On hearing Morgund's voice he forced himself to turn around, 'What?'

'Being rescued by the Uathach.'

Balor grunted before replying, 'If they'd turned up earlier we might have saved the Causeway. What kept them so long?'

'Don't know yet but there's an interesting corpse about a hundred yards over there.'

'Already seen too many bloody corpses,' Balor mumbled in reply.

'This one's Ablach though. Died up here. Someone opened his head for him.'

Balor looked up with a spark of interest, 'Ablach, dead? And killed up here?'

'Interesting isn't it?'

'Serves him right for not coming sooner.'

'Probably what the person who killed him thought as well.'

'What about our lot? I'm too tired to get up and look around. Who made it out of that mess down there?'

'Well, Arthur did...'

'I know Arthur did!' Balor interrupted him, 'He was shouting in my ear every step from the Causeway to the horses!'

'Yours and everyone else's. He must be possessed by the gods. I thought for a second that he was going to order us to charge back into them once we were on our horses.'

'So, who else?' Balor asked.

'You know Cael died at the last bridge?'

'Yes.'

'So we won't ever be short of supplies again.'

Balor looked at Morgund scowling for a second before starting to laugh. 'We'll have to empty a couple of barrels of beer to do justice to his memory.'

'Him and Ruadan,' Morgund said, no longer smiling.

Balor cursed before asking where he fell.

'As we retreated through the West Gate apparently. I didn't see it but unfortunately Ceinwen did. Judging by what Morveren says she went a bit mad after that and she needed help to stop Ceinwen from leaving the shield wall and charging into the Adren.'

Balor cursed again.

'But Morveren's still alive then?'

'Morveren survived. She's over there somewhere sitting with Ceinwen.'

'Who else?' Balor asked once again feeling overcome with tiredness. As Morgund listed the names of those he knew had died and those who were still unaccounted for Balor's concentration ebbed away until all he could think of were the faces of the friends who had died.

Arthur was standing over the dead body of the Uathach chieftain.

'What happened here?' His question was directed to Gwyna but she just stood staring at the sprawled figure of her father and it was Ruraidh who finally answered.

'Gwyna killed him.'

Arthur looked back to the woman by his side.

'What happened here?' he repeated the question to her.

She brought her eyes up to him and her face showed neither remorse nor guilt and she replied, 'I brought you the northern warriors.'

A short silence followed her statement then Ruraidh spoke up again.

'We'd been camped here for over a week. Ablach was undecided whether or not to ride down to the Causeway.' He hesitated as Arthur stared him then took a breath and continued in a matter of fact voice, 'We were divided about what to do. Some counselled that we had no choice but to fight alongside the southerners if we were to have any chance against the Adren host. Others wanted to let you stand alone and die and then either fight them ourselves or turn for the North and hope they left us alone.'

'After taking our horses and plundering what you could from Caer Sulis,' Arthur said without accusation.

Ruraidh took another deep breath and looked for some help from Gwyna but none was forthcoming so he continued, 'Yes, that's what some thought.'

'That's what Ablach wanted.'

'I think he was torn between wishing you dead and needing your warriors to help battle the Adren. Two events spurred him to decide; the two Cithol coming here and Gwyna's arrival.' He paused and looked at Arthur who was staring at him.

'The Cithol came here?'

'Two of them did. I was with Ablach when he spoke to them. I got the impression that there was no Cithol army coming to your aid and I suppose that Ablach read it the same way.'

'Who were they?' Arthur asked.

'A black-skinned captain and a green-eyed witch,' Ruraidh replied, growing nervous under Arthur's intense stare.

'What were their names?'

'I don't remember,' Ruraidh replied, desperate not to reveal what both he and Ablach thought about Seren's reaction to Ablach's crude joke about her carrying another of Arthur's bastards.

'You do remember.'

Ruraidh shot a quick glance at Gwyna who was now watching their exchange with interest.

'Seren and Tyrell or something but it was their message about the Adren that forced Ablach to act one way or the other.' Ruraidh rushed on in his haste to divert away Arthur's attention, 'They warned him about the tunnel under the Causeway and that the Adren were going to use it to trap you between two forces!'

Gwyna swore, 'You mean he knew about it before the confrontation here? Before the Cithol witch spoke up in front of everyone?'

'Yes. I think he believed Arthur's force to be doomed so he chose instead to raid Caer Sulis and head back North.' He turned his attention back to

Arthur and continued, 'It all happened at the same time. As Gwyna was challenging Ablach's authority the Adren surfaced from the tunnel and Gwyna had to act.'

'You slew your father and led the warriors to battle,' Arthur concluded for him as he watched Gwyna. 'What of the two Cithol?'

Gwyna shrugged and Ruraidh looked around him as if he expected to still see them somewhere nearby.

'We left them here,' he finally replied.

'What of Benoc and Hund?' Arthur asked of the other two northern chieftains.

'Neither answered the call though both sent most of their warriors,' Gwyna said.

'And you now lead the northern tribes?' he asked her.

'Together we lead all that will stand against the Adren.'

'Good. Get word to your people for them to go to the safety of Caer Sulis,' Arthur replied and stepping over Ablach's body walked to the nearby cliff edge. The other two followed him and stood on either side as he stared out over the flats. The Adren were still spilling off the Causeway and already the expanse below the cliffs was darkening with their numbers. He studied the host below for a minute and realised that the Adren army was far larger than they had originally guessed. He could see other warriors lined along the cliffs and knew they were realising the same dreadful truth.

He looked to Gwyna and said, 'Your charge saved my warriors' lives.' Then turning to Ruraidh added, 'And without your attack on the tunnel entrance we would never have made it back to the cliffs. We've lost the Causeway when together we may have held it but they've paid for it with thousands of their own soldiers' lives. And they haven't finished paying the toll yet. I want you to hold the cliffs against them to buy me time to get my warriors back to the copse above the Winter Wood. Don't risk being overrun just hold it for a few days then bring your warriors back to the copse.'

They nodded assent and as Arthur turned to go he pointed to Ablach, 'And build a pyre for him.'

'Let the crows pick his bones,' Gwyna retorted.

'As you wish but you'd do better to show those that followed him some respect. Build a pyre.'

As Arthur went to rouse his warriors to begin the journey to Dunraven his thoughts were on Seren and the fact that she had been here on this headland and that she and Gwyna had stood face to face. He wondered if Seren had discovered that he had married Gwyna before he had the chance to tell her himself. He pondered on why it had been she and Terrill who had brought the message about the tunnel under the Causeway and how the Cithol had known that the Adren were going to use it. At the back of his mind was a nagging thought that Ruraidh had concealed something about Seren from him and had diverted his attention away from it before he could discover what it was but he was too weary to pursue the matter any further.

He stopped and looked around the green headland. The Uathach warriors were gathering around Gwyna as she explained how they were going to hold the cliffs against the Adren, while the warriors of the southern tribes were spread out across the grassland in various states of exhaustion. These were all that remained of Britain's warriors; all that were left to stand against the Adren horde now crossing the Causeway.

The Causeway had fallen and he would have to retreat now to the Veiled City and hope that Lord Venning and the Cithol would join them in the battle against the invading Adren. He hoped that with the Cithol standing by them they could hold the Adren at bay in the Winter Wood until Cei managed to destroy the Adren's legacy power source and halt their army's supply line. So much depended upon Cei and Merdynn and he wondered if they had reached the Adren city yet.

But Cei had fallen in the Shadow Lands and Lord Venning had already made a pact with the enemy.

HAVEN

SHADOW LANDS: BOOK THREE

The Shadow Land army is loose in Britain. Arthur and his warriors are forced to retreat before the invading enemy and regroup to defend the Veiled City from the Adren hordes, still hoping Merdynn will succeed in the East. But no word of Merdynn or his warriors has come from the Shadow Lands.

The warriors of Britain fight battle after battle against the greater forces of the enemy - but no army has yet stopped the Adren on their westward conquest and the warriors' rearguard becomes more desperate as the darkness threatens to overwhelm Britain.

Their only hope now is that Arthur can somehow turn the tide of war. A war they are losing.

Haven, the third book in the Shadow Lands series, is available through all online and retail booksellers or it can be ordered direct from www.simonlister.co.uk